PAUL ☑ P9-CDG-326

Praise for *The Windup Girl, the Nebula, Locus, Compton Crook, and John W. Campbell award-winning debut novel by Paolo Bacigalupi:*

"Bacigalupi is a worthy successor to William Gibson: this is cyberpunk without computers."
— *Time Magazine*, Best Books of 2009

"Reminiscent of Philip K. Dick's Blade Runner.... Bacigalupi has created a fully imagined world in *The Windup Girl* that is densely packed with ideas about genetic manipulation, distribution of resources, the social order, and environmental degradation. However, he is never pedantic in addressing these concepts; rather they are expressed through the settings he vividly describes and in the actions of his characters. In short, *The Windup Girl* is science fiction with an environmental message, but one that does not get in the way of its compelling story."
— *Sacramento Book Review*

"This complex, literate and intensely felt tale, which recalls both William Gibson and Ian McDonald at their very best, will garner Bacigalupi significant critical attention and is clearly one of the finest science fiction novels of the year."
— *Publishers Weekly* (starred review)

"Bacigalupi is as unflinching in his examination of the unthinkable cruelty, humiliation and banal evil that humanity inflicts on the Other as he is on the bleak future that our mass consumption society will inevitably unleash. In his fictional vision, there will be no miraculous rescue from our moral or environmental sins. *The Windup Girl* will almost certainly be the most important SF novel of the year for its willingness to confront the most cherished notions of the genre, namely that our future is bright and we will overcome our selfish, cruel nature."
— *BookPage*

"*The Windup Girl* is almost unbearably brutal. It is also extremely good."
— Nancy Kress, Hugo and Nebula award-winning
author of *Steal Across the Sky*

"Written with a feral conviction... provides fertile ground for discussion of many kinds, by many kinds of readers.... An unremittingly harsh work... I can't recall another novel that has articulated the same vision of what it means to be human in the present moment with the same force. It's that vision that insists that Emiko [the 'windup girl'] is human, and that she remains bound at the end of the novel: because we remain bound, and she is us; because at least for now, science fiction remains bound; and because, quite probably, so does our world."
— *Strange Horizons*

"Highly nuanced, violent, and grim... Readers with an interest in political or environmental science fiction or those for whom dystopias are particularly appealing will be intrigued. If they are able to immerse themselves completely into the calorie-mad world of a future Bangkok, they will not be disappointed."
— *School Library Journal*

"Beautifully written with a cast of characters both major and minor who will make it extremely difficult on the reader as to whom to root for, *The Windup Girl* is an important, perhaps even cautionary tale about a very possible future, set in a Thailand one can almost taste and feel. Plan to see it on many a best-of list and most likely a few award short lists as well. It's the end of the world as we know it, so eat your Soylent Green and enjoy the show. Dystopia Rules!"
— Patrick Heffernan, Mysterious Galaxy Books

"One of the best books I've read this year. On a line by line basis, it has the beauty of a well-crafted short story and then you get into the big sweep of the novel. The science fiction of it is thoroughly and frighteningly believable, but that isn't what makes this a great book. What makes *The Windup Girl* beautiful and terrifying is its convincing portrayal of humanity, both as a society and as individuals."
— Mary Robinette Kowal, author of *Shades of Milk and Honey*

"*The Windup Girl* is clearly one of the most significant books of the year, definitely worth Hugo consideration, and the herald of more good work to come from the author."
— *SF Revu*

PAOLO BACIGALUPI

NIGHT SHADE BOOKS
SAN FRANCISCO

First Printing

978-1-59780-202-4

Printed in Canada

Night Shade Books
Please visit us on the web at
http://www.nightshadebooks.com

CONTENTS

POCKETFUL OF DHARMA

Wang Jun stood on the rain-slicked streets of old Chengdu and stared up into the drizzle at Huojianzhu.

It rose into the evening darkness, a massive city core, dwarfing even Chengdu's skyscrapers. Construction workers dangled from its rising skeleton, swinging from one section of growth to the next on long rappelling belts. Others clambered unsecured, digging their fingers into the honeycomb structure, climbing the struts with careless dangerous ease. Soon the growing core would overwhelm the wet-tiled roofs of the old city. Then Huojianzhu, the Living Architecture, would become Chengdu entirely.

It grew on lattices of minerals, laying its own skeleton and following with cellulose skin. Infrastructure strong and broad, growing and branching, it settled roots deep into the green fertile soil of the Sichuan basin. It drew nutrients and minerals from the soil and sun, and the water of the rancid Bing Jiang; sucking at pollutants as willingly as it ate the sunlight which filtered through twining sooty mist.

Within, its veins and arteries grew pipelines to service the waste and food and data needs of its coming occupants. It was an animal vertical city built first in the fertile minds of the Biotects and now growing into reality. Energy pulsed from the growing creature. It would stand a kilometer high and five wide when fully mature. A vast biologic city, which other than its life support would then lie dormant as humanity walked its hollowed arteries, clambered through its veins and nailed memories to its skin in the rituals of habitation.

Wang Jun watched Huojianzhu and dreamed in his small beggar-boy mind of ways and means that might lead him out of the wet streets and hunger and into its comforts. Already sections of it glowed with habitation. People, living high and far above him, roamed the organism's corridors. Only the powerful and wealthy would live so high above.

Those with *guanxi*. Connections. Influence.

His eyes sought the top of the core, through the darkness and rain and mist, but it disappeared long before his eyes could find it. He wondered if the people up high saw the stars while he saw only drizzle. He had heard that if one cut Huojianzhu, its walls would bleed. Some said it cried. He shivered at the rising creature and turned his eyes back to earth to continue pushing with his stick-thin limbs and bent posture through the Chengdu crowds.

Commuters carried black umbrellas or wore blue and yellow plastic ponchos to protect them from the spitting rain. His own hair lay soaked, slicked to the contours of his skull. He shivered and cast about himself, seeking hard for likely marks, so that he nearly tripped over the Tibetan.

The man squatted on the wet pavement with clear plastic covering his wares. Soot and sweat grimed his face, so that his features sheened black and sticky under the harsh halogen glare of the street lamps. The warped and jagged stumps of his teeth showed as he smiled. He pulled a desiccated tiger claw from under the plastic and waved it in Wang Jun's face.

"You want tiger bones?" He leered. "Good for virility."

Wang Jun stopped short before the waving amputated limb. Its owner was long dead so that only the sinews and ragged fur and the bone remained, dried and stringy. He stared at the relic and reached out to touch the jerky tendons and wickedly curving yellowed claws.

The Tibetan jerked it away and laughed again. There was a tarnished silver ring on his finger, studded with chunks of turquoise; a snake twining around his finger and swallowing its tail endlessly.

"You can't afford to touch." He ground phlegm and spit on the pavement beside him, leaving a pool of yellow mucus shot through with the black texturing of Chengdu's air.

"I can," said Wang Jun.

"What have you got in your pockets?"

Wang Jun shrugged, and the Tibetan laughed. "You have nothing, you stunted little boy. Come back when you've got something in your pockets."

He waved his goods of virility at the interested, more moneyed buyers who had gathered. Wang Jun slipped back into the crowd.

It was true what the Tibetan said. He had nothing in his pockets. He had a ratted wool blanket hidden in a Stone-Ailixin cardboard box, a broken VTOL Micro-Machine, and a moldering yellow woolen school hat.

He had come from the green-terraced hills of the countryside with less than that. Already twisted and scarred with the passage of plague, he had come to Chengdu with empty hands and empty pockets and the recollections of a silent dirt village where no thing lived. His body carried recollections of pain so deep that it remained permanently crouched in a muscular memory of that agony.

He had had nothing in his pockets then and he had nothing in his pockets now. It might have bothered him if he had ever known anything but want. Anything but hunger. He could resent the Tibetan's dismissal no more than he might resent the neon logos which hung from the tops of towers and illuminated the pissing rain with flashing reds, yellows, blues, and greens. Electric colors filled the darkness with hypnotic rhythms and glowing dreams. Red Pagoda Cigarettes, Five Star Beer, Shizi Jituan Software, and Heaven City Banking Corporation. Confucius Jiajiu promised warm rice wine comfort while JinLong Pharmaceuticals guaranteed long life, and it all lay beyond him.

He hunkered in a rain-slicked doorway with his twisted bent back and empty pockets and emptier stomach and wide-open eyes looking for the mark who would feed him tonight. The glowing promises hung high above him, more connected to those people who lived in the skyscrapers: people with cash and officials in their pockets. There was nothing up there he knew or understood. He coughed, and cleared the black mucus from his throat. The streets, he knew. Organic rot and desperation, he understood. Hunger, he felt rumbling in his belly.

He watched covetously as people walked past and he called out to them in a polyglot of Mandarin, Chengdu dialect, and the only English words he knew, "Give me money. Give me money." He tugged at their umbrellas and yellow ponchos. He stroked their designer sleeves and powdered skin until they relented and gave money. Those who broke away, he spat upon. The angry ones who seized him, he bit with sharp yellow teeth.

Foreigners were few now in the wet. Late October hurried them homeward, back to their provinces, homes, and countries. Leaner times lay ahead, lean enough that he worried about his future and counted the crumpled paper the people threw to him. He held tight the light aluminum *jiao* coins people tossed. The foreigners always had paper money and often gave, but they grew too few.

He scanned the street, then picked at a damp chip of concrete on the ground. In Huojianzhu, it was said, they used no concrete to build. He wondered what the floors would feel like, the walls. He dimly remembered his home from before he came to Chengdu, a house made of mud, with a dirt floor. He doubted the city core was made of the same. His belly grew emptier. Above him, a video loop of Lu Xieyan, a Guangdong singer, exhorted the people on the street to strike down the Three Wrongs of Religion: Dogmatism, Terrorism, and Splittism. He ignored her screeching indictments and scanned the crowds again.

A pale face bobbed in the flow of Chinese. A foreigner, but he was a strange one. He neither pushed ahead with a purpose, nor gawked about himself at Chengdu's splendors. He seemed at home on the alien street. He wore a black coat which stretched to the ground. It was shiny, so it reflected the reds and blues of neon, and the flash of the street lamps. The patterns were hypnotic.

Wang Jun slid closer. The man was tall, two meters high, and he wore dark glasses so that his eyes were hidden. Wang Jun recognized the glasses and was sure the man saw clearly from behind the inky ovals. Microfibers in the lenses stole the light and amplified and smoothed it so that the man saw day, even as he hid his eyes from others in the night.

Wang Jun knew the glasses were expensive and knew Three-Fingers Gao would buy them if he could steal them. He watched the man and waited as he continued up the street with his assured, arrogant stride. Wang Jun trailed him, stealthy and furtive. When the man turned into an alley and disappeared, Wang Jun rushed to follow.

He peeked into the alley's mouth. Buildings crowded the passageway's darkness. He smelled excrement and dead things moldering. He thought of the Tibetan's tiger claw, dried and dead, with pieces nicked away from the bone and tendons where customers had selected their weight of virility. The foreigner's footsteps echoed and splashed in the darkness; the even footsteps of a man who saw in the dark. Wang Jun slid in after him, crouching and feeling his way blindly. He touched the roughness of the walls. Instant concrete. Stroking the darkness, he followed the receding footsteps.

Whispers broke the dripping stillness. Wang Jun smiled in the darkness, recognizing the sound of a trade. Did the foreigner buy girls? Heroin? So many things for a foreigner to buy. He settled still, to listen.

The whispers grew heated and terminated in a brief yelp of surprise. Someone gagged and then there was a rasping and a splash. Wang Jun trembled and waited, as still as the concrete to which he pressed his body.

The words of his own country echoed, *"Kai deng ba."* Wang Jun's ears pricked at a familiar accent. A light flared and his eyes burned under the sharp glare. When his sight adjusted he stared into the dark eyes of the Tibetan street hawker. The Tibetan smiled slowly showing the encrustations of his teeth and Wang Jun stumbled back, seeking escape.

The Tibetan captured Wang Jun with hard efficiency. Wang Jun bit at the Tibetan's hands and fought, but the Tibetan was quick and he pressed Wang Jun against the wet concrete ground so that all Wang Jun could see were two pairs of boots; the Tibetan's and a companion's. He struggled, then let his body lie limp, understanding the futility of defiance.

"So, you're a fighter," the Tibetan said, and held him down a moment longer to make his lesson clear. Then he hauled Wang Jun upright. His hand clamped painfully at Wang Jun's nape. *"Ni shi shei?"* he asked.

Wang Jun trembled and whined, "No one. A beggar. No one."

The Tibetan looked more closely at him and smiled. "The ugly boy with the empty pockets. Do you want the tiger's claw after all?"

"I don't want anything."

"You will receive nothing," said the Tibetan's companion. The Tibetan smirked. Wang Jun marked the new speaker as Hunanese by his accent.

The Hunanese asked, "What is your name?"

"Wang Jun."

"Which *'Jun'*?"

Wang Jun shrugged. "I don't know."

The Hunanese shook his head and smiled. "A farmer's boy," he said. "What do you plant? Cabbage? Rice?" He laughed. "The Sichuanese are ignorant. You should know how to write your name. I will assume that your 'Jun' is for soldier. Are you a soldier?"

Wang Jun shook his head. "I'm a beggar."

"Soldier Wang, the beggar? No. That won't do. You are simply Soldier Wang." He smiled. "Now tell me, Soldier Wang, why are you here in this dangerous dark alley in the rain?"

Wang Jun swallowed. "I wanted the foreigner's dark glasses."

"Did you?"

Wang Jun nodded.

The Hunanese stared into Wang Jun's eyes, then nodded. "All right, Little Wang. Soldier Wang," he said. "You may have them. Go over there. Take them if you are not afraid." The Tibetan's grip relaxed and Wang Jun was free.

He looked and saw where the foreigner lay, face down in a puddle of water. At the Hunanese's nod, he edged closer to the still body, until he stood above it. He reached down and pulled at the big man's hair until his face rose dripping from the water, and his expensive glasses were accessible. Wang Jun pulled the glasses from the corpse's face and laid its head gently back into the stagnant pool. He shook water from the glasses and the Hunanese and Tibetan smiled.

The Hunanese crooked a finger, beckoning.

"Now, Soldier Wang, I have a mission for you. The glasses are your payment. Put them in your pocket. Take this," a blue datacube appeared in his hand, "and take it to the Renmin Lu bridge across the Bing Jiang. Give it to the person who wears white gloves. That one will give you something extra for your pocket." He leaned conspiratorially closer, encircling Wang Jun's neck and holding him so that their noses pressed together and Wang Jun could smell his stale breath. "If you do not deliver this, my friend will hunt you down and see you die."

The Tibetan smiled.

Wang Jun swallowed and nodded, closing the cube in his small hand. "Go then, Soldier Wang. Dispense your duty." The Hunanese released his neck, and Wang Jun plunged for the lighted streets, with the datacube clutched tight in his hand.

The pair watched him run.

The Hunanese said, "Do you think he will survive?"

The Tibetan shrugged. "We must trust that Palden Lhamo will protect and guide him now."

"And if she does not?"

"Fate delivered him to us. Who can say what fate will deliver him? Perhaps no one will search a beggar child. Perhaps we both will be alive tomorrow to know."

"Or perhaps in another turning of the Wheel."

The Tibetan nodded.

"And if he accesses the data?"

The Tibetan sighed and turned away. "Then that too will be fate. Come, they will be tracking us."

The Bing Jiang ran like an oil slick under the bridge, black and sluggish. Wang Jun perched on the bridge's railing; soot-stained stone engraved with dragons and phoenixes cavorting through clouds. He looked down into the river and watched styrofoam shreddings of packing containers float lazily on the thick surface of the water. Trying to hit a carton, he hawked phlegm and spat. He missed, and his mucus joined the rest of the river's effluent. He looked at the cube again. Turning it in his hands as he had done several times before as he waited for the man with the white gloves. It was blue, with the smoothness of all highly engineered plastics. Its texture reminded him of a tiny plastic chair he had once owned. It had been a brilliant red but smooth like this. He had begged from it until a stronger boy took it.

Now he turned the blue cube in his hands, stroking its surface and probing its black data jack with a speculative finger. He wondered if it might be more valuable than the glasses he now wore. Too large for his small head, they kept slipping down off his nose. He wore them anyway, delighted by the novelty of day-sight in darkness. He pushed the glasses back up on his nose and turned the cube again.

He checked for the man with white gloves and saw none. He turned the cube in his hands. Wondering what might be on it that would kill a foreigner.

The man with white gloves did not come.

Wang Jun coughed and spit again. If the man did not come before he counted ten large pieces of styrofoam, he would keep the cube and sell it.

Twenty styrofoam pieces later, the man with white gloves had not come, and the sky was beginning to lighten. Wang Jun stared at the cube. He considered throwing it in the water. He waited as *nongmin* began filtering across the bridge with their pull-carts laden with produce. Peasants coming in from the countryside, they leaked into the city from the wet fertile fields beyond, with mud between their toes and vegetables on their backs. Dawn was coming. Huojianzhu glistened, shining huge and alive against a lightening sky. He coughed and spit again and hopped off the bridge. He dropped the datacube in a ragged pocket. The Tibetan wouldn't be able to find him anyway.

Sunlight filtered through the haze of the city. Chengdu absorbed the heat. Humidity oozed out of the air, a freak change in temperature, a last wave of heat before winter came on. Wang Jun sweated. He found Three-Fingers Gao in a game room. Gao didn't really have three fingers. He had ten, and he used them all as he controlled a three-dimensional soldier through the high mountains of Tibet against the rebellion. He was known in Chengdu's triad circles as the man who had made TexTel's Chief Rep pay 10,000 yuan a month in protection money until he rotated back to Singapore. Because of the use of three fingers.

Wang Jun tugged Three-Fingers's leather jacket. Distracted, Three-Fingers died under an onslaught of staff-wielding monks.

He scowled at Wang Jun. "What?"

"I got something to sell."

"I don't want any of those boards you tried to sell me before. I told you, they're no good without the hearts."

Wang Jun said, "I got something else."

"What?"

He held out the glasses and Three-Fingers's eyes dilated. He feigned indifference. "Where did you get those?"

"Found them."

"Let me see."

Wang Jun released them to Three-Fingers reluctantly. Three-Fingers put them on, then took them off and tossed them back at Wang Jun. "I'll give you twenty for them." He turned back to start another game.

"I want one hundred."

"*Mei me'er.*" He used Beijing slang. No way. He started the game. His soldier squatted on the plains, with snowy peaks rising before him. He started forward, pushing across short grasses to a hut made of the skin of earlier Chinese soldiers. Wang Jun watched and said, "Don't go in the hut."

"I know."

"I'll take fifty."

Three-Fingers snorted. His soldier spied horsemen approaching and moved so that the hut hid him from their view. "I'll give you twenty."

Wang Jun said, "Maybe BeanBean will give me more."

"I'll give you thirty, go see if BeanBean will give you that." His soldier waited until the horsemen clustered. He launched a rocket into their center. The game machine rumbled as the rocket exploded.

"You have thirty now?"

Three-Fingers turned away from his game and his soldier perished quickly as bioengineered yakmen boiled out of the hut. He ignored the screams of his soldier as he counted out the cash to Wang Jun. Wang Jun left Three-Fingers to his games and celebrated the sale by finding an unused piece of bridge near the Bing Jiang. He settled down to nap under it through the sweltering afternoon heat.

He woke in the evening and he was hungry. He felt the heaviness of coins in his pocket and thought on the possibilities of his wealth. Among the coins, his fingers touched the unfamiliar shape of the datacube. He took it out and turned it in his hands. He had nearly forgotten the origin of his money. Holding the datacube, he was reminded of the Tibetan and the Hunanese and his mission. He considered seeking out the Tibetan and returning it to him, but deep inside he held a suspicion that he would not find the man selling tiger bones tonight. His stomach rumbled. He dropped the datacube back into his pocket and jingled the coins it resided with. Tonight he had money in his pockets. He would eat well.

"How much for *mapo dofu?*"

The cook looked at him from where he stood, swirling a soup in his broad wok, and listening to it sizzle.

"Too expensive for you, Little Wang. Go and find somewhere else to beg. I don't want you bothering my customers."

"*Shushu,* I have money." Wang Jun showed him the coins. "And I want to eat."

The cook laughed. "*Xiao* Wang is rich! Well then, Little Wang, tell me what you care for."

"*Mapo dofu, yu xiang* pork, two *liang* of rice and *Wu Xing* beer." His order tumbled out in a rush.

"Little Wang has a big stomach! Where will you fit all that food, I wonder?" When Wang Jun glared at him he said, "Go, sit, you'll have your feast."

Wang Jun went and sat at a low table and watched as the fire roared and the cook threw chilies into the wok to fry. He wiped at his mouth to keep from drooling as the smell of the food came to his nose. The cook's wife opened a bottle of Five Star for him, and he watched as she poured the beer into a wet glass. The day's heat was dissipating. Rain began to spatter the street restaurant's burlap roof. Wang Jun drank from his beer and watched the other diners, taking in the food they ate and the company they kept. These were people he might have previously harassed for their money. But not tonight. Tonight he was a king. Rich, with money in his pocket.

His thoughts were broken by the arrival of a foreigner. A broad man with long white hair pulled back in a horse's tail. His skin was pale and he wore white gloves. He stepped under the sheltering burlap and cast alien blue eyes across the diners. The Chinese at their tables stared back. When his eyes settled on Wang Jun's bent form, he smiled. He went to squat on a stool across from Wang Jun and said, in accented Mandarin, "You are Little Wang. You have something for me."

Wang Jun stared at the man and then, feeling cocky with the attention of the other Chinese said, "*Ke neng.*" Maybe.

The foreigner frowned, then leaned across the table. The cook's wife came, interrupting, and set down Wang Jun's *mapo dofu,* followed quickly by the pork. She went and scooped out a steaming bowl of rice broader than Wang Jun's hand, and set it before him. Wang Jun picked up chopsticks and began shoveling the food into his mouth, all the while watching the foreigner. His eyes watered at the spiciness of the *dofu* and his mouth tingled with the familiar numbing of ground peppercorns.

The wife asked if the foreigner would eat with him, and Wang Jun eyed the foreigner. He felt the money in his pocket, while his mouth flamed on. He looked at the size of the foreigner and assented reluctantly, feeling his wealth now inadequate. They spoke in *Chengdu hua,* the dialect of the city, so that the foreigner did not understand what they said. The man watched as the wife scooped another bowl of rice and set it in front of him with a pair of chopsticks. He looked down at the white mountain of rice in his bowl and then looked up at Wang Jun. He shook his head, and said, "You have something for me. Give it to me now."

Wang Jun was stung by the foreigner's disregard of the offered food. Because he was unhappy he said, "Why should I give it to you?"

The pale white man frowned and his blue eyes were cold and angry. "Did not the Tibetan tell you to give me something?" He held out a white-gloved hand.

Wang Jun shrugged. "You didn't come to the bridge. Why should I give it to you now?"

"Do you have it?"

Wang Jun became guarded. "No."

"Where is it?"

"I threw it away."

The man reached across the small table and grasped Wang Jun's ragged collar. He pulled him close. "Give it to me now. You are very small, I can take it or you can give it to me. Little Wang, you cannot win tonight. Do not test me."

Wang Jun stared at the foreigner and saw silver flash in the man's breast pocket. On impulse he reached for the glint of sliver and drew a thing up until it was between their two faces. Other people at nearby tables gasped at what Wang Jun held. Wang Jun's hand began to shake, quivering uncontrollably, until the Tibetan's severed finger, with its tarnished silver and turquoise ring still on it, slipped from his horrified grasp and landed in the *yu xiang* pork.

The foreigner smiled, an indifferent, resigned smile. He said, "Give me the datacube before I collect a trophy from you as well." Wang Jun nodded and slowly reached into his pocket. The foreigner's eyes followed his reaching hand.

Wang Jun's free hand reached desperately out to the table and grabbed a handful of scalding *dofu* from its plate. Before the man could react, he drove the contents, full of hot chilies and peppercorns, into those cold blue eyes. As the foreigner howled, Wang Jun sank his sharp yellow teeth into the pale flesh of imprisoning hands. The foreigner dropped Wang Jun to rub frantically at his burning eye sockets, and blood flowed from his damaged hands.

Wang Jun took his freedom and ran for the darkness and alleys he knew best, leaving the foreigner still roaring behind him.

The rain was heavier, and the chill was coming back on Chengdu, harder and colder than before. The concrete and buildings radiated cold, and Wang Jun's breath misted in the air. He hunched in his box, with its logo for Stone-Ailixin Computers on the side. He thought it had been used for satellite phones, from the pictures below the logo. He huddled inside it with the remains of his childhood.

He could still remember the countryside he had come from and, vaguely, a mud-brick home. More clearly, he remembered terrace-sculpted hills and running along those terraces. Playing in warm summer mud with a Micro-Machine VTOL in his hands while his parents labored in brown water around their ankles and green rice shoots sprouted up out of the muck. Later, he had passed those same terraces, lush and unharvested, as he made his way out of his silent village.

Under the cold instant-concrete shadows of the skyscrapers, he stroked his toy VTOL. The wings which folded up and down had broken off and were lost. He turned it over, looking at its die-cast steel frame. He pulled out the datacube and stared at it. Weighed the toy and the cube in his hands. He thought of the Tibetan's finger, severed with its silver snake ring still on it, and shuddered. The white man with the blue eyes would be looking for him. He looked around at his box. He put the Micro-Machine in his pocket but left his ratted blanket. He took his yellow *anchuan maozi,* the traffic safety hat children wore to and from school, stolen from a child even smaller than he. He pulled the yellow wool cap down over his ears, re-pocketed the datacube, and left without looking back.

Three-fingers was crooning karaoke in a bar when Wang Jun found him. A pair of women with smooth skins and hard, empty eyes attended him. They wore red silk *chipao,* styled from Shanghai. The collars were high and formal, but the slits in the dresses went nearly to the women's waists. Three-Fingers glared through the dim red smoky light when

Wang Jun approached.

"What?"

"Do you have a computer that reads these?" He held up the data-cube.

Three-Fingers stared at the cube and reached out for it. "Where did you get that?"

Wang Jun held it out but did not release it. "Off someone."

"Same place you got those glasses?"

"Maybe."

Three-Fingers peered at the datacube. "It's not a standard datacube. See the pins on the inside?" Wang Jun looked at the datasocket. "There's only three pins. You need an adapter to read whatever's on there. And you might not even be able to read it then. Depends what kind of OS it's designed for."

"What do I do?"

"Give it to me."

"No." Wang Jun backed off a step.

One of the women giggled at the interaction between the mini mob boss and street urchin. She stroked Three-Fingers's chest. "Don't worry about the *taofanzhe*. Pay attention to us." She giggled again.

Wang Jun glared. Three-Fingers pushed the hostess off him. "Go away." She made an exaggerated pout, but left with her companion.

Three-Fingers held out his hand. "Let me see it. I can't help you if you don't let me see the *tamade* thing."

Wang Jun frowned but passed the datacube over. Three-Fingers turned it over in his hands. He peered into the socket, then nodded. "It's for HuangLong OS." He tossed it back and said, "It's a medical specialty OS. They use it for things like brain surgery, and DNA mapping. That's pretty specialized. Where'd you get it?"

Wang Jun shrugged. "Someone gave it to me."

"*Fang pi.*" Bullshit.

Wang Jun was silent and they regarded each other, then Three-Fingers said, "*Xing*, I'll buy it off you. Just because I'm curious. I'll give you five yuan. You want to sell it?"

Wang Jun shook his head.

"Fine. Ten yuan, but that's all."

Wang Jun shook his head again.

Three-Fingers Gao frowned. "Did you get rich, suddenly?"

"I don't want to sell it. I want to know what's on it."

"Well, that makes two of us now." They regarded each other for a time longer. Three-Fingers said, "All right. I'll help you. But if there's any value to what's on that, I'm taking three-quarters on the profit."

"*Yi ban.*"

Three-Fingers rolled his eyes. "Fine. Half, then."

"Where are we going?"

Three-Fingers walked fast through chill mist. He led Wang Jun into smaller and smaller alleys. The buildings changed in character from shining modern glass and steel to mud-brick with thatched and tiled roofs. The streets became cobbled and jagged and old women stared out at them from dark wooden doorways. Wang Jun watched the old ladies with suspicion. Their eyes followed him impassively, recording his and Three-Fingers's passage.

Three-Fingers stopped to pull out a box of Red Pagodas. He put one in his mouth. "You smoke?"

Wang Jun took the offered stick and leaned close as Three-Fingers struck a match. It flared high and yellow and then sank low under the pressure of the wet air. Wang Jun drew hard on the cigarette and blew smoke. Three-Fingers lit his own.

"Where are we going?"

Three-Fingers shrugged. "Here." He jerked his head at the building behind them. He smoked for a minute longer, then dropped his cigarette on the damp cobbles and ground it out with a black boot. "Put out your smoke. It's bad for the machines." Wang Jun flicked the butt against a wall. It threw off red sparks where it bounced and then lay smoking on the ground. Three-Fingers pushed open a wooden door. Its paint was peeling and its frame warped so that he shoved hard and the door scraped loudly as they entered.

In the dim light of the room, Wang Jun could see dozens of monitors. They glowed with screen savers and data. He saw columns of characters and numbers, scrolling, connected to distant networks of information. People sat at the monitors in a silence broken only by the sound of the keys being pressed at an incessant rate.

Three-Fingers pulled Wang Jun up to one of the silent technicians and said, "He Dan, can you read this?" He nudged Wang Jun and Wang Jun held up the datacube. He Dan plucked it out of Wang Jun's hand with spidery graceful fingers and brought it close to his eyes in the dimness. With a shrug he began to sort through a pile of adapters. He chose one and connected it to a stray cord, then inserted the adapter into the datacube. He typed on the computer and the borders and workspaces flickered and changed color. A box appeared and he hit a single key in response.

"Where am I?" The voice was so loud that the speakers distorted and crackled. The technicians all jumped as their silence was shattered. He Dan adjusted a speaker control. The voice came again, softer. "Hello?" It held an edge of fear. "Is there anyone there?" it asked.

"Yes," said Wang Jun, impulsively.

"Where am I?" the voice quavered.

"In a computer," said Wang Jun.

Three-Fingers slapped him on the back of the head. "Be quiet."

"What?" said the voice.

They listened silently.

"Hello, did someone say I was in a computer?" it said.

Wang Jun said, "Yes, you're in a computer. What are you?"

"I'm in a computer?" The voice was puzzled. "I was having surgery. How am I in a computer?"

"Who are you?" Wang Jun ignored Three-Fingers's glowering eyes.

"I am Naed Delhi, the nineteenth Dalai Lama. Who are you?"

The typing stopped. No one spoke. Wang Jun heard the faint whine of cooling fans and the high resonances of the monitors humming. Technicians turned to stare at the trio and the computer which spoke. Outside Wang Jun heard someone clear their throat of phlegm and spit. The computer spoke on, heedless of the effect of its words. "Hello?" it said. "Who am I speaking to?"

"I'm Wang Jun."

"Hello. Why can't I see?"

"You're in a computer. You don't have any eyes."

"I can hear. Why can I hear and yet not see?"

He Dan broke in, "Video input is not compatible with the software emulator which runs your program."

"I don't understand."

"You are an artificial intelligence construct. Your consciousness is software. Your input comes from hardware. They are incompatible on the system we have installed you."

The voice quavered, "I am not software. I am the Dalai Lama of the Yellow Hat sect. The nineteenth to be reincarnated as such. It is not my fate to be reincarnated as software. You are probably mistaken."

"Are you really the Dalai Lama?" Wang Jun asked.

"Yes," the computer said.

"How—" Wang Jun began, but Three-Fingers pulled him away from the system before he could phrase his question. He knelt in front of Wang Jun. His hands were shaking as he held Wang Jun by the collar of his shirt. Their faces nearly touched as he hissed out, "Where did you find this cube?"

Wang Jun shrugged. "Someone gave it to me."

Three-Finger's hand blurred and struck Wang Jun's face. Wang Jun jerked at its impact. His face burned. The technicians watched as Three-Fingers hissed, "Don't lie to me. Where did you find this thing?"

Wang Jun touched his face, "From a Tibetan, I got it from a Tibetan who sold tiger bones, and a man from Hunan. And there was a body. A big foreigner. They were his glasses I sold you."

Three-Fingers tilted his head back to stare at the ceiling. "Don't lie to me. Do you know what it means if we've got the Dalai Lama on a datacube that you've been carrying around in your pocket?" He shook Wang Jun. "Do you know what it means?"

Wang Jun whined, "I was supposed to give it to a man with white gloves, but he never came. And there was another man. A foreigner and he killed the Tibetan and took his finger, and he wanted mine too, and I ran and—" his voice rose in a babbling whine.

Three-Fingers's hands settled around Wang Jun's neck and squeezed until Wang Jun's ears rang and blackness scudded across his eyes. Distantly, he heard Three-Fingers say, "Don't cry to me. I'm not your mother. I'll take your tongue out if you make my life any more difficult than it already is. Do you understand?"

Wang Jun nodded in his haze.

Three-Fingers released him, saying, "Good. Go talk to the computer."

Wang Jun breathed deeply and stumbled back to the Dalai Lama.

"How did you get inside the computer?" he asked.

"How do you know I am in a computer?"

"Because we plugged your datacube in and then you started talking."

The computer was silent.

"What's it like in there?" Wang Jun tried.

"Terrible and still," said the computer. Then it said, "I was going to have surgery, and now I am here."

"Did you dream?"

"I don't remember any dreams."

"Are you leading a rebellion against my homeland?"

"You speak Chinese. Are you from China?"

"Yes. Why are you making people fight in Tibet?"

"Where is this computer?"

"Chengdu."

"Oh, my. A long way from Bombay," the computer whispered.

"You came from Bombay?"

"I was having surgery in Bombay."

"Is it lonely in there?"

"I don't remember anything until now. But it is very still here. Deathly still. I can hear you, but cannot feel anything. There is nothing here. I fear that I am not here. It is maddening. All of my senses are lost. I want out of this computer. Help me. Take me back to my body." The computer's voice, vibrating from the speakers, was begging.

"We can sell him," Three-Fingers said abruptly.

Wang Jun stared at Three-Fingers. "You can't sell him."

"Someone wants him if they're chasing you. We can sell him."

The computer said, "You can't sell me. I have to get back to Bombay. I'm sure my surgery can't be completed if I'm not there. I must go back. You must take me back."

Wang Jun nodded in agreement. Three-Fingers smirked. He Dan said, "We need to unplug him. Without some form of stimuli he may go crazy before you can decide what to do with him."

"Wait," said the Dalai Lama. "Please don't unplug me yet. I'm afraid. I'm afraid of being gone again."

"Unplug him," said Three-Fingers.

"Wait," said the computer. "You must listen to me. If my body is dead, you must destroy this computer you keep me in. I fear that I will not reincarnate. Even Palden Lhamo may not be able to find my soul. She is powerful, but though she rides across an ocean of blood astride the skin of her traitorous son, she may not find me. My soul will be trapped here, unnaturally preserved, even as my body decomposes. Promise me, please. You must not leave me—"

He Dan shut off the computer.

Three-Fingers raised his eyebrows at He Dan.

He Dan shrugged. "It could be that it is the Dalai Lama. If there are people chasing the beggar-child, it lends credence to its claims. It would not be hard to upload his identity matrix while he was undergoing surgery."

"Who would do that?"

He Dan shrugged. "He is at the center of so many different political conflicts, it would be impossible to say. In a datacube, he makes a convenient hostage. Tibetan extremists, Americans, us, perhaps the EU; they would all be interested in having such a hostage."

Three-Fingers said, "If I'm going to sell him, I'll need to know who put him in there."

He Dan nodded, and then the door exploded inward. Splinters of wood flew about and shafts of light illuminated the dim room. Outside there was a whine of VTOLs and then there were bright lights lancing through the door, followed by the rapid thud of heavy boots. Wang Jun ducked instinctively as something seemed to suck the air out of the room and the monitors exploded, showering glass on the technicians and Wang Jun. People were shouting everywhere around him and Wang Jun smelled smoke. He stood up and pulled the datacube out of its adapter and rolled underneath a table as a barrage of pellets ratcheted across the wall above him.

He saw Three-Fingers fumble with something at his belt and then stiffen as red blossoms appeared on his chest. Other technicians were falling, all of them sprouting bloody stains on their bodies. Wang Jun huddled deeper under the table as forms in black armor came through the door. He put the datacube in his mouth, thinking he might swallow it before they could find him. More explosions came and suddenly the wall beside him was gone in a cacophony of bricks and rubble. He scrambled over the collapsed wall as shouts filled the air. Hunched low and running, he became nothing except a small child shadow. An irrelevant shadow in the rain and the play of lights from the troops left behind.

He crouched in a doorway's shadow, turning the datacube in his hands, stroking its blue plastic surface with reverential fascination. Rain fell in a cold mist and his nose dripped with the accumulated moisture. He shivered. The datacube was cold. He wondered if the Dalai Lama felt anything inside. People walked along the side-street, ignoring his small shadow in the doorway. They rose as forms out of the mist, became distinct and individual under the street lamps and then disappeared back into shadows.

He had seen the VTOLs rise from a distance, their running lights illuminating their forms in the darkness. He had watched their wings lower and lock above the wet tile roofs. Then they were gone in a hissing acceleration. Against his better judgment he had returned, joining other residents in a slow scavenging across the rubble of the destroyed building. They moved in a methodical stooped walk. Picking at brick. Turning shattered monitor screens. Fumbling at the pockets of the bodies left behind. He had found no trace of Three-Fingers and doubted he was alive. He Dan he found, but only in pieces.

He turned the datacube again in his hands.

"Where did you get that?"

He jerked skittishly and moved to run, but a hand was holding him and he was immobile. It was a Chinese woman and she wore white gloves. He stared at the hand which held him.

"Do you have something for me?" she asked. Her Mandarin was clear and educated, perfect, as though she came from Beijing itself.

"I don't know."

"Is that yours?"

"No."

"Were you supposed to give it to me?"

"I don't know."

"I missed you at the bridge."

"Why didn't you come?"

"There were delays," she said, and her eyes became hooded and dark.

Wang Jun reached out to hand her the datacube. "You have to be careful with it. It has the Dalai Lama."

"I know. I was coming to you. I was afraid I had lost you. Come." She motioned him. "You are cold. There is a bed and food waiting for you." She motioned again and he followed her out of the doorway and into the rain.

She led him through the wet streets. In his mind, the images of VTOLs and exploding monitors and Three-Fingers's blossoming red mortality made him wary as they crossed intersections and bore along the old streets of Chengdu.

The woman held his hand firm in hers, and she bore him with direction and purpose so that no matter how many twists and turns they took, they were always closer to the organic skeleton of the city core. It rose above them, glowing. Dwarfing them and the constructors who swung from it on gossamer lines. They swarmed it as ants might, slowly growing their nest.

Then they were under its bones, walking through the wet organic passageways of the growing creature. Wang Jun smelled compost and death. The air grew warm and humid as they headed deeper into the architectural animal. Glowing chips embedded in the woman's wrists passed them through construction checkpoints until they came to a lift, a cage that rose up through Huojianzhu's internals, sliding on smooth organic rails. Through the bars of the cage Wang Jun saw levels completed, shining and habitable, the walls with the appearance of polished steel, and fluorescent lamps, glowing, in their brackets. He saw levels where only the segmented superstructure of the beast existed. A monster with its bones exposed; wet slick things sheened with a biological ooze. Hardening silicon mucus coated the bones, flowed, and built up successive layers to form walls. Huojianzhu grew and where it grew the Biotects and constructors oversaw, guiding and ensuring that its growth followed their carefully imagined intentions. The beautiful woman, and Wang Jun with her, rose higher.

They came to a level nearly complete. Her feet echoed in a hallway, and she came to a door. Her hand leaned gently on the surface of the door and its skin moved slightly under her pressure so that Wang Jun was unsure if the door molded to her hand or reached out to caress it. The door swung open and Wang Jun saw the luxury of the heights of which he had always dreamed.

In a room with a bed so soft his back ached and with pillows so fluffy he believed he smothered, he woke. There were voices. "—a beggar. No one," she said.

"Then blank him and turn him out."

"He helped us."

"Leave his pocket with money, then."

Their voices became distant, and though he wished he could stay awake, he slept again.

Wang Jun sank into the enveloping cushions of a chair so deep that his feet could not touch the polished elegance of the real wooden floors. He was well rested now, having climbed finally out of the womb of bedding and pillows which had tangled him. Around him, *shanshui* paintings hung from smooth white walls, and recessed shelves held intricately fired vases from China's dynasties, long dead and gone. The kitchen he had already made acquaintance with, watching the lady who looked Chinese but wasn't as she prepared a mountain of food for him on burners that flared like suns, and made tea with water that scalded as it came from the faucet. In other rooms, lights glowed on and off as he entered and departed, and there was carpet, soft expanses of pale fiber that were always warm under his feet. Now he sat in the enveloping chair and watched with dark eyes as the lady and her foreign companion paced before him. Behind them, the Dalai Lama's cube sat on a shelf, blue and small.

"*Sile?*"

Wang Jun started at the sound of her voice, and he felt his heart beating. Outside the windows of the apartment thick Chengdu mist hung, stagnant and damp. No more rain. He struggled out of the chair and went to look out the windows. He could not see the lights of Chengdu's old city below. The mist was too thick. The woman watched him as her counterpart spoke. "Yeah, either the Chinese or the Europeans blew his head full of holes. They're just annoyed because they lost him."

"What should we do?"

"I'm waiting for an indication from the embassy. The Tibetans want us to destroy him. Keep whining about how his soul won't be reborn, if we don't destroy it."

She laughed. "Why not write him onto a new body?"

"Don't be sacrilegious."

"That's how they see it? Fanatics can be so—"

"—intractable," he finished for her.

"So this whole mission is a waste?"

"He's not much good to us without his body. The Tibetans won't recognize him if we write him onto a new body and he's no good as leverage against the Chinese if he doesn't have a following."

She sighed. "I wish we didn't have to work with them."

"Without the Tibetans, we wouldn't even have known to look for the kid."

"Well, now they're threatening that if we don't give him back, the Pali Lama is going to flay our skins, or something."

"Palden Lhamo," said the man.

"What?"

He repeated, "Palden Lhamo. She's a Tibetan goddess. Supposed to be the protector of Tibet and our digital friend." He jerked his head at the datacube sitting on its shelf. "The paintings of her show her riding a mule across seas of blood and using the flayed skin of her son as a saddle blanket."

"What a lovely culture they've got."

"You should see the paintings: red hair, necklaces of skulls—"

"Enough."

Wang Jun said, "Can I open the window?"

The woman looked over at the man; he shrugged.

"*Suibian,*" she said.

Wang Jun undid the securing clasps and rolled the wide window open. Chill air washed into the room. He peered down into the orange glow of the mist, leaning far out into the air. He stroked the spongy organic exoskeleton of the building, a resilient honeycomb of holes. Below, he could just make out the shifting silhouettes of constructors clambering across the surface of the structure. Behind him the conversation continued.

"So what do we do?"

He waved at the datacube. "We could always plug his eminence into a computer and ask him for advice."

Wang Jun's ears perked up. He wanted to hear the man inside the computer again.

"Would the Chinese be interested in a deal, even if his body is gone?"

"Maybe. They'd probably keep his cube in a desk drawer. Let it gather dust. If he never reincarnated, it would be fine with them. One less headache for them to deal with."

"Maybe we'll be able to trade him for something still, then."

"Not much, though. So what if he does reincarnate? It'll be twenty years before he has an effect on them." He sighed. "Trade talks start tomorrow. This operation's starting to look like a scrub at the home office. They're already rumbling about extracting us before the talks begin. At least the EU didn't get him."

"Well, I'll be glad to get back to California."

"Yeah."

Wang Jun turned from his view and asked, "Will you kill him?"

The pair exchanged looks. The man turned away, muttering under his breath. Wang Jun held in his response to the man's rudeness. Instead he said, "I'm hungry."

"He's hungry, *again*," muttered the man.

"We only have instants, now," said the woman.

"*Xing*," said Wang Jun. The woman went into the kitchen and Wang Jun's eyes fastened on the dark blue sheen of the datacube, sitting on its shelf.

"I'm cold," said the man. "Close the window."

Wang Jun sniffed at the aroma of frying food coming from the woman and the kitchen. His belly rumbled, but he went to the window. "Okay."

* * *

The mist clung to him as he clung to the superstructure of the biologic city. His fingers dug into its spongy honeycomb skin and he heard the rush of Chengdu far below, but could not see it through the mist. He heard curses and looked up. Light silhouetted the beautiful woman who looked Chinese but wasn't and the man as they peered out of their luxury apartment window from high above.

He dug a fist deeper into the honeycomb wall and waved at them with his free hand, and then climbed lower with the self-confident ease of a beggar monkey. He looked up again to see the man make to climb out the window, and then the woman pulled him back in.

He descended. Slipping deeper into the mist, clambering for the slick safety of the pavement far below. He passed constructors and Biotects, working late-night shifts. They all hung precariously from the side of the mountainous building, but only he was so daring as to climb the skin of the creature without the protection of a harness. They watched him climb by with grave eyes, but they made no move to stop him. Who were they to care if his fingers slipped and he fell to the infinitely distant pavement? He passed them and continued his descent.

When he looked up again, seeking the isolated window from which he had issued, it was gone. Lost in the thickness of the chill mist. He guessed the man and woman would not follow. That they would have more pressing concerns than to find a lone beggar boy with a useless datacube somewhere in the drizzling streets of Chengdu. He smiled to himself. They would pack and go home to their foreign country and leave him to remain in Chengdu. Beggars always remained.

His arms began to shake with strain as his descent continued. The climb was already taking him longer than he had guessed possible. The sheer size of the core was greater than he had ever imagined. His fingers dug into the spongy biomass of Huojianzhu's skin, seeking another hold. The joints of his fingers ached and his arms trembled. It was cold this high even though the night air was still. The wet mist and the damp spongy walls he clung to chilled his fingers, numbing them and making him unsure of his handholds. He watched where he placed each hand in an agony of care, seeking stability and safety with every grip.

For the first time he wondered how long it would be until he fell. The descent was too long, and the clinging chill was sinking deeper into his bones. The mists parted and he could see the lights of Chengdu proper, spread out below him. His hopes sank as he saw finally how high he hung above the city.

He dug for another handhold and when he set his weight against it, the spongy mass gave way and he was suddenly dangling by a single weak hand while the Chengdu lights spun crazily below him. He scrabbled desperately for another handhold. He dug his feet deep into the spongy surface and found one. He saw where his slipping hand had torn away the wall. There was a deep rent, and from it, the milky blood of the bio-structure dripped slowly. His heart beat faster staring at Huojianzhu's mucus wound and he imagined himself slipping and falling; spattering across the pavement while his blood ran slick and easy into the street gutters. He fought to control his rising panic as his arms trembled and threatened to give way. Then he forced himself to move his limbs and descend, to seek some respite from the climb, a hope of survival on the harsh skin of the core.

He spoke to himself. Told himself that he would survive. That he would not fall and die on the pavement of the street. Not he. Not *Xiao* Wang. No. Not *Xiao* Wang at all. Not Little Wang anymore. Wang Jun; Soldier Wang. Twisted and bent though he was, Soldier Wang would survive. He smiled to himself. Wang Jun would survive. He continued his descent with shaking arms and numbed fingers, picking each hold carefully, and eventually when he began to believe that he could climb no more, he found a hole in Huojianzhu's skin and swung himself into the safety of the ducts of the animal structure.

Standing on a firm surface he turned and looked out at Chengdu's spread lights. In a few more years all of Chengdu would be overwhelmed by the spreading core. He wondered where a beggar boy would run then. What streets would be left open for those such as he? He reached into his pocket and felt the hard edges of the datacube. He drew it from his pocket, and gazed on its smooth blue perfect surface. Its perfect geometric edges. So much consternation over the man who lived inside. He hefted the cube. It was light. Too light to hold the whole of a person. He remembered his brief interaction with the Dalai Lama, in a dark room under the glow of monitors. He squeezed the cube tight in his hand and then went to the edge of the duct. Chengdu lay below him.

He cocked his arm to throw. Winding it back to launch the Dalai Lama in his silicon cell out into the empty air. To arc and fall, faster and faster, until he shattered against the distant ground and was released, to begin again his cycle of rebirth. He held his arm cocked, then whipped it forward in a trajectory of launch. When his arm had completed its swing, the datacube and the Dalai Lama still sat safe in his palm. Smooth and blue and undamaged.

He considered it. Stroking it, feeling its contours in his hand. Then he slid it back into his pocket and swung himself out, once again onto the skin of Huojianzhu. He smiled as he climbed, digging his fingers into the living flesh of the building. He wondered how long this infinity of climbing would last, and if he would reach the streets whole or as a bloody pulp. Chengdu seemed a long way below.

The datacube rested in his pocket. If he fell, it would shatter and the Dalai Lama would be released. If he survived? For now he would keep it. Later, perhaps, he would destroy it. The Dalai Lama was asleep in the cube, and would not overly mind the longer wait. And, Wang Jun thought, who in all the world of important people could say, as he could say, that he had the Dalai Lama in his pocket?

THE FLUTED GIRL

The fluted girl huddled in the darkness clutching Stephen's final gift in her small pale hands. Madame Belari would be looking for her. The servants would be sniffing through the castle like feral dogs, looking under beds, in closets, behind the wine racks, all their senses hungry for a whiff of her. Belari never knew the fluted girl's hiding places. It was the servants who always found her. Belari simply wandered the halls and let the servants search her out. The servants thought they knew all her hiding places.

The fluted girl shifted her body. Her awkward position already strained her fragile skeleton. She stretched as much as the cramped space allowed, then folded herself back into compactness, imagining herself as a rabbit, like the ones Belari kept in cages in the kitchen: small and soft with wet warm eyes, they could sit and wait for hours. The fluted girl summoned patience and ignored the sore protest of her folded body.

Soon she had to show herself, or Madame Belari would get impatient and send for Burson, her head of security. Then Burson would bring his jackals and they would hunt again, crisscrossing every room, spraying pheromone additives across the floors and following her neon tracks to her hidey-hole. She had to leave before Burson came. Madame Belari punished her if the staff wasted time scrubbing out pheromones.

The fluted girl shifted her position again. Her legs were beginning to ache. She wondered if they could snap from the strain. Sometimes she was surprised at what broke her. A gentle bump against a table and she was shattered again, with Belari angry at the careless treatment of her investment.

The fluted girl sighed. In truth, it was already time to leave her hidey-hole, but still she craved the silence, the moment alone. Her sister Nia never understood. Stephen though…he had understood. When the fluted girl told him of her hidey-hole, she thought he forgave because he was kind. Now she knew better. Stephen had bigger secrets than the silly fluted girl. He had secrets bigger than anyone had guessed. The fluted girl turned his tiny vial in her hands, feeling its smooth glass shape, knowing the amber drops it held within. Already, she missed him.

Beyond her hidey-hole, footsteps echoed. Metal scraped heavily across stone. The fluted girl peered out through a crack in her makeshift fortress. Below her, the castle's pantry lay jumbled with dry goods. Mirriam was looking for her again, poking behind the refrigerated crates of champagne for Belari's party tonight. They hissed and leaked mist as Mirriam struggled to shove them aside and look deeper into the dark recesses behind. The fluted girl had known Mirriam when they were both children in the town. Now, they were as different as life and death.

Mirriam had grown, her breasts burgeoning, her hips widening, her rosy face smiling and laughing at her fortune. When they both came to Belari, the fluted girl and Mirriam had been the same height. Now, Mirriam was a grown woman, a full two feet taller than the fluted girl, and filled out to please a man. And she was loyal. She was a good servant for Belari. Smiling, happy to serve. They'd all been that way when they came up from the town to the castle: Mirriam, the fluted girl, and her sister Nia. Then Belari decided to make them into fluted girls. Mirriam got to grow, but the fluted girls were going to be stars.

Mirriam spied a stack of cheeses and hams piled carelessly in one corner. She stalked it while the fluted girl watched and smiled at the plump girl's suspicions. Mirriam hefted a great wheel of Danish cheese and peered into the gap behind. "Lidia? Are you there?"

The fluted girl shook her head. No, she thought. But you guessed well. A year ago, I would have been. I could have moved the cheeses, with effort. The champagne would have been too much, though. I would never have been behind the champagne.

Mirriam stood up. Sweat sheened her face from the effort of moving the bulky goods that fed Belari's household. Her face looked like a bright shiny apple. She wiped her brow with a sleeve. "Lidia, Madame Belari is getting angry. You're being a selfish girl. Nia is already waiting for you in the practice room."

Lidia nodded silently. Yes, Nia would be in the practice room. She was the good sister. Lidia was the bad one. The one they had to search for. Lidia was the reason both fluted girls were punished. Belari had given up on discipline for Lidia directly. She contented herself with punishing both sisters and letting guilt enforce compliance. Sometimes it worked. But not now. Not with Stephen gone. Lidia needed quiet now. A place where no one watched her. A place alone. Her secret place which she showed to Stephen and which he had examined with such surprised sad eyes. Stephen's eyes had been brown. When he looked at her, she thought that his eyes were almost as soft as Belari's rabbits. They were safe eyes. You could fall into those safe brown eyes and never worry about breaking a bone.

Mirriam sat heavily on a sack of potatoes and scowled around her, acting for her potential audience. "You're being a selfish girl. A vicious selfish girl to make us all search this way."

The fluted girl nodded. Yes, I am a selfish girl, she thought. I am a selfish girl, and you are a woman, and yet we are the same age, and I am smarter than you. You are clever but you don't know that hidey-holes are best when they are in places no one looks. You look for me under and behind and between, but you don't look up. I am above you, and I am watching you, just as Stephen watched us all.

Mirriam grimaced and got up. "No matter. Burson will find you." She brushed the dust from her skirts. "You hear me? Burson will find you." She left the pantry.

Lidia waited for Mirriam to go away. It galled her that Mirriam was right. Burson would find her. He found her every time, if she waited too long. Silent time could only be stolen for so many minutes. It lasted as long as it took Belari to lose patience and call the jackals. Then another hidey-hole was lost.

Lidia turned Stephen's tiny blown-glass bottle in her delicate fingers a final time. A parting gift, she understood, now that he was gone, now that he would no longer comfort her when Belari's depredations became too much. She forced back tears. No more time to cry. Burson would be looking for her.

She pressed the vial into a secure crack, tight against the stone and roughhewn wood of the shelving where she hid, then worked a vacuum jar of red lentils back until she had an opening. She squeezed out from behind the legume wall that lined the pantry's top shelves.

It had taken weeks for her to clear out the back jars and make a place for herself, but the jars made a good hidey-hole. A place others neglected to search. She had a fortress of jars, full of flat innocent beans, and behind that barrier, if she was patient and bore the strain, she could crouch for hours. She climbed down.

Carefully, carefully, she thought. We don't want to break a bone. We have to be careful of the bones. She hung from the shelves as she gently worked the fat jar of red lentils back into place then slipped down the last shelves to the pantry floor.

Barefoot on cold stone flagging, Lidia studied her hidey-hole. Yes, it looked good still. Stephen's final gift was safe up there. No one looked able to fit in that few feet of space, not even a delicate fluted girl. No one would suspect she folded herself so perfectly into such a place. She was slight as a mouse, and sometimes fit into surprising places. For that, she could thank Belari. She turned and hurried from the pantry, determined to let the servants catch her far away from her last surviving hidey-hole.

By the time Lidia reached the dining hall, she believed she might gain the practice rooms without discovery. There might be no punishments. Belari was kind to those she loved, but uncompromising when they disappointed her. Though Lidia was too delicate to strike, there were other punishments. Lidia thought of Stephen. A small part of her was happy that he was beyond Belari's tortures.

Lidia slipped along the dining hall's edge, shielded by ferns and blooming orchids. Between the lush leaves and flowers, she caught glimpses of the dining table's long ebony expanse, polished mirror-bright each day by the servants and perpetually set with gleaming silver. She studied the room for observers. It was empty.

The rich warm smell of greenery reminded her of summer, despite the winter season that slashed the mountains around the castle. When she and Nia had been younger, before their surgeries, they had run in the mountains, amongst the pines. Lidia slipped through the orchids: one from Singapore; another from Chennai; another, striped like a tiger, engineered by Belari. She touched the delicate tiger blossom, admiring its lurid color.

We are beautiful prisoners, she thought. Just like you.

The ferns shuddered. A man exploded from the greenery, springing on her like a wolf. His hands wrenched her shoulders. His fingers plunged into her pale flesh and Lidia gasped as they stabbed her nerves into paralysis. She collapsed to the slate flagstones, a butterfly folding as Burson pressed her down.

She whimpered against the stone, her heart hammering inside her chest at the shock of Burson's ambush. She moaned, trembling under his weight, her face hard against the castle's smooth gray slate. On the stone beside her, a pink and white orchid lay beheaded by Burson's attack.

Slowly, when he was sure of her compliance, Burson allowed her to move. His great weight lessened, lifting away from her like a tank rolling off a crushed hovel. Lidia forced herself to sit up. Finally she stood, an unsteady pale fairy dwarfed by the looming monster that was Belari's head of security.

Burson's mountainous body was a cragged landscape of muscle and scars, all juts of strength and angry puckered furrows of combat. Mirriam gossiped that he had previously been a gladiator, but she was romantic and Lidia suspected his scars came from training handlers, much as her own punishments came from Belari.

Burson held her wrist, penning it in a rocklike grasp. For all its unyielding strength, his grip was gentle. After an initial disastrous breakage, he had learned what strain her skeleton could bear before it shattered.

Lidia struggled, testing his hold on her wrist, then accepted her capture. Burson knelt, bringing his height to match hers. Red-rimmed eyes studied her. Augmented irises bloodshot with enhancements scanned her skin's infrared pulse.

Burson's slashed face slowly lost the green blush of camouflage, abandoning stone and foliage colors now that he stood in open air. Where his hand touched her though, his skin paled, as though powdered by flour, matching the white of her own flesh.

"Where have you been hiding?" he rumbled.

"Nowhere."

Burson's red eyes narrowed, his brows furrowing over deep pits of interrogation. He sniffed at her clothing, hunting for clues. He brought his nose close to her face, her hair, snuffled at her hands. "The kitchens," he murmured.

Lidia flinched. His red eyes studied her closely, hunting for more details, watching the unintentional reactions of her skin, the blush of discovery she could not hide from his prying eyes. Burson smiled. He hunted with the wild fierce joy of his bloodhound genetics. It was difficult to tell where the jackal, dog, and human blended in the man. His joys were hunting, capture, and slaughter.

Burson straightened, smiling. He took a steel bracelet from a pouch. "I have something for you, Lidia." He slapped the jewelry onto Lidia's wrist. It writhed around her thin arm, snakelike, chiming as it locked. "No more hiding for you."

A current charged up Lidia's arm and she cried out, shivering as electricity rooted through her body. Burson supported her as the current cut off. He said, "I'm tired of searching for Belari's property."

He smiled, tight-lipped, and pushed her toward the practice rooms. Lidia allowed herself to be herded.

Belari was in the performance hall when Burson brought Lidia before her. Servants bustled around her, arranging tables, setting up the round stage, installing the lighting. The walls were hung in pale muslin shot through with electric charges, a billowing sheath of charged air that crackled and sparked whenever a servant walked near.

Belari seemed unaware of the fanciful world building around her as she tossed orders at her events coordinator. Her black body armor was open at the collar, in deference to the warmth of human activity. She spared Burson and Lidia a quick glance, then turned her attention back to her servant, still furiously scribbling on a digital pad. "I want everything to be perfect tonight, Tania. Nothing out of place. Nothing amiss. Perfect."

"Yes, Madame."

Belari smiled. Her face was mathematically sculpted into beauty, structured by focus-groups and cosmetic traditions that stretched back generations. Cocktails of disease prophylaxis, cell-scouring cancer inhibitors, and Revitia kept Belari's physical appearance at twenty-eight, much as Lidia's own Revitia treatments kept her frozen in the first throes of adolescence. "And I want Vernon taken care of."

"Will he want a companion?"

Belari shook her head. "No. He'll confine himself to harassing me, I'm sure." She shivered. "Disgusting man."

Tania tittered. Belari's chill gaze quieted her. Belari surveyed the performance hall. "I want everything in here. The food, the champagne, everything. I want them packed together so that they feel each other when the girls perform. I want it very tight. Very intimate."

Tania nodded and scribbled more notes on her pad. She tapped the screen authoritatively, sending orders to the staff. Already, servants would be receiving messages in their earbuds, reacting to their mistress's demands.

Belari said, "I want Tingle available. With the champagne. It will whet their appetites."

"You'll have an orgy if you do."

Belari laughed. "That's fine. I want them to remember tonight. I want them to remember our fluted girls. Vernon particularly." Her laughter quieted, replaced by a hard-edged smile, brittle with emotion. "He'll be angry when he finds out about them. But he'll want them, anyway. And he'll bid like the rest."

Lidia watched Belari's face. She wondered if the woman knew how clearly she broadcast her feelings about the Pendant Entertainment executive. Lidia had seen him once, from behind a curtain. She and Stephen had watched Vernon Weir touch Belari, and watched Belari first shy from his touch and then give in, summoning the reserves of her acting skill to play the part of a seduced woman.

Vernon Weir had made Belari famous. He'd paid the expense of her body sculpting and made her a star, much as Belari now invested in Lidia and her sister. But Master Weir extracted a price for his aid, Faustian devil that he was. Stephen and Lidia had watched as Weir took his pleasure from Belari, and Stephen had whispered to her that when Weir was gone, Belari would summon Stephen and reenact the scene, but with Stephen as the victim, and then he would pretend, as she did, that he was happy to submit.

Lidia's thoughts broke off. Belari had turned to her. The angry welt from Stephen's attack was still visible on her throat, despite the cell-knitters she popped like candy. Lidia thought it must gall her to have a scar out of place. She was careful of her image. Belari seemed to catch the focus of Lidia's gaze. Her lips pursed and she pulled the collar of her body armor close, hiding the damage. Her green eyes narrowed. "We've been looking for you."

Lidia ducked her head. "I'm sorry, Mistress."

Belari ran a finger under the fluted girl's jaw, lifting her downcast face until they were eye to eye. "I should punish you for wasting my time."

"Yes, Mistress. I'm sorry." The fluted girl lowered her eyes. Belari wouldn't hit her. She was too expensive to fix. She wondered if Belari would use electricity, or isolation, or some other humiliation cleverly devised.

Instead, Belari pointed to the steel bracelet. "What's this?"

Burson didn't flinch at her question. He had no fear. He was the only servant who had no fear. Lidia admired him for that, if nothing else. "To track her. And shock her." He smiled, pleased with himself. "It causes no physical destruction."

Belari shook her head. "I need her without jewelry tonight. Take it off."

"She will hide."

"No. She wants to be star. She'll be good now, won't you, Lidia?"

Lidia nodded.

Burson shrugged and removed the bracelet, unperturbed. He leaned his great scarred face close to Lidia's ear. "Don't hide in the kitchens the next time. I will find you." He stood away, smiling his satisfaction. Lidia narrowed her eyes at Burson and told herself she had won a victory that Burson didn't know her hidey-hole yet. But then Burson smiled at her and she wondered if he did know already, if he was playing with her the way a cat played with a maimed mouse.

Belari said, "Thank you, Burson," then paused, eyeing the great creature who looked so manlike yet moved with the feral quickness of the wilds. "Have you tightened our security?"

Burson nodded. "Your fief is safe. We are checking the rest of the staff, for background irregularities."

"Have you found anything?"

Burson shook his head. "Your staff love you."

Belari's voice sharpened. "That's what we thought about Stephen. And now I wear body armor in my own fief. I can't afford the appearance of lost popularity. It affects my share price too much."

"I've been thorough."

"If my stock falls, Vernon will have me wired for TouchSense. I won't have it."

"I understand. There will be no more failures."

Belari frowned at the monster looming over her. "Good. Well, come on then." She motioned for Lidia to join her. "Your sister has been waiting for you." She took the fluted girl by the hand and led her out of the performance hall.

Lidia spared a glance back. Burson was gone. The servants bustled, placing orchid cuttings on tables, but Burson had disappeared, either blended into the walls or sped away on his errands of security.

Belari tugged Lidia's hand. "You led us on a merry search. I thought we would have to spray the pheromones again."

"I'm sorry."

"No harm. This time." Belari smiled down at her. "Are you nervous about tonight?"

Lidia shook her head. "No."

"No?"

Lidia shrugged. "Will Master Weir purchase our stock?"

"If he pays enough."

"Will he?"

Belari smiled. "I think he will, yes. You are unique. Like me. Vernon likes to collect rare beauty."

"What is he like?"

Belari's smile stiffened. She looked up, concentrating on their path through the castle. "When I was a girl, very young, much younger than you, long before I became famous, I used to go to a playground. A man came to watch me on the swings. He wanted to be my friend. I didn't like him, but being near him made me dizzy. Whatever he said made perfect sense. He smelled bad, but I couldn't pull away from him." Belari shook her head. "Someone's mother chased him away." She looked down at Lidia. "He had a chemical cologne, you understand?"

"Contraband?"

"Yes. From Asia. Not legal here. Vernon is like that. Your skin crawls but he draws you to him."

"He touches you."

Belari looked down at Lidia sadly. "He likes my old crone experience in my young girl body. But he hardly discriminates. He touches everyone." She smiled slightly. "But not you, perhaps. You are too valuable to touch."

"Too delicate."

"Don't sound so bitter. You're unique. We're going to make you a star." Belari looked down at her protégé hungrily. "Your stock will rise, and you will be a star."

Lidia watched from her windows as Belari's guests began to arrive. Aircars snaked in under security escort, sliding low over the pines, green and red running lights blinking in the darkness.

Nia came to stand behind Lidia. "They're here."

"Yes."

Snow clotted thickly on the trees, like heavy cream. The occasional blue sweeps of search beams highlighted the snow and the dark silhouettes of the forest; Burson's ski patrols, hoping to spy out the telltale red exhalations of intruders crouched amongst pine shadows. Their beams swept over the ancient hulk of a ski lift that climbed up from the town. It was rusting, silent except when the wind caught its chairs and sent its cables swaying. The empty seats swung lethargically in the freezing air, another victim of Belari's influence. Belari hated competition. Now, she was the only patron of the town that sparkled in the deep of the valley far below.

"You should get dressed," Nia said.

Lidia turned to study her twin. Black eyes like pits watched her from between elfin lids. Her skin was pale, stripped of pigment, and she was thin, accenting the delicacy of her bone structure. That was one true thing about her, about both of them: their bones were theirs. It was what had attracted Belari to them in the first place, when they were just eleven. Just old enough for Belari to strip them from their parents.

Lidia's gaze returned to the view. Deep in the tight crease of the mountain valley, the town shimmered with amber lights.

"Do you miss it?" she asked.

Nia slipped closer. "Miss what?"

Lidia nodded down at the shimmering jewel. "The town."

Their parents had been glassblowers, practicing the old arts abandoned in the face of efficient manufacturing, breathing delicate works into existence, sand running liquid under their supervision. They had moved to Belari's fief for patronage, like all the town's artisans: the potters, the blacksmiths, the painters. Sometimes Belari's peers noticed an artist and his influence grew. Niels Kinkaid had made his fortune from Belari's favor, turning iron to her will, outfitting her fortress with its great hand-wrought gates and her gardens with crouching sculptural surprises: foxes and children peering from amongst lupine and monkshood in the summers and deep drifted snow in the winters. Now he was almost famous enough to float his own stock.

Lidia's parents had come for patronage, but Belari's evaluating eye had not fallen on their artistry. Instead, she selected the biological accident of their twin daughters: delicate and blond with cornflower eyes that watched the world blinkless as they absorbed the fief's mountain wonders. Their trade flourished now thanks to the donation of their children.

Nia jostled Lidia gently, her ghostly face serious. "Hurry and dress. You mustn't be late."

Lidia turned away from her black-eyed sister. Of their original features, little remained. Belari had watched them grow in the castle for two years and then the pills began. Revitia treatments at thirteen froze their features in the matrix of youth. Then had come the eyes, drawn from twins in some far foreign land. Lidia sometimes wondered if in India, two dusky girl children looked out at the world from cornflower eyes, or if they walked the mud streets of their village guided only by the sound of echoes on cow-dung walls and the scrape of their canes on the dirt before them.

Lidia studied the night beyond the windows with her stolen black eyes. More aircars dropped guests on the landing pads then spread gossamer wings and let the mountain winds bear them away.

More treatments had followed: pigment drugs drained color from their skins, leaving them Kabuki pale, ethereal shadows of their former mountain sun-blushed selves, and then the surgeries began. She remembered waking after each successive surgery, crippled, unable to move for weeks despite the wide-bore needles full of cell-knitters and nutrient fluids the doctor flushed through her slight body. The doctor would hold her hand after the surgeries, wipe the sweat from her pale brow and whisper, "Poor girl. Poor poor girl." Then Belari would come and smile at the progress and say that Lidia and Nia would soon be stars.

Gusts of wind tore snow from the pines and sent it swirling in great tornado clouds around the arriving aristocracy. The guests hurried through the driving snow while the blue search beams of Burson's ski patrols carved across the forests. Lidia sighed and turned from the windows, obedient finally to Nia's anxious hope that she would dress.

Stephen and Lidia went on picnics together when Belari was away from the fief. They would leave the great gray construct of Belari's castle and walk carefully across the mountain meadows, Stephen always helping her, guiding her fragile steps through fields of daisies, columbine, and lupine until they peered down over sheer granite cliffs to the town far below. All about them glacier-sculpted peaks ringed the valley like giants squatting in council, their faces adorned with snow even in summer, like beards of wisdom. At the edge of the precipice, they ate a picnic lunch and Stephen told stories of the world before the fiefs, before Revitia made stars immortal.

He said the country had been democratic. That people once voted for their lieges. That they had been free to travel between any fief they liked. Everyone, he said, not just stars. Lidia knew there were places on the coasts where this occurred. She had heard of them. But it seemed difficult to credit. She was a child of a fief.

"It's true," Stephen said. "On the coasts, the people choose their own leader. It's only here, in the mountains, that it's different." He grinned at her. His soft brown eyes crinkled slightly, showing his humor, showing that he already saw the skepticism on her face.

Lidia laughed. "But who would pay for everything? Without Belari who would pay to fix the roads and make the schools?" She picked an aster and twirled it between her fingers, watching the purple spokes blur around the yellow center of the flower.

"The people do."

Lidia laughed again. "They can't afford to do that. They hardly have enough to feed themselves. And how would they know what to do?

Without Belari, no one would even know what needs fixing, or improving." She tossed the flower away, aiming to send it over the cliff. Instead, the wind caught it, and it fell near her.

Stephen picked up the flower and flicked it over the edge easily. "It's true. They don't have to be rich, they just work together. You think Belari knows everything? She hires advisors. People can do that as well as she."

Lidia shook her head. "People like Mirriam? Ruling a fief? It sounds like madness. No one would respect her."

Stephen scowled. "It's true," he said stubbornly, and because Lidia liked him and didn't want him to be unhappy, she agreed that it might be true, but in her heart, she thought that Stephen was a dreamer. It made him sweet, even if he didn't understand the true ways of the world.

"Do you like Belari?" Stephen asked suddenly.

"What do you mean?"

"Do you like her?"

Lidia gave him a puzzled look. Stephen's brown eyes studied her intensely. She shrugged. "She's a good liege. Everyone is fed and cared for. It's not like Master Weir's fief."

Stephen made a face of disgust. "Nothing is like Weir's fief. He's barbaric. He put one of his servants on a spit." He paused. "But still, look at what Belari has done to you."

Lidia frowned. "What about me?"

"You're not natural. Look at your eyes, your skin and…" he turned his eyes away, his voice lowering, "your bones. Look what she did to your bones."

"What's wrong with my bones?"

"You can barely walk!" he cried suddenly. "You should be able to walk!"

Lidia glanced around nervously. Stephen was talking critically. Someone might be listening. They seemed alone, but people were always around: security on the hillsides, others out for walks. Burson might be there, blended with the scenery, a stony man hidden amongst the rocks. Stephen had a hard time understanding about Burson. "I can walk," she whispered fiercely.

"How many times have you broken a leg or an arm or a rib?"

"Not in a year." She was proud of it. She had learned to be careful.

Stephen laughed incredulously. "Do you know how many bones I've broken in my life?" He didn't wait for an answer. "None. Not a single bone. Never. Do you even remember what it's like to walk without worrying that you'll trip, or bump into someone? You're like glass."

Lidia shook her head and looked away. "I'm going to be star. Belari will float us on the markets."

"But you can't walk," Stephen said. His eyes had a pitying quality that made Lidia angry.

"I can too. And it's enough."

"But—"

"No!" Lidia shook her head. "Who are you to say what I do? Look what Belari does to you, but still you are loyal! I may have had surgeries, but at least I'm not her toy."

It was the only time Stephen became angry. For a moment the rage in his face made Lidia think he would strike her and break her bones. A part of her hoped he would, that he would release the terrible frustration brewing between them, two servants each calling the other slave.

Instead, Stephen mastered himself and gave up the argument. He apologized and held her hand and they were quiet as the Sun set, but it was already too late and their quiet time was ruined. Lidia's mind had gone back to the days before the surgeries, when she ran without care, and though she would not admit it to Stephen, it felt as though he had ripped away a scab and revealed an aching bitter wound.

The performance hall trembled with anticipation, a room full of people high on Tingle and champagne. The muslin on the walls flickered like lightning as Belari's guests, swathed in brilliant silks and sparkling gold, swirled through the room in colorful clouds of revelry, clumping together with conversation, then breaking apart with laughter as they made their social rounds.

Lidia slipped carefully amongst the guests, her pale skin and diaphanous shift a spot of simplicity amongst the gaudy colors and wealth. Some of the guests eyed her curiously, the strange girl threading through their pleasure. They quickly dismissed her. She was merely another creature of Belari's, intriguing to look at, perhaps, but of no account. Their attention always returned to the more important patterns of gossip and association swirling around them. Lidia smiled. Soon, she thought, you will recognize me. She slipped up against a wall, near a table piled high with finger sandwiches, small cuts of meat and plates of plump strawberries.

Lidia scanned the crowds. Her sister was there, across the room, dressed in an identical diaphanous shift. Belari stood surrounded by mediascape names and fief lieges, her green gown matching her eyes, smiling, apparently at ease, even without her newfound habit of body armor.

Vernon Weir slipped up behind Belari, stroking her shoulder. Lidia saw Belari shiver and steel herself against Weir's touch. She wondered how he could not notice. Perhaps he was one of those who took pleasure in the repulsion he inflicted. Belari smiled at him, her emotions under control once again.

Lidia took a small plate of meats from the table. The meat was drizzled with raspberry reduction and was sweet. Belari liked sweet things, like the strawberries she was eating now with the Pendant Entertainment executive at the far end of the table. The sweet addiction was another side effect of the Tingle.

Belari caught sight of Lidia and led Vernon Weir toward her. "Do you like the meat?" she asked, smiling slightly.

Lidia nodded, finishing carefully.

Belari's smile sharpened. "I'm not surprised. You have a taste for good ingredients." Her face was flushed with Tingle. Lidia was glad they were in public. When Belari took too much Tingle she hungered and became erratic. Once, Belari had crushed strawberries against her skin, making her pale flesh blush with the juice, and then, high with the erotic charge of overdose, she had forced Lidia's tongue to Nia's juice-stained flesh and Nia's tongue to hers, while Belari watched, pleased with the decadent performance.

Belari selected a strawberry and offered it to Lidia. "Here. Have one, but don't stain yourself. I want you perfect." Her eyes glistened with excitement. Lidia steeled herself against memory and accepted the berry.

Vernon studied Lidia. "She's yours?"

Belari smiled fondly. "One of my fluted girls."

Vernon knelt and studied Lidia more closely. "What unusual eyes you have."

Lidia ducked her head shyly.

Belari said, "I had them replaced."

"Replaced?" Vernon glanced up at her. "Not altered?"

Belari smiled. "We both know nothing that beautiful comes artificially." She reached down and stroked Lidia's pale blond hair, smiling with satisfaction at her creation. "When I got her, she had the most beautiful blue eyes. The color of the flowers you find here in the mountains in the summer." She shook her head. "I had them replaced. They were beautiful, but not the look I wished for."

Vernon stood up again. "She is striking. But not as beautiful as you."

Belari smiled cynically at Vernon. "Is that why you want me wired for TouchSense?"

Vernon shrugged. "It's a new market, Belari. With your response, you could be a star."

"I'm already a star."

Vernon smiled. "But Revitia is expensive."

"We always come back to that, don't we, Vernon?"

Vernon gave her a hard look. "I don't want to be at odds with you, Belari. You've been wonderful for us. Worth every penny of your reconstruction. I've never seen a finer actress. But this is Pendant, after all. You could have bought your stock a long time ago if you weren't so attached to immortality." He eyed Belari coldly. "If you want to be immortal, you will wire TouchSense. Already we're seeing massive acceptance in the marketplace. It's the future of entertainment."

"I'm an actress, not a marionette. I don't crave people inside my skin."

Vernon shrugged. "We all pay a price for our celebrity. Where the markets move, we must follow. None of us is truly free." He looked at Belari meaningfully. "Certainly not if we want to live forever."

Belari smiled slyly. "Perhaps." She nodded at Lidia. "Run along. It's almost time." She turned back to Vernon. "There's something I'd like you to see."

Stephen gave her the vial the day before he died. Lidia had asked what it was, a few amber drops in a vial no larger than her pinky. She had smiled at the gift, feeling playful, but Stephen had been serious.

"It's freedom," he said.

She shook her head, uncomprehending.

"If you ever choose, you control your life. You don't have to be Belari's pet."

"I'm not her pet."

He shook his head. "If you ever want escape," he held up the vial, "it's here." He handed it to her and closed her pale hand around the tiny bottle. It was handblown. Briefly, she wondered if it came from her parents' workshop. Stephen said, "We're small people here. Only people like Belari have control. In other places, other parts of the world, it's different. Little people still matter. But here," he smiled sadly, "all we have is our lives."

Comprehension dawned. She tried to pull away but Stephen held her firmly. "I'm not saying you want it now, but someday, perhaps you will. Perhaps you'll decide you don't want to cooperate with Belari anymore. No matter how many gifts she showers on you." He squeezed her hand gently. "It's quick. Almost painless." He looked into her eyes with the soft brown kindness that had always been there.

It was a gift of love, however misguided, and because she knew it would make him happy, she nodded and agreed to keep the vial and put it in her hidey-hole, just in case. She couldn't have known that he had already chosen his own death, that he would hunt Belari with a knife, and almost succeed.

No one noticed when the fluted girls took their places on the center dais. They were merely oddities, pale angels, entwined. Lidia put her mouth to her sister's throat, feeling her pulse threading rapidly under her white, white skin. It throbbed against her tongue as she sought out the tiny bore hole in her sister's body. She felt the wet touch of Nia's tongue on her own throat, nestling into her flesh like a small mouse seeking comfort.

Lidia stilled herself, waiting for the attention of the people, patient and focused on her performance. She felt Nia breathe, her lungs expanding inside the frail cage of her chest. Lidia took her own breath. They began to play, first her own notes, running out through unstopped keys in her flesh, and then Nia's notes beginning as well. The open sound, haunting moments of breath, pressed through their bodies.

The melancholy tones trailed off. Lidia moved her head, breathing in, mirroring Nia as she pressed her lips again to her sister's flesh. This time, Lidia kissed her sister's hand. Nia's mouth sought the delicate hollow of her clavicle. Music, mournful, as hollow as they were, breathed out from their bodies. Nia breathed into Lidia and the exhalation of her lungs slipped out through Lidia's bones, tinged with emotion, as though the warm air of her sister came to life within her body.

Around the girls, the guests fell quiet. The silence spread, like ripples from a stone thrown into a placid pool, speeding outward from their epicenter to lap at the farthest edges of the room. All eyes turned to the pale girls on stage. Lidia could feel their eyes, hungry, yearning, almost physical as their gazes pressed against her. She moved her hands beneath her sister's shift, clasping her close. Her sister's hands touched her hips, closing stops in her fluted body. At their new embrace a sigh of yearning came from the crowd, a whisper of their own hungers made musical.

Lidia's hands found the keys to her sister, her tongue touching Nia's throat once more. Her fingers ran along the knuckles of Nia's spine, finding the clarinet within her, stroking keys. She pressed the warm breath of herself into her sister and she felt Nia breathing into her. Nia's sound was dark and melancholy, her own tones, brighter, higher, ran in counterpoint, a slowly developing story of forbidden touch.

They stood embraced. Their body music built, notes intertwining seductively as their hands stroked one another's bodies, bringing forth a complex rising tide of sound. Suddenly, Nia wrenched at Lidia's shift and Lidia's fingers tore away Nia's own. They stood revealed, pale elfin creatures of music. The guests around them gasped as the notes poured out brighter now, unmuffled by clinging clothes. The girls' musical graftings shone: cobalt boreholes in their spines, glinting stops and keys made of brass and ivory that ran along their fluted frames and contained a hundred possible instruments within the structure of their bodies.

Nia's mouth crept up Lidia's arm. Notes spilled out of Lidia as bright as water jewels. Laments of desire and sin flowed from Nia's pores. Their embraces became more frenzied, a choreography of lust. The spectators pressed closer, incited by the spectacle of naked youth and music intertwined.

Around her, Lidia was vaguely aware of their watching eyes and flushed expressions. The Tingle and the performance were doing their work on the guests. She could feel the heat rising in the room. She and Nia sank slowly to the floor, their embraces becoming more erotic and elaborate, the sexual tension of their musical conflict increasing as they entwined. Years of training had come to this moment, this carefully constructed weave of harmonizing flesh.

We perform pornography, Lidia thought. Pornography for the profit of Belari. She caught a glimpse of her patron's gleaming pleasure, Vernon Weir dumbstruck beside her. Yes, she thought, look at us, Master Weir, look and see what pornography we perform, and then it was her turn to play upon her sister, and her tongue and hands stroked Nia's keys.

It was a dance of seduction and acquiescence. They had other dances, solos and duets, some chaste, others obscene, but for their debut, Belari had chosen this one. The energy of their music increased, violent, climactic, until at last she and Nia lay upon the floor, expended, sheathed in sweat, bare twins tangled in musical lasciviousness. Their body music fell silent.

Around them, no one moved. Lidia tasted salt on her sister's skin as they held their pose. The lights dimmed, signaling completion.

Applause exploded around them. The lights brightened. Nia drew herself upright. Her lips quirked in a smile of satisfaction as she helped Lidia to her feet. You see? Nia's eyes seemed to say. We will be stars. Lidia found herself smiling with her sister. Despite the loss of Stephen, despite Belari's depredations, she was smiling. The audience's adoration washed over her, a balm of pleasure.

They curtsied to Belari as they had been trained, making obeisance first to their patron, the mother goddess who had created them. Belari smiled at the gesture, however scripted it was, and joined the applause of her guests. The people's applause increased again at the girls' good grace, then Nia and Lidia were curtseying to the corners of the compass, gathering their shifts and leaving the stage, guided by Burson's hulking presence to their patron.

The applause continued as they crossed the distance to Belari. Finally, at Belari's wave, the clapping gave way to respectful silence. She smiled at her assembled guests, placing her arms around the slight shoulders of the girls and said, "My lords and ladies, our Fluted Girls," and applause burst over them again, one final explosion of adulation before the guests fell to talking, fanning themselves, and feeling the flush of their own skins which the girls had inspired.

Belari held the fluted girls closely and whispered in their ears, "You did well." She hugged them carefully.

Vernon Weir's eyes roved over Lidia and Nia's exposed bodies. "You outdo yourself, Belari," he said.

Belari inclined her head slightly at the compliment. Her grip on Lidia's shoulder became proprietary. Belari's voice didn't betray her tension. She kept it light, comfortably satisfied with her position, but her fingers dug into Lidia's skin. "They are my finest."

"Such an extraordinary crafting."

"It's expensive when they break a bone. They're terribly fragile." Belari smiled down at the girls affectionately. "They hardly remember what it's like to walk without care."

"All the most beautiful things are fragile." Vernon touched Lidia's cheek. She forced herself not to flinch. "It must have been complex to build them."

Belari nodded. "They are intricate." She traced a finger along the boreholes in Nia's arm. "Each note isn't simply affected by the placement of fingers on keys; but also by how they press against one another, or the floor; if an arm is bent or if it is straightened. We froze their hormone levels so that they wouldn't grow, and then we began designing their instruments. It takes an enormous amount of skill for them to play and to dance."

"How long have you been training them?"

"Five years. Seven if you count the surgeries that began the process."

Vernon shook his head. "And we never heard of them."

"You would have ruined them. I'm going to make them stars."

"We made you a star."

"And you'll unmake me as well, if I falter."

"So you'll float them on the markets?"

Belari smiled at him. "Of course. I'll retain a controlling interest, but the rest, I will sell."

"You'll be rich."

Belari smiled, "More than that, I'll be independent."

Vernon mimed elaborate disappointment. "I suppose this means we won't be wiring you for TouchSense."

"I suppose not."

The tension between them was palpable. Vernon, calculating, looking for an opening while Belari gripped her property and faced him. Vernon's eyes narrowed.

As though sensing his thoughts, Belari said, "I've insured them."

Vernon shook his head ruefully. "Belari, you do me a disservice." He sighed. "I suppose I should congratulate you. To have such loyal subjects, and such wealth, you've achieved more than I would have thought possible when we first met."

"My servants are loyal because I treat them well. They are happy to serve."

"Would your Stephen agree?" Vernon waved at the sweetmeats in the center of the refreshment table, drizzled with raspberry and garnished with bright green leaves of mint.

Belari smiled. "Oh yes, even him. Do you know that just as Michael and Renee were preparing to cook him, he looked at me and said 'Thank you'?" She shrugged. "He tried to kill me, but he did have the most eager urge to please, even so. At the very end, he told me he was sorry, and that the best years of his life had been in service to me." She wiped at a theatrical tear. "I don't know how it is, that he could love me so, and still so desire to have me dead." She looked away from Vernon, watching the other guests. "For that, though, I thought I would serve him, rather than simply stake him out as a warning. We loved each other, even if he was a traitor."

Vernon shrugged sympathetically. "So many people dislike the fief structure. You try to tell them that you provide far more security than what existed before, and yet still they protest, and," he glanced meaningfully at Belari, "sometimes more."

Belari shrugged. "Well, my subjects don't protest. At least not until Stephen. They love me."

Vernon smiled. "As we all do. In any case, serving him chilled this way." He lifted a plate from the table. "Your taste is impeccable."

Lidia's face stiffened as she followed the conversation. She looked at the array of finely sliced meats and then at Vernon as he forked a bite into his mouth. Her stomach turned. Only her training let her remain still. Vernon and Belari's conversation continued, but all Lidia could think was that she had consumed her friend, the one who had been kind to her.

Anger trickled through her, filling her porous body with rebellion. She longed to attack her smug patron, but her rage was impotent. She was too weak to hurt Belari. Her bones were too fragile, her physique too delicate. Belari was strong in all things as she was weak. Lidia stood trembling with frustration, and then Stephen's voice whispered comforting wisdom inside her head. She could defeat Belari. Her pale skin flushed with pleasure at the thought.

As though sensing her, Belari looked down. "Lidia, go put on clothes and come back. I'll want to introduce you and your sister to everyone before we take you public."

Lidia crept toward her hidey-hole. The vial was still there, if Burson had not found it. Her heart hammered at the thought: that the vial might be missing, that Stephen's final gift had been destroyed by the monster. She slipped through dimly lit servants' tunnels to the kitchen, anxiety pulsing at every step.

The kitchen was busy, full of staff preparing new platters for the guests. Lidia's stomach turned. She wondered if more trays bore Stephen's remains. The stoves flared and the ovens roared as Lidia slipped through the confusion, a ghostly waif sliding along the walls. No one paid her attention. They were too busy laboring for Belari, doing her bidding without thought or conscience: slaves, truly. Obedience was all Belari cared for.

Lidia smiled grimly to herself. If obedience was what Belari loved, she was happy to provide a true betrayal. She would collapse on the floor, amongst her mistress's guests, destroying Belari's perfect moment, shaming her and foiling her hopes of independence.

The pantry was silent when Lidia slipped through its archway. Everyone was busy serving, running like dogs to feed Belari's brood. Lidia wandered amongst the stores, past casks of oil and sacks of onions, past the great humming freezers that held whole sides of beef within their steel bowels. She reached the broad tall shelves at the pantry's end and climbed past preserved peaches, tomatoes, and olives to the high-stored legumes. She pushed aside a vacuum jar of lentils and felt within.

For a moment, as she slid her hand around the cramped hiding place, she thought the vial was missing, but then her grasp closed on the tiny blown-glass bulb.

She climbed down, careful not to break any bones, laughing at herself as she did, thinking that it hardly mattered now, and hurried back through the kitchen, past the busy, obedient servants, and then down the servants' tunnels, intent on self-destruction.

As she sped through the darkened tunnels, she smiled, glad that she would never again steal through dim halls hidden from the view of aristocracy. Freedom was in her hands. For the first time in years she controlled her own fate.

Burson lunged from the shadows, his skin shifting from black to flesh as he materialized. He seized her and jerked her to a halt. Lidia's body strained at the abrupt capture. She gasped, her joints creaking. Burson gathered her wrists into a single massive fist. With his other hand, he turned her chin upward, subjecting her black eyes to the interrogation of his red-rimmed orbs. "Where are you going?"

His size could make you mistake him for stupid, she thought. His slow rumbling voice. His great animal-like gaze. But he was observant where Belari was not. Lidia trembled and cursed herself for foolishness. Burson studied her, his nostrils flaring at the scent of fear. His eyes watched the blush of her skin. "Where are you going?" he asked again. Warning laced his tone.

"Back to the party," Lidia whispered.

"Where have you been?"

Lidia tried to shrug. "Nowhere. Changing."

"Nia is already there. You are late. Belari wondered about you."

Lidia said nothing. There was nothing she could say to make Burson lose his suspicions. She was terrified that he would pry open her clenched hand and discover the glass vial. The servants said it was impossible to lie to Burson. He discovered everything.

Burson eyed her silently, letting her betray herself. Finally he said, "You went to your hidey-hole." He sniffed at her. "Not in the kitchen, though. The pantry." He smiled, revealing hard sharp teeth. "High up."

Lidia held her breath. Burson couldn't let go of a problem until it was solved. It was bred into him. His eyes swept over her skin. "You're nervous." He sniffed. "Sweating. Fear."

Lidia shook her head stubbornly. The tiny vial in her hand was slick, she was afraid she would drop it, or move her hands and call attention to it. Burson's great strength pulled her until they were nose to nose. His fist squeezed her wrists until she thought they would shatter. He studied her eyes. "So afraid."

"No." Lidia shook her head again.

Burson laughed, contempt and pity in the sound. "It must be terrifying to know you can be broken, at any time." His stone grip relaxed. Blood rushed back into her wrists. "Have your hidey-hole, then. Your secret is safe with me."

For a moment, Lidia wasn't sure what he meant. She stood before the giant security officer, frozen still, but then Burson waved his hand irritably and slipped back into the shadows, his skin darkening as he disappeared. "Go."

Lidia stumbled away, her legs wavering, threatening to give out. She forced herself to keep moving, imagining Burson's eyes burning into her pale back. She wondered if he still watched her or if he had already lost interest in the harmless spindly fluted girl, Belari's animal who hid in the closets and made the staff hunt high and low for the selfish mite.

Lidia shook her head in wonderment. Burson had not seen. Burson, for all his enhancements, was blind, so accustomed to inspiring terror that he could no longer distinguish fear from guilt.

A new gaggle of admirers swarmed around Belari, people who knew she was soon to be independent. Once the fluted girls floated on the market, Belari would be nearly as powerful as Vernon Weir, valuable not only for her own performances, but also for her stable of talent. Lidia moved to join her, the vial of liberation hidden in her fist.

Nia stood near Belari, talking to Claire Paranovis from SK Net. Nia nodded graciously at whatever the woman was saying, acting as Belari had trained them: always polite, never ruffled, always happy to talk, nothing to hide, but stories to tell. That was how you handled the media. If you kept them full, they never looked deeper. Nia looked comfortable in her role.

For a moment, Lidia felt a pang of regret at what she was about to do, then she was beside Belari, and Belari was smiling and introducing her to the men and women who surrounded her with fanatic affection.

Mgumi Story. Kim Song Lee. Maria Blyst. Takashi Ghandi. More and more names, the global fraternity of media elites.

Lidia smiled and bowed while Belari fended off their proffered hands of congratulation, protecting her delicate investment. Lidia performed as she had been trained, but in her hand the vial lay sweaty, a small jewel of power and destiny. Stephen had been right. The small only controlled their own termination, sometimes not even that. Lidia watched the guests take slices of Stephen, commenting on his sweetness. Sometimes, not even that.

She turned from the crowd of admirers and drew a strawberry from the pyramids of fruit on the refreshment table. She dipped it in cream and rolled it in sugar, tasting the mingled flavors. She selected another strawberry, red and tender between her spidery fingers, a sweet medium for a bitter freedom earned.

With her thumb, she popped the tiny cork out of the vial and sprinkled amber jewels on the lush berry. She wondered if it would hurt, or if it would be quick. It hardly mattered, soon she would be free. She would cry out and fall to the floor and the guests would step back, stunned at Belari's loss. Belari would be humiliated, and more important, would lose the value of the fluted twins. Vernon Weir's lecherous hands would hold her once again.

Lidia gazed at the tainted strawberry. Sweet, Lidia thought. Death should be sweet. She saw Belari watching her, smiling fondly, no doubt happy to see another as addicted to sweets as she. Lidia smiled inwardly, pleased that Belari would see the moment of her rebellion. She raised the strawberry to her lips.

Suddenly a new inspiration whispered in her ear.

An inch from death, Lidia paused, then turned and held out the strawberry to her patron.

She offered the berry as obeisance, with the humility of a creature utterly owned. She bowed her head and proffered the strawberry in the palm of her pale hand, bringing forth all her skill, playing the loyal servant desperately eager to please. She held her breath, no longer aware of the room around her. The guests and conversations all had disappeared. Everything had gone silent.

There was only Belari and the strawberry and the frozen moment of delicious possibility.

THE PEOPLE OF SAND AND SLAG

"Hostile movement! Well inside the perimeter! Well inside!" I stripped off my Immersive Response goggles as adrenaline surged through me. The virtual cityscape I'd been about to raze disappeared, replaced by our monitoring room's many views of SesCo's mining operations. On one screen, the red phosphorescent tracery of an intruder skated across a terrain map, a hot blip like blood spattering its way toward Pit 8.

Jaak was already out of the monitoring room. I ran for my gear.

I caught up with Jaak in the equipment room as he grabbed a TS-101 and slashbangs and dragged his impact exoskeleton over his tattooed body. He draped bandoleers of surgepacks over his massive shoulders and ran for the outer locks. I strapped on my own exoskeleton, pulled my 101 from its rack, checked its charge, and followed.

Lisa was already in the HEV, its turbofans screaming like banshees when the hatch dilated. Sentry centaurs leveled their 101s at me, then relaxed as friend/foe data spilled into their heads-up displays. I bolted across the tarmac, my skin pricking under blasts of icy Montana wind and the jet wash of Hentasa Mark V engines. Overhead, the clouds glowed orange with light from SesCo's mining bots.

"Come on, Chen! Move! Move! Move!"

I dove into the hunter. The ship leaped into the sky. It banked, throwing me against a bulkhead, then the Hentasas cycled wide and the hunter punched forward. The HEV's hatch slid shut. The wind howl muted.

I struggled forward to the flight cocoon and peered over Jaak's and Lisa's shoulders to the landscape beyond.

"Have a good game?" Lisa asked.

I scowled. "I was about to win. I made it to Paris."

We cut through the mists over the catchment lakes, skimming inches above the water, and then we hit the far shore. The hunter lurched as its anti-collision software jerked us away from the roughening terrain. Lisa overrode the computers and forced the ship back down against the soil, driving us so low I could have reached out and dragged my hands through the broken scree as we screamed over it.

Alarms yowled. Jaak shut them off as Lisa pushed the hunter lower. Ahead, a tailings ridge loomed. We ripped up its face and dropped sickeningly into the next valley. The Hentasas shuddered as Lisa forced them to the edge of their design buffer. We hurtled up and over another ridge. Ahead, the ragged cutscape of mined mountains stretched to the horizon. We dipped again into mist and skimmed low over another catchment lake, leaving choppy wake in the thick golden waters.

Jaak studied the hunter's scanners. "I've got it." He grinned. "It's moving, but slow."

"Contact in one minute," Lisa said. "He hasn't launched any countermeasures."

I watched the intruder on the tracking screens as they displayed real-time data fed to us from SesCo's satellites. "It's not even a masked target. We could have dropped a mini on it from base if we'd known he wasn't going to play hide-and-seek."

"Could have finished your game," Lisa said.

"We could still nuke him," Jaak suggested.

I shook my head. "No, let's take a look. Vaporizing him won't leave us anything and Bunbaum will want to know what we used the hunter for."

"Thirty seconds."

"He wouldn't care, if someone hadn't taken the hunter on a joyride to Cancun."

Lisa shrugged. "I wanted to swim. It was either that, or rip off your kneecaps."

The hunter lunged over another series of ridges.

Jaak studied his monitor. "Target's moving away. He's still slow. We'll get him."

"Fifteen seconds to drop," Lisa said. She unstrapped and switched the hunter to software. We all ran for the hatch as the HEV yanked itself skyward, its autopilot desperate to tear away from the screaming hazard of the rocks beneath its belly.

We plunged out the hatch, one, two, three, falling like Icarus. We slammed into the ground at hundreds of kilometers per hour. Our exoskeletons shattered like glass, flinging leaves into the sky. The shards fluttered down around us, black metallic petals absorbing our enemy's radar and heat detection while we rolled to jarred vulnerable stops in muddy scree.

The hunter blew over the ridge, Hentasas shrieking, a blazing target. I dragged myself upright and ran for the ridge, my feet churning through yellow tailings mud and rags of jaundiced snow. Behind me, Jaak was down with smashed arms. The leaves of his exoskeleton marked his roll path, a long trail of black shimmering metal. Lisa lay a hundred yards away, her femur rammed through her thigh like a bright white exclamation mark.

I reached the top of the ridge and stared down into the valley.

Nothing.

I dialed up the magnification of my helmet. The monotonous slopes of more tailings rubble spread out below me. Boulders, some as large as our HEV, some cracked and shattered by high explosives, shared the slopes with the unstable yellow shale and fine grit of waste materials from SesCo's operations.

Jaak slipped up beside me, followed a moment later by Lisa, her flight suit's leg torn and bloodied. She wiped yellow mud off her face and ate it as she studied the valley below. "Anything?"

I shook my head. "Nothing yet. You okay?"

"Clean break."

Jaak pointed. "There!"

Down in the valley, something was running, flushed by the hunter. It slipped along a shallow creek, viscous with tailings acid. The ship herded it toward us. Nothing. No missile fire. No slag. Just the running creature. A mass of tangled hair. Quadrupedal. Splattered with mud.

"Some kind of bio-job?" I wondered.

"It doesn't have any hands," Lisa murmured.

"No equipment either."

Jaak muttered. "What kind of sick bastard makes a bio-job without hands?"

I searched the nearby ridgelines. "Decoy, maybe?"

Jaak checked his scanner data, piped in from the hunter's more aggressive instruments. "I don't think so. Can we put the hunter up higher? I want to look around."

At Lisa's command, the hunter rose, allowing its sensors a fuller reach. The howl of its turbofans became muted as it gained altitude.

Jaak waited as more data spat into his heads-up display. "Nope, nothing. And no new alerts from any of the perimeter stations, either. We're alone."

Lisa shook her head. "We should have just dropped a mini on it from base."

Down in the valley, the bio-job's headlong run slowed to a trot. It seemed unaware of us. Closer now, we could make out its shape: A shaggy quadruped with a tail. Dreadlocked hair dangled from its shanks like ornaments, tagged with tailings mud clods. It was stained around its legs from the acids of the catchment ponds, as though it had forded streams of urine.

"That's one ugly bio-job," I said.

Lisa shouldered her 101. "Bio-melt when I'm done with it."

"Wait!" Jaak said. "Don't slag it!"

Lisa glanced over at him, irritated. "What now?"

"That's not a bio-job at all," Jaak whispered. "That's a dog."

He stood suddenly and jumped over the hillside, running headlong down the scree toward the animal.

"Wait!" Lisa called, but Jaak was already fully exposed and blurring to his top speed.

The animal took one look at Jaak, whooping and hollering as he came roaring down the slope, then turned and ran. It was no match for Jaak. Half a minute later he overtook the animal.

Lisa and I exchanged glances. "Well," she said, "it's awfully slow if it's a bio-job. I've seen centaurs walk faster."

By the time we caught up with Jaak and the animal, Jaak had it cornered in a dull gully. The animal stood in the center of a trickling ditch of sludgy water, shaking and growling and baring its teeth at us as we surrounded it. It tried to break around us, but Jaak kept it corralled easily.

Up close, the animal seemed even more pathetic than from a distance, a good thirty kilos of snarling mange. Its paws were slashed and bloody and patches of fur were torn away, revealing festering chemical burns underneath.

"I'll be damned," I breathed, staring at the animal. "It really looks like a dog."

Jaak grinned. "It's like finding a goddamn dinosaur."

"How could it live out here?" Lisa's arm swept the horizon. "There's nothing to live on. It's got to be modified." She studied it closely, then glanced at Jaak. "Are you sure nothing's coming in on the perimeter? This isn't some kind of decoy?"

Jaak shook his head. "Nothing. Not even a peep."

I leaned in toward the creature. It bared its teeth in a rictus of hatred. "It's pretty beat up. Maybe it's the real thing."

Jaak said, "Oh yeah, it's the real thing all right. I saw a dog in a zoo once. I'm telling you, this is a dog."

Lisa shook her head. "It can't be. It would be dead, if it were a real dog."

Jaak just grinned and shook his head. "No way. Look at it." He reached out to push the hair out of the animal's face so that we could see its muzzle.

The animal lunged and its teeth sank into Jaak's arm. It shook his arm violently, growling as Jaak stared down at the creature latched onto his flesh. It yanked its head back and forth, trying to tear Jaak's arm off. Blood spurted around its muzzle as its teeth found Jaak's arteries.

Jaak laughed. His bleeding stopped. "Damn. Check that out." He lifted his arm until the animal dangled fully out of the stream, dripping. "I got me a pet."

The dog swung from the thick bough of Jaak's arm. It tried to shake his arm once again, but its movements were ineffectual now that it hung off the ground. Even Lisa smiled.

"Must be a bummer to wake up and find out you're at the end of your evolutionary curve."

The dog growled, determined to hang on.

Jaak laughed and drew his monomol knife. "Here you go, doggy." He sliced his arm off, leaving it in the bewildered animal's mouth.

Lisa cocked her head. "You think we could make some kind of money on it?"

Jaak watched as the dog devoured his severed arm. "I read somewhere that they used to eat dogs. I wonder what they taste like."

I checked the time in my heads-up display. We'd already killed an hour on an exercise that wasn't giving any bonuses. "Get your dog, Jaak, and get it on the hunter. We aren't going to eat it before we call Bunbaum."

"He'll probably call it company property," Jaak groused.

"Yeah, that's the way it always goes. But we still have to report. Might as well keep the evidence, since we didn't nuke it."

We ate sand for dinner. Outside the security bunker, the mining robots rumbled back and forth, ripping deeper into the earth, turning it into a mush of tailings and rock acid that they left in exposed ponds when they hit the water table, or piled into thousand-foot mountainscapes of waste soil. It was comforting to hear those machines cruising back and forth all day. Just you and the bots and the profits, and if nothing got bombed while you were on duty, there was always a nice bonus.

After dinner we sat around and sharpened Lisa's skin, implanting blades along her limbs so that she was like a razor from all directions. She'd considered monomol blades, but it was too easy to take a limb off accidentally, and we lost enough body parts as it was without adding to the mayhem. That kind of garbage was for people who didn't have to work: aesthetes from New York City and California.

Lisa had a DermDecora kit for the sharpening. She'd bought it last time we'd gone on vacation and spent extra to get it, instead of getting one of the cheap knock-offs that were cropping up. We worked on cutting her skin down to the bone and setting the blades. A friend of ours in L.A said that he just held DermDecora parties so everyone could do their modifications and help out with the hard-to-reach places.

Lisa had done my glowspine, a sweet tracery of lime landing lights that ran from my tailbone to the base of my skull, so I didn't mind helping her out, but Jaak, who did all of his modification with an old-time scar and tattoo shop in Hawaii, wasn't so pleased. It was a little frustrating because her flesh kept trying to close before we had the blades set, but eventually we got the hang of it, and an hour later, she started looking good.

Once we finished with Lisa's front settings, we sat around and fed her. I had a bowl of tailings mud that I drizzled into her mouth to speed her integration process. When we weren't feeding her, we watched the dog. Jaak had shoved it into a makeshift cage in one corner of our common room. It lay there like it was dead.

Lisa said, "I ran its DNA. It really is a dog."

"Bunbaum believe you?"

She gave me a dirty look. "What do you think?"

I laughed. At SesCo, tactical defense responders were expected to be fast, flexible, and deadly, but the reality was our SOP was always the same: drop nukes on intruders, slag the leftovers to melt so they couldn't regrow, hit the beaches for vacation. We were independent and trusted as far as tactical decisions went, but there was no way SesCo was going to believe its slag soldiers had found a dog in their tailings mountains.

Lisa nodded. "He wanted to know how the hell a dog could live out here. Then he wanted to know why we didn't catch it sooner. Wanted to know what he pays us for." She pushed her short blond hair off her face and eyed the animal. "I should have slagged it."

"What's he want us to do?"

"It's not in the manual. He's calling back."

I studied the limp animal. "I want to know how it was surviving. Dogs are meat eaters, right?"

"Maybe some of the engineers were giving it meat. Like Jaak did."

Jaak shook his head. "I don't think so. The sucker threw up my arm almost right after he ate it." He wiggled his new stump where it was rapidly regrowing. "I don't think we're compatible for it."

I asked, "But we could eat it, right?"

Lisa laughed and took a spoonful of tailings. "We can eat anything. We're the top of the food chain."

"Weird how it can't eat us."

"You've probably got more mercury and lead running through your blood than any pre-weeviltech animal ever could have had."

"That's bad?"

"Used to be poison."

"Weird."

Jaak said, "I think I might have broken it when I put it in the cage." He studied it seriously. "It's not moving like it was before. And I heard something snap when I stuffed it in."

"So?"

Jaak shrugged. "I don't think it's healing."

The dog did look kind of beat up. It just lay there, its sides going up and down like a bellows. Its eyes were half-open, but didn't seem to be focused on any of us. When Jaak made a sudden movement, it twitched for a second, but it didn't get up. It didn't even growl.

Jaak said, "I never thought an animal could be so fragile."

"You're fragile, too. That's not such a big surprise."

"Yeah, but I only broke a couple bones on it, and now look at it. It just lies there and pants."

Lisa frowned thoughtfully. "It doesn't heal." She climbed awkwardly to her feet and went to peer into the cage. Her voice was excited. "It really is a dog. Just like we used to be. It could take weeks for it to heal. One broken bone, and it's done for."

She reached a razored hand into the cage and sliced a thin wound into its shank. Blood oozed out, and kept oozing. It took minutes for it to begin clotting. The dog lay still and panted, clearly wasted.

She laughed. "It's hard to believe we ever lived long enough to evolve out of that. If you chop off its legs, they won't regrow." She cocked her head, fascinated. "It's as delicate as rock. You break it, and it never comes back together." She reached out to stroke the matted fur of the animal. "It's as easy to kill as the hunter."

The comm buzzed. Jaak went to answer.

Lisa and I stared at the dog, our own little window into pre-history.

Jaak came back into the room. "Bunbaum's flying out a biologist to take a look at it."

"You mean a bio-engineer," I corrected him.

"Nope. Biologist. Bunbaum said they study animals."

Lisa sat down. I checked her blades to see if she'd knocked anything loose. "There's a dead-end job."

"I guess they grow them out of DNA. Study what they do. Behavior, shit like that."

"Who hires them?"

Jaak shrugged. "Pau Foundation has three of them on staff. Origin of life guys. That's who's sending out this one. Mushi-something. Didn't get his name."

"Origin of life?"

"Sure, you know, what makes us tick. What makes us alive. Stuff like that."

I poured a handful of tailings mud into Lisa's mouth. She gobbled it gratefully. "Mud makes us tick," I said.

Jaak nodded at the dog. "It doesn't make that dog tick."

We all looked at the dog. "It's hard to tell what makes it tick."

Lin Musharraf was a short guy with black hair and a hooked nose that dominated his face. He had carved his skin with swirling patterns of glow implants, so he stood out as cobalt spirals in the darkness as he jumped down from his chartered HEV.

The centaurs went wild about the unauthorized visitor and corralled him right up against his ship. They were all over him and his DNA kit, sniffing him, running their scanners over his case, pointing their 101s into his glowing face and snarling at him.

I let him sweat for a minute before calling them away. The centaurs backed off, swearing and circling, but didn't slag him. Musharraf looked shaken. I couldn't blame him. They're scary monsters: bigger and faster than a man. Their behavior patches make them vicious, their sentience upgrades give them the intelligence to operate military equipment, and their basic fight/flight response is so impaired that they only know how to attack when they're threatened. I've seen a half-slagged centaur tear a man to pieces barehanded and then join an assault on enemy ridge fortifications, dragging its whole melted carcass forward with just its arms. They're great critters to have at your back when the slag starts flying.

I guided Musharraf out of the scrum. He had a whole pack of memory addendums blinking off the back of his skull: a fat pipe of data retrieval, channeled direct to the brain, and no smash protection. The centaurs could have shut him down with one hard tap to the back of the head. His cortex might have grown back, but he wouldn't have been the same. Looking at those blinking triple fins of intelligence draping down the back of his head, you could tell he was a typical lab rat. All brains, no survival instincts. I wouldn't have stuck mem-adds into my head even for a triple bonus.

"You've got a dog?" Musharraf asked when we were out of reach of the centaurs.

"We think so." I led him down into the bunker, past our weapons racks and weight rooms to the common room where we'd stored the dog. The dog looked up at us as we came in, the most movement it had made since Jaak put it in the cage.

Musharraf stopped short and stared. "Remarkable."

He knelt in front of the animal's cage and unlocked the door. He held out a handful of pellets. The dog dragged itself upright. Musharraf backed away, giving it room, and the dog followed stiff and wary, snuffling after the pellets. It buried its muzzle in his brown hand, snorting and gobbling at the pellets.

Musharraf looked up. "And you found it in your tailings pits?"

"That's right."

"Remarkable."

The dog finished the pellets and snuffled his palm for more. Musharraf laughed and stood. "No more for you. Not right now." He opened his DNA kit, pulled out a sampler needle and stuck the dog. The sampler's chamber filled with blood.

Lisa watched. "You talk to it?"

Musharraf shrugged. "It's a habit."

"But it's not sentient."

"Well, no, but it likes to hear voices." The chamber finished filling. He withdrew the needle, disconnected the collection chamber and fitted it into the kit. The analysis software blinked alive and the blood disappeared into the heart of the kit with a soft vacuum hiss.

"How do you know?"

Musharraf shrugged. "It's a dog. Dogs are that way."

We all frowned. Musharraf started running tests on the blood, humming tunelessly to himself as he worked. His DNA kit peeped and squawked. Lisa watched him run his tests, clearly pissed off that SesCo had sent out a lab rat to retest what she had already done. It was easy to understand her irritation. A centaur could have run those DNA tests.

"I'm astounded that you found a dog in your pits," Musharraf muttered.

Lisa said, "We were going to slag it, but Bunbaum wouldn't let us."

Musharraf eyed her. "How restrained of you."

Lisa shrugged. "Orders."

"Still, I'm sure your thermal surge weapon presented a powerful temptation. How good of you not to slag a starving animal."

Lisa frowned suspiciously. I started to worry that she might take Musharraf apart. She was crazy enough without people talking down to her. The memory addendums on the back of his head were an awfully tempting target: one slap, down goes the lab rat. I wondered if we sank him in a catchment lake if anyone would notice him missing. A biologist, for Christ's sake.

Musharraf turned back to his DNA kit, apparently unaware of his hazard. "Did you know that in the past, people believed that we should have compassion for all things on Earth? Not just for ourselves, but for all living things?"

"So?"

"I would hope you will have compassion for one foolish scientist and not dismember me today."

Lisa laughed. I relaxed. Encouraged, Musharraf said, "It truly is remarkable that you found such a specimen amongst your mining operations. I haven't heard of a living specimen in ten or fifteen years."

"I saw one in a zoo, once," Jaak said.

"Yes, well, a zoo is the only place for them. And laboratories, of course. They still provide useful genetic data." He was studying the results of the tests, nodding to himself as information scrolled across the kit's screen.

Jaak grinned. "Who needs animals if you can eat stone?"

Musharraf began packing up his DNA kit. "Weeviltech. Precisely. We transcended the animal kingdom." He latched his kit closed and nodded to us all. "Well, it's been quite enlightening. Thank you for letting me see your specimen."

"You're not going to take it with you?"

Musharraf paused, surprised. "Oh no. I don't think so."

"It's not a dog, then?"

"Oh no, it's quite certainly a real dog. But what on Earth would I do with it?" He held up a vial of blood. "We have the DNA. A live one is hardly worth keeping around. Very expensive to maintain, you know. Manufacturing a basic organism's food is quite complex. Clean rooms, air filters, special lights. Re-creating the web of life isn't easy. Far more simple to release oneself from it completely than to attempt to re-create it." He glanced at the dog. "Unfortunately, our furry friend over there would never survive weeviltech. The worms would eat him as quickly as they eat everything else. No, you would have to manufacture the animal from scratch. And really, what would be the point of that? A bio-job without hands?" He laughed and headed for his HEV.

We all looked at each other. I jogged after the doctor and caught up with him at the hatch to the tarmac. He had paused on the verge of opening it. "Your centaurs know me now?" he asked.

"Yeah, you're fine."

"Good." He dilated the hatch and strode out into the cold.

I trailed after him. "Wait! What are we supposed to do with it?"

"The dog?" The doctor climbed into the HEV and began strapping in. Wind whipped around us, carrying stinging grit from the tailings piles. "Turn it back to your pits. Or you could eat it, I suppose. I understand that it was a real delicacy. There are recipes for cooking animals. They take time, but they can give quite extraordinary results."

Musharraf's pilot started cycling up his turbofans.

"Are you kidding?"

Musharraf shrugged and shouted over the increasing scream of the engines. "You should try it! Just another part of our heritage that's atrophied since weeviltech!"

He yanked down the flight cocoon's door, sealing himself inside. The turbofans cycled higher and the pilot motioned me back from their wash as the HEV slowly lifted into the air.

Lisa and Jaak couldn't agree on what we should do with the dog. We had protocols for working out conflict. As a tribe of killers, we needed them. Normally, consensus worked for us, but every once in a while, we just got tangled up and stuck to our positions, and after that, not much could get done without someone getting slaughtered. Lisa and Jaak dug in, and after a couple days of wrangling, with Lisa threatening to cook the thing in the middle of the night while Jaak wasn't watching, and Jaak threatening to cook her if she did, we finally went with a majority vote. I got to be the tie-breaker.

"I say we eat it," Lisa said.

We were sitting in the monitoring room, watching satellite shots of the tailings mountains and the infrared blobs of the mining bots while they ripped around in the earth. In one corner, the object of our discussion lay in its cage, dragged there by Jaak in an attempt to sway the result. He spun his observation chair, turning his attention away from the theater maps. "I think we should keep it. It's cool. Old-timey, you know? I mean, who the hell do you know who has a real dog?"

"Who the hell wants the hassle?" Lisa responded. "I say we try real meat." She cut a line in her forearm with her razors. She ran her finger along the resulting blood beads and tasted them as the wound sealed.

They both looked at me. I looked at the ceiling. "Are you sure you can't decide this without me?"

Lisa grinned. "Come on, Chen, you decide. It was a group find. Jaak won't pout, will you?"

Jaak gave her a dirty look.

I looked at Jaak. "I don't want its food costs to come out of group bonuses. We agreed we'd use part of it for the new Immersive Response. I'm sick of the old one."

Jaak shrugged. "Fine with me. I can pay for it out of my own. I just won't get any more tats."

I leaned back in my chair, surprised, then looked at Lisa. "Well, if Jaak wants to pay for it, I think we should keep it."

Lisa stared at me, incredulous. "But we could cook it!"

I glanced at the dog where it lay panting in its cage. "It's like having a zoo of our own. I kind of like it."

Musharraf and the Pau Foundation hooked us up with a supply of food pellets for the dog and Jaak looked up an old database on how to splint its busted bones. He bought water filtration so that it could drink.

I thought I'd made a good decision, putting the costs on Jaak, but I didn't really foresee the complications that came with having an un-modified organism in the bunker. The thing shit all over the floor, and sometimes it wouldn't eat, and it would get sick for no reason, and it was slow to heal so we all ended up playing nursemaid to the thing while it lay in its cage. I kept expecting Lisa to break its neck in the middle of the night, but even though she grumbled, she didn't assassinate it.

Jaak tried to act like Musharraf. He talked to the dog. He logged onto the libraries and read all about old-time dogs. How they ran in packs.

How people used to breed them.

We tried to figure out what kind of dog it was, but we couldn't narrow it down much, and then Jaak discovered that all the dogs could interbreed, so all you could do was guess that it was some kind of big sheep dog, with maybe a head from a Rottweiler, along with maybe some other kind of dog, like a wolf or coyote or something.

Jaak thought it had coyote in it because they were supposed to have been big adapters, and whatever our dog was, it must have been a big adapter to hang out in the tailings pits. It didn't have the boosters we had, and it had still lived in the rock acids. Even Lisa was impressed by that.

I was carpet bombing Antarctic Recessionists, swooping low, driving the suckers further and further along the ice floe. If I got lucky, I'd drive the whole village out onto a vestigial shelf and sink them all before they knew what was happening. I dove again, strafing and then spinning away from their return slag.

It was fun, but mostly just a way to kill time between real bombing runs. The new IR was supposed to be as good as the arcades, full immersion and feedback, and portable to boot. People got so lost they had to take intravenous feedings or they withered away while they were inside.

I was about to sink a whole load of refugees when Jaak shouted. "Get out here! You've got to see this!"

I stripped off my goggles and ran for the monitoring room, adrenaline amping up. When I got there, Jaak was just standing in the center of the room with the dog, grinning.

Lisa came tearing in a second later. "What? What is it?" Her eyes scanned the theater maps, ready for bloodshed.

Jaak grinned. "Look at this." He turned to the dog and held out his hand. "Shake."

The dog sat back on its haunches and gravely offered him its paw. Jaak grinned and shook the paw, then tossed it a food pellet. He turned to us and bowed.

Lisa frowned. "Do it again."

Jaak shrugged and went through the performance a second time.

"It thinks?" she asked.

Jaak shrugged. "Got me. You can get it to do things. The libraries are full of stuff on them. They're trainable. Not like a centaur or anything, but you can make them do little tricks, and if they're certain breeds, they can learn special stuff, too."

"Like what?"

"Some of them were trained to attack. Or to find explosives."

Lisa looked impressed. "Like nukes and stuff?"

Jaak shrugged. "I guess."

"Can I try?" I asked.

Jaak nodded. "Go for it."

I went over to the dog and stuck out my hand. "Shake."

It stuck out its paw. My hackles went up. It was like sending signals to aliens. I mean, you expect a bio-job or a robot to do what you want it to. Centaur, go get blown up. Find the op-force. Call reinforcements. The HEV was like that, too. It would do anything. But it was designed.

"Feed it," Jaak said, handing me a food pellet. "You have to feed it when it does it right."

I held out the food pellet. The dog's long pink tongue swabbed my palm.

I held out my hand again. "Shake." I said. It held out its paw. We shook hands. Its amber eyes stared up at me, solemn.

"That's some weird shit," Lisa said. I shivered, nodding, and backed away. The dog watched me go.

That night in my bunk, I lay awake, reading. I'd turned out the lights and only the book's surface glowed, illuminating the bunkroom in a soft green aura. Some of Lisa's art buys glimmered dimly from the walls: a bronze hanging of a phoenix breaking into flight, stylized flames glowing around it; a Japanese woodblock print of Mount Fuji and another of a village weighed down under thick snows; a photo of the three of us in Siberia after the Peninsula campaign, grinning and alive amongst the slag.

Lisa came into the room. Her razors glinted in my book's dim light, flashes of green sparks that outlined her limbs as she moved.

"What are you reading?" She stripped and squeezed into bed with me.

I held up the book and read out loud.

Cut me I won't bleed. Gas me I won't breathe.
Stab me, shoot me, slash me, smash me
I have swallowed science
I am God.
Alone.

I closed the book and its glow died. In the darkness, Lisa rustled under the covers.

My eyes adjusted. She was staring at me. "'Dead Man,' right?"

"Because of the dog," I said.

"Dark reading." She touched my shoulder, her hand warm, the blades embedded, biting lightly into my skin.

"We used to be like that dog," I said.

"Pathetic."

"Scary."

We were quiet for a little while. Finally I asked, "Do you ever wonder what would happen to us if we didn't have our science? If we didn't have our big brains and our weeviltech and our cellstims and—"

"And everything that makes our life good?" She laughed. "No." She rubbed my stomach. "I like all those little worms that live in your belly." She started to tickle me.

Wormy, squirmy in your belly,
wormy squirmy feeds you Nelly.
Microweevils eat the bad,
and give you something good instead.

I fought her off, laughing. "That's no Yearly."

"Third Grade. Basic bio-logic. Mrs. Alvarez. She was really big on weeviltech."

She tried to tickle me again but I fought her off. "Yeah, well Yearly only wrote about immortality. He wouldn't take it."

Lisa gave up on the tickling and flopped down beside me again. "Blah, blah, blah. He wouldn't take any gene modifications. No c-cell inhibitors. He was dying of cancer and he wouldn't take the drugs that would have saved him. Our last mortal poet. Cry me a river. So what?"

"You ever think about why he wouldn't?"

"Yeah. He wanted to be famous. Suicide's good for attention."

"Seriously, though. He thought being human meant having animals. The whole web of life thing. I've been reading about him. It's weird shit. He didn't want to live without them."

"Mrs. Alvarez hated him. She had some rhymes about him, too. Anyway, what were we supposed to do? Work out weeviltech and DNA patches for every stupid species? Do you know what that would have cost?" She nuzzled close to me. "If you want animals around you, go to a zoo. Or get some building blocks and make something, if it makes you happy. Something with hands, for god's sake, not like that dog." She stared at the underside of the bunk above. "I'd cook that dog in a second."

I shook my head. "I don't know. That dog's different from a bio-job. It looks at us, and there's something there, and it's not us. I mean, take any bio-job out there, and it's basically us, poured into another shape, but not that dog. . . ." I trailed off, thinking.

Lisa laughed. "It shook hands with you, Chen. You don't worry about a centaur when it salutes." She climbed on top of me. "Forget the dog. Concentrate on something that matters." Her smile and her razor blades glinted in the dimness.

I woke up to something licking my face. At first I thought it was Lisa, but she'd climbed into her own bunk. I opened my eyes and found the dog.

It was a funny thing to have this animal licking me, like it wanted to talk, or say hello or something. It licked me again, and I thought that it had come a long way from when it had tried to take off Jaak's arm. It put its paws up on my bed, and then in a single heavy movement, it was up on the bunk with me, its bulk curled against me.

It slept there all night. It was weird having something other than Lisa lying next to me, but it was warm and there was something friendly about it. I couldn't help smiling as I drifted back to sleep.

We flew to Hawaii for a swimming vacation and we brought the dog with us. It was good to get out of the northern cold and into the gentle Pacific. Good to stand on the beach, and look out to a limitless horizon. Good to walk along the beach holding hands while black waves crashed on the sand.

Lisa was a good swimmer. She flashed through the ocean's metallic sheen like an eel out of history and when she surfaced, her naked body glistened with hundreds of iridescent petroleum jewels.

When the Sun started to set, Jaak lit the ocean on fire with his 101. We all sat and watched as the Sun's great red ball sank through veils of smoke, its light shading deeper crimson with every minute. Waves rushed flaming onto the beach. Jaak got out his harmonica and played while Lisa and I made love on the sand.

We'd intended to amputate her for the weekend, to let her try what she had done to me the vacation before. It was a new thing in L.A., an experiment in vulnerability.

She was beautiful, lying there on the beach, slick and excited with all of our play in the water. I licked oil opals off her skin as I sliced off her limbs, leaving her more dependent than a baby. Jaak played his harmonica and watched the Sun set, and watched as I rendered Lisa down to her core.

After our sex, we lay on the sand. The last of the Sun was dropping below the water. Its rays glinted redly across the smoldering waves. The sky, thick with particulates and smoke, shaded darker.

Lisa sighed contentedly. "We should vacation here more often."

I tugged on a length of barbed wire buried in the sand. It tore free and I wrapped it around my upper arm, a tight band that bit into my skin. I showed it to Lisa. "I used to do this all the time when I was a kid." I smiled. "I thought I was so bad-ass."

Lisa smiled. "You are."

"Thanks to science." I glanced over at the dog. It was lying on the sand a short distance away. It seemed sullen and unsure in its new environment, torn away from the safety of the acid pits and tailings mountains of its homeland. Jaak sat beside the dog and played. Its ears twitched to the music. He was a good player. The mournful sound of the harmonica carried easily over the beach to where we lay.

Lisa turned her head, trying to see the dog. "Roll me."

I did what she asked. Already, her limbs were regrowing. Small stumps, which would build into larger limbs. By morning, she would be whole, and ravenous. She studied the dog. "This is as close as I'll ever get to it," she said.

"Sorry?"

"It's vulnerable to everything. It can't swim in the ocean. It can't eat anything. We have to fly its food to it. We have to scrub its water. Dead end of an evolutionary chain. Without science, we'd be as vulnerable as it." She looked up at me. "As vulnerable as I am now." She grinned. "This is as close to death as I've ever been. At least, not in combat."

"Wild, isn't it?"

"For a day. I liked it better when I did it to you. I'm already starving."

I fed her a handful of oily sand and watched the dog, standing uncertainly on the beach, sniffing suspiciously at some rusting scrap iron that stuck out of the beach like a giant memory fin. It pawed up a chunk of red plastic rubbed shiny by the ocean and chewed on it briefly, before dropping it. It started licking around its mouth. I wondered if it had poisoned itself again.

"It sure can make you think," I muttered. I fed Lisa another handful of sand. "If someone came from the past, to meet us here and now, what do you think they'd say about us? Would they even call us human?"

Lisa looked at me seriously. "No, they'd call us gods."

Jaak got up and wandered into the surf, standing knee-deep in the black smoldering waters. The dog, driven by some unknown instinct, followed him, gingerly picking its way across the sand and rubble.

The dog got tangled in a cluster of wire our last day on the beach. Really ripped the hell out of it: slashes through its fur, broken legs, practically strangled. It had gnawed one of its own paws half off trying to get free. By the time we found it, it was a bloody mess of ragged fur and exposed meat.

Lisa stared down at the dog. "Christ, Jaak, you were supposed to be watching it."

"I went swimming. You can't keep an eye on the thing all the time."

"It's going to take forever to fix this," she fumed.

"We should warm up the hunter," I said. "It'll be easier to work on it back home." Lisa and I knelt down to start cutting the dog free. It whimpered and its tail wagged feebly as we started to work.

Jaak was silent.

Lisa slapped him on his leg. "Come on, Jaak, get down here. It'll bleed out if you don't hurry up. You know how fragile it is."

Jaak said, "I think we should eat it."

Lisa glanced up, surprised. "You do?"

He shrugged. "Sure."

I looked up from where I was tearing away tangled wires from around the dog's torso. "I thought you wanted it to be your pet. Like in the zoo."

Jaak shook his head. "Those food pellets are expensive. I'm spending half my salary on food and water filtration, and now this bullshit." He waved his hand at the tangled dog. "You have to watch the sucker all the time. It's not worth it."

"But still, it's your friend. It shook hands with you."

Jaak laughed. "You're my friend." He looked down at the dog, his face wrinkled with thought. "It's, it's…an animal."

Even though we had all idly discussed what it would be like to eat the dog, it was a surprise to hear him so determined to kill it. "Maybe you should sleep on it." I said. "We can get it back to the bunker, fix it up, and then you can decide when you aren't so pissed off about it."

"No." He pulled out his harmonica and played a few notes, a quick jazzy scale. He took the harmonica out of his mouth. "If you want to put up the money for his feed, I'll keep it, I guess, but otherwise...." He shrugged.

"I don't think you should cook it."

"You don't?" Lisa glanced at me. "We could roast it, right here, on the beach."

I looked down at the dog, a mass of panting, trusting animal. "I still don't think we should do it."

Jaak looked at me seriously. "You want to pay for the feed?"

I sighed. "I'm saving for the new Immersive Response."

"Yeah, well, I've got things I want to buy too, you know." He flexed his muscles, showing off his tattoos. "I mean, what the fuck good does it do?"

"It makes you smile."

"Immersive Response makes you smile. And you don't have to clean up after its crap. Come on, Chen. Admit it. You don't want to take care of it either. It's a pain in the ass."

We all looked at each other, then down at the dog.

Lisa roasted the dog on a spit, over burning plastics and petroleum skimmed from the ocean. It tasted okay, but in the end it was hard to understand the big deal. I've eaten slagged centaur that tasted better.

Afterward, we walked along the shoreline. Opalescent waves crashed and roared up the sand, leaving jewel slicks as they receded and the Sun sank red in the distance.

Without the dog, we could really enjoy the beach. We didn't have to worry about whether it was going to step in acid, or tangle in barbwire half-buried in the sand, or eat something that would keep it up vomiting half the night.

Still, I remember when the dog licked my face and hauled its shaggy bulk onto my bed, and I remember its warm breathing beside me, and sometimes, I miss it.

THE PASHO

he acrid scent of burning dung carried easily on the dry wind. Raphel Ka' Korum breathed once, deeply, tasting memory, then fastened his electrostatic scarf over his face and turned to receive his luggage from the passengers still on the fat wheel.

Wind gusted around them. Scarves came loose and flapped wildly in the stinging air and brown hands snatched at the ragged free-flying banners before tucking them, sparking and crackling, over dust-caked noses and mouths. A man, Kai by his crucifix, Keli by his silk shirt, handed down Raphel's leather satchel, then pressed his palms together and ducked his head in ritual sterile farewell. Raphel did the same. The rest of the passengers, a motley conglomeration of basin people all stuffed tightly in the bed of the fat wheel, made gestures of their own, observing scrupulous politeness to his Pasho's robes and attainment marks.

The fat wheel slowly rolled away. Its bulbous jelly tires crunched on the Dry Basin's hardpan. Raphel watched the beat-up vehicle recede. Its passengers observed him in turn, their eyes full of questions at the Keli Pasho who disembarked in the center of the desert. Raphel turned to face his village.

The round haci of the Jai huddled in the barren basin like a small mob of conical-hatted refugees, their pointed heads jammed tight together, their adobe robes splattered with white Jai geometric patterns. Around them, clay-clotted fields lay tilled and patient as wind blew across them, ripping dust devils into the air and sending them dancing across the pale plain. In the far distance, the bones of the old city stuck up from the basin in a tangled mass of steel and concrete ruin, silent and abandoned for more generations than even the Jai could remember.

Raphel unwrapped his scarf and once again breathed deeply, taking in the scents of home, sniffing at nostalgia, letting it fill the depths of his lungs. Dust and burning dung and sage blown from the distant hills intermingled. Somewhere within the village, meat was grilling. A coyote or rabbit, likely stunned into sonic paralysis and skinned before it regained consciousness, now dripping fat onto open coals. Raphel inhaled again and licked his lips. Already they chapped in the aridity. His skin, long accustomed to Keli's lush humidity, felt tight on his face, as though he wore a mask that would fall away at any moment.

He glanced back wistfully at the receding fat wheel, a child's toy slowly creeping toward the distant muddy line where blue sky finally touched yellow clay. Sighing, Raphel shouldered his satchel and headed for the village.

The few scattered haci at the village outskirts quickly sidled close. They formed a tightly packed mass of thick walls and claustrophobic alleys. Streets twisted randomly, inviting invaders to stumble into cul-de-sacs and death courts. Sonic bulbs dangled overhead, their beaks gaping, eager to scream.

Raphel wandered amongst the Jai defenses along a path of childhood memories. He recognized Bia' Giomo's haci, and remembered how she had paid in sugar rocks when he brought her water from the well. He recognized the thick blue door to Evia's courtyard, and remembered hiding together beneath her parents' bed, stifling laughter while her parents groaned and creaked above them. His mother had written to him that Bia' Giomo had passed beyond and that Evia was called Bia' Dosero and now lived at Clear Spring Village.

Raphel turned another corner, and recognized Old Martiz squatting outside his haci. Red beans boiled over the old man's dung fire, slowly congealing into porridge. Raphel smiled and started to greet the old man, but as soon as Martiz saw Raphel, he grabbed his bean pot and scrambled backward, desperate to keep Quaran.

Raphel hastily pulled his scarf back over his face and ducked his head in apology. Martiz softened enough to set down his beans and press his palms together. Raphel returned the ancient gesture. He could have told Martiz the source of the Quaran gesture and how it had spread during the Cleansing, but Martiz was unlikely to care. For the Jai it was custom, and that was enough. Jai observed the old ways. In Keli, people shook hands and hardly observed Quaran at all. The trading culture easily discarded careful traditions of past survival. The Jai had longer memories.

Raphel skirted Martiz by the prescribed two meters of sunlight and threaded deeper into the village. The alley narrowed to a tight path between squeezing walls. He turned sideways and scraped through a kill-slot, its walls pressing against his chest and shoulder blades. At the far end of the kill-slot, he paused to brush ineffectually at the adobe dust that clung to his white robes.

Children's laughter echoed. Young Jai boys, their robes bright crimson splashes against the pale yellow clay of the haci, dashed down the alley toward him. They stopped short, staring at his Pasho's white robes and attainment marks, then pressed their brown hands together and ducked their heads in careful respect. A moment later they were past him and continuing their chase, slipping through the kill-slot with the easy limberness of basin lizards.

Raphel turned to watch them, remembering when he had dashed down the self-same alley, chasing friends, pretending that he was a hook-hand crusader, pretending he himself led the war against the Keli. It seemed a long time ago. The boys' red flapping robes disappeared beyond the kill-slot, leaving Raphel alone in the alley.

Raphel cleared his throat and swallowed several times, trying to relieve its constricting dryness. He inhaled again, deeply, hungry for the scent of his native place. His scarf crackled and he breathed sterile air.

"A Pasho's responsibilities are often convoluted. How can one know in advance the consequences of an action? It is a Pasho's duty to peer into the nooks and crannies of possibility and only proceed with caution. Slow change is a virtue. For a society to survive the upheavals of technology, the race and culture must adapt. It is not enough that clever fingers learn to work a plough in a few short days, the culture must also be readied for its expanding population, its shift to agriculture, the willy-nilly follow-on ripples of technology introduction. Without proper preparation, moral and philosophical, how can any culture be trusted with a technology as casually violent as a gun?"

—Pasho Giles Martin, CS 152.
(Lectures on Moral Change)

"You must be very proud, Bia' Pasho." Bia' Hanna smiled at Raphel as she spoke. Gold flashed in her mouth and the crow's feet at the edges of her desert eyes deepened.

"Proud?" Raphel's mother laughed. She took a pot of newly boiled tea from the hearth fire and turned to eye Raphel where he sat separated from them by three meters, electrostatic scarf covering his face. "Proud that my only son abandons his family for ten years? Proud that he turns from his family in favor of Keli and its thousand lakes?" She shook her head and poured tea into Bia' Hanna's clay cup. The thick black liquid, its source leaves dried and fermented over her own hearthfire, sent up smoke-laden scents as it splashed into the glazed clay.

"But a Pasho, a Jai Pasho." Bia' Hanna's marriage bangles clinked as her wrinkled hand reached for the steaming cup. She and all her friends sat in Raphel's family home, clustered around his mother, a bright seething mass of laughing blue-swathed married women all happy and excited to be invited for the occasion of a family reunion.

Bia' Hanna's gold teeth flashed at Raphel again. She was proud of the dental work she had received at the border of Keli and smiled willingly and widely. "Yes, you must be so proud. Your son returned to you and a Pasho already, at his age." She sipped her tea appreciatively. "You make the best smoke tea, Bia' Pasho."

"Stop already with this 'Bia' Pasho' nonsense. I was Bia' Raphel before. I am Bia' Raphel now, whatever my foolish son has done." Raphel's mother turned to refill another woman's cup, one hand deftly holding the blackened steel pot, the other twining around the blue folds of her skirts, keeping them from dragging on the floor.

Bia' Hanna laughed. "So modest. But look how handsome he is with his attainment marks." She pointed at Raphel. "Look at his hands, Jai Bia'. The script on his face, so much knowledge on his skin, and that only a tiny portion of what sloshes inside his shaven head."

Raphel ducked his head and stared at his hands, vaguely embarrassed at the women's sudden attention. On the back of his left hand were his first attainment marks: the old alphabet in tiny script. From there, lettering the color of dried blood marched up his arms and stole under his robes. Denotations of rising rank, ritually applied over the years, the chanted mnemonic devices of the ten thousand stanzas, hooks into the core of Pasho knowledge, each one a memory aid and mark of passage. They covered his body in the spiking calligraphy of the ancients, sometimes a mere symbol to hook a bound tome's worth of knowledge, something to recall, and ensure that all Pasho trained later might have access to an unchanging spring of wisdom.

Raphel looked up in time to catch the quirk of a smile on his mother's face. Bia' Hanna also spied his mother's quickly hidden pleasure. Bia' Hanna slapped his mother on the hip as she turned to pour for another woman. "Ah there! You see, Jai Bia'? You see how the mother flushes with pride at the son's accomplishment? You watch, she'll be seeking a wife for him before the sun touches the basin rim." She cackled, her gold teeth glinting in the dim light of the family haci. "Lock up your daughters, Jai Bia', she'll want to harvest them all for her tattooed son!"

The other women laughed and joined in the teasing, commenting on Bia' Pasho's good fortune. They shot smiles and evaluating glances in Raphel's direction His mother laughed and accepted their jokes and adulation, Bia' Raphel no longer: Bia' Pasho. Mother of the Pasho. A great honor.

"Look! He thirsts!" Bia' Hanna cried, and motioned toward Raphel's empty cup. "You ignore our new Pasho!"

Raphel smiled. "No, Bia', I only wait to speak between your outbursts."

"Cheeky Pasho. If we didn't keep Quaran, I'd redden your bottom. Don't forget it was I who caught you uprooting bean plants when you were no higher than my hip."

The women laughed. Bia' Hanna played to her audience, waving her arms in outrage. "He said he only wished to help—"

"It's true!"

"—And what was left? Nothing but shredded greens! As though the dust devils had torn through it. It's a good thing he has a new profession, Bia' Pasho. Your fields would never survive his return."

The Jai women all laughed as Bia' Hanna continued, recalling Raphel's childhood transgressions: rock sugar that disappeared whenever a woman blinked, electrostatic masks reversed, goats with flaming tails, the tales poured out of her golden mouth. Finally, her fountain of memory apparently depleted, she paused and eyed Raphel. "Tell me, revered Pasho, do the Keli people really eat fish? Straight from their lakes?"

Raphel laughed. "They ask if we really eat coyote."

"Yes, yes. But custom, Raphel . . . you didn't eat fish, did you?"

The women fell silent, watching him, their breath unconsciously held for the answer.

Raphel smiled slightly. "No. Of course not."

Bia' Hanna laughed. "There, you see Jai Bia'? Blood will tell. You can take the Jai to Keli, but blood will tell. Blood always tells."

The women nodded knowingly, pretending satisfaction, but their eyes betrayed relief that he had not broken Jai custom. A Jai would die before eating tainted flesh. Jai observed the old ways.

The women's conversations began again. Raphel was forgotten in the speculation over what day the rain would come and whether Bia' Renado's daughter had been seen too often in the company of a married hook hand.

Raphel glanced toward the doorway. Sunlight burned in the courtyard beyond. Male voices filtered in with the heat and light: his father and his hook-hand friends. Soon he would join them. They would push a ritual cup of mez toward him, and then step back carefully, keeping Quaran. Ten heartbeats later, he would raise his cup from the courtyard stones and they would toast the blue sky, pour a splash into the dust, and drink until the harsh liquor evaporated from the baked earth. They would perform the ritual again and again, pouring and drinking, getting drunker and drunker until the sun touched the horizon and the bones of the old city turned red in the failing light.

If Raphel listened carefully, he could make out the men's conversation. His father's voice, laughing: "He didn't get his smarts from me. It must have been his grandfather," and then all the hook hands laughing as they recalled Old Gawar, a man whose hook knives swirled like tornadoes and who spat on the graves of the Pasho he had delivered during the Keli crusade. Legendary deeds from a legendary time. Now, Keli's fat wheels wandered the Dry Basin with impunity, Jai children listened to earbuds full of Keli transmitter stations and spoke with Keli slang, and Old Gawar's grandchild was stained from head to toe with the Keli Pasho's secrets.

Raphel remembered his grandfather: a withered skinny man who wore his red robes cut open so that the virile white fur of his bony chest tufted out for all to see. A man among men. A great Jai, even at a century and a half. Raphel remembered the old man's black hawk eyes, piercing, as he dragged Raphel close to whisper deeds of bloodshed, teaching him a Jai's understanding of life, muttering darkness into Raphel's ears until his mother caught them and dragged Raphel away, scolding Old Gawar for frightening the boy, and Gawar, sitting paralyzed in his chair, watching and smiling and content, his black bloody eyes on his descendant.

Raphel shook his head at the memory. Even in far away Keli the old man had whispered bloodshed into his dreams. A hard man to forget. In Keli, more so. Vestiges of his presence lingered everywhere: monuments to the Keli dead, lakes poisonous with burn residue, the hackings of hook knives on marble statues, the skeletal ruins of buildings burned and never reconstructed. Where Raphel dreamed of his grandfather, the Keli people tossed in nightmare.

Raphel stood carefully and wrapped his robes around him. The women swayed back, unconsciously keeping Quaran, three meters indoors, two meters in clean sunlight, and so it would continue for ten days or until he was dead. Tradition. In Keli, they no longer observed the old ways. Here, it was pointless to explain that the scourge was long gone. The custom was too deeply ingrained, as rigidly respected as handwashing before meals, and planting days before the rains.

Raphel slipped into the oven heat of the courtyard. His father and the other hook hands called to him. Raphel waved, but did not join the drinking. Soon he would join them and drink himself into a mez stupor, but not until his pilgrimage was complete.

"Mez, is, of course, poisonous in large doses, and even in small amounts the toxins build up over time, impairing a disproportionate number of the male population.

"The Jai follow a ritual of distillation for the desert plant that renders its toxins less potent, but custom dictates that they allow a certain percentage to remain. Early efforts to reform the brewing of mez were met with hostility. If a Pasho were to seek to reform the practice, it would best come from within the community as there is too much distrust in the Jai for outside influences."

—Pasho Eduard, CS 1404.
(Recovered document, Dry Basin Circuit, XI 333)

The haci was old, older than most in the village, and sat near its center, at the joining of three alleys. It commanded a good killing view of their confluence and its walls were thick, built for a time when bullets had been more than myths and blood flowed down the alleys many times each generation.

Up close, the haci showed its age. Settlement cracks crept along its clay walls. Long lines like vines threaded across its face, breeding ruin into its structure. Its thick wooden doors were thrown open, exposing peeling sky-blue paint and silvered splintered wood. A fraying electro-static curtain swayed in the doorway, black and red interwoven, in Jai traditional style.

Raphel stood at the haci's curtained doorway, peering into the darkness. From inside, metal scraped rhythmically. It was a comforting sound. A Jai sound. He had grown up listening to that familiar rasp, listening at his grandfather's knee as the old man told stories. The metal continued its scraping. In his mind, Raphel was eight again, sucking sugar rocks and squatting beside his grandfather as the man whispered bloodshed.

"I burned Keli to the ground," the old man had said and his eyes had blazed as though he could see the pillage still. "I burned Heli, Seli, and Keli. Last of all I burned Keli. Its canals were no defense. Its green gardens burned in our napalm bath. Keli's women fled before us, those silly girls with long black braids and silver belts. We burned that city and taught those soft water people what it is to rule the Jai. We are not ruled by bureaucrats. The Jai control our own destinies. We are not the dirty Kai who choose slavery and have no words. We bathe every morning, charge our sonics in the afternoon, and write dust epitaphs for our enemies under the stars." He had chuckled. "We burned Keli. Burned it to the ground."

Raphel called into the haci's dimness, "Grandfather?"

The scrape of metal stopped. Then started again. Over a nearby wall, children played a game with stones, trying to knock one another's casts away from a central stake. Their shrieks of pleasure and disappointment echoed in the heat.

"Grandfather?" Raphel called again.

The scrape of metal stopped. Raphel leaned close to the doorway's curtain. Wind rustled through the courtyard, hot breeze making the curtain sway gently. Raphel strained his ears. The slow sigh of breathing came from within. Finally a voice rasped. "So, you've come back."

"Yes, Grandfather."

"Let me see."

Raphel pushed aside the curtain and slipped inside, his fingers tingling in the curtain's static. Inside, the air was cool. He tightened his scarf, pulling it close around his face as he waited for his eyes to adjust to the dimness. Shapes slowly resolved. His grandfather sat near the hearth, a slumped shadow. A hook knife and a sharpening stone glimmered in his hands. The hearth was cold and black. At one side of the room the man's pallet lay on the floor, its bedding knotted and unmade. His clothing was scattered carelessly. Only the hook knives on the walls seemed cared for. Their edges shone in the dim light, prizes from men sent beyond.

The old man's shadow body shifted. The hook knife in his hand glinted. "A Pasho. A Keli Pasho."

"Yes, Grandfather."

"Your mother must be pleased."

"Yes."

The old man laughed, then coughed. "Brainless woman. Wringing her hands so her bangles always chime. Probably already seeking a match for you." He laughed again. "I suppose you think you are an important man now that you've committed the ten thousand stanzas to memory?"

"No."

The old man jerked his head toward a picture on the wall. "Why not? Your image comes before you."

Raphel turned to examine the photograph, a picture of himself wrapped in Pasho robes, standing and smiling with the head of the Keli Pasho. His tattoos were newly inscribed, still dark and clear on his skin. The elder man's were faded into the folds of his skin, as though the knowledge inscribed had settled deeply into the old Pasho's being. "I don't ask the people to revere me," Raphel said.

"And yet they do. Ahh, of course they do. The Pasho make sure of that. Your dogs go before you, spreading your pictures, telling stories of your wisdom." The old man laughed. "Everyone believes a Pasho when he speaks. The all-seeing all-benevolent Pasho. Who would beg wisdom from a Jai when a Pasho sits among them?"

"I am Jai, and Pasho. They are not incompatible."

"You think not?" The black shadow of the man coughed laughter, a harsh explosion of humor that faded into labored breathing. His hook knife glinted movement and then he was sharpening again. The sharp scrape of metal on stone was rhythmic, filling the haci. He rasped, "I burned Keli to the ground. Would you do the same? Your Pasho friends are there. Keli girls are there. I slaughtered them all. That is Jai."

Raphel squatted on the hard-packed dirt of the haci, three meters from his grandfather. He pulled his robes around him and settled to the ground, cross-legged. "No mean feat to burn a water city."

The old man glanced up slyly before returning to his sharpening. "Even water burns."

"Napalm. That weapon should have been forgotten."

"According to the Pasho. But Jai have long memories. We keep our own records and have very long memories, don't we, Grandson?"

"Keli people, also. Your name is remembered there still."

"Is it?"

"They spit when they speak of you."

The old man wheezed laughter. "That's good." He stopped his sharpening and looked up at Raphel, eyes narrowed with suspicion. "And did you spit with them?"

"What do you think?"

The old man pointed his hook knife at Raphel. "I think your skin cries out for Keli's clear pools and your fingers tingle to touch a Keli girl's silken braid. That is what I think." He returned to his sharpening. "I think your nose twitches for the scent of lilac on the thousand lakes."

"I may have studied in Keli, Grandfather, but I am still Jai."

"So you say," the old man muttered. He set down his knife and sharpening stone and turned toward a shelf beside him. His thin fingers came up with a thick glass bottle. "Will you drink?"

Raphel hastily gathered his robes and made to stand. "I should pour."

The old man laughed and cringed away. "And break Quaran?" He shook his head. "You have been in Keli too long. Keep your distance, Grandson." He uncorked the bottle and poured two clay cups of mez. The bright tingling scent of the liquor filled the dim room. The old man carefully lowered himself to the floor and pushed the cup until it sat midway between himself and his grandson before dragging his crippled body slowly back into the shadows and hoisting himself up to his seat against the hearthwall. Raphel waited the requisite ten beats of the heart, then leaned forward and pulled the clay cup close.

"To our ancestors." The old man raised his cup to the heavens, then poured a splash on the ground. "May they not be abandoned by their descendants."

"May we always honor them." Raphel mirrored his grandfather's motions, pouring the liquor onto the ground. Its drops clustered like opals on the dirt. The white heat of the liquor burned in his chest as he drank.

His grandfather watched him drink. "Not as smooth as Keli's rice wine, is it?"

"No."

"Well, you're fortunate. The Keli sell their wine here, now. Many drink it."

"I've seen."

The old man leaned forward. "Why do they peddle their wine in the Dry Basin, Grandson? Do they not see we are Jai? Do they not understand they have no business here?"

"If it bothers you, you could sell mez to Keli."

"Mez is for Jai. Baji is for Keli."

Raphel sighed. "Do you somehow become less Jai if you drink their rice wine? Does it seep into a man and turn him all at once into something different?" He took another sip of the burning mez. "Even you have drunk rice wine."

The old man waved his hand dismissively. "Only when I sacked their water city."

"But still, it touched your desert tongue." Raphel smiled. "Did it make you Keli?"

Old Gawar flashed a hard smile. "Ask the Keli people."

"It is the same for me."

"You? You are a chained pet. I'm sure the Keli enjoyed your toothless desert bite. You're not Jai. You're one of them, now."

"It's not so. Keli people know instantly that I am Jai: my accent, my eyes, my hook knife, my laugh, my observance of the old ways. No matter how long I walk Keli's bridges or swim in their thousand lakes, I will never be Keli."

The old man made a face of irritation. "And because Keli rejects you, you believe you are Jai?"

Raphel toasted his grandfather with his clay cup of mez. "I am sure of it."

"No!" The old man slammed his cup down. It shattered, splashing liquor and leaving shards. He swept the shards away, careless of their sharp points. "You are not Jai! If you were Jai, you would not sit there talking. You would draw your hook knife and cut me down for insulting you."

"That is not Jai. That is you, Grandfather."

The old man reached for the edge of his hearth and slowly pulled himself upright, a crippled skeletal hawk of a man, eyes bright with the fires of past bloodshed. His voice, full of conviction, rasped as he clutched the hearth's chimney for support. "What I do is Jai. I am Jai." He pulled himself taller. "You Pasho want the Jai to set down our hook knives and bury our sonics so no one will hear their wail. You keep technology from us and give it to Keli. You cannot deny history. We Jai have letters, we keep our own records of the past. We know Pasho trickery. When I burned Keli, the Pasho fell like wheat under my hook knife. I stained their white robes red. Tell me that they have forgotten me. Tell me they don't seek to bury the Jai still!"

Raphel made placating motions with his hands, urging his grandfather back to his seat. "That time is past. We Jai no longer make war on Keli, nor the Pasho who happen to live there."

Old Gawar smiled thinly and rubbed at his crippled leg. "War never ends. I taught you that."

"You squat in Keli's nightmares still."

"A pity they don't learn their lesson and stay on their side of the mountains." Old Gawar chuckled and slowly eased himself back to his seat. "When we burn Keli next, we won't show mercy. The Keli accent will not poison our children's ears again."

"You can't keep the outside world from the Dry Basin forever."

"So says the Pasho. My own grandson, who comes to betray us."

"Knowledge is a Jai birthright as much as a Keli's."

"Don't feed me carrion. You come like all Pasho, with knowledge out-stretched in one hand while you wait to seize influence with the other. You sit cross-legged, meditating like the ancient wise ones, and then you advise our people to sink water veins, to lend themselves to your road projects and factories, but I know your true object."

"We're building civilization, Grandfather."

"You are the death of us."

"Because Jai wells will be full, even when the dry season doubles?"

"Is that what you offer?" The old man laughed bitterly. "Water wells always full? A better breed of the red bean plant? Something to make our lives easier? To make our children live longer?" He shook his head. "I've watched your cult of the Open Eye long enough to know what Pasho are about. Even the Keli who worship you couldn't pull salvation from your tattooed fists when we attacked. We Jai slaughtered those soft water people like goats. You are not a savior. You are the death of us. Get out, Grandson. Get out of my home. Whatever you are, you are not Jai."

"Writing is the key to survival. A culture which can write, can remember, and share its knowledge widely. The First Attainment mark must always be the alphabet, the key to all other knowledge. With an alphabet, what I write today may be learned a thousand years from now, by some young student who will never know me except through my hand on paper. When all of us are dust, our learning will survive and we hope, with time, civilization will thrive again."

—Pasho Mirriam Milliner, CS 13. (On Survival)

The sharp clicking of his mother's tongue woke him, a gentle tap tap from the vicinity of his doorway.

He had been dreaming of Keli. Dreaming that he stood again in front of the Pasho libraries and stared up at Milliner's statue. Dreaming that he ran his fingers along the hook knife hackings at its base, that he stared up at the founder of the Pasho order, carved in marble mid-escape. Milliner fled with one hand forward, Pasho's open eye on his palm. His other arm clutched a pile of torn pages, falling free. His head was turned back, his eyes fastened on the destruction he fled.

Raphel's mother clicked her tongue again. Raphel opened his eyes in time to see her withdraw behind the wool hanging curtain. Her marriage bangles clicked on her wrists as she let the curtain fall, turning the room back to dimness. Fully awake, he noticed other morning sounds: the virile crowing of roosters challenging one another across the village, children shouting beyond the high slit windows in the haci's walls. Sunlight pierced into the room in tiny shafts, illuminating dust motes stirred by his mother's presence.

In the Pasho towers, he had woken each day with the dawn. His cell had faced east and filled early with the sterile light. He would wake and go to his window and stare into the bright dawn, letting it bathe him as it glinted across the mirror stillness of the thousand lakes. The sharp hard light reflected like mica splashes and turned the land molten as far as he could see, blinding him and obscuring green Keli's bridges.

Soon after, his master would come to his door, a soft Keli man, fed well on the fish of Keli's lakes, his tattoos well set into the comfortable folds of his flesh. "Come desert Pasho," he would laugh. "Let us see what destruction Gawar's grandson has in store for us this morning. How many books will you tear through today?" To him, all men had been the same. Jai or Keli made no difference. Only study mattered.

"Raphel?" his mother whispered. "Pasho?" Her tongue clicked again from behind the curtain, a faint probing of his room's silence.

Raphel sat up slowly. "You don't need to call me 'Pasho,' Mother. I am still your son."

Her voice came back, muffled. "That may be. But your skin is covered with knowledge and everyone calls me Bia' Pasho."

"But I am the same."

His mother didn't answer.

Raphel kicked off his blankets and scratched at his dry skin. It was peeling in the aridity. He shivered. It had been cold in the night. He had forgotten that about the basin, that its nights, even in the dry season could be so cold. In Keli the nights were hot, even when the sun went down. Humid warmth saturated everything. Sometimes he would lie in his bed and think he could squeeze the air with his fists and warm water would run down his arms. He scratched again, wistful for the smooth suppleness of skin always caressed with liquid warmth. The air in the basin seemed to be an enemy, attacking him much as his grandfather had the day before.

Raphel began pulling his robes on, covering the sharp knifelike script of his attainment marks. It was an old language, more basic than the Jai, more direct in its impulses, less careful of offense, an impatient tongue, for lightning-quick, impulsive people. He began tying the stays of his robes, quickly hiding the learning hooks covering his body: The One Hundred Books, The Rituals of Arrival and Release, The Scientific Principles, The Rituals of Cleansing, Essentials of the Body, Bio Logic, The Rituals of Quaran, Chemic Knowledge, Plant and Animal Observation, Matica, Physical Matica, Principles of Construction, Earth Studies; Core Tech: Paper, Ink, Steel, Plastic, Plague, Production Line, Projectiles, Fertilizer, Soap . . . ten thousand chanted stanzas, interlinked and attached to symbol rhyme to aid their stability. Knowledge locked in verse from a time when books were hard to make and harder to protect, from a time when Pasho wandered like dandelion seeds between far-flung villages, holding up their palms in greeting to show the Open Eye and beg their free movement, dispensing their knowledge as far as their seed-pod minds could carry them, hoping to set down roots, and begin schools where they would seed new Pasho further afield.

"Raphel?"

His mother's voice broke his thoughts. Hurriedly, Raphel finished dressing and pushed the curtain aside.

His mother gasped. "Raphel! Your scarf !" She stumbled away from him desperate to keep Quaran.

Raphel ducked back into his room. He found his electrostatic scarf and wrapped it over his face. When he emerged again, his mother stood at the far side of their common room. She pointed at a cup of smoke tea sitting three meters from their hearth. Safe distance. Raphel skirted the hearth and squatted with his tea. A sweet bean porridge sat cooled beside it. The fire coals were already floating in a bucket of gray water, black and cold.

"How long have you been awake?" he asked.

"Hours. You slept late. You must have been tired."

Raphel sipped the cool smoke tea. "It's dark in the room. I'm used to the sun waking me."

His mother began sweeping the hard-packed floor with a straw broom, carefully avoiding coming too close. Raphel watched her cleaning process. Nine more days of ritual isolation.

When his grandfather had burned Keli, he and his army had camped at the village edge to keep Quaran. They had sung songs of blood and fire across the intervening distance, but did not enter the village until Quaran had passed. The Jai kept to the old ways. It had been absurd for him to think the old man would welcome him with open arms.

His mother swept dust out the door, then turned. Her tongue clicked uncertainly. Finally she said, "There is a girl I would like you to meet.

She's from a very good family."

Raphel smiled and sipped his tea. "Already seeking a match?"

"The girl is visiting Bia' Hardez. Her aunt. She's a good Jai girl."

"What point is there? I won't complete Quaran for more than a week."

"Mala is returning to her family at Kettle Rock. If you wanted to see her you would have to go there, and then still pass Quaran in a foreign village. Mala is willing. You will meet outside, with clean sunlight between you."

Raphel stifled a teasing smile. "You turn from the old ways?"

"There is no harm meeting in clean sunlight. She does not fear you. You traveled from Keli. If you are not dead now, you never will be."

"Grandfather would disapprove."

"An untrampled scorpion troubles no one."

"And you were always such a proper Jai lady."

His mother clicked her tongue. "My hook knife is still sharp." She nodded at his finished tea. "Throw your cup away, and make sure it breaks in clean sunlight. No one can use it now."

"A stone cannot be a pillow, the Keli cannot be friends."
—Jai Proverb. Recorded CS 1404, Pasho Eduard.
(Recovered Document, Dry Basin Circuit, XI 333)

Five days into Quaran, Raphel met his potential match on the edge of the village, separated by two meters of sterile light. The black ringlets of Mala's hair shimmered in the bright sun and her eyes were deepened by the black lines of an eye pigment that Keli girls favored. Mala's skirt and blouse were of the old Jai patterns, black and red interwoven diamonds, shot through with gold threads. Her arms were bare of bangles, inviting a man to marry her and swathe her in blue.

Within sight, but out of earshot, Raphel's mother and Bia' Hardez sat on the yellow plain, a pair of blue billowing matrons. Their gold bangles glittered sharply in the sunlight. In the distance, the old city stood silent, black bones against the sky. Raphel remembered exploring the city's tangled ruins where hawks roosted and coyotes trotted arrogantly down streets twice the width of Keli's greatest avenues. He remembered gathering spent shells from the mangled city, hunting for prizes from the vicious protracted wars that had destroyed the place.

Wind gusted. The chaperoning women tucked their blue skirts tighter around them. Mala pulled away her electrostatic scarf. Raphel noticed it was from Keli. The solar pack was distinctly from beyond the mountains, though with a Jai pattern to its weave. He pushed the thought away and studied the smooth lines of the girl's brown skin. She was like a bird, her face thin and graceful. Her cheekbones were sharp, but she was beautiful. At her questioning eyes, he pulled away his own scarf. They studied each other.

Finally she said, "You're much more handsome than in your pictures. Even with all those tattoos."

"You expected worse?"

Mala laughed. She pushed her windblown hair back from her face, showing the knife curve of her throat and jaw. "I thought you might have aged. You're young to be a Pasho. I thought my aunt exaggerated."

Raphel glanced back at the pair of women in married blue, gossiping and watching with speculative eyes for signs of a match. "No. Bia' Hardez is honest about those things. She matched my cousin."

"I've never seen a young Pasho."

"My teachers were dedicated."

"How long were you in Keli?"

"Ten years."

She shook her head. "I wouldn't have lasted a week. All that water. My grandfather told me it rained for months there."

"It's very pretty. When the rain touches the lakes, it makes rings, thousands and thousands of ring ripples all across them. You can stand on the marble bridges there and the rain can be as gentle as feathers."

The girl turned her eyes toward the old city. "I could never have lived in the rain." Her eyes remained fixed on the blackened ruins. "They say the Keli people shake hands. With strangers even. And they eat fish."

Raphel nodded. "It's true. I've seen it."

She wrapped her arms around herself and shuddered. "Disgusting. Bia' Hardez told me that your grandfather would as soon kill you as have you return."

Raphel shrugged. "He is traditional. He doesn't like that I went to Keli."

"Most families would welcome a Pasho back into their family."

"You've heard of my grandfather."

"Oh yes. One of mine died in Keli on his crusade. When they burned the city."

Raphel thought of the chips in Milliner's statue, and wondered if her grandfather had been one of the hook hands who failed to topple it. Or if he had raged through the Pasho libraries, burning and killing and setting the severed heads of delivered Pasho beside the busts of Plato and Einstein. He pushed the thought away. "Do they sing songs for him in Kettle Rock?"

"Of course. He is remembered well."

"That's good."

Mala turned back to him, her dark accented eyes evaluating. "My aunt thinks a Pasho would be a good match for me." She stopped and pushed her hair back. She looked again toward the ruined city in the distance, then back at him. She gave a little shrug.

Finally Raphel said, "But you think differently."

"A husband should be from your native place."

"The basin is still my home."

"But your grandfather disowns you. My family is traditional."

"Your aunt sees no difficulty."

"She doesn't live in Kettle Rock. I have to face my family." She shook her head, studying him. "There is something not right about you. Something not Jai."

Raphel scowled. "And what is that, do you think?"

She cocked her head, examining him. "Too difficult to say. Maybe it's the taint of Keli in you. Maybe some water rose has captured your heart, some girl with a black braid and a silver belt around her hips. Those Keli girls are soft, I've heard. Not like Jai. Not like desert girls. We are hawks. They are little sparrows." She laughed. "No. I don't think you are the man for me. I am a traditional girl."

Raphel laughed. "You think you are traditional? You wear a Keli scarf and line your eyes like a Keli girl, and you still call yourself Jai?"

She shrugged. "I wouldn't expect you to understand."

"I am Jai. My hook knife is sharp."

"So you say." She shook her head. "Go back to Keli, Raphel. Find a soft water girl who will love whatever desert bite you have left. Your grandfather is right. You don't belong here." She wrapped her scarf back across her face.

Raphel watched her walk away from him, her skirts molded across her hips as she swayed into the wind. For a moment he imagined following her but he forced himself to stand still. Pursuit would only lead to humiliation. He turned and strode away before the watching chaperones could see he had been discarded.

"The path of a Pasho is not one of simple reading. Knowledge is dangerous. We know this from the First Age, when people studied quickly quickly,

like ants. We know this because there is so little left of what they constructed. Knowledge is always two-edged. For every benefit, there is hazard. For every good, evil. Carelessness and convenient solutions lead to chaos.

"It is not for a Pasho simply to gain knowledge, but to deserve knowledge. Our libraries are locked and the concepts inside are graded into levels of attainment. We do not keep this knowledge under lock and key because we crave power, as outsiders often accuse. We keep it because we fear it.

"The process of becoming Pasho is not a process of study, but a process of wisdom. Milliner knew knowledge must spread again, but this time, it must spread without destruction accompanying it. Knowledge and technology are not things to be handed to any man who demands them. That path can only lead to disaster. We saw this in the First Age. We moved too quickly and were punished for it. This time we move slowly, slowly like the turtle and hope that there is no Second Cleansing."

—Pasho Cho Gan, CS 580. (Pasho Wisdom, Vol. XX)

"I went to be matched yesterday."

Old Gawar sat outside the door of his haci, surrounded by piles of red chilies, drying. The hot spice scent saturated the air, making Raphel cough. The old man smirked as he plucked dried chilies out of various piles, turned them speculatively between his gnarled fingers, then set them in his mortar and ground them into red dust before dumping the flakes into a clay urn. "So my grandson comes to see me again, does he?"

"What did you tell Bia' Hardez?"

The old man laughed. "Mala rejected you, did she?" He studied Raphel's angry face for an answer, then went back to grinding chilies, shaking his head and grinning. "Even your brainless mother should have known better than to arrange a meeting with that girl."

"You poisoned my name with her."

His grandfather laughed and crushed new chilies into dust. "Never." His vigorous movements sent up red powder clouds as he worked. "But I'm not surprised. Her grandfather fought with me. He died like a desert lion. We fought across Keli's bridges together. We stormed her towers. Mala would be too proud to take a fish-eater for a husband. I don't know what your mother was thinking. I'm brave, but I would never send my hook hands into an unwinnable battle." He dumped more finished chilies into the storage urn. "You should meet with the Renali family. They have a daughter."

"The ones who sell rice wine from Keli?" Raphel scowled. "You think too little of me."

The old man laughed. "Oh? My grandson is Jai after all?"

"I have never been anything else."

"Would you burn Keli?"

"We are not at war."

"War never ends. Even now they send their goods and people closer to us. Even good girls like Mala wear Keli scarves. How long before we are like the Kai, just another tribe who look and dress and talk like the Keli people? Wars such as this never end. If you want to prove you are Jai, you will help me wage war again, and put Keli in its place."

Raphel laughed. "What war can you wage?"

Old Gawar's eyes flicked up to Raphel, then back down to his grinding. A smile quirked at the corners of his mouth. "My hook knife is still sharp. Even now I counsel with the basin villages. There are many who would war on Keli. If you are Jai, you will help us."

Raphel shook his head. "Pasho do not deal war. If you want to gather more water for the village, I can help. If you want to feed our children better, this too I can accomplish. What you ask, I cannot give."

"Cannot? Or will not?" The old man studied Raphel, then smiled, showing worn yellowed teeth. "The all-seeing all-giving knowledge of the Pasho." He spat. "One hand open with an eye, the other behind the back with a noose. Look at the dirty Kai, well under the yoke of Keli now. They took your knowledge."

"They had no letters before us, nor basic hygiene. They were starving. Now they are fat and comfortable."

"And indistinguishable from Keli people. Pasho came and gave them letters and now they are not Kai." He spat again.

Raphel inclined his head. "You call my knowledge Keli knowledge, and yet, if we leave the knowledge for Keli alone, only then will you be right. If we use it for Jai purposes, then it is Jai. Knowledge knows no master. You complain about Keli electrostatics, but you won't use my knowledge."

"The Jai will not work in factories. We are not traders. We plant in the wet season. We war in the dry season. That is Jai."

"Then the Jai will pass into memory, and Keli will flourish."

The old man laughed. "No, Keli will burn, and we will write their epitaphs in the mud of that sweltering place. Already I send hook hands to the corners of the basin. Thousands answer the call. Don't look so surprised. Keli encroaches too much. Their fat wheels, their scarves, their liquor, and their transmitter stations invade on every side. If you are Jai, you will help us raze Keli once and for all."

"Pasho are neutral. We do not deal in war."

The old man waved a hand at Raphel in irritation. It was glazed red with the residue of dried chilies. "You think you don't deal in war? Just because blood doesn't flow down our alleys? Electrostatics and cosmetics from Keli one day, earbuds the next? Your Pasho gifts to Keli kill us day by day. Where does this end? With the Jai eating fish? This is certainly war, whatever you Pasho and your protégés claim." His black eyes turned hard as he stared up at Raphel. "If you are Jai, you will use that knowledge on your skin for Jai purposes, and you will make war."

Raphel frowned. "What knowledge do you want so badly, Grandfather? Something to leak radiation into Keli's lakes and fish, something to sicken their women and sterilize their men? A virus keyed to their climate? Something that will leave corpses on their water bridges, and nothing but wind on the thousand lakes?" Raphel waved his hand toward the edge of the village. "What does the old city tell us, if we seek so much destructive power? I sit five paces from you even now, thanks to ancient follies."

"Don't lecture me, boy. I learned the first one thousand stanzas myself."

"Before trying to destroy everything the Pasho built. A frustrated child, breaking clay because it wouldn't mold to his satisfaction."

"No! I would not mold to theirs! Their grand design is the death of the Jai. In a thousand years, will there be anything to distinguish us from Keli? Will our women wear silver belts, and theirs perhaps wear gold bangles on their wrists, and what then? What of the Jai?"

Raphel shook his head. "I cannot give what you ask for. A few knowledgeable men could sweep the planet clean of all that remains of us. We Pasho guide knowledge now. Our ancestors moved quickly, quickly, as impatient as ants. We move slowly now, with care. We understand that knowledge is simply a terrible ocean we must cross, and hope that wisdom lies on the other side. It is not some toy casually used for our pleasure."

Old Gawar made a face. "Elegantly spoken."

"Rhetoric. A Pasho must speak well, or die in distant lands."

"You speak well to cover black deeds. You let children die of the yellow sickness and men bleed dry from war wounds. We guess at knowledge you already possess. We know that you hold keys to a thousand locks, and that you part them out sparingly, according to Pasho design." The old man picked up a chili and dropped it into his mortar bowl. He picked up another and dropped it in with its cousin. "So sparingly."

He looked up at Raphel. "I don't want the knowledge the Pasho call appropriate. I want the Jai to survive. When the Keli are forgotten and the Kai are remembered as slaves, I want the Jai to write history. Jai drink mez. We wear gold not silver. We write dust epitaphs for our vanquished enemies and watch them blow away in the desert wind. This is what it is to be Jai. The Pasho would rub all this away and blend us into a toothless race of servants. I will not allow it. I tell you, Grandson, Keli will burn. Best of all, it will burn because the Keli never managed to pry war knowledge from your selfish tattooed fists." The old man smiled thinly. "If nothing else, I must thank you Pasho for your neutrality. It serves me nearly as well. Go back to Keli, Grandson. Tell them Gawar Ka' Korum is coming again."

"A Pasho must always be respectful on his circuit. It is natural for a people to resist the presence and ideas of an outsider. In all cases, patience and subtlety are the Pasho's best tools. Our work is already generations long, and will be many more generations before it is complete. There is no hurry. Speed is what brought our ancestors to ruin. We guess, we move slowly, we wait. If we are not welcomed in a new place, we must pass on and wait for invitation. If we meet challenges, we must bend before them. Knowledge and influence are fragile things. Our reputation for neutrality, morality, and humanity must take the place of steel and sonics. Men make war. Pasho never."

—Pasho Nalina Desai, CS 955.
(Lecture 121: On Circuit Travel Etiquette)

On the ninth day of Raphel's return, the rains came. Thick gray clouds banked on the horizon, building until they filled the southern sky. They came across the basin, their bellies heavy with water. Slowly they opened and the gray paint of falling water streaked the air. The yellow plains darkened as the sun disappeared behind the onrushing clouds. Dust puffed where fat raindrops struck. Minutes later, dust turned to mud as water thundered out of the sky. By the tenth day of Raphel's Quaran, a fine bright sheen of grass, nearly phosphorescent in its new life, covered the yellow plains outside the village as the rains continued to pour down.

In the family haci, Raphel's mother worked at a celebratory feast made doubly joyful by the rain's arrival. Bowls of spiced mutton, cool yogurt, and thick red bean soup propagated around the hearth. She smiled at the rain, stirred pots over the fire and didn't complain that the wood gathered from the far hills had been dampened by the sudden rush of water. She reached out to touch Raphel often, a nearly superstitious movement that she repeated again and again, assuring herself that her son once again truly stood within her home.

In the afternoon, she sent him to fetch his grandfather. She sent him with an umbrella bought from a Keli trader, a big black thing. When Raphel protested that he didn't mind the rain, she clicked her tongue and sent him out anyway, saying that if anyone knew how to make an umbrella it should be the Keli and there was no shame in using it.

Raphel made his way through the village, dodging flooding alleys and the curtains of rain that poured off the haci roofs. Lightning flickered high above. Thunder rolled distantly. A young girl in black and red dashed down the alley toward him, smiling at his bare face, now unhidden by an electrostatic mask. His umbrella protected him from much of the dumping rain, but the girl was soaked, and clearly didn't care. Raphel turned to watch as she deliberately jumped into puddles and yellow flows, splashing mud and water and laughing at the wet.

His grandfather's courtyard was empty, its red chilies removed indoors. Raphel stood dripping outside.

"Grandfather?"

The rasping voice was surprised. "You're still here?"

Raphel pulled aside the curtain and slipped inside. He carefully shook his umbrella outside the door, and left it leaning there. His grandfather sat beside the hearth, working on another hook knife. Several lay around his feet, all of them gleaming with oil and sharpening.

"Bia' wants you to come for dinner."

The old man snorted. "She won't live in my haci but she invites me for dinner." He looked up and studied Raphel's uncovered face. "You've completed Quaran, then?"

"Today."

"You return and the land turns green. Auspicious. And you haven't left for Keli."

Raphel sighed. He sat on the hard-packed floor near his grandfather's feet. "I am Jai, Grandfather. Whatever you think, this is my home. I am here to stay."

"I suppose it's good to see your face. Despite your tattoos."

Raphel squeezed the wet hem of his robe. It was spattered with mud. Water ran out between his fingers. "I feel like I'm finally home." He looked outside to the gray curtain of water pouring off the haci's roof.

"It amazes me that I ever hated the sound of rain. In Keli it rained all the time, and no one cared. Or else they hated it. I think it's the finest sound I've ever heard."

"You sound like a Jai. If you picked up your hook knife, I'd almost believe you belong."

Raphel shook his head and grinned. "Pasho are neutral, Grandfather."

The old man's laughter was mocking. He reached for his bottle of mez. "Drink with me then, Pasho."

Raphel climbed back to his feet. "This time, I will serve you. As I should have done the day I arrived."

"And break Quaran? I think not."

Raphel took the bottle from his grandfather and set the clay cups on the ground. "You're right. We should observe the old ways. It's what distinguishes us from Keli people. We are true to our history." The long sleeves of his Pasho's robes dragged around the paired cups as he began pouring.

"Don't spill," his grandfather scolded.

Raphel smiled. He tucked his sleeves out of the way. "I'm not used to my robes, yet." He finished pouring the clear bright liquor into the paired cups. He capped the bottle carefully and handed a cup to his grandfather.

They held their cups to the sky, poured drops to their ancestors and drained them together. A moment later, Gawar's cup fell from his nerveless hand. It shattered. Clay fragments skittered across the hard-packed dirt. The old man's jaw locked. Air whistled between his clenched teeth as he fought to breathe. "Mez?" The word squeezed out.

Raphel ducked his head apologetically and pressed his palms together in farewell. "Undistilled. A common enough death for a Jai. You were right, Grandfather. War never ends. You taught the Pasho that. They have not forgotten. Even now you squat in their nightmares."

His grandfather grimaced and forced words out between his clenched teeth. "The Pasho side with Keli?"

Raphel shrugged apologetically. "Knowledge must be protected, Grandfather—" He broke off as his grandfather spasmed. Spittle leaked from the corner of the old man's mouth. Raphel leaned close and used the sleeve of his white robe to wipe the shaking man's drool. "I'm sorry, Grandfather. The Keli are too soft to withstand a Jai crusade. You would have slaughtered them like goats and turned all the Pasho work to ash: Keli's libraries, its hospitals, its factories. We Pasho cannot afford an open war; mez seemed the best alternative."

His grandfather's eyes were wide, stunned. He grunted, trying to form words. Raphel held the old man's hand as another spasm swept through him. The old man strained. Raphel leaned close to hear his whisper.

"You betray us all."

Raphel shook his head. "No, Grandfather, only you. Knowledge is a Jai birthright as much as Keli's. Your bloody crusade would have left ashes for our children. Now, instead of war, I will teach our people to sink water veins and help them plant crops that weather the hottest days of dry season, and we will flourish. Never fear, Grandfather, I am still Jai, whatever you think of my Pasho's tattoos. Your hook knife has dulled, but mine is still sharp."

Old Gawar's body stilled. His head lolled. Raphel wiped the death froth from his grandfather's mouth, the last residue of his passing. Outside, rain fell steadily, softening the air and soaking the thirsty ground with the life-giving water of the wet season.

THE CALORIE MAN

"**N**o mammy, no pappy, poor little bastard. Money? You give money?" The urchin turned a cartwheel and then a somersault in the street, stirring yellow dust around his nakedness.

Lalji paused to stare at the dirty blond child who had come to a halt at his feet. The attention seemed to encourage the urchin; the boy did another somersault. He smiled up at Lalji from his squat, calculating and eager, rivulets of sweat and mud streaking his face. "Money? You give money?"

Around them, the town was nearly silent in the afternoon heat. A few dungareed farmers led mulies toward the fields. Buildings, pressed from WeatherAll chips, slumped against their fellows like drunkards, rain-stained and sun-cracked, but, as their trade name implied, still sturdy. At the far end of the narrow street, the lush sprawl of SoyPRO and HiGro began, a waving rustling growth that rolled into the blue-sky distance. It was much as all the villages Lalji had seen as he traveled upriver, just another farming enclave paying its intellectual property dues and shipping calories down to New Orleans.

The boy crawled closer, smiling ingratiatingly, nodding his head like a snake hoping to strike. "Money? Money?"

Lalji put his hands in his pockets in case the beggar child had friends and turned his full attention on the boy. "And why should I give money to you?"

The boy stared up at him, stalled. His mouth opened, then closed. Finally he looped back to an earlier, more familiar part of his script, "No mammy? No pappy?" but it was a query now, lacking conviction.

Lalji made a face of disgust and aimed a kick at the boy. The child scrambled aside, falling on his back in his desperation to dodge, and this pleased Lalji briefly. At least the boy was quick. He turned and started back up the street. Behind him, the urchin's wailing despair echoed. "Noooo maaaammy! Nooo paaaapy!" Lalji shook his head, irritated. The child might cry for money, but he failed to follow. No true beggar at all. An opportunist only—most likely the accidental creation of strangers who had visited the village and were open-fisted when it came to blond beggar children. AgriGen and Midwest Grower scientists and land factotums would be pleased to show ostentatious kindness to the villagers at the core of their empire.

Through a gap in the slumped hovels, Lalji caught another glimpse of the lush waves of SoyPRO and HiGro. The sheer sprawl of calories stimulated tingling fantasies of loading a barge and slipping it down through the locks to St. Louis or New Orleans and into the mouths of waiting megodonts. It was impossible, but the sight of those emerald fields was more than enough assurance that no child could beg with conviction here. Not surrounded by SoyPRO. Lalji shook his head again, disgusted, and squeezed down a footpath between two of the houses.

The acrid reek of WeatherAll's excreted oils clogged the dim alley. A pair of cheshires sheltering in the unused space scattered and molted ahead of him, disappearing into bright sunlight. Just beyond, a kinetic shop leaned against its beaten neighbors, adding the scents of dung and animal sweat to the stink of WeatherAll. Lalji leaned against the shop's plank door and shoved inside.

Shafts of sunlight pierced the sweet manure gloom with lazy gold beams. A pair of hand-painted posters scabbed to one wall, partly torn but still legible. One said: "Unstamped calories mean starving families. We check royalty receipts and IP stamps." A farmer and his brood stared hollow-eyed from beneath the scolding words. PurCal was the sponsor. The other poster was AgriGen's trademarked collage of kink-springs, green rows of SoyPRO under sunlight and smiling children along with the words "We Provide Energy for the World." Lalji studied the posters sourly.

"Back already?" The owner came in from the winding room, wiping his hands on his pants and kicking straw and mud off his boots. He eyed Lalji. "My springs didn't have enough stored. I had to feed the mulies extra, to make your joules."

Lalji shrugged, having expected the last-minute bargaining, so much like Shriram's that he couldn't muster the interest to look offended. "Yes? How much?"

The man squinted up at Lalji, then ducked his head, his body defensive. "F-Five hundred." His voice caught on the amount, as though gagging on the surprising greed scampering up his throat.

Lalji frowned and pulled his mustache. It was outrageous. The calories hadn't even been transported. The village was awash with energy. And despite the man's virtuous poster, it was doubtful that the calories feeding his kinetic shop were equally upstanding. Not with tempting green fields waving within meters of the shop. Shriram often said that using stamped calories was like dumping money into a methane composter.

Lalji tugged his mustache again, wondering how much to pay for the joules without calling excessive attention to himself. Rich men must have been all over the village to make the kinetic man so greedy. Calorie executives, almost certainly. It would fit. The town was close to the center. Perhaps even this village was engaged in growing the crown jewels of AgriGen's energy monopolies. Still, not everyone who passed through would be as rich as that. "Two hundred."

The kinetic man showed a relieved smile along with knotted yellow teeth, his guilt apparently assuaged by Lalji's bargaining. "Four."

"Two. I can moor on the river and let my own winders do the same work."

The man snorted. "It would take weeks."

Lalji shrugged. "I have time. Dump the joules back into your own springs. I'll do the job myself."

"I've got family to feed. Three?"

"You live next to more calories than some rich families in St. Louis. Two."

The man shook his head sourly but he led Lalji into the winding room. The manure haze thickened. Big kinetic storage drums, twice as tall as a man, sat in a darkened corner, mud and manure lapping around their high-capacity precision kink-springs. Sunbeams poured between open gaps in the roof where shingles had blown away. Dung motes stirred lazily.

A half-dozen hyper-developed mulies crouched on their treadmills, their rib cages billowing slowly, their flanks streaked with salt lines of sweat residue from the labor of winding Lalji's boat springs. They blew air through their nostrils, nervous at Lalji's sudden scent, and gathered their squat legs under them. Muscles like boulders rippled under their bony hides as they stood. They eyed Lalji with resentful near-intelligence. One of them showed stubborn yellow teeth that matched its owner's.

Lalji made a face of disgust. "Feed them."

"I already did."

"I can see their bones. If you want my money, feed them again."

The man scowled. "They aren't supposed to get fat, they're supposed to wind your damn springs." But he dipped double handfuls of SoyPRO into their feed canisters.

The mulies shoved their heads into the buckets, slobbering and grunting with need. In its eagerness, one of them started briefly forward on its treadmill, sending energy into the winding shop's depleted storage springs before seeming to realize that its work was not demanded and that it could eat without molestation.

"They aren't even designed to get fat," the kinetic man muttered.

Lalji smiled slightly as he counted through his wadded bluebills and handed over the money. The kinetic man unjacked Lalji's kink-springs from the winding treadmills and stacked them beside the slavering mulies. Lalji lifted a spring, grunting at its heft. Its mass was no different than when he had brought it to the winding shop, but now it fairly seemed to quiver with the mulies' stored labor.

"You want help with those?" The man didn't move. His eyes flicked toward the mulies' feed buckets, still calculating his chances of interrupting their meal.

Lalji took his time answering, watching as the mulies rooted for the last of their calories. "No." He hefted the spring again, getting a better grip. "My helpboy will come for the rest."

As he turned for the door, he heard the man dragging the feed buckets away from the mulies and their grunts as they fought for their sustenance. Once again, Lalji regretted agreeing to the trip at all.

Shriram had been the one to broach the idea. They had been sitting under the awning of Lalji's porch in New Orleans, spitting betel nut juice into the alley gutters and watching the rain come down as they played chess. At the end of the alley, cycle rickshaws and bicycles slipped through the midmorning gray, pulses of green and red and blue as they passed the alley's mouth draped under rain-glossed corn polymer ponchos.

The chess game was a tradition of many years, a ritual when Lalji was in town and Shriram had time away from his small kinetic company where he rewound people's home and boat springs. Theirs was a good friendship, and a fruitful one, when Lalji had unstamped calories that needed to disappear into the mouth of a hungry megodont.

Neither of them played chess well, and so their games often devolved into a series of trades made in dizzying succession; a cascade of destruction that left a board previously well-arrayed in a tantrum wreck, with both opponents blinking surprise, trying to calculate if the mangle had been worth the combat. It was after one of these tit-for-tat cleansings that Shriram had asked Lalji if he might go upriver. Beyond the southern states.

Lalji had shaken his head and spit bloody betel juice into the overflowing gutter. "No. Nothing is profitable so far up. Too many joules to get there. Better to let the calories float to me." He was surprised to discover that he still had his queen. He used it to take a pawn.

"And if the energy costs could be defrayed?"

Lalji laughed, waiting for Shriram to make his own move. "By who? AgriGen? The IP men? Only their boats go up and down so far." He frowned as he realized that his queen was now vulnerable to Shriram's remaining knight.

Shriram was silent. He didn't touch his pieces. Lalji looked up from the board and was surprised by Shriram's serious expression. Shriram said, "I would pay. Myself and others. There is a man who some of us would like to see come south. A very special man."

"Then why not bring him south on a paddle wheel? It is expensive to go up the river. How many gigajoules? I would have to change the boat's springs, and then what would the IP patrols ask? 'Where are you going, strange Indian man with your small boat and your so many springs? Going far? To what purpose?'" Lalji shook his head. "Let this man take a ferry, or ride a barge. Isn't this cheaper?" He waved at the game board. "It's your move. You should take my queen."

Shriram waggled his head thoughtfully from side to side but didn't make any move toward the chess game. "Cheaper, yes...."

"But?"

Shriram shrugged. "A swift, inconsequential boat would attract less attention."

"What sort of man is this?"

Shriram glanced around, suddenly furtive. Methane lamps burned like blue fairies behind the closed glass of the neighbors' droplet-spattered windows. Rain sheeted off their roofs, drumming wet into the empty alley. A cheshire was yowling for a mate somewhere in the wet, barely audible under the thrum of falling water.

"Is Creo inside?"

Lalji raised his eyebrows in surprise. "He has gone to his gymnasium. Why? Should it matter?"

Shriram shrugged and gave an embarrassed smile. "Some things are better kept between old friends. People with strong ties."

"Creo has been with me for years."

Shriram grunted noncommittally, glanced around again and leaned close, pitching his voice low, forcing Lalji to lean forward as well. "There is a man who the calorie companies would like very much to find." He tapped his balding head. "A very intelligent man. We want to help him."

Lalji sucked in his breath. "A generipper?"

Shriram avoided Lalji's eyes. "In a sense. A calorie man."

Lalji made a face of disgust. "Even better reason not to be involved. I don't traffic with those killers."

"No, no. Of course not. But still…you brought that huge sign down once, did you not? A few greased palms, so smooth, and you float into town and suddenly Lakshmi smiles on you, such a calorie bandit, and now with a name instead as a dealer of antiques. Such a wonderful misdirection."

Lalji shrugged. "I was lucky. I knew the man to help move it through the locks."

"So? Do it again."

"If the calorie companies are looking for him, it would be danger-ous."

"But not impossible. The locks would be easy. Much easier than carry-ing unlicensed grains. Or even something as big as that sign. This would be a man. No sniffer dog would find him of interest. Place him in a barrel. It would be easy. And I would pay. All your joules, plus more."

Lalji sucked at his narcotic betel nut, spit red, spit red again, consid-ering. "And what does a second-rate kinetic man like you think this calorie man will do? Generippers work for big fish, and you are such a small one."

Shriram grinned haplessly and gave a self-deprecating shrug. "You do not think Ganesha Kinetic could not some day be great? The next AgriGen, maybe?" and they had both laughed at the absurdity and Shriram dropped the subject.

An IP man was on duty with his dog, blocking Lalji's way as he re-turned to his boat lugging the kink-spring. The brute's hairs bristled as Lalji approached and it lunged against its leash, its blunt nose quivering to reach him. With effort, the IP man held the creature back. "I need to sniff you." His helmet lay on the grass, already discarded, but still he was sweating under the swaddling heat of his gray slash-resistant uniform and the heavy webbing of his spring gun and bandoliers.

Lalji held still. The dog growled, deep from its throat, and inched forward. It snuffled his clothing, bared hungry teeth, snuffled again, then its black ruff iridesced blue and it relaxed and wagged its stubby tail. It sat. A pink tongue lolled from between smiling teeth. Lalji smiled sourly back at the animal, glad that he wasn't smuggling calories and wouldn't have to go through the pantomimes of obeisance as the IP man demanded stamps and then tried to verify that the grain shipment had paid its royalties and licensing fees.

At the dog's change in color, the IP man relaxed somewhat, but still he studied Lalji's features carefully, hunting for recognition against memorized photographs. Lalji waited patiently, accustomed to the scrutiny. Many men tried to steal the honest profits of AgriGen and its peers, but to Lalji's knowledge, he was unknown to the protectors of intellectual property. He was an antiques dealer, handling the junk of the previous century, not a calorie bandit staring out from corporate photo books.

Finally, the IP man waved him past. Lalji nodded politely and made his way down the stairs to the river's low stage where his needleboat was moored. Out on the river, cumbrous grain barges wallowed past, riding low under their burdens.

Though there was a great deal of river traffic, it didn't compare with harvest time. Then the whole of the Mississippi would fill with calories pouring downstream, pulled from hundreds of towns like this one. Barges would clot the arterial flow of the river system from high on the Missouri, the Illinois, and the Ohio and the thousand smaller tributaries. Some of those calories would float only as far as St. Louis where they would be chewed by megodonts and churned into joules, but the rest, the vast majority, would float to New Orleans where the great calorie companies' clippers and dirigibles would be loaded with the precious grains. Then they would cross the Earth on tradewinds and sea, in time for the next season's planting, so that the world could go on eating.

Lalji watched the barges moving slowly past, wallowing and bloated with their wealth, then hefted his kink-spring and jumped aboard his needleboat.

Creo was lying on deck as Lalji had left him, his muscled body oiled and shining in the sun, a blond Arjuna waiting for glorious battle. His cornrows spread around his head in a halo, their tipped bits of bone lying like foretelling stones on the hot deck. He didn't open his eyes as Lalji jumped aboard. Lalji went and stood in Creo's sun, eclipsing his tan. Slowly, the young man opened his blue eyes.

"Get up." Lalji dropped the spring on Creo's rippled stomach.

Creo let out a whuff and wrapped his arms around the spring. He sat up easily and set it on the deck. "Rest of the springs wound?"

Lalji nodded. Creo took the spring and went down the boat's narrow stairs to the mechanical room. When he returned from fitting the spring into the gearings of the boat's power system, he said, "Your springs are shit, all of them. I don't know why you didn't bring bigger ones. We have to rewind, what, every twenty hours? You could have gotten all the way here on a couple of the big ones."

Lalji scowled at Creo and jerked his head toward the guard still standing at the top of the riverbank and looking down on them. He lowered his voice. "And then what would the MidWest Authority be saying as we are going upriver? All their IP men all over our boat, wondering where we are going so far? Boarding us and then wondering what we are doing with such big springs. Where have we gotten so many joules? Wondering what business we have so far upriver." He shook his head. "No, no. This is better. Small boat, small distance, who worries about Lalji and his stupid blond helpboy then? No one. No, this is better."

"You always were a cheap bastard."

Lalji glanced at Creo. "You are lucky it is not forty years ago. Then you would be paddling up this river by hand, instead of lying on your lazy back letting these fancy kink-springs do the work. Then we would be seeing you use those muscles of yours."

"If I was lucky, I would have been born during the Expansion and we'd still be using gasoline."

Lalji was about to retort but an IP boat slashed past them, ripping a deep wake. Creo lunged for their cache of spring guns. Lalji dove after him and slammed the cache shut. "They're not after us!"

Creo stared at Lalji, uncomprehending for a moment, then relaxed. He stepped away from the stored weapons. The IP boat continued upriver, half its displacement dedicated to massive precision kink-springs and the stored joules that gushed from their unlocking molecules. Its curling wake rocked the needleboat. Lalji steadied himself against the rail as the IP boat dwindled to a speck and disappeared between obstructing barge chains.

Creo scowled after the boat. "I could have taken them."

Lalji took a deep breath. "You would have gotten us killed." He glanced at the top of the riverbank to see if the IP man had noticed their panic. He wasn't even visible. Lalji silently gave thanks to Ganesha.

"I don't like all of them around," Creo complained. "They're like ants.

Fourteen at the last lock. That one, up on the hill. Now these boats."

"It is the heart of calorie country. It is to be expected."

"You making a lot of money on this trip?"

"Why should you care?"

"Because you never used to take risks like this." Creo swept his arm, indicating the village, the cultivated fields, the muddy width of river gurgling past, and the massive barges clogging it. "No one comes this far upriver."

"I'm making enough money to pay you. That's all you should concern yourself with. Now go get the rest of the springs. When you think too much, your brain makes mush."

Creo shook his head doubtfully but jumped for the dock and headed up the steps to the kinetic shop. Lalji turned to face the river. He took a deep breath.

The IP boat had been a close call. Creo was too eager to fight. It was only with luck that they hadn't ended up as shredded meat from the IP men's spring guns. He shook his head tiredly, wondering if he had ever had as much reckless confidence as Creo. He didn't think so. Not even when he was a boy. Perhaps Shriram was right. Even if Creo was trustworthy, he was still dangerous.

A barge chain, loaded with TotalNutrient Wheat, slid past. The happy sheaves of its logo smiled across the river's muddy flow, promising "A Healthful Tomorrow" along with folates, B vitamins, and pork protein. Another IP boat slashed upriver, weaving amongst the barge traffic. Its complement of IP men studied him coldly as they went by. Lalji's skin crawled. Was it worth it? If he thought too much, his businessman's instinct—bred into him through thousands of years of caste practice—told him no. But still, there was Gita. When he balanced his debts each year on Diwali, how did he account for all he owed her? How did one pay off something that weighed heavier than all his profits, in all his lifetimes?

The NutriWheat wallowed past, witlessly inviting, and without answers.

"You wanted to know if there was something that would be worth your trip upriver."

Lalji and Shriram had been standing in the winding room of Ganesha Kinetic, watching a misplaced ton of SuperFlavor burn into joules. Shriram's paired megodonts labored against the winding spindles, ponderous and steady as they turned just-consumed calories into kinetic energy and wound the shop's main storage springs.

Priti and Bidi. The massive creatures barely resembled the elephants that had once provided their template DNA. Generippers had honed them to a perfect balance of musculature and hunger for a single purpose: to inhale calories and do terrible labors without complaint. The smell of them was overwhelming. Their trunks dragged the ground.

The animals were getting old, Lalji thought, and on the heels of that thought came another: he, too, was getting old. Every morning he found gray in his mustache. He plucked it, of course, but more gray hairs always sprouted. And now his joints ached in the mornings as well. Shriram's own head shone like polished teak. At some point, he'd turned bald. Fat and bald. Lalji wondered when they had turned into such old men.

Shriram repeated himself, and Lalji shook away his thoughts. "No, I am not interested in anything upriver. That is the calorie companies' province. I have accepted that when you scatter my ashes it will be on the Mississippi, and not the holy Ganges, but I am not so eager to find my next life that I wish my corpse to float down from Iowa."

Shriram twisted his hands nervously and glanced around. He lowered his voice, even though the steady groan of the spindles was more than enough to drown their sounds. "Please, friend, there are people…who want…to kill this man."

"And I should care?"

Shriram made placating motions with his hands. "He knows how to make calories. AgriGen wants him, badly. PurCal as well. He has rejected them and their kind. His mind is valuable. He needs someone trustworthy to bring him downriver. No friend of the IP men."

"And just because he is an enemy of AgriGen I should help him? Some former associate of the Des Moines clique? Some ex-calorie man with blood on his hands and you think he will help you make money?"

Shriram shook his head. "You make it sound as if this man is unclean."

"We are talking of generippers, yes? How much morality can he have?"

"A geneticist. Not a generipper. Geneticists gave us megodonts." He waved at Priti and Bidi. "Me, a livelihood."

Lalji turned on Shriram. "You take refuge in these semantics, now? You, who starved in Chennai when the Nippon genehack weevil came? When the soil turned to alcohol? Before U-Tex and HiGro and the rest all showed up so conveniently? You, who waited on the docks when the seeds came in, saw them come and then saw them sit behind their fences and guards, waiting for people with the money to buy? What traffic would I have with this sort of people? I would sooner spit on him, this calorie man. Let the PurCal devils have him, I say."

The town was as Shriram had described it. Cottonwoods and willows tangled the edges of the river and over them, the remains of the bridge, some of it still spanning the river in a hazy network of broken trusses and crumbling supports. Lalji and Creo stared up at the rusting construction, a web of steel and cable and concrete, slowly collapsing into the river.

"How much do you think the steel would bring?" Creo asked.

Lalji filled his cheek with a handful of PestResis sunflower seeds and started cracking them between his teeth. He spit the hulls into the river one by one. "Not much. Too much energy to tear it out, then to melt it." He shook his head and spat another hull. "A waste to make something like that with steel. Better to use Fast-Gen hardwoods, or WeatherAll."

"Not to cover that distance. It couldn't be done now. Not unless you were in Des Moines, maybe. I heard they burn coal there."

"And they have electric lights that go all night and computers as large as a house." Lalji waved his hand dismissively and turned to finish securing the needleboat. "Who needs such a bridge now? A waste. A ferry and a mulie would serve just as well." He jumped ashore and started climbing the crumbling steps that led up from the river. Creo followed.

At the top of the steep climb, a ruined suburb waited. Built to serve the cities on the far side of the river when commuting was common and petroleum cheap, it now sprawled in an advanced state of decay. A junk city built with junk materials, as transient as water, willingly abandoned when the expense of commuting grew too great.

"What the hell is this place?" Creo muttered.

Lalji smiled cynically. He jerked his head toward the green fields across the river, where SoyPRO and HiGro undulated to the horizon. "The very cradle of civilization, yes? AgriGen, Midwest Growers Group, PurCal, all of them have fields here."

"Yeah? That excite you?"

Lalji turned and studied a barge chain as it wallowed down the river below them, its mammoth size rendered small by the height. "If we could turn all their calories into traceless joules, we'd be wealthy men."

"Keep dreaming." Creo breathed deeply and stretched. His back cracked and he winced at the sound. "I get out of shape when I ride your boat this long. I should have stayed in New Orleans."

Lalji raised his eyebrows. "You're not happy to be making this touristic journey?" He pointed across the river. "Somewhere over there, perhaps in those very acres, AgriGen created SoyPRO. And everyone thought they were such wonderful people." He frowned. "And then the weevil came, and suddenly there was nothing else to eat."

Creo made a face. "I don't go for those conspiracy theories."

"You weren't even born when it happened." Lalji turned to lead Creo into the wrecked suburb. "But I remember. No such accident had ever happened before."

"Monocultures. They were vulnerable."

"Basmati was no monoculture!" Lalji waved his hand back toward the green fields. "SoyPRO is monoculture. PurCal is monoculture. Generippers make monoculture."

"Whatever you say, Lalji."

Lalji glanced at Creo, trying to tell if the young man was still arguing with him, but Creo was carefully studying the street wreckage and Lalji let the argument die. He began counting streets, following memorized directions.

The avenues were all ridiculously broad and identical, large enough to run a herd of megodonts. Twenty cycle rickshaws could ride abreast easily, and yet the town had only been a support suburb. It boggled Lalji's mind to consider the scale of life before.

A gang of children watched them from the doorway of a collapsed house. Half its timbers had been removed, and the other half were splintered, rising from the foundation like carcass bones where siding flesh had been stripped away.

Creo showed the children his spring gun and they ran away. He scowled at their departing forms. "So what the hell are we picking up here? You got a lead on another antique?"

Lalji shrugged.

"Come on. I'm going to be hauling it in a couple minutes anyway. What's with the secrecy?"

Lalji glanced at Creo. "There's nothing for you to haul. 'It' is a man. We're looking for a man."

Creo made a sound of disbelief. Lalji didn't bother responding.

Eventually, they came to an intersection. At its center, an old signal light lay smashed. Around it, the pavement was broken through by grasses gone to seed. Dandelions stuck up their yellow heads. On the far side of the intersection, a tall brick building squatted, a ruin of a civil center, yet still standing, built with better materials than the housing it had served.

A cheshire bled across the weedy expanse. Creo tried to shoot it. Missed.

Lalji studied the brick building. "This is the place."

Creo grunted and shot at another cheshire shimmer.

Lalji went over and inspected the smashed signal light, idly curious to see if it might have value. It was rusted. He turned in a slow circle, studying the surroundings for anything at all that might be worth taking downriver. Some of the old Expansion's wreckage still had worthy artifacts. He'd found the Conoco sign in such a place, in a suburb soon to be swallowed by SoyPRO, perfectly intact, seemingly never mounted in the open air, never subjected to the angry mobs of the energy Contraction. He'd sold it to an AgriGen executive for more than an entire smuggled cargo of HiGro.

The AgriGen woman had laughed at the sign. She'd mounted it on her wall, surrounded by the lesser artifacts of the Expansion: plastic cups, computer monitors, photos of racing automobiles, brightly colored children's toys. She'd hung the sign on her wall and then stood back and murmured that at one point, it had been a powerful company…global, even.

Global.

She'd said the word with an almost sexual yearning as she stared up at the sign's ruddy polymers.

Global.

For a moment, Lalji had been smitten by her vision: a company that pulled energy from the remotest parts of the planet and sold it far away within weeks of extraction; a company with customers and investors on every continent, with executives who crossed time zones as casually as Lalji crossed the alley to visit Shriram.

The AgriGen woman had hung the sign on her wall like the head of a trophy megodont and in that moment, next to a representative of the most powerful energy company in the world, Lalji had felt a sudden sadness at how very diminished humanity had become.

Lalji shook away the memory and again turned slowly in the intersection, seeking signs of his passenger. More cheshires flitted amongst the ruins, their smoky shimmer shapes pulsing across the sunlight and passing into shadows. Creo pumped his spring gun and sprayed disks. A shimmer tumbled to stillness and became a matted pile of calico and blood.

Creo repumped his spring gun. "So where is this guy?"

"I think he will come. If not today, then tomorrow or the next." Lalji headed up the steps of the civil center and slipped between its shattered doors. Inside, it was nothing but dust and gloom and bird droppings. He found stairs and made his way upward until he found a broken window with a view. A gust of wind rattled the window pane and tugged his mustache. A pair of crows circled in the blue sky. Below, Creo pumped his spring gun and shot more cheshire shimmers. When he hit, angry yowls filtered up. Blood swatches spattered the weedy pavement as more animals fled.

In the distance, the suburb's periphery was already falling to agriculture. Its time was short. Soon the houses would be plowed under and a perfect blanket of SoyPRO would cover it. The suburb's history, as silly and transient as it had been, would be lost, churned under by the march of energy development. No loss, from the standpoint of value, but still, some part of Lalji cringed at the thought of time erased. He spent too much time trying to recall the India of his boyhood to take pleasure in the disappearance. He headed back down the dusty stairs to Creo.

"See anyone?"

Lalji shook his head. Creo grunted and shot at another cheshire, narrowly missing. He was good, but the nearly invisible animals were hard targets. Creo pumped his spring gun and fired again. "Can't believe how many cheshires there are."

"There is no one to exterminate them."

"I should collect the skins and take them back to New Orleans."

"Not on my boat."

Many of the shimmers were fleeing, finally understanding the quality of their enemy. Creo pumped again and aimed at a twist of light further down the street.

Lalji watched complacently. "You will never hit it."

"Watch." Creo aimed carefully.

A shadow fell across them. "Don't shoot."

Creo whipped his spring gun around.

Lalji waved a hand at Creo. "Wait! It's him!"

The new arrival was a skinny old man, bald except for a greasy fringe of gray and brown hair, his heavy jaw thick with gray stubble. Hemp sacking covered his body, dirty and torn, and his eyes had a sunken, knowing quality that unearthed in Lalji the memory of a long-ago sadhu, covered with ash and little else: the tangled hair, the disinterest in his clothing, the distance in the eyes that came from enlightenment. Lalji shook away the memory. This man was no holy man. Just a man, and a generipper, at that.

Creo resighted his spring gun on the distant cheshire. "Down south, I get a bluebill for every one I kill."

The old man said, "There are no bluebills for you to collect here."

"Yeah, but they're pests."

"It's not their fault we made them too perfectly." The man smiled hesitantly, as though testing a facial expression. "Please." He squatted down in front of Creo. "Don't shoot."

Lalji placed a hand on Creo's spring gun. "Let the cheshires be."

Creo scowled, but he let his gun's mechanism unwind with a sigh of releasing energy.

The calorie man said, "I am Charles Bowman." He looked at them expectantly, as though anticipating recognition. "I am ready. I can leave."

Gita was dead, of that Lalji was now sure.

At times, he had pretended that it might not be so. Pretended that she might have found a life, even after he had gone.

But she was dead, and he was sure of it.

It was one of his secret shames. One of the accretions to his life that clung to him like dog shit on his shoes and reduced himself in his own eyes: as when he had thrown a rock and hit a boy's head, unprovoked, to see if it was possible; or when he had dug seeds out of the dirt and eaten them one by one, too starved to share. And then there was Gita. Always Gita. That he had left her and gone instead to live close to the calories. That she had stood on the docks and waved as he set sail, when it was she who had paid his passage price.

He remembered chasing her when he was small, following the rustle of her salwar kameez as she dashed ahead of him, her black hair and black eyes and white, white teeth. He wondered if she had been as beautiful as he recalled. If her oiled black braid had truly gleamed the way he remembered when she sat with him in the dark and told him stories of Arjuna and Krishna and Ram and Hanuman. So much was lost. He wondered sometimes if he even remembered her face correctly, or if he had replaced it with an ancient poster of a Bollywood girl, one of the old ones that Shriram kept in the safe of his winding shop and guarded jealously from the influences of light and air.

For a long time he thought he would go back and find her. That he might feed her. That he would send money and food back to his blighted land that now existed only in his mind, in his dreams, and in half-awake hallucinations of deserts, red and black saris, of women in dust, and their black hands and silver bangles, and their hunger, so many of the last memories of hunger.

He had fantasized that he would smuggle Gita back across the shining sea, and bring her close to the accountants who calculated calorie burn quotas for the world. Close to the calories, as she had said, once so long ago. Close to the men who balanced price stability against margins of error and protectively managed energy markets against a flood of food. Close to those small gods with more power than Kali to destroy the world.

But she was dead by now, whether through starvation or disease, and he was sure of it.

And wasn't that why Shriram had come to him? Shriram who knew more of his history than any other. Shriram, who had found him after he arrived in New Orleans, and known him for a fellow countryman: not just another Indian long settled in America, but one who still spoke the dialects of desert villages and who still remembered their country as it had existed before genehack weevil, leafcurl, and root rust. Shriram, who had shared a place on the floor while they both worked the winding sheds for calories and nothing else, and were grateful for it, as though they were nothing but genehacks themselves.

Of course Shriram had known what to say to send him upriver. Shriram had known how much he wished to balance the unbalanceable.

They followed Bowman down empty streets and up remnant alleys, winding through the pathetic collapse of termite-ridden wood, crumbling concrete foundations, and rusted rebar too useless to scavenge and too stubborn to erode. Finally, the old man squeezed them between the stripped hulks of a pair of rusted automobiles. On the far side, Lalji and Creo gasped.

Sunflowers waved over their heads. A jungle of broad squash leaves hugged their knees. Dry corn stalks rattled in the wind. Bowman looked back at their surprise, and his smile, so hesitant and testing at first, broadened with unrestrained pleasure. He laughed and waved them onward, floundering through a garden of flowers and weeds and produce, catching his torn hemp cloth on the dried stems of cabbage gone to seed and the cling of cantaloupe vines. Creo and Lalji picked their way through the tangle, wending around purple lengths of eggplants, red orb tomatoes, and dangling orange ornament chilies. Bees buzzed heavily between the sunflowers, burdened with saddlebags of pollen.

Lalji paused in the overgrowth and called after Bowman. "These plants. They are not engineered?"

Bowman paused and came thrashing back, wiping sweat and vegetal debris off his face, grinning. "Well, engineered, that is a matter of definition, but no, these are not owned by calorie companies. Some of them are even heirloom." He grinned again. "Or close enough."

"How do they survive?"

"Oh, that." He reached down and yanked up a tomato. "Nippon gene-hack weevils, or curl.111.b, or perhaps cibiscosis bacterium, something like that?" He bit into the tomato and let the juice run down his gray bristled chin. "There isn't another heirloom planting within hundreds of miles. This is an island in an ocean of SoyPRO and HiGro. It makes a formidable barrier." He studied the garden thoughtfully, took another bite of tomato. "Now that you have come, of course, only a few of these plants will survive." He nodded at Lalji and Creo. "You will be carrying some infection or another and many of these rarities can only survive in isolation." He plucked another tomato and handed it to Lalji. "Try it."

Lalji studied its gleaming red skin. He bit into it and tasted sweetness and acid. Grinning, he offered it to Creo, who took a bite and made a face of disgust. "I'll stick with SoyPRO." He handed it back to Lalji, who finished it greedily.

Bowman smiled at Lalji's hunger. "You're old enough to remember, I think, what food used to be. You can take as much of this as you like, before we go. It will all die anyway." He turned and thrashed again through the garden overgrowth, shoving aside dry corn stalks with crackling authoritative sweeps of his arms.

Beyond the garden a house lay collapsed, leaning as though it had been toppled by a megodont, its walls rammed and buckled. The collapsed roof had an ungainly slant, and at one end, a pool of water lay cool and deep, rippled with water skippers. Scavenged gutter had been laid to sluice rainwater from the roof into the pond.

Bowman slipped around the pool's edge and disappeared down a series of crumbled cellar steps. By the time Lalji and Creo followed him down, he had wound a handlight and its dim bulb was spattering the cellar with illumination as its spring ran its course. He cranked the light again while he searched around, then struck a match and lit a lantern. The wick burned high on vegetable oil.

Lalji studied the cellar. It was sparse and damp. A pair of pallets lay on the broken concrete floor. A computer was tucked against a corner, its mahogany case and tiny screen gleaming, its treadle worn with use. An unruly kitchen was shoved against a wall with jars of grains arrayed on pantry shelves and bags of produce hanging from the ceiling to defend against rodents.

The man pointed to a sack on the ground. "There, my luggage."

"What about the computer?" Lalji asked.

Bowman frowned at the machine. "No. I don't need it."

"But it's valuable."

"What I need, I carry in my head. Everything in that machine came from me. My fat burned into knowledge. My calories pedaled into data analysis." He scowled. "Sometimes, I look at that computer and all I see is myself whittled away. I was a fat man once." He shook his head emphatically. "I won't miss it."

Lalji began to protest but Creo startled and whipped out his spring gun. "Someone else is here."

Lalji saw her even as Creo spoke: a girl squatting in the corner, hidden by shadow, a skinny, staring, freckled creature with stringy brown hair. Creo lowered his spring gun with a sigh.

Bowman beckoned. "Come out, Tazi. These are the men I told you about."

Lalji wondered how long she had been sitting in the cellar darkness, waiting. She had the look of a creature who had almost molded with the basement: her hair lank, her dark eyes nearly swallowed by their pupils. He turned on Bowman. "I thought there was only you."

Bowman's pleased smile faded. "Will you go back because of it?"

Lalji eyed the girl. Was she a lover? His child? A feral adoptee? He couldn't guess. The girl slipped her hand into the old man's. Bowman patted it reassuringly. Lalji shook his head. "She is too many. You, I have agreed to take. I prepared a way to carry you, to hide you from boarders and inspections. Her," he waved at the girl, "I did not agree to. It is risky to take someone like yourself, and now you wish to compound the danger with this girl? No." He shook his head emphatically. "It cannot be done."

"What difference does it make?" Bowman asked. "It costs you nothing. The current will carry us all. I have food enough for both of us." He went over to the pantry and started to pull down glass jars of beans, lentils, corn, and rice. "Look, here."

Lalji said, "We have more than enough food."

Bowman made a face. "SoyPRO, I suppose?"

"Nothing wrong with SoyPRO," Creo said.

The old man grinned and held up a jar of green beans floating in brine. "No. Of course not. But a man likes variety." He began filling his bag with more jars, letting them clink carefully. He caught Creo's snort of disgust and smiled, ingratiating suddenly. "For lean times, if nothing else." He dumped more jars of grains into the sack.

Lalji chopped the air with his hand. "Your food is not the issue. Your girl is the issue, and she is a risk!"

Bowman shook his head. "No risk. No one is looking for her. She can travel in the open, even."

"No. You must leave her. I will not take her."

The old man looked down at the girl, uncertain. She gazed back, extricated her hand from his. "I'm not afraid. I can live here still. Like before."

Bowman frowned, thinking. Finally, he shook his head. "No." He faced Lalji. "If she cannot go, then I cannot. She fed me when I worked. I deprived her of calories for my research when they should have gone to her. I owe her too much. I will not leave her to the wolves of this place." He placed his hands on her shoulders and placed her ahead of him, between himself and Lalji.

Creo made a face of disgust. "What difference does it make? Just bring her. We've got plenty of space."

Lalji shook his head. He and Bowman stared at one another across the cellar. Creo said, "What if he gives us the computer? We could call it payment."

Lalji shook his head stubbornly. "No. I do not care about the money. It is too dangerous to bring her."

Bowman laughed. "Then why come all this way if you are afraid? Half the calorie companies want to kill me and you talk about risk?"

Creo frowned. "What's he talking about?"

Bowman's eyebrows went up in surprise. "You haven't told your partner about me?"

Creo looked from Lalji to Bowman and back. "Lalji?"

Lalji took a deep breath, his eyes still locked on Bowman. "They say he can break the calorie monopolies. That he can pirate SoyPRO."

Creo boggled for a moment. "That's impossible!"

Bowman shrugged. "For you, perhaps. But for a knowledgeable man? Willing to dedicate his life to DNA helixes? More than possible. If one is willing to burn the calories for such a project, to waste energy on statistics and genome analysis, to pedal a computer through millions upon millions of cycles. More than possible." He wrapped his arms around his skinny girl and held her to him. He smiled at Lalji. "So. Do we have any agreement?"

Creo shook his head, puzzling. "I thought you had a money plan, Lalji, but this…" He shook his head again. "I don't get it. How the hell do we make money off this?"

Lalji gave Creo a dirty look. Bowman smiled, patiently waiting. Lalji stifled an urge to seize the lantern and throw it in his face, such a confident man, so sure of himself, so loyal.…

He turned abruptly and headed for the stairs. "Bring the computer, Creo. If his girl makes any trouble, we dump them both in the river, and still keep his knowledge."

Lalji remembered his father pushing back his thali, pretending he was full when dal had barely stained the steel plate. He remembered his mother pressing an extra bite onto his own. He remembered Gita, watching, silent, and then all of them unfolding their legs and climbing off the family bed, bustling around the hovel, ostentatiously ignoring him as he consumed the extra portion. He remembered roti in his mouth, dry like ashes, and forcing himself to swallow anyway.

He remembered planting. Squatting with his father in desert heat, yellow dust all around them, burying seeds they had stored away, saved when they might have been eaten, kept when they might have made Gita fat and marriageable, his father smiling, saying, "These seeds will make hundreds of new seeds and then we will all eat well."

"How many seeds will they make?" Lalji had asked.

And his father had laughed and spread his arms fully wide, and seemed so large and great with his big white teeth and red and gold earrings and crinkling eyes as he cried, "Hundreds! Thousands if you pray!" And Lalji had prayed, to Ganesha and Lakshmi and Krishna and Rani Sati and Ram and Vishnu, to every god he could think of, joining the many villagers who did the same as he poured water from the well over tiny seeds and sat guard in the darkness against the possibility that the precious grains might be uprooted in the night and transported to some other farmer's field.

He sat every night while cold stars turned overhead, watching the seed rows, waiting, watering, praying, waiting through the days until his father finally shook his head and said it was no use. And yet still he had hoped, until at last he went out into the field and dug up the seeds one by one, and found them already decomposed, tiny corpses in his hand, rotted. As dead in his palm as the day he and his father had planted them.

He had crouched in the darkness and eaten the cold dead seeds, knowing he should share, and yet unable to master his hunger and carry them home. He wolfed them down alone, half-decayed and caked with dirt: his first true taste of PurCal.

In the light of early morning, Lalji bathed in the most sacred river of his adopted land. He immersed himself in the Mississippi's silty flow, cleansing the weight of sleep, making himself clean before his gods. He pulled himself back aboard, slick with water, his underwear dripping off his sagging bottom, his brown skin glistening, and toweled himself dry on the deck as he looked across the water to where the rising sun cast gold flecks on the river's rippled surface.

He finished drying himself and dressed in new clean clothes before going to his shrine. He lit incense in front of the gods, placed U-Tex and SoyPRO before the tiny carved idols of Krishna and his lute, benevolent Lakshmi, and elephant-headed Ganesha. He knelt in front of the idols, prostrated himself, and prayed.

They had floated south on the river's current, winding easily through bright fall days and watching as leaves changed and cool weather came on. Tranquil skies had arched overhead and mirrored on the river, turning the mud of the Mississippi's flow into shining blue, and they had followed that blue road south, riding the great arterial flow of the river as creeks and tributaries and the linked chains of barges all crowded in with them and gravity did the work of carrying them south.

He was grateful for their smooth movement downriver. The first of the locks were behind them, and having watched the sniffer dogs ignore Bowman's hiding place under the decking, Lalji was beginning to hope that the trip would be as easy as Shriram had claimed. Nonetheless, he prayed longer and harder each day as IP patrols shot past in their fast boats, and he placed extra SoyPRO before Ganesha's idol, desperately hoping that the Remover of Obstacles would continue to do so.

By the time he finished his morning devotions, the rest of the boat was stirring. Creo came below and wandered into the cramped galley. Bowman followed, complaining of SoyPRO, offering heirloom ingredients that Creo shook off with suspicion. On deck, Tazi sat at the edge of the boat with a fishing line tossed into the water, hoping to snare one of the massive lethargic LiveSalmon that occasionally bumped against the boat's keel in the warm murk of the river.

Lalji unmoored and took his place at the tiller. He unlocked the kink-springs and the boat whirred into the deeper current, stored joules dripping from its precision springs in a steady flow as molecules unlocked, one after another, reliable from the first kink to the last. He positioned the needleboat amongst the wallowing grain barges and locked the springs again, allowing the boat to drift.

Bowman and Creo came back up on deck as Creo was asking, "...you know how to grow SoyPRO?"

Bowman laughed and sat down beside Tazi. "What good would that do? The IP men would find the fields, ask for the licenses, and if none were provided, the fields would burn and burn and burn."

"So what good are you?"

Bowman smiled and posed a question instead. "SoyPRO—what is its most precious quality?"

"It's high calorie."

Bowman's braying laughter carried across the water. He tousled Tazi's hair and the pair of them exchanged amused glances. "You've seen too many billboards from AgriGen. 'Energy for the world' indeed, indeed. Oh, AgriGen and their ilk must love you very much. So malleable, so...tractable." He laughed again and shook his head. "No. Anyone can make high-calorie plants. What else?"

Nettled, Creo said, "It resists the weevil."

Bowman's expression became sly. "Closer, yes. Difficult to make a plant that fights off the weevil, the leafcurl rust, the soil bacterium which chew through their roots... so many blights plague us now, so many beasts assail our plantings, but come now, what, best of all, do we like about SoyPRO? We of AgriGen who 'provide energy to the world'?" He waved at a chain of grain barges slathered with logos for SuperFlavor. "What makes SuperFlavor so perfect from a CEO's perspective?" He turned toward Lalji. "You know, Indian, don't you? Isn't it why you've come all this distance?"

Lalji stared back at him. When he spoke, his voice was hoarse. "It's sterile."

Bowman's eyes held Lalji's for a moment. His smile slipped. He ducked his head. "Yes. Indeed, indeed. A genetic dead-end. A one-way street. We now pay for a privilege that nature once provided willingly, for just a little labor." He looked up at Lalji. "I'm sorry. I should have thought. You would have felt our accountants' optimum demand estimates more than most."

Lalji shook his head. "You cannot apologize." He nodded at Creo. "Tell him the rest. Tell him what you can do. What I was told you can do."

"Some things are perhaps better left unsaid."

Lalji was undaunted. "Tell him. Tell me. Again."

Bowman shrugged. "If you trust him, then I must trust him as well, yes?" He turned to Creo. "Do you know cheshires?"

Creo made a noise of disgust. "They're pests."

"Ah, yes. A bluebill for every dead one. I forgot. But what makes our cheshires such pests?"

"They molt. They kill birds."

"And?" Bowman prodded.

Creo shrugged.

Bowman shook his head. "And to think it was for people like you that I wasted my life on research and my calories on computer cycles.

"You call cheshires a plague, and truly, they are. A few wealthy patrons, obsessed with Lewis Carroll, and suddenly they are everywhere, breeding with heirloom cats, killing birds, wailing in the night, but most importantly, their offspring, an astonishing ninety-two percent of the time, are cheshires themselves, pure, absolute. We create a new species in a heartbeat of evolutionary time, and our songbird populations disappear almost as quickly. A more perfect predator, but most importantly, one that spreads.

"With SoyPRO, or U-Tex, the calorie companies may patent the plants and use intellectual property police and sensitized dogs to sniff out their property, but even IP men can only inspect so many acres. Most importantly, the seeds are sterile, a locked box. Some may steal a little here and there, as you and Lalji do, but in the end, you are nothing but a small expense on a balance sheet fat with profit because no one except the calorie companies can grow the plants.

"But what would happen if we passed SoyPRO a different trait, stealthily, like a man climbing atop his best friend's wife?" He waved his arm to indicate the green fields that lapped at the edges of the river. "What if someone were to drop bastardizing pollens amongst these crown jewels that surround us? Before the calorie companies harvested and shipped the resulting seeds across the world in their mighty clipper fleets, before the licensed dealers delivered the patented crop seed to their customers. What sorts of seeds might they be delivering then?"

Bowman began ticking traits off with his fingers. "Resistant to weevil and leafcurl, yes. High calorie, yes, of course. Genetically distinct and therefore unpatentable?" He smiled briefly. "Perhaps. But best of all, fecund. Unbelievably fecund. Ripe, fat with breeding potential." He leaned forward. "Imagine it. Seeds distributed across the world by the very cuckolds who have always clutched them so tight, all of those seeds lusting to breed, lusting to produce their own fine offspring full of the same pollens that polluted the crown jewels in the first place." He clapped his hands. "Oh, what an infection that would be! And how it would spread!"

Creo stared, his expression contorting between horror and fascination. "You can do this?"

Bowman laughed and clapped his hands again. "I'm going to be the next Johnny Appleseed."

Lalji woke suddenly. Around him, the darkness of the river was nearly complete. A few windup LED beacons glowed on grain barges, powered by the flow of the current's drag against their ungainly bodies. Water lapped against the sides of the needleboat and the bank where they had tied up. Beside him on the deck the others lay bundled in blankets.

Why had he wakened? In the distance, a pair of village roosters were challenging one another across the darkness. A dog was barking, incensed by whatever hidden smells or sounds caused dogs to startle and defend their territory. Lalji closed his eyes and listened to the gentle undulation of the river, the sounds of the distant village. If he pressed his imagination, he could almost be lying in the early dawn of another village, far away, long ago dissolved.

Why was he awake? He opened his eyes again and sat up. He strained his eyes against the darkness. A shadow appeared on the river blackness, a subtle blot of movement.

Lalji shook Bowman awake, his hand over Bowman's mouth. "Hide!" he whispered.

Lights swept over them. Bowman's eyes widened. He fought off his blankets and scrambled for the hold. Lalji gathered Bowman's blankets with his own, trying to obscure the number of sleepers as more lights flashed brightly, sliding across the deck, pasting them like insects on a collection board.

Abandoning its pretense of stealth, the IP boat opened its springs and rushed in. It slammed against the needleboat, pinning it to the shoreline as men swarmed aboard. Three of them, and two dogs.

"Everyone stay calm! Keep your hands in sight!"

Handlight beams swept across the deck, dazzlingly bright. Creo and Tazi clawed out of their blankets and stood, surprised. The sniffer dogs growled and lunged against their leashes. Creo backed away from them, his hands held before him, defensive.

One of the IP men swept his handlight across them. "Who owns this boat?"

Lalji took a breath. "It's mine. This is my boat." The beam swung back and speared his eyes. He squinted into the light. "Have we done something wrong?"

The leader didn't answer. The other IP men fanned out, swinging their lights across the boat, marking the people on deck. Lalji realized that except for the leader, they were just boys, barely old enough to have mustaches and beards at all. Just peachfuzzed boys carrying spring guns and covered in armor that helped them swagger.

Two of them headed for the stairs with the dogs as a fourth jumped aboard from the secured IP boat. Handlight beams disappeared into the bowels of the needleboat, casting looming shadows from inside the stairway. Creo had somehow managed to end up backed against the needleboat's cache of spring guns. His hand rested casually beside the catches. Lalji stepped toward the captain, hoping to head off Creo's impulsiveness.

The captain swung his light on him. "What are you doing here?"

Lalji stopped and spread his hands helplessly. "Nothing."

"No?"

Lalji wondered if Bowman had managed to secure himself. "What I mean is that we only moored here to sleep."

"Why didn't you tie up at Willow Bend?"

"I'm not familiar with this part of the river. It was getting dark. I didn't want to be crushed by the barges." He wrung his hands. "I deal with antiques. We were looking in the old suburbs to the north. It's not illeg—" A shout from below interrupted him. Lalji closed his eyes regretfully. The Mississippi would be his burial river. He would never find his way to the Ganges.

The IP men came up dragging Bowman. "Look what we found! Trying to hide under the decking!"

Bowman tried to shake them off. "I don't know what you're talking about—"

"Shut up!" One of the boys shoved a club into Bowman's stomach. The old man doubled over. Tazi lunged toward them, but the captain corralled her and held her tightly as he flashed his light over Bowman's features. He gasped.

"Cuff him. We want him. Cover them!" Spring guns came up all around. The captain scowled at Lalji. "An antiques dealer. I almost believed you." To his men he said, "He's a generipper. From a long time ago. See if there's anything else on board. Any disks, any computers, any papers."

One of them said, "There's a treadle computer below."

"Get it."

In moments the computer was on deck. The captain surveyed his captives. "Cuff them all." One of the IP boys made Lalji kneel and started patting him down while a sniffer dog growled over them.

Bowman was saying, "I'm really very sorry. Perhaps you've made a mistake. Perhaps...."

Suddenly the captain shouted. The IP men's handlights swung toward the sound. Tazi was latched onto the captain's hand, biting him. He was shaking at her as though she were a dog, struggling with his other hand to get his spring gun free. For a brief moment everyone watched the scuffle between the girl and the much larger man. Someone—Lalji thought it was an IP man—laughed. Then Tazi was flung free and the captain had his gun out and there was a sharp hiss of disks. Handlights thudded on the deck and rolled, casting dizzy beams of light.

More disks hissed through the darkness. A rolling light beam showed the captain falling, crashing against Bowman's computer, silver disks embedded in his armor. He and the computer slid backwards. Darkness again. A splash. The dogs howled, either released and attacking or else wounded. Lalji dove and lay prone on the decking as metal whirred past his head.

"Lalji!" It was Creo's voice. A gun skittered across the planking. Lalji scrambled toward the sound.

One of the handlight beams had stabilized. The captain was sitting up, black blood lines trailing from his jaw as he leveled his pistol at Tazi. Bowman lunged into the light, shielding the girl with his body. He curled as disks hit him.

Lalji's fingers bumped the spring gun. He clutched after it blindly. His hand closed on it. He jacked the pump, aimed toward bootfalls, and let the spring gun whir. The shadow of one of the IP men, the boys, was above him, falling, bleeding, already dead as he hit the decking.

Everything went silent.

Lalji waited. Nothing moved. He waited still, forcing himself to breathe quietly, straining his eyes against the shadows where the handlights didn't illuminate. Was he the only one alive?

One by one, the three remaining handlights ran out of juice. Darkness closed in. The IP boat bumped gently against the needleboat. A breeze rustled the willow banks, carrying the muddy reek of fish and grasses. Crickets chirped.

Lalji stood. Nothing. No movement. Slowly he limped across the deck.

He'd twisted his leg somehow. He felt for one of the handlights, found it by its faint metallic gleam, and wound it. He played its flickering beam across the deck.

Creo. The big blond boy was dead, a disk caught in his throat. Blood pooled from where it had hit his artery. Not far away, Bowman was ribboned with disks. His blood ran everywhere. The computer was missing. Gone overboard. Lalji squatted beside the bodies, sighing. He pulled Creo's bloodied braids off his face. He had been fast. As fast as he had believed he was. Three armored IP men and the dogs as well. He sighed again.

Something whimpered. Lalji flicked his light toward the source, afraid of what he would find, but it was only the girl, seemingly unhurt, crawling to Bowman's body. She looked up into the glare of Lalji's light, then ignored him and crouched over Bowman. She sobbed, then stifled herself. Lalji locked the handlight's spring and let darkness fall over them.

He listened to the night sounds again, praying to Ganesha that there were no others out on the river. His eyes adjusted. The shadow of the grieving girl kneeling amongst lumped bodies resolved from the blackness. He shook his head. So many dead for such an idea. That such a man as Bowman might be of use. And now such a waste. He listened for signs others had been alerted but heard nothing. A single patrol, it seemed, uncoordinated with any others. Bad luck. That was all. One piece of bad luck breaking a string of good. Gods were fickle.

He limped to the needleboat's moorings and began untying. Unbidden, Tazi joined him, her small hands fumbling with the knots. He went to the tiller and unlocked the kink-springs. The boat jerked as the screws bit and they swept into the river darkness. He let the springs fly for an hour, wasting joules but anxious to make distance from the killing place, then searched the banks for an inlet and anchored. The darkness was nearly total.

After securing the boat, he searched for weights and tied them around the ankles of the IP men. He did the same with the dogs, then began shoving the bodies off the deck. The water swallowed them easily. It felt unclean to dump them so unceremoniously, but he had no intention of taking time to bury them. With luck, the men would bump along under water, picked at by fish until they disintegrated.

When the IP men were gone, he paused over Creo. So wonderfully quick. He pushed Creo overboard, wishing he could build a pyre for him.

Lalji began mopping the decks, sluicing away the remaining blood. The moon rose, bathing them in pale light. The girl sat beside the body of her chaperone. Eventually, Lalji could avoid her with his mopping no more. He knelt beside her. "You understand he must go into the river?"

The girl didn't respond. Lalji took it as assent. "If there is anything you wish to have of his, you should take it now." The girl shook her head. Lalji hesitantly let his hand rest on her shoulder. "It is no shame to be given to a river. An honor, even, to go to a river such as this."

He waited. Finally, she nodded. He stood and dragged the body to the edge of the boat. He tied it with weights and levered the legs over the lip. The old man slid out of his hands. The girl was silent, staring at where Bowman had disappeared into the water.

Lalji finished his mopping. In the morning he would have to mop again, and sand the stains, but for the time it would do. He began pulling in the anchors. A moment later, the girl was with him again, helping. Lalji settled himself at the tiller. Such a waste, he thought. Such a great waste.

Slowly, the current drew their needleboat into the deeper flows of the river. The girl came and knelt beside him. "Will they chase us?"

Lalji shrugged. "With luck? No. They will look for something larger than us to make so many of their men disappear. With just the two of us now, we will look like very small inconsequential fish to them. With luck."

She nodded, seeming to digest this information. "He saved me, you know. I should be dead now."

"I saw."

"Will you plant his seeds?"

"Without him to make them, there will be no one to plant them."

Tazi frowned. "But we've got so many." She stood and slipped down into the hold. When she returned, she lugged the sack of Bowman's food stores. She began pulling jars from the sack: rice and corn, soybeans and kernels of wheat.

"That's just food," Lalji protested.

Tazi shook her head stubbornly. "They're his Johnny Appleseeds. I wasn't supposed to tell you. He didn't trust you to take us all the way. To take me. But you could plant them, too, right?"

Lalji frowned and picked up a jar of corn. The kernels nestled tightly together, hundreds of them, each one unpatented, each one a genetic infection. He closed his eyes and in his mind he saw a field: row upon row of green rustling plants, and his father, laughing, with his arms spread wide as he shouted, "Hundreds! Thousands if you pray!"

Lalji hugged the jar to his chest, and slowly, he began to smile.

The needleboat continued downstream, a bit of flotsam in the Mississippi's current. Around it, the crowding shadow hulks of the grain barges loomed, all of them flowing south through the fertile heartland toward the gateway of New Orleans; all of them flowing steadily toward the vast wide world.

THE TAMARISK HUNTER

A big tamarisk can suck 73,000 gallons of river water a year. For $2.88 a day, plus water bounty, Lolo rips tamarisk all winter long.

Ten years ago, it was a good living. Back then, tamarisk shouldered up against every riverbank in the Colorado River Basin, along with cottonwoods, Russian olives, and elms. Ten years ago, towns like Grand Junction and Moab thought they could still squeeze life from a river.

Lolo stands on the edge of a canyon, Maggie the camel his only companion. He stares down into the deeps. It's an hour's scramble to the bottom. He ties Maggie to a juniper and starts down, boot-skiing a gully. A few blades of green grass sprout neon around him, piercing juniper-tagged snow clods. In the late winter, there is just a beginning surge of water down in the deeps; the ice is off the river edges. Up high, the mountains still wear their ragged snow mantles. Lolo smears through mud and hits a channel of scree, sliding and scattering rocks. His jugs of tamarisk poison gurgle and slosh on his back. His shovel and rockbar snag on occasional junipers as he skids by. It will be a long hike out. But then, that's what makes this patch so perfect. It's a long way down, and the riverbanks are largely hidden.

It's a living; where other people have dried out and blown away, he has remained: a tamarisk hunter, a water tick, a stubborn bit of weed. Everyone else has been blown off the land as surely as dandelion seeds, set free to fly south or east, or most of all north where watersheds sometimes still run deep and where even if there are no more lush ferns or deep cold fish runs, at least there is still water for people.

Eventually, Lolo reaches the canyon bottom. Down in the cold shadows, his breath steams.

He pulls out a digital camera and starts shooting his proof. The Bureau of Reclamation has gotten uptight about proof. They want different angles on the offending tamarisk, they want each one photographed before and after, the whole process documented, GPS'd, and uploaded directly by the camera. They want it done on-site. And then they still sometimes come out to spot check before they calibrate his headgate for water bounty.

But all their due diligence can't protect them from the likes of Lolo. Lolo has found the secret to eternal life as a tamarisk hunter. Unknown to the Interior Department and its BuRec subsidiary, he has been seeding new patches of tamarisk, encouraging vigorous brushy groves in previously cleared areas. He has hauled and planted healthy root balls up and down the river system in strategically hidden and inaccessible corridors, all in a bid for security against the swarms of other tamarisk hunters that scour these same tributaries. Lolo is crafty. Stands like this one, a quarter-mile long and thick with salt-laden tamarisk, are his insurance policy.

Documentation finished, he unstraps a folding saw, along with his rockbar and shovel, and sets his poison jugs on the dead salt bank. He starts cutting, slicing into the roots of the tamarisk, pausing every thirty seconds to spread Garlon 4 on the cuts, poisoning the tamarisk wounds faster than they can heal. But some of the best tamarisk, the most vigorous, he uproots and sets aside, for later use.

$2.88 a day, plus water bounty.

It takes Maggie's rolling bleating camel stride a week to make it back to Lolo's homestead. They follow the river, occasionally climbing above it onto cold mesas or wandering off into the open desert in a bid to avoid the skeleton sprawl of emptied towns. Guardie choppers buzz up and down the river like swarms of angry yellowjackets, hunting for porto-pumpers and wildcat diversions. They rush overhead in a wash of beaten air and gleaming National Guard logos. Lolo remembers a time when the guardies traded potshots with people down on the riverbanks, tracer-fire and machine-gun chatter echoing in the canyons. He remembers the glorious hiss and arc of a Stinger missile as it flashed across redrock desert and blue sky and burned a chopper where it hovered.

But that's long in the past. Now, guardie patrols skim up the river unmolested.

Lolo tops another mesa and stares down at the familiar landscape of an eviscerated town, its curving streets and subdivision cul-de-sacs all sitting silent in the sun. At the very edge of the empty town, one-acre ranchettes and snazzy five-thousand-square-foot houses with dead-stick trees and dust-hill landscaping fringe a brown tumbleweed golf course. The sandtraps don't even show anymore.

When California put its first calls on the river, no one really worried. A couple towns went begging for water. Some idiot newcomers with bad water rights stopped grazing their horses, and that was it. A few years later, people started showering real fast. And a few after that, they showered once a week. And then people started using the buckets. By then, everyone had stopped joking about how "hot" it was. It didn't really matter how "hot" it was. The problem wasn't lack of water or an excess of heat, not really. The problem was that 4.4 million acre-feet of water were supposed to go down the river to California. There was water; they just couldn't touch it.

They were supposed to stand there like dumb monkeys and watch it flow on by.

"Lolo?"

The voice catches him by surprise. Maggie startles and groans and lunges for the mesa edge before Lolo can rein her around. The camel's great padded feet scuffle dust and Lolo flails for his shotgun where it nestles in a scabbard at the camel's side. He forces Maggie to turn, shotgun half-drawn, holding barely to his seat and swearing.

A familiar face, tucked amongst juniper tangle.

"Goddamnit!" Lolo lets the shotgun drop back into its scabbard. "Jesus Christ, Travis. You scared the hell out of me."

Travis grins. He emerges from amongst the junipers' silver bark rags, one hand on his gray fedora, the other on the reins as he guides his mule out of the trees. "Surprised?"

"I could've shot you!"

"Don't be so jittery. There's no one out here 'cept us water ticks."

"That's what I thought the last time I went shopping down there. I had a whole set of new dishes for Annie and I broke them all when I ran into an ultralight parked right in the middle of the main drag."

"Meth flyers?"

"Beats the hell out of me. I didn't stick around to ask."

"Shit. I'll bet they were as surprised as you were."

"They almost killed me."

"I guess they didn't."

Lolo shakes his head and swears again, this time without anger. Despite the ambush, he's happy to run into Travis. It's lonely country, and Lolo's been out long enough to notice the silence of talking to Maggie. They trade ritual sips of water from their canteens and make camp together. They swap stories about BuRec and avoid discussing where they've been ripping tamarisk and enjoy the view of the empty town far below, with its serpentine streets and quiet houses and shining untouched river.

It isn't until the sun is setting and they've finished roasting a magpie that Lolo finally asks the question that's been on his mind ever since Travis's sun-baked face came out of the tangle. It goes against etiquette, but he can't help himself. He picks magpie out of his teeth and says, "I thought you were working downriver."

Travis glances sidelong at Lolo and in that one suspicious uncertain look, Lolo sees that Travis has hit a lean patch. He's not smart like Lolo. He hasn't been reseeding. He's got no insurance. He hasn't been thinking ahead about all the competition, and what the tamarisk endgame looks like, and now he's feeling the pinch. Lolo feels a twinge of pity. He likes Travis. A part of him wants to tell Travis the secret, but he stifles the urge. The stakes are too high. Water crimes are serious now, so serious Lolo hasn't even told his wife, Annie, for fear of what she'll say. Like all of the most shameful crimes, water theft is a private business, and at the scale Lolo works, forced labor on the Straw is the best punishment he can hope for.

Travis gets his hackles down over Lolo's invasion of his privacy and says, "I had a couple cows I was running up here, but I lost 'em. I think something got 'em."

"Long way to graze cows."

"Yeah, well, down my way even the sagebrush is dead. Big Daddy Drought's doing a real number on my patch." He pinches his lip, thoughtful. "Wish I could find those cows."

"They probably went down to the river."

Travis sighs. "Then the guardies probably got 'em."

"Probably shot 'em from a chopper and roasted 'em."

"Californians."

They both spit at the word. The sun continues to sink. Shadows fall across the town's silent structures. The rooftops gleam red, a ruby cluster decorating the blue river necklace.

"You think there's any stands worth pulling down there?" Travis asks.

"You can go down and look. But I think I got it all last year. And someone had already been through before me, so I doubt much is coming up."

"Shit. Well, maybe I'll go shopping. Might as well get something out of this trip."

"There sure isn't anyone to stop you."

As if to emphasize the fact, the thud-thwap of a guardie chopper breaks the evening silence. The black-fly dot of its movement barely shows against the darkening sky. Soon it's out of sight and cricket chirps swallow the last evidence of its passing.

Travis laughs. "Remember when the guardies said they'd keep out looters? I saw them on TV with all their choppers and Humvees and them all saying they were going to protect everything until the situation improved." He laughs again. "You remember that? All of them driving up and down the streets?"

"I remember."

"Sometimes I wonder if we shouldn't have fought them more."

"Annie was in Lake Havasu City when they fought there. You saw what happened." Lolo shivers. "Anyway, there's not much to fight for once they blow up your water treatment plant. If nothing's coming out of your faucet, you might as well move on."

"Yeah, well, sometimes I think you still got to fight. Even if it's just for pride." Travis gestures at the town below, a shadow movement. "I remember when all that land down there was selling like hotcakes and they were building shit as fast as they could ship in the lumber. Shopping malls and parking lots and subdivisions, anywhere they could scrape a flat spot."

"We weren't calling it Big Daddy Drought, back then."

"Forty-five thousand people. And none of us had a clue. And I was a real estate agent." Travis laughs, a self-mocking sound that ends quickly. It sounds too much like self-pity for Lolo's taste. They're quiet again, looking down at the town wreckage.

"I think I might be heading north," Travis says finally.

Lolo glances over, surprised. Again he has the urge to let Travis in on his secret, but he stifles it. "And do what?"

"Pick fruit, maybe. Maybe something else. Anyway, there's water up there."

Lolo points down at the river. "There's water."

"Not for us." Travis pauses. "I got to level with you, Lolo. I went down to the Straw."

For a second, Lolo is confused by the non sequitur. The statement is too outrageous. And yet Travis's face is serious. "The Straw? No kidding? All the way there?"

"All the way there." He shrugs defensively. "I wasn't finding any tamarisk, anyway. And it didn't actually take that long. It's a lot closer than it used to be. A week out to the train tracks, and then I hopped a coal train, and rode it right to the interstate, and then I hitched."

"What's it like out there?"

"Empty. A trucker told me that California and the Interior Department drew up all these plans to decide which cities they'd turn off when." He looks at Lolo significantly. "That was after Lake Havasu. They figured out they had to do it slow. They worked out some kind of formula: how many cities, how many people they could evaporate at a time without making too much unrest. Got advice from the Chinese, from when they were shutting down their old communist industries. Anyway, it looks like they're pretty much done with it. There's nothing moving out there except highway trucks and coal trains and a couple truck stops."

"And you saw the Straw?"

"Oh sure, I saw it. Out toward the border. Big old mother. So big you couldn't climb on top of it, flopped out on the desert like a damn silver snake. All the way to California." He spits reflexively. "They're spraying with concrete to keep water from seeping into the ground and they've got some kind of carbon-fiber stuff over the top to stop the evaporation. And the river just disappears inside. Nothing but an empty canyon below it. Bone-dry. And choppers and Humvees everywhere, like a damn hornets' nest. They wouldn't let me get any closer than a half mile on account of the eco-crazies trying to blow it up. They weren't nice about it, either."

"What did you expect?"

"I dunno. It sure depressed me, though: They work us out here and toss us a little water bounty and then all that water next year goes right down into that big old pipe. Some Californian's probably filling his swimming pool with last year's water bounty right now."

Cricket-song pulses in the darkness. Off in the distance, a pack of coyotes starts yipping. The two of them are quiet for a while. Finally, Lolo chucks his friend on the shoulder. "Hell, Travis, it's probably for the best. A desert's a stupid place to put a river, anyway."

Lolo's homestead runs across a couple acres of semi-alkaline soil, conveniently close to the river's edge. Annie is out in the field when he crests the low hills that overlook his patch. She waves, but keeps digging, planting for whatever water he can collect in bounty.

Lolo pauses, watching Annie work. Hot wind kicks up, carrying with it the scents of sage and clay. A dust devil swirls around Annie, whipping her bandana off her head. Lolo smiles as she snags it; she sees him still watching her and waves at him to quit loafing.

He grins to himself and starts Maggie down the hill, but he doesn't stop watching Annie work. He's grateful for her. Grateful that every time he comes back from tamarisk hunting she is still here. She's steady. Steadier than the people like Travis who give up when times get dry. Steadier than anyone Lolo knows, really. And if she has nightmares sometimes, and can't stand being in towns or crowds and wakes up in the middle of the night calling out for family she'll never see again, well, then it's all the more reason to seed more tamarisk and make sure they never get pushed off their patch like she was pushed.

Lolo gets Maggie to kneel down so he can dismount, then leads her over to a water trough, half-full of slime and water skippers. He gets a bucket and heads for the river while Maggie groans and complains behind him. The patch used to have a well and running water, but like everyone else, they lost their pumping rights and BuRec stuffed the well with Quickcrete when the water table dropped below the Minimum Allowable Reserve. Now he and Annie steal buckets from the river, or, when the Interior Department isn't watching, they jump up and down on a footpump and dump water into a hidden underground cistern he built when the Resource Conservation and Allowable Use Guidelines went into effect.

Annie calls the guidelines "RaCAUG" and it sounds like she's hawking spit when she says it, but even with their filled-in well, they're lucky. They aren't like Spanish Oaks or Antelope Valley or River Reaches: expensive places that had rotten water rights and turned to dust, money or no, when Vegas and L.A. put in their calls. And they didn't have to bail out of Phoenix Metro when the Central Arizona Project got turned off and then had its aqueducts blown to smithereens when Arizona wouldn't stop pumping out of Lake Havasu.

Pouring water into Maggie's water trough, and looking around at his dusty patch with Annie out in the fields, Lolo reminds himself how lucky he is. He hasn't blown away. He and Annie are dug in. Calies may call them water ticks, but fuck them. If it weren't for people like him and Annie, they'd dry up and blow away the same as everyone else. And if Lolo moves a little bit of tamarisk around, well, the Calies deserve it, considering what they've done to everyone else.

Finished with Maggie, Lolo goes into the house and gets a drink of his own out of the filter urn. The water is cool in the shadows of the adobe house. Juniper beams hang low overhead. He sits down and connects his BuRec camera to the solar panel they've got scabbed onto the roof. Its charge light blinks amber. Lolo goes and gets some more water. He's used to being thirsty, but for some reason he can't get enough today. Big Daddy Drought's got his hands around Lolo's neck today.

Annie comes in, wiping her forehead with a tanned arm. "Don't drink too much water," she says. "I haven't been able to pump. Bunch of guardies around."

"What the hell are they doing around? We haven't even opened our headgates yet."

"They said they were looking for you."

Lolo almost drops his cup.

They know.

They know about his tamarisk reseeding. They know he's been splitting and planting root-clusters. That he's been dragging big healthy chunks of tamarisk up and down the river. A week ago he uploaded his claim on the canyon tamarisk—his biggest stand yet—almost worth an acre-foot in itself in water bounty. And now the guardies are knocking on his door.

Lolo forces his hand not to shake as he puts his cup down. "They say what they want?" He's surprised his voice doesn't crack.

"Just that they wanted to talk to you." She pauses. "They had one of those Humvees. With the guns."

Lolo closes his eyes. Forces himself to take a deep breath. "They've always got guns. It's probably nothing."

"It reminded me of Lake Havasu. When they cleared us out. When they shut down the water treatment plant and everyone tried to burn down the BLM office."

"It's probably nothing." Suddenly he's glad he never told her about his tamarisk hijinks. They can't punish her the same. How many acre-feet is he liable for? It must be hundreds. They'll want him, all right. Put him on a Straw work crew and make him work for life, repay his water debt forever. He's replanted hundreds, maybe thousands of tamarisk, shuffling them around like a cardsharp on a poker table, moving them from one bank to another, killing them again and again and again, and always happily sending in his "evidence."

"It's probably nothing," he says again.

"That's what people said in Havasu."

Lolo waves out at their newly tilled patch. The sun shines down hot and hard on the small plot. "We're not worth that kind of effort." He forces a grin. "It probably has to do with those enviro crazies who tried to blow up the Straw. Some of them supposedly ran this way. It's probably that."

Annie shakes her head, unconvinced. "I don't know. They could have asked me the same as you."

"Yeah, but I cover a lot of ground. See a lot of things. I'll bet that's why they want to talk to me. They're just looking for eco-freaks."

"Yeah, maybe you're right. It's probably that." She nods slowly, trying to make herself believe. "Those enviros, they don't make any sense at all. Not enough water for people, and they want to give the river to a bunch of fish and birds."

Lolo nods emphatically and grins wider. "Yeah. Stupid." But suddenly he views the eco-crazies with something approaching brotherly affection. The Californians are after him, too.

Lolo doesn't sleep all night. His instincts tell him to run, but he doesn't have the heart to tell Annie, or to leave her. He goes out in the morning hunting tamarisk and fails at that as well. He doesn't cut a single stand all day. He considers shooting himself with his shotgun, but chickens out when he gets the barrels in his mouth. Better alive and on the run than dead. Finally, as he stares into the twin barrels, he knows that he has to tell Annie, tell her he's been a water thief for years and that he's got to run north. Maybe she'll come with him. Maybe she'll see reason. They'll run together. At least they have that. For sure, he's not going to let those bastards take him off to a labor camp for the rest of his life.

But the guardies are already waiting when Lolo gets back. They're squatting in the shade of their Humvee, talking. When Lolo comes over the crest of the hill, one of them taps the other and points. They both stand. Annie is out in the field again, turning over dirt, unaware of what's about to happen. Lolo reins in and studies the guardies. They lean against their Humvee and watch him back.

Suddenly Lolo sees his future. It plays out in his mind the way it does in a movie, as clear as the blue sky above. He puts his hand on his shotgun. Where it sits on Maggie's far side, the guardies can't see it. He keeps Maggie angled away from them and lets the camel start down the hill.

The guardies saunter toward him. They've got their Humvee with a .50 caliber on the back and they've both got M-16s slung over their shoulders. They're in full bulletproof gear and they look flushed and hot. Lolo rides down slowly. He'll have to hit them both in the face. Sweat trickles between his shoulder blades. His hand is slick on the shotgun's stock.

The guardies are playing it cool. They've still got their rifles slung, and they let Lolo keep approaching. One of them has a wide smile. He's maybe forty years old, and tanned. He's been out for a while, picking up a tan like that. The other raises a hand and says, "Hey there, Lolo."

Lolo's so surprised he takes his hand off his shotgun. "Hale?" He recognizes the guardie. He grew up with him. They played football together a million years ago, when football fields still had green grass and sprinklers sprayed their water straight into the air. Hale. Hale Perkins. Lolo scowls. He can't shoot Hale.

Hale says. "You're still out here, huh?"

"What the hell are you doing in that uniform? You with the Calies now?"

Hale grimaces and points to his uniform patches: Utah National Guard.

Lolo scowls. Utah National Guard. Colorado National Guard. Arizona National Guard. They're all the same. There's hardly a single member of the "National Guard" that isn't an out-of-state mercenary. Most of the local guardies quit a long time ago, sick to death of goose-stepping family and friends off their properties and sick to death of trading potshots with people who just wanted to stay in their homes. So even if there's still a Colorado National Guard, or an Arizona or a Utah, inside those uniforms with all their expensive nightsight gear and their brand-new choppers flying the river bends, it's pure California.

And then there are a few like Hale.

Lolo remembers Hale as being an OK guy. Remembers stealing a keg of beer from behind the Elks Club one night with him. Lolo eyes him. "How you liking that Supplementary Assistance Program?" He glances at the other guardie. "That working real well for you? The Calies a big help?"

Hale's eyes plead for understanding. "Come on, Lolo. I'm not like you. I got a family to look after. If I do another year of duty, they let Shannon and the kids base out of California."

"They give you a swimming pool in your back yard, too?"

"You know it's not like that. Water's scarce there, too."

Lolo wants to taunt him, but his heart isn't in it. A part of him wonders if Hale is just smart. At first, when California started winning its water lawsuits and shutting off cities, the displaced people just followed the water—right to California. It took a little while before the bureaucrats realized what was going on, but finally someone with a sharp pencil did the math and realized that taking in people along with their water didn't solve a water shortage. So the immigration fences went up.

But people like Hale can still get in.

"So what do you two want?" Inside, Lolo's wondering why they haven't already pulled him off Maggie and hauled him away, but he's willing to play this out.

The other guardie grins. "Maybe we're just out here seeing how the water ticks live."

Lolo eyes him. This one, he could shoot. He lets his hand fall to his shotgun again. "BuRec sets my headgate. No reason for you to be out here."

The Calie says, "There were some marks on it. Big ones."

Lolo smiles tightly. He knows which marks the Calie is talking about. He made them with five different wrenches when he tried to dismember the entire headgate apparatus in a fit of obsession. Finally he gave up trying to open the bolts and just beat on the thing, banging the steel of the gate, smashing at it, while on the other side he had plants withering. After that, he gave up and just carried buckets of water to his plants and left it at that. But the dents and nicks are still there, reminding him of a period of madness. "It still works, don't it?"

Hale holds up a hand to his partner, quieting him. "Yeah, it still works. That's not why we're here."

"So what do you two want? You didn't drive all the way out here with your machine gun just to talk about dents in my headgate."

Hale sighs, put-upon, trying to be reasonable. "You mind getting down off that damn camel so we can talk?"

Lolo studies the two guardies, figuring his chances on the ground. "Shit." He spits. "Yeah, OK. You got me." He urges Maggie to kneel and climbs off her hump. "Annie didn't know anything about this. Don't get her involved. It was all me."

Hale's brow wrinkles, puzzled. "What are you talking about?"

"You're not arresting me?"

The Calie with Hale laughs. "Why? Cause you take a couple buckets of water from the river? Cause you probably got an illegal cistern around here somewhere?" He laughs again. "You ticks are all the same. You think we don't know about all that crap?"

Hale scowls at the Calie, then turns back to Lolo. "No, we're not here to arrest you. You know about the Straw?"

"Yeah." Lolo says it slowly, but inside, he's grinning. A great weight is suddenly off him. They don't know. They don't know shit. It was a good plan when he started it, and it's a good plan still. Lolo schools his face to keep the glee off, and tries to listen to what Hale's saying, but he can't, he's jumping up and down and gibbering like a monkey. They don't know—

"Wait." Lolo holds up his hand. "What did you just say?"

Hale repeats himself. "California's ending the water bounty. They've got enough Straw sections built up now that they don't need the program. They've got half the river enclosed. They got an agreement from the Department of Interior to focus their budget on seep and evaporation control. That's where all the big benefits are. They're shutting down the water bounty payout program." He pauses. "I'm sorry, Lolo."

Lolo frowns. "But a tamarisk is still a tamarisk. Why should one of those damn plants get the water? If I knock out a tamarisk, even if Cali doesn't want the water, I could still take it. Lots of people could use the water."

Hale looks pityingly at Lolo. "We don't make the regulations, we just enforce them. I'm supposed to tell you that your headgate won't get opened next year. If you keep hunting tamarisk, it won't do any good." He looks around the patch, then shrugs. "Anyway, in another couple years they were going to pipe this whole stretch. There won't be any tamarisk at all after that."

"What am I supposed to do, then?"

"California and BuRec is offering early buyout money." Hale pulls a booklet out of his bulletproof vest and flips it open. "Sort of to soften the blow." The pages of the booklet flap in the hot breeze. Hale pins the pages with a thumb and pulls a pen out of another vest pocket. He marks something on the booklet, then tears off a perforated check. "It's not a bad deal."

Lolo takes the check. Stares at it. "Five hundred dollars?"

Hale shrugs sadly. "It's what they're offering. That's just the paper codes. You confirm it online. Use your BuRec camera phone, and they'll deposit it in whatever bank you want. Or they can hold it in trust until you get into a town and want to withdraw it. Any place with a BLM office, you can do that. But you need to confirm before April 15. Then BuRec'll send out a guy to shut down your headgate before this season gets going."

"Five hundred dollars?"

"It's enough to get you north. That's more than they're offering next year."

"But this is my patch."

"Not as long as we've got Big Daddy Drought. I'm sorry, Lolo."

"The drought could break any time. Why can't they give us a couple more years? It could break any time." But even as he says it, Lolo doesn't believe. Ten years ago, he might have. But not now. Big Daddy Drought's here to stay. He clutches the check and its keycodes to his chest.

A hundred yards away, the river flows on to California.

POP SQUAD

The familiar stench of unwashed bodies, cooked food, and shit washes over me as I come through the door. Cruiser lights flicker through the blinds, sparkling in rain and illuminating the crime scene with strobes of red and blue fire. A kitchen. A humid mess. A chunky woman huddles in the corner, clutching closed her nightgown. Fat thighs and swaying breasts under stained silk. Squad goons crowding her, pushing her around, making her sit, making her cower. Another woman, young-looking and pretty, pregnant and black-haired, is slumped against the opposite wall, her blouse spackled with spaghetti remains. Screams from the next room: kids.

I squeeze my fingers over my nose and breathe through my mouth, fighting off nausea as Pentle wanders in, holstering his Grange. He sees me and tosses me a nosecap. I break it and snort lavender until the stink slides off. Children come scampering in with Pentle, a brood of three tangling around his knees—the screamers from the other room. They gallop around the kitchen and disappear again, screaming still, into the living room where data sparkles like fairy dust on the wallscreens and provides what is likely their only connection to the outside world.

"That's everyone," Pentle says. He's got a long skinny face and a sour small mouth that always points south. Weights seem to hang off his cheeks. Fat caterpillar brows droop over his eyes. He surveys the kitchen, mouth corners dragging lower. It's always depressing to come into these scenes. "They were all inside when we broke down the door."

I nod absently as I shake monsoon water from my hat. "Great. Thanks." Liquid beads scatter on the floor, joining puddles of wet from the pop squad along with the maggot debris of the spaghetti dinner. I put my hat back on. Water still manages to drip off the brim and slip under my collar, a slick rivulet of discomfort. Someone closes the door to the outside. The shit smell thickens, eggy and humid. The nosecap barely holds it off. Old peas and bits of cereal crunch under my feet. They squish with the spaghetti, the geologic layers of past feedings. The kitchen hasn't been self-cleaned in years.

The older woman coughs and pulls her nightgown tighter around her cellulite and I wonder, as I always do when I come into situations like this, what made her choose this furtive nasty life of rotting garbage and brief illicit forays into daylight. The pregnant girl seems to have slipped even further into herself since I arrived. She stares into space. You'd have to touch her pulse to know that she's alive. It amazes me that women can end up like this, seduced so far down into gutter life that they arrive here, fugitives from everyone who would have kept them and held them and loved them and let them see the world outside.

The children run in from the living room again, playing chase: a blond, no more than five; another, younger and with brown braids, topless and in makeshift diapers, less than three; and a knee-high toddler boy, scrap diaper bunched around little muscle thighs, wearing a T-shirt stained with tomato sauce that says "Who's the Cutest?" The T-shirt would be an antique if it wasn't stained.

"You need anything else?" Pentle asks. He wrinkles his nose as new reek wafts from the direction of the kids.

"You get photos for the prosecutor?"

"Got 'em." Pentle holds out a digicam and thumbs through the images of the ladies and the three children, all of them staring out from the screen like little smeared dolls. "You want me to take them in, now?"

I look over the women. The kids have run out again. From the other room, their howls echo as they chase around. Their shrieks are piercing. Even from a distance they hurt my head. "Yeah. I'll deal with the kids."

Pentle gets the women up off the floor and shuffles out the door, leaving me standing alone in the middle of the kitchen. It's all so familiar: a typical floor plan from Builders United. Custom undercab lighting, black mirror tile on the floors, clever self-clean nozzles hidden behind deco trim lines, so much like the stuff Alice and I have that I can almost forget where I am. It's a negative image of our apartment's kitchen: light vs. dark, clean vs. dirty, quiet vs. loud. The same floor plan, everything about it the same, and yet, nothing in it is. It's archeological. I can look at the layers of gunk and grime and noise and see what must have underlain it before…when these people worried about color coordinating and classy appliances.

I open the fridge (smudgefree nickel, how practical). Ours contains pineapples and avocados and endive and corn and coffee and brazil nuts from Angel Spire's hanging gardens. This one holds a shelf cluttered with ground mycoprotein bars and wadded piles of nutrition supplement sacs like the kind they hand out at the government rejoo clinics. Other than a bag of slimy lettuce, there isn't anything unprocessed in the fridge at all. No vegetables except in powder jars, ditto for fruit. A stack of self-warming dinner bins for fried rice and laap and spaghetti just like the one still lying on the kitchen table in a puddle of its own sauce, and that's it.

I close the fridge and straighten. There's something here in the mess and the screaming in the next room and the reek of the one kid's poopy pants, but I'm stumped as to what it is. They could have lived up in the light and air. Instead, they hid in the dark under wet jungle canopy and turned pale and gave up their lives.

The kids race back in, chasing each other all in a train, laughing and shrieking. They stop and look around, surprised, maybe, that their moms have disappeared. The littlest one has a stuffed dinosaur by the nose. It's got a long green neck and a fat body. A brontosaurus, I think, with big cartooney eyes and black felt lashes. It's funny about the dinosaur, because they've been gone so long, but here one is, showing up as a stuffed toy. And then it's funny again, because when you think about it, a dinosaur toy is really extinct twice.

"Sorry, kids. Mommy's gone."

I pull out my Grange. Their heads kick back in successive jerks, bang bang bang down the line, holes appearing on their foreheads like paint and their brains spattering out the back. Their bodies flip and skid on the black mirror floor. They land in jumbled piles of misaligned limbs. For a second, gunpowder burn makes the stench bearable.

Up out of the jungle like a bat out of hell, climbing out of Rhinehurst Supercluster's holdout suburban sprawl and then rising through jungle overstory. Blasting across the Causeway toward Angel Spire and the sea. Monkeys diving off the rail line like grasshoppers, pouring off the edge ahead of my cruiser and disappearing into the mangrove and kudzu and mahogany and teak, disappearing into the wet bowels of greenery tangle. Dumping the cruiser at squad center, no time for mopdown, don't need it anyway. My hat, my raincoat, my clothes into hazmat bags, and then out again on the other side, rushing to pull on a tux before catching a masslift up 188 stories, rising into the high clear air over the jungle fur of carbon sequestration project N22.

Mma Telogo has a new concerto. Alice is his diva viola, his prize, and Hua Chiang and Telogo have been circling her like ravens, picking apart her performance, corvid eyes on her, watching and hungry for fault, but now they call her ready. Ready to banish Banini from his throne. Ready to challenge for a place in the immortal canon of classical performance. And I'm late. Caught in a masslift on Level 55, packed in with the breath and heat of upper-deck diners and weekenders climbing the spire while the seconds tick by, listening to the climate fans buzz and whir while we all sweat and wilt, waiting for some problem on the line to clear.

Finally we're rising again, our stomachs dropping into our shoes, our ears popping as we soar into the heavens, flying under magnetic acceleration…and then slowing so fast we almost leave the floor. Our stomachs catch up. I shove out through hundreds of people, waving my cop badge when anyone complains, and sprint through the glass arch of the Ki Performance Center. I dive between the closing slabs of the attention doors.

The autolocks thud home behind me, sealing the performance space. It's comforting. I'm inside, enfolded in the symphony, as though its hands have cupped themselves around me and pulled me into a chamber of absolute focus. The lights dim. Conversational thrum falls away. I find my way to my seat more by feel than sight. Dirty looks from men in topaz hats and women in spectacle eyes as I squeeze across them. Gauche, I know. Absurdly late to an event that happens once in a decade. Plopping down just as Hua Chiang steps up to the podium.

His hands rise like crane wings. Bows and horns and flutes flash with movement and then the music comes, first a hint, like blowing mist, and then building, winding through a series of repeated stanzas that I have heard Alice play perhaps ten thousand times. Notes I heard first so long ago, stumbling and painful, that now spill like water and burst like ice flowers. The music settles, pianissimo again, the lovely delicate motifs that I know from Alice's practice. An introduction only, she has told me, intended to file away the audience's last thoughts of the world outside, repeated stanzas until Hua Chiang accepts that the audience is completely his and then Alice's viola rises, and the other players move to support her, fifteen years of practice coming to fruition.

I look down at my hands, overwhelmed. It's different in the concert hall. Different than all those days when she cursed and practiced and swore at Telogo and claimed his work couldn't be performed. Different even from when she finished her practices early, smiling, hands calloused in new ways, face flushed, eager to drink a cool white wine with me on our balcony in the light of the setting sun and watch the sky as monsoon clouds parted and starlight shone down on our companionship. Tonight, her part joins the rest of the symphony and I can't speak or think for the beauty of the whole.

Later, I'll hear whether Telogo has surpassed Banini for sheer audacity. I'll hear how critics compare living memories of ancient performances and see how critical opinion shifts to accommodate this new piece in a canon that stretches back more than a century, and that hangs like a ghost over everything that Alice and her director Hua Chiang hope for: a performance that will knock Banini off his throne and perhaps depress him enough to stop rejoo and stuff him in his grave. For me, competing against that much history would be a heavy weight. I'm glad I've got a job where forgetting is the most important part. Working on the pop squad means your brain takes a vacation and your hands do the work. And when you leave work, you've left it for good.

Except now, as I look down at my hands, I'm surprised to find pinpricks of blood all over them. A fine spray. The misty remains of the little kid with the dinosaur. My fingers smell of rust.

The tempo accelerates. Alice is playing again. Notes writhe together so fluidly that it seems impossible they aren't generated electronically, and yet the warmth and phrasing is hers, achingly hers, I've heard it in the morning, when she practiced on the balcony, testing herself, working again and again against the limitations of her self. Disciplining her fingers and hands, forcing them to accept Telogo's demands, the ones that years ago she had called impossible and which now run so cleanly through the audience.

The blood is all over my hands. I pick at it, scrape it away in flakes. It had to be the kid with the dinosaur. He was closest when he took the bullet. Some of his residue is stuck tight, bonded to my own skin. I shouldn't have skipped mopdown.

I pick.

The man next to me, tan face and rouged lips, frowns. I'm ruining a moment of history for him, something he has waited years to hear.

I pick more carefully. Silently. The blood flakes off. Dumb kid with the dumb dinosaur that almost made me miss the performance.

The cleanup crew noticed the dinosaur toy too. Caught the irony. Joked and snorted nosecaps and started bagging the bodies for compost. Made me late. Stupid dinosaur.

The music cascades into silence. Hua Chiang's hands fall. Applause. Alice stands at Chiang's urging and the applause increases. Craning my neck, I can see her, nineteen-year-old face flushed, smile bright and triumphant, enveloped in our adulation.

We end up at a party thrown by Maria Illoni, one of the symphony's high donors. She made her money on global warming mitigation for New York City, before it went under. Her penthouse is in Shoreline Curve, daringly arcing over the seawalls and the surf, a sort of flip of the finger to the ocean that beat her storm surge calculations. A spidery silver vine over dark water and the bob of the boat communities out in the deeps. New York obviously never got its money back: Illoni's outdoor patio runs across the entire top floor of the Shoreline and platforms additional petals of spun hollowform carbon out into the air.

From the far side of the Curve, you can see beyond the incandescent cores of the superclusters to the old city sprawl, dark except along where maglines radiate. A strange mangle of wreckage and scavenge and disrepair. In the day, it looks like some kind of dry red fungal collapse, a weave of jungle canopy and old suburban understory, but at night, all that's visible is the skeleton of glowing infrastructure, radial blooms in the darkness, and I breathe deeply, enjoying all the freshness and openness that's missing from those steaming hideouts I raid with the pop squad.

Alice sparkles in the heat, perfectly slim, well curved—an armful of beautiful girl. The fall air is under thirty-three degrees and pleasant, and I feel infinitely tender toward her. I pull her close. We slip into a forest of century-old bonsai sculptures created by Maria's husband. Alice murmurs that he spends all his time here on the roof, staring at branches, studying their curves, and occasionally, perhaps every few years, wiring a branch and guiding it in a new direction. We kiss in the shadows they provide, and Alice is beautiful and everything is perfect.

But I'm distracted.

When I hit the kids with my Grange, the littlest one—the one with that stupid dinosaur—flipped over. A Grange is built for nitheads, not little kids, so the bullet plowed through the kid and he flipped and his dinosaur went flying. It sailed, I mean really sailed, through the air. And now I can't get it out of my mind: that dinosaur flying. And then hitting the wall and bouncing onto the black mirror floor. So fast and so slow. Bang bang bang down the line…and then the dinosaur in the air.

Alice pulls away, seeming to sense my inattention. I straighten up. Try to focus on her.

She says, "I thought you weren't going to make it. When we were tuning, I looked out and your seat was empty."

I force a grin. "But I did. I made it."

Barely. I stood around too long with the cleanup guys while the dinosaur lay in a puddle and sopped up the kid's blood. Double extinct. The kid and the dinosaur both. Dead one way, and then dead again. There's a weird symmetry there.

She cocks her head, studying me. "Was it bad?"

"What?" *The brontosaurus?* "The call?" I shrug. "Just a couple crazy ladies. Not armed or anything. It was easy."

"I can't imagine it. Cutting rejoo like that." She sighs and reaches out to touch a bonsai, perfectly guided over the decades by the map that only Michael Illoni can see or understand. "Why give all this up?"

I don't have an answer. I rewind the crime scene in my mind. I have the same feeling that I did when I stood on spaghetti maggots and went through their fridge. There's something there in the stink and noise and darkness, something hot and obsessive and ripe. But I don't know what it is.

"The ladies looked old," I say. "Like week-old balloons, all puffy and droopy."

Alice makes a face of distaste. "Can you imagine trying to perform Telogo without rejoo? We wouldn't have had the time. Half of us would have been past our prime, and we'd have needed understudies, and then the understudies would have had to find understudies. Fifteen years. And these women throw it all away. How can they throw away something as beautiful as Telogo?"

"You thinking about Kara?"

"She would have played Telogo twice as well as I did."

"I don't believe that."

"Believe it. She was the best. Before she went kid-crazy." She sighs. "I miss her."

"You could still visit her. She's not dead yet."

"She might as well be. She's already twenty years older than when we knew her." She shakes her head. "No. I'd rather remember her in her prime, not out at some single-sex work camp growing vegetables and losing the last of her talent. I couldn't stand listening to her play now. It would kill me to hear all of that gone." She turns abruptly. "That reminds me, my rejoo booster is tomorrow. Can you take me?"

"Tomorrow?" I hesitate. I'm supposed to be on another shift popping kids. "It's kind of short notice."

"I know. I meant to ask sooner, but with the concert coming up, I forgot." She shrugs. "It's not that important. I can go by myself." She glances at me sidelong. "But it is nicer when you come."

What the hell. I don't really want to work anyway. "Okay, sure. I'll get Pentle to cover for me." Let him deal with the dinosaurs.

"Really?"

I shrug. "What can I say? I'm a sweet guy."

She smiles and stands on tiptoe to kiss me. "If we weren't going to live forever, I'd marry you."

I laugh. "If we weren't going to live forever, I'd get you pregnant."

We look at each other. Alice laughs unsteadily and takes it as a joke. "Don't be gross."

Before we can talk any more, Illoni pops out from behind a bonsai and grabs Alice by the arm. "There you are! I've been looking everywhere for you. You can't hide yourself like this. You're the woman of the hour."

She pulls Alice away with all the confidence that must have made New York believe she could save it. She barely even looks at me as they hustle off. Alice smiles tolerantly and motions for me to follow. Then Maria's calling to everyone and pulling them all together and she climbs up on a fountain's rim and pulls Alice up beside her. She starts talking about art and sacrifice and discipline and beauty.

I tune it out. There's only so much self-congratulation you can take. It's obvious Alice is one of the best in the world. Talking about it just makes it seem banal. But the donors need to feel like they're part of the moment, so they all want to squeeze Alice and make her theirs, so they talk and talk and talk.

Maria's saying, "...wouldn't be standing here congratulating ourselves, if it weren't for our lovely Alice. Hua Chiang and Telogo did their work well, but in the final moment it was Alice's execution in the face of Telogo's ambitious piece that has made it resonate so strongly already with the critics. We have her to thank for the piece's flawlessness."

Everyone starts applauding and Alice blushes prettily, not accustomed to adulation from her peers and competitors. Maria shouts over the cheering, "I've made several calls to Banini, and it is more than apparent that he has no answer to our challenge and so I expect the next eighty years are ours. And Alice's!" The applause is almost deafening.

Maria waves for attention again and the applause fades into scattered whistles and catcalls which finally taper off enough to allow Maria to continue. "To commemorate the end of Banini's age, and the beginning of a new one, I would like to present Alice with a small token of affection—" and here she leans down and picks up a jute-woven gift bag shot with gold as she says, "Of course a woman likes gold and jewels, and strings for her viola, but I thought this was a particularly apt gift for the evening...."

I'm leaning against the woman next to me, trying to see, as Maria holds the bag dramatically above her head and calls out to the crowd, "For Alice, our slayer of *dinosaurs!*" and pulls the green brontosaurus out of the bag.

It's just like the one the kid had.

Its big eyes look right at me. For a second it seems to blink at me with its big black lashes and then the crowd laughs and applauds as they all get the joke. *Banini = dinosaur.* Ha ha.

Alice takes the dinosaur and holds it by the neck and swings it over her head and everybody laughs again but I can't see anything anymore because I'm lying on the ground caught in the jungle swelter of people's legs and I can't breathe.

"Are you sure you're okay?"

"Sure. No problem. I told you. I'm fine."

It's true, I guess. Sitting next to Alice in the waiting room, I don't feel dizzy or anything, even if I am tired. Last night, she put the dinosaur on the bedside table, right in with her collection of little jeweled music boxes, and the damn thing looked at me all night long. Finally at four A.M. I couldn't stand it anymore and I shoved it under the bed. But in the morning, she found it and put it back, and it's been looking at me ever since.

Alice squeezes my hand. The rejoo clinic's a small one, private, carefully appointed with holographic windows of sailboats on the Atlantic so it feels open and airy even though its daylight is piped in through mirror collectors. It's not one of the big public monsters out in the clusters that got started after rejoo's patents expired. You pay a little more than you do for the Medicaid generics, but you don't rub shoulders with a bunch of starving gamblers and nitheads and drunks who all still want their rejoo even if they're wasting every day of their endless lives.

The nurses are quick and efficient. Pretty soon, Alice is on her back hooked up to an IV bladder with me sitting beside her on the bed, and we're watching rejoo push into her.

It's just a clear liquid. I always thought it should be fizzy and green for growing things. Or maybe not green, but definitely fizzy. It always feels fizzy when it goes in.

Alice takes a quick breath and reaches out for me, her slender pale fingers brushing my thigh. "Hold my hand."

The elixir of life pulses into her, filling her, flushing her. She pants shallowly. Her eyes dilate. She isn't watching me anymore. She's somewhere deep inside, reclaiming what was lost over the last eighteen months. No matter how many times I do it, I'm surprised when I watch it come over someone, the way it seems to swallow them and then they come back to the surface more whole and alive than when they started.

Alice's eyes focus. She smiles. "Oh, God. I can never get used to that."

She tries to stand up, but I hold her down and beep the nurse. Once we've got her unhooked, I lead her back out to the car. She leans heavily against me, stumbling and touching me. I can almost feel the fizzing and tingling through her skin. She climbs into the car. When I'm inside, she looks over at me and laughs. "I can't believe how good I feel."

"Nothing like winding back the clock."

"Take me home. I want to be with you. "

I push the start button on the car and we slide out of our parking space. We hook onto the magline out of Center Spire. Alice watches the city slide by outside the windows. All the shoppers and the businessmen and the martyrs and the ghosts, and then we're out in the open, on the high track over the jungle, speeding north again, for Angel Spire.

"It's so wonderful to be alive," she says, "It doesn't make any sense."

"What doesn't?"

"Cutting rejoo."

"If people made sense, we wouldn't have psychologists." And we wouldn't buy dinosaur toys for kids who were never going to make it anyway. I grit my teeth. None of them make any sense. Stupid moms.

Alice sighs and runs her hands across her thighs, kneading herself, hiking up her skirt and digging her fingers into her flesh. "But it still doesn't make any sense. It feels so good. You'd have to be crazy to stop rejoo."

"Of course they're crazy. They kill themselves, they make babies they don't know how to take care of, they live in shitty apartments in the dark, they never go out, they smell bad, they look terrible, they never have anything good again—" I'm starting to shout. I shut my mouth.

Alice looks over at me. "Are you okay?"

"I'm fine."

But I'm not. I'm mad. Mad at the ladies and their stupid toy-buying. Pissed off that these dumb women tease their dumb terminal kids like that; treat them like they aren't going to end up as compost. "Let's not talk about work right now. Let's just go home." I force a grin. "I've already got the day off. We should take advantage of it."

Alice is still looking at me. I can see the questions in her eyes. If she weren't on the leading edge of a rejoo high, she'd keep pressing, but she's so wrapped up in the tingling of her rebuilt body that she lets it go. She laughs and runs her fingers up my leg and starts to play with me. I override the magline's safeties with my cop codes and we barrel across the Causeway toward Angel Spire with the sun on the ocean and Alice smiling and laughing and the bright air whirling around us.

Three A.M. Another call, windows down, howling through the humidity and swelter of Newfoundland. Alice wants me to come home, come back, relax, but I can't. I don't want to. I'm not sure what I want, but it's not brunch with Belgian waffles or screwing on the living room floor or a trip to the movies or…anything, really.

I can't do it, anyway. We got home, and I couldn't do it. Nothing felt right. Alice said it didn't matter, that she wanted to practice.

Now I haven't seen her for more than a day.

I've been on duty, catching up on calls. I've been going for twenty-four hours straight, powered on coppers'-little-helpers and mainlined caffeine and my hat and trench coat and hands are pinprick-sprayed with the residue of work.

Along the coastline the sea runs high and hot, splashing in over the breakwaters. Lights ahead, the glow of coalfoundries and gasification works. The call takes me up the glittering face of Palomino Cluster. Nice real estate. Up the masslifts and smashing through a door with Pentle backing me, knowing what we're going to find but never knowing how much these ones will fight.

Bedlam. A lady, this one a pretty brown girl who might have had a great life if she didn't decide she needed a baby, and a kid lying in the corner in a box screaming and screaming. And the lady's screaming too, screaming at the little kid in its box, like she's gone out of her mind.

As we come in through the door, she starts screaming at us. The kid keeps screaming. The lady keeps screaming. It's like a bunch of screwdrivers jamming in my ears; it goes on and on. Pentle grabs the lady and tries to hold her but she and the kid just keep screaming away and suddenly I can't breathe. I can barely stand. The kid screams and screams and screams: screwdrivers and glass and icepicks in my head.

So I shoot the thing. I pull out my Grange and put a bullet in the little sucker. Fragments of box and baby spray the air.

I don't do that, normally; it's against procedure to waste the kid in front of the mother.

But there we all are, staring at the body, bloodmist and gunpowder all over and my ears ringing from the shot and for one pristine crystal second, it's quiet.

Then the woman's screaming at me again and Pentle's screaming too because I screwed up the evidence before he could get a picture, and then the lady's all over me, trying to claw my eyes out. Pentle drags her off and then she's calling me a bastard and a killer and bastard and monkey man and a fucking pig and that I've got dead eyes.

And that really gets me: I've got dead eyes. This lady's headed into a rejoo collapse and won't last another twenty years and she'll spend all of it in a single-sex work camp. She's young, a lot like Alice, maybe the last of them to cross the line into rejoo, right when she came of age—not an old workhorse like me who was already forty when it went generic—and now she'll be dead in an eye blink. But I'm the one with dead eyes.

I take my Grange and shove it into her forehead. "You want to die too?"

"Go ahead! Do it! Do it!" She doesn't stop for a second, just keeps howling and spitting. "Fucking bastard! Bastard fuckingfuckfuck-ing— Do it! Do it!" She's crying.

Even though I want to see her brains pop out the back of her head,

I don't have the heart. She'll die soon enough. Another twenty years and she's done for. The paperwork isn't worth it.

Pentle cuffs her while she babbles to the baby in the box, just a lump of blood and limp doll parts now. "My baby my poor baby I didn't know I'm sorry my baby my poor baby I'm sorry…." Pentle muscles her out to the car.

For a while I can hear her in the hall. *My baby my poor baby my poor baby….* And then she's gone down the lifts and it's a relief just to be standing there with the wet smells of the apartment and the dead body.

She was using a dresser drawer as her bassinet.

I run my fingers along the splintered edge, fondle the brass pulls. If nothing else, these ladies are resourceful, making the things we can't buy anymore. If I close my eyes, I can almost remember a whole industry around these little guys. Little outfits. Little chairs. Little beds. Everything made little.

Little dinosaurs.

"She couldn't make it shut up."

I jerk my hands away from the baby box, startled. Pentle has come up behind me. "Huh?"

"She couldn't make it stop crying. Didn't know what to do with it. Didn't know how to make it calm down. That's how the neighbors heard."

"Dumb."

"Yeah. She didn't even have a tag-teamer. How the heck was she going to do grocery shopping?"

He gets out his camera and tries a couple shots of the baby. There's not a whole lot left. A 12mm Grange is built for junkies, nitheads going crazy, 'bot assassins. It's overkill for an unarmored thing like this. When the new Granges came out, Grange ran an ad campaign on the sides of our cruisers. "Grange: Unstoppable." Or something like that. There was this one that said "Point Blank Grange" with a photo of a completely mangled nithead. That one was in all our lockers.

Pentle tries another angle on the drawer, going for a profile, trying to make the best of a bad situation. "I like how she used a drawer," he says.

"Yeah. Resourceful."

"I saw this one where the lady made a whole little table and chair set for her kid. Handmade it all. I couldn't believe how much energy she put into it." He makes shapes with his hand. "Little scalloped edges, shapes painted on the top: squares and triangles and things."

"If you're going to die doing something, I guess you want to do a good job of it."

"I'd rather be parasailing. Or go to a concert. I heard Alice was great the other night."

"Yeah. She was." I study the baby's body as Pentle takes some more shots. "If you had to do it, how do you think you'd make one of them be quiet?"

Pentle nods at my Grange. "I'd tell it to shut up."

I grimace and holster the gun. "Sorry about that. It's been a rough week. I've been up too long. Haven't been sleeping." *Too many dinosaurs looking at me.*

Pentle shrugs. "Whatever. It would have been better to get an intact image—" He snaps another picture. "—but even if she gets off this time, you got to figure in another year or two we'll be busting down her door again. These girls have a damn high recidivism." He takes another photo.

I go to a window and open it. Salt air flows in like fresh life, cleaning out the wet shit and body stinks. Probably the first fresh air the apartment's had since the baby was born. Got to keep the windows closed or the neighbors might hear. Got to stay locked in. I wonder if she's got a boyfriend, some rejoo dropout who's going to show up with groceries and find her gone. Probably worth staking out the apartment, just to see. Keep the feminists off us for only bagging the women. I take a deep breath of sea air to get something fresh in my lungs, then light a cigarette and turn back to the room with its clutter and stink.

Recidivism. Fancy word for girls with a compulsion. Like a nithead or a coke freak, but weirder, more self-destructive. At least being a junkie is fun. Who the hell chooses to live in dark apartments with shitty diapers, instant food, and no sleep for years on end? The whole breeding thing is an anachronism—twenty-first-century ritual torture we don't need anymore. But these girls keep trying to turn back the clock and pop out the pups, little lizard brains compelled to pass on some DNA. And there's a new batch every year, little burps of offspring cropping up here and there, the convulsions of a species trying to restart itself and get evolution rolling again, like we can't tell that we've already won.

I'm keying through the directory listings in my cruiser, fiddling through ads and keywords and search preferences, trying to zero in on something that doesn't come up no matter how I go after it.

Dinosaur.

Toys.

Stuffed animals.

Nothing. Nobody sells stuff like that dinosaur. But I've run into two of them now.

Monkeys scamper over the roof of my car. One of them lands on my forward impact rails and looks at me, yellow eyes wide, before another jumps it and they fall off the carbon petal pullout where I'm parked. Somewhere down below, suburban crumble keeps small herds of them. I remember when this area was tundra. It was a long time ago. I've talked to techs in the carbon sink business who talk about flipping the climate and building an icecap, but it's a slow process, an accretion of centuries most likely. Assuming I don't get shot by a crazy mom or a nithead, I'll see it happen. But for now, it's monkeys and jungle.

Forty-eight hours on call and two more cleanups and Alice wants me to take the weekend off and play, but I can't. I'm living on perkies, now. She feels good about her work, and wants me all day. We've done it before. Lying together, enjoying the silence and our own company, the pleasure of just being together with nothing needing to be done. There's something wonderful about peace and silence and sea breezes twisting the curtains on the balcony.

I should go home. In a week, maybe, she'll be back at worrying, doubting herself, thrashing herself to work harder, to practice longer, to listen and feel and move inside of music that's so complex it might as well be the mathematics of chaos for anyone but her. But in reality, she has time. All the time in the world, and it makes me happy that she has it, that fifteen years isn't too long to prepare for something as heartstoppingly beautiful as what she did with Telogo.

I want to spend this time with her, to enjoy her bliss. But I don't want to go back and sleep with that dinosaur. I can't.

I call her from the cruiser.

"Alice?"

She looks out at me from the dash. "Are you coming home? I could meet you for lunch."

"Do you know where Maria got that dinosaur toy?"

She shrugs. "Maybe one of the shops on the Span? Why?"

"Just wondering." I pause. "Could you go get it for me?"

"Why? Why can't we do something fun? I'm on vacation. I just had my rejoo. I feel great. If you want to see my dinosaur, why don't you come home and get it?"

"Alice, please."

Scowling, she disappears from the screen. In a few minutes she's back, holding it up to the screen, shoving it in my face. I can feel my heart beating faster. It's cool in the cruiser, but I break into a sweat when I see the dinosaur on the screen. I clear my throat. "What's it say on the tag?"

Frowning, she turns the thing over, runs her fingers through its fur. She holds up the tag to the camera. It comes in blurry as the camera focuses, then it's there, clear and sharp. "*Ipswitch Collectibles.*"

Of course. Not a toy at all.

The woman who runs Ipswitch is old, as old a rejoo as I've ever met. The wrinkles on her face look so much like plastic that it's hard to tell what's real and what may be a mask. Her eyes are sunken little blue coals and her hair is so white I think of weddings and silk. She must have been ninety when rejoo hit.

Whatever the name of it, Ipswitch Collectibles is full of toys: dolls staring down from their racks, different faces and shapes and colors of hair, some of them soft, some of them made of hard bright plastics; tiny trains that run around miniature tracks and spout steam from their pinky-sized smokestacks; figurines from old-time movies and comics in action poses: Superman, Dolphina, Rex Mutinous. And, under a shelf of hand-carved wooden cars, a bin full of stuffed dinosaurs in green and blue and red. A tyrannosaurus rex. A pterodactyl. The brontosaurus.

"I've got a few stegosauruses in the back."

I look up, startled. The old woman watches me from behind the counter, a strange wrinkly buzzard, studying me with those sharp blue eyes, examining me like I'm carrion.

I pick out the brontosaurus and hold it up by the neck. "No. These're fine."

A bell rings. The shop's main doors to the concourse slide open. A woman steps through, hesitant. Her hair is pulled back in a ponytail and she hasn't applied any makeup, and I can tell, even before she's all the way through the door, that she's one of them: a mom.

She hasn't been off rejoo long; she still looks fresh and young, despite the plumpness that comes with kids. She still looks good. But even without rejoo-collapse telltales, I know what she's done to herself. She's got the tired look of a person at war with the world. None of us look like that. No one has to look like that. Nitheads look less besieged. She's trying to act like the person she was before, like the actress or the financial advisor or the code engineer or the biologist or the waitress or whatever, putting on clothes from her life before, that used to fit perfectly and don't now, making herself look like a person who walks without fear in the open air, and who doesn't now.

As she wanders the aisles, I spy a stain on her shoulder. It's small but obvious if you know what to look for, a light streak of green on a creamy blouse. The kind of thing that never happens to anyone except women with children. No matter how hard she tries, she doesn't fit anymore. Not with us.

Ipswitch Collectibles, like others of its ilk, is a trap door of sorts—a rabbit hole down into the land of illicit motherhood: the place of mashed pea stains, sound-proofed walls, and furtive forays into daylight for resupply and survival. If I stand here long enough, holding my magic brontosaurus by the neck, I'll slip through entirely and see their world as it overlaps with my own, see it with the queer double vision of these women who have learned to turn a drawer into a crib, and know how to fold and pin an old shirt into a diaper, and know that *"collectibles"* really means *"toys."*

The woman slips in the direction of the train sets. She chooses one and places it on the counter. It's a bright wooden thing, each car a different color, each connected by a magnet.

The old woman takes the train and says, "Oh yes, this is a fine piece. I had grandchildren who played with trains like this when they were just a little more than one."

The mother doesn't say anything, just holds out her wrist for the charge, her eyes down on the train. She fingers the blue and yellow engine nervously.

I come up to the counter. "I'll bet you sell a lot of them."

The mother jerks. For a second she looks like she'll run, but she steadies. The old woman's eyes turn on me. Dark sunken blue cores, infinitely knowledgeable. "Not many. Not now. Not many collectors around for this sort of thing. Not now."

The transaction clears. The woman hustles out of the store, not looking back. I watch her go.

The old woman says, "That dinosaur is forty-seven, if you want it." Her tone says that she already knows I won't be buying.

I'm not a collector.

* * *

Nighttime. More dark-of-night encounters with illicit motherhood. The babies are everywhere, popping up like toadstools after rain. I can't keep up with them. I had to leave my last call before the cleanup crew came. Broke the chain of evidence, but what can you do? Everywhere I go, the baby world is ripping open around me, melons and seedpods and fertile wombs splitting open and vomiting babies onto the ground. We're drowning in babies. The jungle seems to seethe with them, the hidden women down in the suburb swelter, and as I shoot along the maglines on my way to bloody errands, the jungle's tendril vines curl up from below, reaching out to me.

I've got the mom's address in my cruiser. She's hidden now. Back down the rabbit hole. Pulled the lid down tight over her head. Lying low with her brood, reconnected with the underground of women who have all decided to kill themselves for the sake of squeezing out pups. Back in the swelter of locked doors and poopy diapers amongst the sorority who give train sets to little creatures who actually play with them instead of putting them on an end table and making you look at them every damn day....

The woman. The *collector*. I've been holding off on hitting her. It doesn't seem fair. It seems like I should wait for her to make her mistake before I pop her kids. But knowing that she's out there tickles my mind. I catch myself again and again, reaching to key in the homing on her address.

But then another call comes, another cleanup, and I let myself pretend I don't know about her, that I haven't perforated her hidey-hole and can now peer in on her whenever I like. The woman we don't know about—yet. Who hasn't made a mistake—yet. Instead I barrel down the rails to another call, slicing through jungle overstory where it impinges around the tracks, blasting toward another woman's destiny who was less lucky and less clever than the one who likes to collect. And these other women hold me for a little while. But in the end, parked on the edge of the sea, with monkeys screeching from the jungle and rain spackling my windshield, I punch in the collector's address.

I'll just drive by.

It could have been a rich house, before carbon sequestration. Before we all climbed into the bright air of the spires and superclusters. But now it exists at the very edge of what is left of suburbs. I'm surprised it even has electric or any services running to it at all. The jungle surrounds it, envelopes it. The road to it, off the maglines and off the maintenance routes, is heaved and split and perforated with encroaching trees. She's smart. She's as close to wilderness as it is possible to live. Beyond is only shadow tangle and green darkness. Monkeys scamper away from the spray of my headlights. The houses around her have already been abandoned. Any day now, they'll stop serving this area entirely. In another couple years, this portion will be completely overgrown. We'll cut off services and the last of the spires will go online and the jungle will swallow this place completely.

I sit outside the house for a while, looking at it. She's a smart one. To live this far out. No neighbors to hear the screaming. But if I think about it, she would have been smarter to move into the jungle entirely, and live with all the other monkeys that just can't keep themselves from breeding. I guess at the end of the day, even these crazy ladies are still human. They can't leave civilization totally behind. Or don't know how, anyway.

I get out of my car, pull my Grange, and hit the door.

As I slam through, she looks up from where she sits at her kitchen table. She isn't even surprised. A little bit of her seems to deflate, and that's all. Like she knew it was going to happen all along. Like I said: a smart one.

A kid runs in from the other room, attracted by the noise of me coming through the door. Maybe one and a half or two years old. It stops and stares, little tow-headed thing, its hair already getting long like hers. We stare at each other. Then it turns and scrambles into its mother's lap.

The woman closes her eyes. "Go on, then. Do it."

I point my Grange, my 12mm hand cannon. Zero in on the kid. The lady wraps her arms around it. It's not a clear shot. It'll rip right through and take out the mom. I angle differently, looking for the shot. Nothing.

She opens her eyes. "What are you waiting for?"

We stare at each other. "I saw you in the toy store. A couple days ago."

She closes her eyes again, regretful, understanding her mistake. She doesn't let go of the kid. I could just take it out of her arms, throw it on the floor and shoot it. But I don't. Her eyes are still closed.

"Why do you do it?" I ask.

Her eyes open again. She's confused. I'm breaking the script. She's mapped this out in her own mind. Probably a thousand times. Had to. Had to know this day would be coming. But here I am, all alone, and her kid's not dead yet. And I keep asking her questions.

"Why do you keep having these kids?"

She just stares at me. The kid squirms around on her and tries to start nursing. She lifts her blouse a little and the kid dives under. I can see the hanging bulges of the lady's breasts, these heavy swinging mammaries, so much larger than I remember them from the store when they were hidden under bra and blouse. They sag while the kid sucks. The woman just stares at me. She's on some kind of autopilot, feeding the kid. Last meal.

I take my hat off and put it on the table and sit. I put my Grange down, too. It just doesn't seem right to blow the sucker away while it's nursing. I take out a cigarette and light it. Take a drag. The woman watches me the way anyone watches a predator. I take another drag on my cigarette and offer it to her.

"Smoke?"

"I don't." She jerks her head toward her kid.

I nod. "Ah. Right. Bad for the new lungs. I heard that, once. Can't remember where." I grin. "Can't remember when."

She stares at me. "What are you waiting for?"

I look down at my pistol, lying on the table. The heavy machine weight of slugs and steel, a monster weapon. Grange 12mm Recoilless Hand Cannon. Standard issue. Stop a nitfitter in his tracks. Take out the whole damn heart if you hit them right. Pulverize a baby. "You had to stop taking rejoo to have the kid, right?"

She shrugs. "It's just an additive. They don't have to make rejoo that way."

"But otherwise we'd have a big damn population problem, wouldn't we?"

She shrugs again.

The gun sits on the table between us. Her eyes flick toward the gun, then to me, then back to the gun. I take a drag on the cigarette. I can tell what she's thinking, looking at that big old steel hand cannon on her table. It's way out of her reach, but she's desperate, so it looks a lot closer to her, almost close enough. Almost.

Her eyes go back up to me. "Why don't you just do it? Get it over with?"

It's my turn to shrug. I don't really have an answer. I should be taking pictures and securing her in the car, and popping the kid, and calling in the cleanup squad, but here we sit. She's got tears in her eyes. I watch her cry. Mammaries and fatty limbs and a frightening sort of wisdom, maybe coming from knowing that she won't last forever. A contrast to Alice with her smooth smooth skin and high bright breasts. This woman is fecund. Hips and breasts and belly fertile, surrounded by her messy kitchen, the jungle outside. The soil of life. She seems settled in all of this, a damp Gaia creature.

A dinosaur.

I should be cuffing her. I've got her and her kid. I should be shooting the kid. But I don't. Instead, I've got a hard-on. She's not beautiful exactly, but I've got a hard-on. She sags, she's round, she's breasty and hippy and sloppy; I can barely sit because my pants are so tight. I try not to stare at the kid nursing. At her exposed breasts. I take another drag on my cigarette. "You know, I've been doing this job for a long time."

She stares at me dully, doesn't say anything.

"I've always wanted to know why you women do this." I nod at the kid. It's come off her breast, and now the whole thing is exposed, this huge sagging thing with its heavy nipple. She doesn't cover up. When I look up, she's studying me, seeing me looking at her breast. The kid scrambles down and watches me, too, solemn-eyed. I wonder if it can feel the tension in the room. If it knows what's coming. "Why the kid? Really. Why?"

She purses her lips. I think I can see anger in the tightening of her teary eyes, anger that I'm playing with her. That I'm sitting here, talking to her with my Grange on her grimy table, but then her eyes go down to that gun and I can almost see the gears clicking. The calculations. The she-wolf gathering herself.

She sighs and scoots her chair forward. "I just wanted one. Ever since I was a little girl."

"Play with dolls, all that? *Collectibles?*"

She shrugs. "I guess." She pauses. Eyes back to the gun. "Yeah. I guess I did. I had a little plastic doll, and I used to dress it up. And I'd play tea with it. You know, we'd make tea, and then I'd pour some on her face, to make her drink. It wasn't a great doll. Voice input, but not much repertoire. My parents weren't rich. 'Let's go shopping.' *'Okay, for what?'* 'For watches.' *'I love watches.'* Simple. Like that. But I liked it. And then one day I called her my baby. I don't know why. I did, though, and the doll said, *'I love you mommy.'*"

Her eyes turn wet as she speaks. "And I just knew I wanted to have a baby. I played with her all the time, and she'd pretend she was my baby, and then my mother caught us doing it and said I was a stupid girl, and I shouldn't talk that way, girls didn't have babies anymore, and she took the doll away."

The kid is down on the floor, shoving blocks under the table. Stacking and unstacking. It catches sight of me. It's got blue eyes and a shy smile. I get a twitch of it, again, and then it scrambles up off the floor, and buries its face in its mother's breasts, hiding. It peeks out at me, and giggles and hides again.

I nod at the kid. "Who's the dad?"

Stone cold face. "I don't know. I got a sample shipped from a guy I found online. We didn't want to meet. I erased everything about him as soon as I got the sample."

"Too bad. Things would have been better if you'd kept in touch."

"Better for you."

"That's what I said." I notice that the ash on my cigarette has gotten long, a thin gray penis hanging limp off the end of my smoke. I give it a twitch and it falls. "I still can't get over the rejoo part."

Inexplicably, she laughs. Brightens even. "Why? Because I'm not so in love with myself that I just want to live forever and ever?"

"What were you going to do? Keep it in the house until—"

"Her," she interrupts suddenly. "Keep *her* in the house. *She* is a girl and *her* name is Melanie."

At her name, the kid looks over at me. She sees my hat on the table and grabs it. Then climbs down off her mother's lap and carries it over to me. She holds it out to me, arms fully extended, an offering. I try to take it but she pulls the hat away.

"She wants to put it on your head."

I look at the lady, confused. She's smiling slightly, sadly. "It's a game she plays. She likes to put hats on my head."

I look at the girl again. She's getting antsy, holding the hat. She makes little grunts of meaning at me and waves the hat invitingly. I lean down. The girl puts the hat on my head, and beams. I sit up and set it more firmly.

"You're smiling," she says.

I look up at her. "She's cute."

"You like her, don't you?"

I look at the girl again, thinking. "Can't say. I've never really looked at them before."

"Liar."

My cigarette is dead. I stub it out on the kitchen table. She watches me do it, frowning, pissed off that I'm messing up her messy table, maybe, but then she seems to remember the gun. And I do, too. A chill runs up my spine. For a moment, when I leaned down to the girl, I'd forgotten about it. I could be dead, right now. Funny how we forget and remember and forget these things. Both of us. Me and the lady. One minute we're having a conversation, the next we're waiting for the killing to start.

This lady seems like she would have been a nice date. She's got spunk. You can tell that. It almost comes out before she remembers the gun. You can watch it flicker back and forth. She's one person, then another person: alive, thinking, remembering, then bang, she's sitting in a kitchen full of crusty dishes, coffee rings on her countertop and a cop with a hand cannon sitting at the kitchen table.

I spark up another cigarette. "Don't you miss the rejoo?"

She looks down at her daughter, holds out her arms. "No. Not a bit." The girl climbs back onto her mother's lap.

I let the smoke curl out of my mouth. "But there's no way you were going to get away with this. It's insane. You have to drop off of rejoo; you have to find a sperm donor who's willing to drop off, too, so two people kill themselves for a kid; you've got to birth the kid alone, and then you've got to keep it hidden, and then you'd eventually need an ID card so you could get it started on rejoo, because nobody's going to dose an undocumented patient, and you've got to know that none of this would ever work. But here you are."

She scowls at me. "I could have done it."

"You didn't."

Bang. She's back in the kitchen again. She slumps in her chair, holding the kid. "So why don't you just hurry up and do it?"

I shrug. "I was just curious about what you breeders are thinking."

She looks at me, hard. Angry. "You know what I'm thinking? I'm thinking we need something new. I've been alive for one hundred and eighteen years and I'm thinking that it's not just about me. I'm thinking I want a baby and I want to see what she sees today when she wakes up and what she'll find and see that I've never seen before because that's new. Finally, something new. I love seeing things through her little eyes and not through dead eyes like yours."

"I don't have dead eyes."

"Look in the mirror. You've all got dead eyes."

"I'm a hundred and fifty and I feel just as good as I did the day I went on."

"I'll bet you can't even remember. No one remembers." Her eyes are on the gun again, but they come up off it to look at me. "But I do. Now. And it's better this way. A thousand times better than living forever."

I make a face. "Live through your kid and all that?"

"You wouldn't understand. None of you would."

I look away. I don't know why. I'm the one with the gun. I'm running everything, but she's looking at me, and something gets tight inside me when she says that. If I was imaginative, I'd say it was some little bit of old primal monkey trying to drag itself out of the muck and make itself heard. Some bit of the critter we were before. I look at the kid—the girl—and she's looking back at me. I wonder if they all do the trick with the hat, or if this one's special somehow. If they all like to put hats on their killers' heads. She smiles at me and ducks her head back under her mother's arm. The woman's got her eyes on my gun.

"You want to shoot me?" I ask.

Her eyes come up. "No."

I smile slightly. "Come on. Be honest."

Her eyes narrow. "I'd blow your head off if I could."

Suddenly I'm tired. I don't care anymore. I'm sick of the dirty kitchen and the dark rooms and the smell of dirty makeshift diapers. I give the Grange a push, shove it closer to her. "Go ahead. You going to kill an old life so you can save one that isn't even going to last? I'm going to live forever, and that little girl won't last longer than seventy years even if she's lucky—which she won't be—and you're practically already dead. But you want to waste my life?" I feel like I'm standing on the edge of a cliff. Possibility seethes around me. "Give it a shot."

"What do you mean?"

"I'm giving you your shot. You want to try for it? This is your chance." I shove the Grange a little closer, baiting her. I'm tingling all over. My head feels light, almost dizzy. Adrenaline rushes through me. I push the Grange even closer to her, suddenly not even sure if I'll fight her for the gun, or if I'll just let her have it. "This is your chance."

She doesn't give a warning.

She flings herself across the table. Her kid flies out of her arms. Her fingers touch the gun at the same time as I yank it out of reach. She lunges again, clawing across the table. I jump back, knocking over my chair. I step out of range. She stretches toward the gun, fingers wide and grasping, desperate still, even though she knows she's already lost. I point the gun at her.

She stares at me, then puts her head down on the table and sobs.

The girl is crying too. She sits bawling on the floor, her little face screwed up and red, crying along with her mother who's given every-thing in that one run at my gun: all her hopes and years of hidden dedication, all her need to protect her progeny, everything. And now she lies sprawled on a dirty table and cries while her daughter howls from the floor. The girl keeps screaming and screaming.

I sight the Grange on the girl. She's exposed, now. She's squalling and holding her hands out to her mother, but she doesn't get up. She just holds out her hands, waiting to be picked up and held by a lady who doesn't have anything left to give. She doesn't notice me or the gun.

One quick shot and she's gone, paint hole in the forehead and brains on the wall just like spaghetti and the crying's over and all that's left is gunpowder burn and cleanup calls.

But I don't fire.

Instead, I holster my Grange and walk out the door, leaving them to their crying and their grime and their lives.

It's raining again, outside. Thick ropes of water spout off the eaves and spatter the ground. All around me the jungle seethes with the chatter of monkeys. I pull up my collar and resettle my hat. Behind me, I can barely hear the crying anymore.

Maybe they'll make it. Anything is possible. Maybe the kid will make it to eighteen, get some black market rejoo and live to be a hundred and fifty. More likely, in six months, or a year, or two years, or ten, a cop will bust down the door and pop the kid. But it won't be me.

I run for my cruiser, splashing through mud and vines and wet. And for the first time in a long time, the rain feels new.

YELLOW CARD MAN

Machetes gleam on the warehouse floor, reflecting a red conflagration of jute and tamarind and kink-springs. They're all around now. The men with their green headbands and their slogans and their wet wet blades. Their calls echo in the warehouse and on the street. Number one son is already gone. Jade Blossom he cannot find, no matter how many times he treadles her phone number. His daughters' faces have been split wide like blister rust durians.

More fires blaze. Black smoke roils around him. He runs through his warehouse offices, past computers with teak cases and iron treadles and past piles of ash where his clerks burned files through the night, obliterating the names of people who aided the Tri-Clipper.

He runs, choking on heat and smoke. In his own gracious office he dashes to the shutters and fumbles with their brass catches. He slams his shoulder against those blue shutters while the warehouse burns and brown-skinned men boil through the door and swing their slick red knives...

Tranh wakes, gasping.

Sharp concrete edges jam against the knuckles of his spine. A salt-slick thigh smothers his face. He shoves away the stranger's leg. Sweat-sheened skin glimmers in the blackness, impressionistic markers for the bodies that shift and shove all around him. They fart and groan and turn, flesh on flesh, bone against bone, the living and the heat-smothered dead all together.

A man coughs. Moist lungs and spittle gust against Tranh's face. His spine and belly stick to the naked sweating flesh of the strangers around him. Claustrophobia rises. He forces it down. Forces himself to lie still, to breathe slowly, deeply, despite the heat. To taste the swelter darkness with all the paranoia of a survivor's mind. He is awake while others sleep. He is alive while others are long dead. He forces himself to lie still, and listen.

Bicycle bells are ringing. Down below and far away, ten thousand bodies below, a lifetime away, bicycle bells chime. He claws himself out of the mass of tangled humanity, dragging his hemp sack of possessions with him. He is late. Of all the days he could be late, this is the worst possible one. He slings the bag over a bony shoulder and feels his way down the stairs, finding his footing in the cascade of sleeping flesh. He slides his sandals between families, lovers, and crouching hungry ghosts, praying that he will not slip and break an old man's bone. Step, feel, step, feel.

A curse rises from the mass. Bodies shift and roll. He steadies himself on a landing amongst the privileged who lie flat, then wades on. Downward ever downward, round more turnings of the stair, wading down through the carpet of his countrymen. Step. Feel. Step. Feel. Another turn. A hint of gray light glimmers far below. Fresh air kisses his face, caresses his body. The waterfall of anonymous flesh resolves into individuals, men and women sprawled across one another, pillowed on hard concrete, propped on the slant of the windowless stair. Gray light turns gold. The tinkle of bicycle bells comes louder now, clear like the ring of cibiscosis chimes.

Tranh spills out of the highrise and into a crowd of congee sellers, hemp weavers, and potato carts. He puts his hands on his knees and gasps, sucking in swirling dust and trampled street dung, grateful for every breath as sweat pours off his body. Salt jewels fall from the tip of his nose, spatter the red paving stones of the sidewalk with his moisture. Heat kills men. Kills old men. But he is out of the oven; he has not been cooked again, despite the blast furnace of the dry season.

Bicycles and their ringing bells flow past like schools of carp, commuters already on their way to work. Behind him the highrise looms, forty stories of heat and vines and mold. A vertical ruin of broken windows and pillaged apartments. A remnant glory from the old energy Expansion now become a heated tropic coffin without air conditioning or electricity to protect it from the glaze of the equatorial sun. Bangkok keeps its refugees in the pale blue sky, and wishes they would stay there. And yet he has emerged alive, despite the Dung Lord, despite the white shirts, despite old age, he has once again clawed his way down from the heavens.

Tranh straightens. Men stir woks of noodles and pull steamers of *baozi* from their bamboo rounds. Gray high-protein U-Tex rice gruel fills the air with the scents of rotting fish and fatty acid oils. Tranh's stomach knots with hunger and a pasty saliva coats his mouth, all that his dehydrated body can summon at the scent of food. Devil cats swirl around the vendors' legs like sharks, hoping for morsels to drop, hoping for theft opportunities. Their shimmering chameleon-like forms flit and flicker, showing calico and siamese and orange tabby markings before fading against the backdrop of concrete and crowding hungry people that they brush against. The woks burn hard and bright with green-tinged methane, giving off new scents as rice noodles splash into hot oil. Tranh forces himself to turn away.

He shoves through the press, dragging his hemp bag along with him, ignoring who it hits and who shouts after him. Incident victims crouch in the doorways, waving severed limbs and begging from others who have a little more. Men squat on tea stools and watch the day's swelter build as they smoke tiny rolled cigarettes of scavenged gold leaf tobacco and share them from lip to lip. Women converse in knots, nervously fingering yellow cards as they wait for white shirts to appear and stamp their renewals.

Yellow card people as far as the eye can see: an entire race of people, fled to the great Thai Kingdom from Malaya where they were suddenly unwelcome. A fat clot of refugees placed under the authority of the Environment Ministry's white shirts as if they were nothing but another invasive species to be managed, like cibiscosis, blister rust, and genehack weevil. Yellow cards, yellow men. *Huang ren* all around, and Tranh is late for his one opportunity to climb out of their mass. One opportunity in all his months as a yellow card Chinese refugee. And now he is late. He squeezes past a rat seller, swallowing another rush of saliva at the scent of roasted flesh, and rushes down an alley to the water pump. He stops short.

Ten others stand in line before him: old men, young women, mothers, boys.

He slumps. He wants to rage at the setback. If he had the energy—if he had eaten well yesterday or the day before or even the day before that he would scream, would throw his hemp bag on the street and stamp on it until it turned to dust—but his calories are too few. It is just another opportunity squandered, thanks to the ill luck of the stairwells. He should have given the last of his baht to the Dung Lord and rented body-space in an apartment with windows facing east so that he could see the rising sun, and wake early.

But he was cheap. Cheap with his money. Cheap with his future. How many times did he tell his sons that spending money to make more money was perfectly acceptable? But the timid yellow card refugee that he has become counseled him to save his baht. Like an ignorant peasant mouse he clutched his cash to himself and slept in pitch-black stairwells. He should have stood like a tiger and braved the night curfew and the ministry's white shirts and their black batons…. And now he is late and reeks of the stairwells and stands behind ten others, all of whom must drink and fill a bucket and brush their teeth with the brown water of the Chao Phraya River.

There was a time when he demanded punctuality of his employees, of his wife, of his sons and concubines, but it was when he owned a spring-wound wristwatch and could gaze at its steady sweep of minutes and hours. Every so often, he could wind its tiny spring, and listen to it tick, and lash his sons for their lazy attitudes. He has become old and slow and stupid or he would have foreseen this. Just as he should have foreseen the rising militancy of the Green Headbands. When did his mind become so slack?

One by one, the other refugees finish their ablutions. A mother with gap teeth and blooms of gray *fa' gan* fringe behind her ears tops her bucket, and Tranh slips forward.

He has no bucket. Just the bag. The precious bag. He hangs it beside the pump and wraps his sarong more tightly around his hollow hips before he squats under the pump head. With a bony arm he yanks the pump's handle. Ripe brown water gushes over him. The river's blessing. His skin droops off his body with the weight of the water, sagging like the flesh of a shaved cat. He opens his mouth and drinks the gritty water, rubs his teeth with a finger, wondering what protozoa he may swallow. It doesn't matter. He trusts luck, now. It's all he has.

Children watch him bathe his old body while their mothers scavenge through PurCal mango peels and Red Star tamarind hulls hoping to find some bit of fruit not tainted with cibiscosis.111mt.6…. Or is it 111mt.7? Or mt.8? There was a time when he knew all the bio-engineered plagues which ailed them. Knew when a crop was about to fail, and whether new seedstock had been ripped. Profited from the knowledge by filling his clipper ships with the right seeds and produce. But that was a lifetime ago.

His hands are shaking as he opens his bag and pulls out his clothes. Is it old age or excitement that makes him tremble? Clean clothes. Good clothes. A rich man's white linen suit.

The clothes were not his, but now they are, and he has kept them safe. Safe for this opportunity, even when he desperately wanted to sell them for cash or wear them as his other clothes turned to rags. He drags the trousers up his bony legs, stepping out of his sandals and balancing one foot at a time. He begins buttoning the shirt, hurrying his fingers as a voice in his head reminds him that time is slipping away.

"Selling those clothes? Going to parade them around until someone with meat on his bones buys them off you?"

Tranh glances up—he shouldn't need to look; he should know the voice—and yet he looks anyway. He can't help himself. Once he was a tiger. Now he is nothing but a frightened little mouse who jumps and twitches at every hint of danger. And there it is: Ma. Standing before him, beaming. Fat and beaming. As vital as a wolf.

Ma grins. "You look like a wire-frame mannequin at Palawan Plaza."

"I wouldn't know. I can't afford to shop there." Tranh keeps putting on his clothes.

"Those are nice enough to come from Palawan. How did you get them?"

Tranh doesn't answer.

"Who are you fooling? Those clothes were made for a man a thousand times your size."

"We can't all be fat and lucky." Tranh's voice comes out as a whisper. Did he always whisper? Was he always such a rattletrap corpse whispering and sighing at every threat? He doesn't think so. But it's hard for him to remember what a tiger should sound like. He tries again, steadying his voice. "We can't all be as lucky as Ma Ping who lives on the top floors with the Dung Lord himself." His words still come out like reeds shushing against concrete.

"Lucky?" Ma laughs. So young. So pleased with himself. "I earn my fate. Isn't that what you always used to tell me? That luck has nothing to do with success? That men make their own luck?" He laughs again. "And now look at you."

Tranh grits his teeth. "Better men than you have fallen." Still the awful timid whisper.

"And better men than you are on the rise." Ma's fingers dart to his wrist. They stroke a wristwatch, a fine chronograph, ancient, gold and diamonds—Rolex. From an earlier time. A different place. A different world. Tranh stares stupidly, like a hypnotized snake. He can't tear his eyes away.

Ma smiles lazily. "You like it? I found it in an antique shop near Wat

Rajapradit. It seemed familiar."

Tranh's anger rises. He starts to reply, then shakes his head and says nothing. Time is passing. He fumbles with his final buttons, pulls on the coat and runs his fingers through the last surviving strands of his lank gray hair. If he had a comb… He grimaces. It is stupid to wish. The clothes are enough. They have to be.

Ma laughs. "Now you look like a Big Name."

Ignore him, says the voice inside Tranh's head. Tranh pulls his last paltry baht out of his hemp bag—the money he saved by sleeping in the stairwells, and which has now made him so late—and shoves it into his pockets.

"You seem rushed. Do you have an appointment somewhere?"

Tranh shoves past, trying not to flinch as he squeezes around Ma's bulk.

Ma calls after him, laughing. "Where are you headed, Mr. Big Name? Mr. Three Prosperities! Do you have some intelligence you'd like to share with the rest of us?"

Others look up at the shout: hungry yellow card faces, hungry yellow card mouths. Yellow card people as far as the eye can see, and all of them looking at him now. Incident survivors. Men. Women. Children. Knowing him, now. Recognizing his legend. With a change of clothing and a single shout he has risen from obscurity. Their mocking calls pour down like a monsoon rain:

"*Wei!* Mr. Three Prosperities! Nice shirt!"

"Share a smoke, Mr. Big Name!"

"Where are you going so fast all dressed up?"

"Getting married?"

"Getting a tenth wife?"

"Got a job?"

"Mr. Big Name! Got a job for me?"

"Where you going? Maybe we should all follow Old Multinational!"

Tranh's neck prickles. He shakes off the fear. Even if they follow it will be too late for them to take advantage. For the first time in half a year, the advantage of skills and knowledge are on his side. Now there is only time.

He jogs through Bangkok's morning press as bicycles and cycle rickshaws and spring-wound scooters stream past. Sweat drenches him. It soaks his good shirt, damps even his jacket. He takes it off and slings it over an arm. His gray hair clings to his egg-bald liver-spotted skull, waterlogged. He pauses every other block to walk and recover his breath as his shins begin to ache and his breath comes in gasps and his old man's heart hammers in his chest.

He should spend his baht on a cycle rickshaw but he can't make himself do it. He is late. But perhaps he is too late? And if he is too late, the extra baht will be wasted and he will starve tonight. But then, what good is a suit soaked with sweat?

Clothes make the man, he told his sons; the first impression is the most important. Start well, and you start ahead. Of course you can win someone with your skills and your knowledge but people are animals first. Look good. Smell good. Satisfy their first senses. Then when they are well-disposed toward you, make your proposal.

Isn't that why he beat Second Son when he came home with a red tattoo of a tiger on his shoulder, as though he was some calorie gangster? Isn't that why he paid a tooth doctor to twist even his daughters' teeth with cultured bamboo and rubber curves from Singapore so that they were as straight as razors?

And isn't that why the Green Headbands in Malaya hated us Chinese? Because we looked so good? Because we looked so rich? Because we spoke so well and worked so hard when they were lazy and we sweated every day?

Tranh watches a pack of spring-wound scooters flit past, all of them Thai-Chinese manufactured. Such clever fast things—a megajoule kink-spring and a flywheel, pedals and friction brakes to regather kinetic energy. And all their factories owned one hundred percent by Chiu Chow Chinese. And yet no Chiu Chow blood runs in the gutters of this country. These Chiu Chow Chinese are loved, despite the fact that they came to the Thai Kingdom as *farang*.

If we had assimilated in Malaya like the Chiu Chow did here, would we have survived?

Tranh shakes his head at the thought. It would have been impossible. His clan would have had to convert to Islam as well, and forsake all their ancestors in Hell. It would have been impossible. Perhaps it was his people's karma to be destroyed. To stand tall and dominate the cities of Penang and Malacca and all the western coast of the Malayan Peninsula for a brief while, and then to die.

Clothes make the man. Or kill him. Tranh understands this, finally. A white tailored suit from Hwang Brothers is nothing so much as a target. An antique piece of gold mechanization swinging on your wrist is nothing if not bait. Tranh wonders if his sons' perfect teeth still lie in the ashes of Three Prosperities' warehouses, if their lovely time pieces now attract sharks and crabs in the holds of his scuttled clipper ships.

He should have known. Should have seen the rising tide of bloodthirsty subsects and intensifying nationalism. Just as the man he followed two months ago should have known that fine clothes were no protection. A man in good clothes, a yellow card to boot, should have known that he was nothing but a bit of bloodied bait before a Komodo lizard. At least the stupid melon didn't bleed on his fancy clothes when the white shirts were done with him. That one had no habit of survival. He forgot that he was no longer a Big Name.

But Tranh is learning. As he once learned tides and depth charts, markets and bio-engineered plagues, profit maximization and how to balance the dragon's gate, he now learns from the devil cats who molt and fade from sight, who flee their hunters at the first sign of danger. He learns from the crows and kites who live so well on scavenge. These are the animals he must emulate. He must discard the reflexes of a tiger. There are no tigers except in zoos. A tiger is always hunted and killed. But a small animal, a scavenging animal, has a chance to strip the bones of a tiger and walk away with the last Hwang Brothers suit that will ever cross the border from Malaya. With the Hwang clan all dead and the Hwang patterns all burned, nothing is left except memories and antiques, and one scavenging old man who knows the power and the peril of good appearance.

An empty cycle rickshaw coasts past. The rickshaw man looks back at Tranh, eyes questioning, attracted by the Hwang Brothers fabrics that flap off Tranh's skinny frame. Tranh raises a tentative hand. The cycle rickshaw slows.

Is it a good risk? To spend his last security so frivolously?

There was a time when he sent clipper fleets across the ocean to Chennai with great stinking loads of durians because he guessed that the Indians had not had time to plant resistant crop strains before the new blister rust mutations swept over them. A time when he bought black tea and sandalwood from the river men on the chance that he could sell it in the South. Now he can't decide if he should ride or walk. What a pale man he has become! Sometimes he wonders if he is actually a hungry ghost, trapped between worlds and unable to escape one way or the other.

The cycle rickshaw coasts ahead, the rider's blue jersey shimmering in the tropic sun, waiting for a decision. Tranh waves him away. The rickshaw man stands on his pedals, sandals flapping against calloused heels and accelerates.

Panic seizes Tranh. He raises his hand again, chases after the rickshaw. "Wait!" His voice comes out as a whisper.

The rickshaw slips into traffic, joining bicycles and the massive shambling shapes of elephantine megodonts. Tranh lets his hand fall, obscurely grateful that the rickshaw man hasn't heard, that the decision of spending his last baht has been made by some force larger than himself.

All around him, the morning press flows. Hundreds of children in their sailor suit uniforms stream through school gates. Saffron-robed monks stroll under the shade of wide black umbrellas. A man with a conical bamboo hat watches him and then mutters quietly to his friend. They both study him. A trickle of fear runs up Tranh's spine.

They are all around him, as they were in Malacca. In his own mind, he calls them foreigners, *farang*. And yet it is he who is the foreigner here. The creature that doesn't belong. And they know it. The women hanging sarongs on the wires of their balconies, the men sitting barefoot while they drink sugared coffee. The fish sellers and curry men. They all know it, and Tranh can barely control his terror.

Bangkok is not Malacca, he tells himself. Bangkok is not Penang. We have no wives, or gold wristwatches with diamonds, or clipper fleets to steal anymore. Ask the snakeheads who abandoned me in the leech jungles of the border. They have all my wealth. I have nothing. I am no tiger. I am safe.

For a few seconds he believes it. But then a teak-skinned boy chops the top off a coconut with a rusty machete and offers it to Tranh with a smile and it's all Tranh can do not to scream and run.

Bangkok is not Malacca. They will not burn your warehouses or slash your clerks into chunks of shark bait. He wipes sweat off his face. Perhaps he should have waited to wear the suit. It draws too much attention. There are too many people looking at him. Better to fade like a devil cat and slink across the city in safe anonymity, instead of strutting around like a peacock.

Slowly the streets change from palm-lined boulevards to the open wastelands of the new foreigner's quarter. Tranh hurries toward the river, heading deeper into the manufacturing empire of white *farang*.

Gweilo, yang guizi, farang. So many words in so many languages for these translucent-skinned sweating monkeys. Two generations ago when the petroleum ran out and the *gweilo* factories shut down, everyone assumed they were gone for good. And now they are back. The monsters of the past returned, with new toys and new technologies. The nightmares his mother threatened him with, invading Asiatic coasts. Demons truly; never dead.

And he goes to worship them: the ilk of AgriGen and PurCal with their monopolies on U-Tex rice and TotalNutrient Wheat; the blood-brothers of the bio-engineers who generipped devil cats from story-book inspiration and set them loose in the world to breed and breed and breed; the sponsors of the Intellectual Property Police who used to board his clipper fleets in search of IP infringements, hunting like wolves for unstamped calories and generipped grains as though their engineered plagues of cibiscosis and blister rust weren't enough to keep their profits high…

Ahead of him, a crowd has formed. Tranh frowns. He starts to run, then forces himself back to a walk. Better not to waste his calories, now. A line has already formed in front of the foreign devil Tennyson Brothers' factory. It stretches almost a *li*, snaking around the corner, past the bicycle gear logo in the wrought-iron gate of Sukhumvit Research Corporation, past the intertwined dragons of PurCal East Asia, and past Mishimoto & Co., the clever Japanese fluid dynamics company that Tranh once sourced his clipper designs from.

Mishimoto is full of windup import workers, they say. Full of illegal generipped bodies that walk and talk and totter about in their herky-jerky way—and take rice from real men's bowls. Creatures with as many as eight arms like the Hindu gods, creatures with no legs so they cannot run away, creatures with eyes as large as teacups which can only see a bare few feet ahead of them but inspect everything with enormous magnified curiosity. But no one can see inside, and if the Environment Ministry's white shirts know, then the clever Japanese are paying them well to ignore their crimes against biology and religion. It is perhaps the only thing a good Buddhist and a good Muslim and even the *farang* Grahamite Christians can agree on: windups have no souls.

When Tranh bought Mishimoto's clipper ships so long ago, he didn't care. Now he wonders if behind their high gates, windup monstrosities labor while yellow cards stand outside and beg.

Tranh trudges down the line. Policemen with clubs and spring guns patrol the hopefuls, making jokes about *farang* who wish to work for *farang*. Heat beats down, merciless on the men lined up before the gate.

"Wah! You look like a pretty bird with those clothes."

Tranh starts. Li Shen and Hu Laoshi and Lao Xia stand in the line, clustered together. A trio of old men as pathetic as himself. Hu waves a newly rolled cigarette in invitation, motioning him to join them. Tranh nearly shakes at the sight of the tobacco, but forces himself to refuse it. Three times Hu offers, and finally Tranh allows himself to accept, grateful that Hu is in earnest, and wondering where Hu has found this sudden wealth. But then, Hu has a little more strength than the rest of them. A cart man earns more if he works as fast as Hu.

Tranh wipes the sweat off his brow. "A lot of applicants."

They all laugh at Tranh's dismay.

Hu lights the cigarette for Tranh. "You thought you knew a secret, maybe?"

Tranh shrugs and draws deeply, passes the cigarette to Lao Xia. "A rumor. Potato God said his elder brother's son had a promotion. I thought there might be a niche down below, in the slot the nephew left behind."

Hu grins. "That's where I heard it, too. 'Eee. He'll be rich. Manage fifteen clerks. Eee! He'll be rich.' I thought I might be one of the fifteen."

"At least the rumor was true," Lao Xia says. "And not just Potato God's nephew promoted, either." He scratches the back of his head, a convulsive movement like a dog fighting fleas. *Fa' gan*'s gray fringe stains the crooks of his elbows and peeps from the sweaty pockets behind his ears where his hair has receded. He sometimes jokes about it: nothing a little money can't fix. A good joke. But today he is scratching and the skin behind his ears is cracked and raw. He notices everyone watching and yanks his hand down. He grimaces and passes the cigarette to Li Shen.

"How many positions?" Tranh asks.

"Three. Three clerks."

Tranh grimaces. "My lucky number."

Li Shen peers down the line with his bottle-thick glasses. "Too many of us, I think, even if your lucky number is 555."

Lao Xia laughs. "Amongst the four of us, there are already too many." He taps the man standing in line just ahead of them. "Uncle. What was your profession before?"

The stranger looks back, surprised. He was a distinguished gentleman, once, by his scholar's collar, by his fine leather shoes now scarred and blackened with scavenged charcoal. "I taught physics."

Lao Xia nods. "You see? We're all overqualified. I oversaw a rubber plantation. Our own professor has degrees in fluid dynamics and materials design. Hu was a fine doctor. And then there is our friend of the Three Prosperities. Not a trading company at all. More like a multi-national." He tastes the words. Says them again, "Multi-national." A strange, powerful, seductive sound.

Tranh ducks his head, embarrassed. "You're too kind."

"*Fang pi.*" Hu takes a drag on his cigarette, keeps it moving. "You were the richest of us all. And now here we are, old men scrambling for young men's jobs. Every one of us ten thousand times overqualified."

The man behind them interjects, "I was executive legal council for Standard & Commerce."

Lao Xia makes a face. "Who cares, dog fucker? You're nothing now."

The banking lawyer turns away, affronted. Lao Xia grins, sucks hard on the hand-rolled cigarette and passes it again to Tranh. Hu nudges Tranh's elbow as he starts to take a puff. "Look! There goes old Ma."

Tranh looks over, exhales smoke sharply. For a moment he thinks Ma has followed him, but no. It is just coincidence. They are in the *farang* factory district. Ma works for the foreign devils, balancing their books. A kink-spring company. Springlife. Yes, Springlife. It is natural that Ma should be here, comfortably riding to work behind a sweating cycle-rickshaw man.

"Ma Ping," Li Shen says. "I heard he's living on the top floor now. Up there with the Dung Lord himself."

Tranh scowls. "I fired him, once. Ten thousand years ago. Lazy and an embezzler."

"He's so fat."

"I've seen his wife," Hu says. "And his sons. They both have fat on them. They eat meat every night. The boys are fatter than fat. Full of U-Tex proteins."

"You're exaggerating."

"Fatter than us."

Lao Xia scratches a rib. "Bamboo is fatter than you."

Tranh watches Ma Ping open a factory door and slip inside. The past is past. Dwelling on the past is madness. There is nothing for him there. There are no wrist watches, no concubines, no opium pipes or jade sculptures of Quan Yin's merciful form. There are no pretty clipper ships slicing into port with fortunes in their holds. He shakes his head and offers the nearly spent cigarette to Hu so that he can recover the last tobacco for later use. There is nothing for him in the past. Ma is in the past. Three Prosperities Trading Company is the past. The sooner he remembers this, the sooner he will climb out of this awful hole.

From behind him, a man calls out, "*Wei!* Baldy! When did you cut the line? Go to the back! You line up, like the rest of us!"

"Line up?" Lao Xia shouts back. "Don't be stupid!" He waves at the line ahead. "How many hundreds are ahead of us? It won't make any difference where he stands."

Others begin to attend the man's complaint. Complain as well. "Line up! *Pai dui! Pai dui!*" The disturbance increases and police start down the line, casually swinging their batons. They aren't white shirts, but they have no love for hungry yellow cards.

Tranh makes placating motions to the crowd and Lao Xia. "Of course. Of course. I'll line up. It's of no consequence." He makes his farewells and plods his way down the winding yellow card snake, seeking its distant tail.

Everyone is dismissed long before he reaches it.

A scavenging night. A starving night. Tranh hunts through dark alleys avoiding the vertical prison heat of the towers. Devil cats seethe and scatter ahead of him in rippling waves. The lights of the methane lamps flicker, burn low and snuff themselves, blackening the city. Hot velvet darkness fetid with rotting fruit swaddles him. The heavy humid air sags. Still swelter darkness. Empty market stalls. On a street corner, theater men turn in stylized cadences to stories of Ravana. On a thoroughfare, swingshift megodonts shuffle homeward like gray mountains, their massed shadows led by the gold trim glitter of union handlers.

In the alleys, children with bright silver knives hunt unwary yellow cards and drunken Thais, but Tranh is wise to their feral ways. A year ago, he would not have seen them, but he has the paranoid's gift of survival, now. Creatures like them are no worse than sharks: easy to predict, easy to avoid. It is not these obviously feral hunters who churn Tranh's guts with fear, it is the chameleons, the everyday people who work and shop and smile and *wai* so pleasantly—and riot without warning—who terrify Tranh.

He picks through the trash heaps, fighting devil cats for signs of food, wishing he was fast enough to catch and kill one of those nearly invisible felines. Picking up discarded mangos, studying them carefully with his old man's eyes, holding them close and then far away, sniffing at them, feeling their blister rusted exteriors and then tossing them aside when they show red mottle in their guts. Some of them still smell good, but even crows won't accept such a taint. They would eagerly peck apart a bloated corpse but they will not feed on blister rust.

Down the street, the Dung Lord's lackeys shovel the day's animal leavings into sacks and throw them into tricycle carriers: the night harvest. They watch him suspiciously. Tranh keeps his eyes averted, avoiding challenge, and scuffles on. He has nothing to cook on an illegally stolen shit fire anyway, and nowhere to sell manure on the black market. The Dung Lord's monopoly is too strong. Tranh wonders how it might be to find a place in the dung shovelers' union, to know that his survival was guaranteed feeding the composters of Bangkok's methane reclamation plants. But it is an opium dream; no yellow card can slither into that closed club.

Tranh lifts another mango and freezes. He bends low, squinting. Pushes aside broadsheet complaints against the Ministry of Trade and handbills calling for a new gold-sheathed River Wat. He pushes aside black slime banana peels and burrows into the garbage. Below it all, stained and torn but still legible, he finds a portion of what was once a great advertising board that perhaps stood over this marketplace: —*ogistics. Shipping. Tradin*— and behind the words, the glorious silhouette of *Dawn Star*: one part of Three Prosperities' tri-clipper logo, running before the wind as fast and sleek as a shark: a high-tech image of palm-oil spun polymers and sails as sharp and white as a gull's.

Tranh turns his face away, overcome. It's like unearthing a grave and finding himself within. His pride. His blindness. Fom a time when he thought he might compete with the foreign devils and become a shipping magnate. A Li Ka Shing or a reborn Richard Kuok for the New Expansion. Rebuild the pride of Nanyang Chinese shipping and trading. And here, like a slap in the face, a portion of his ego, buried in rot and blister rust and devil-cat urine.

He searches around, pawing for more portions of the sign, wondering if anyone treadles a phone call to that old phone number, if the secretary whose wages he once paid is still at her desk, working for a new master, a native Malay perhaps, with impeccable pedigree and religion. Wondering if the few clippers he failed to scuttle still ply the seas and islands of the archipelago. He forces himself to stop his search. Even if he had the money he would not treadle that number. Would not waste the calories. Could not stand the loss again.

He straightens, scattering devil cats who have slunk close. There is nothing here in this market except rinds and unshoveled dung. He has wasted his calories once again. Even the cockroaches and the blood beetles have been eaten. If he searches for a dozen hours, he will still find nothing. Too many people have come before, picking at these bones.

Three times he hides from white shirts as he makes his way home, three times ducking into shadows as they strut past. Cringing as they wander close, cursing his white linen suit that shows so clearly in darkness. By the third time, superstitious fear runs hot in his veins. His rich man's clothes seem to attract the patrols of the Environment Ministry, seem to hunger for the wearer's death. Black batons twirl from casual hands no more than inches away from his face. Spring guns glitter silver in the darkness. His hunters stand so close that he can count the wicked bladed disk cartridges in their jute bandoliers. A white shirt pauses and pisses in the alley where Tranh crouches, and only fails to see him because his partner stands on the street and wants to check the permits of the dung gatherers.

Each time, Tranh stifles his panicked urge to tear off his too-rich clothes and sink into safe anonymity. It is only a matter of time before the white shirts catch him. Before they swing their black clubs and make his Chinese skull a mash of blood and bone. Better to run naked through the hot night than strut like a peacock and die. And yet he cannot quite abandon the cursed suit. Is it pride? Is it stupidity? He keeps it though, even as its arrogant cut turns his bowels watery with fear.

By the time he reaches home, even the gas lights on the main thoroughfares of Sukhumvit Road and Rama IV are blackened. Outside the Dung Lord's tower, street stalls still burn woks for the few laborers lucky enough to have night work and curfew dispensations. Pork tallow candles flicker on the tables. Noodles splash into hot woks with a sizzle. White shirts stroll past, their eyes on the seated yellow cards, ensuring that none of the foreigners brazenly sleep in the open air and sully the sidewalks with their snoring presence.

Tranh joins the protective loom of the towers, entering the nearly extra-territorial safety of the Dung Lord's influence. He stumbles toward the doorways and the swelter of the highrise, wondering how high he will be forced to climb before he can shove a niche for himself on the stairwells.

"You didn't get the job, did you?"

Tranh cringes at the voice. It's Ma Ping again, sitting at a sidewalk table, a bottle of Mekong whiskey beside his hand. His face is flushed with alcohol, as bright as a red paper lantern. Half-eaten plates of food lie strewn around his table. Enough to feed five others, easily.

Images of Ma war in Tranh's head: the young clerk he once sent packing for being too clever with an abacus, the man whose son is fat, the man who got out early, the man who begged to be rehired at Three Prosperities, the man who now struts around Bangkok with Tranh's last precious possession on his wrist—the one item that even the snakeheads didn't steal. Tranh thinks that truly fate is cruel, placing him in such proximity to one he once considered so far beneath him.

Despite his intention to show bravado, Tranh's words come out as a mousy whisper. "What do you care?"

Ma shrugs, pours whiskey for himself. "I wouldn't have noticed you in the line, without that suit." He nods at Tranh's sweat-damp clothing. "Good idea to dress up. Too far back in line, though."

Tranh wants to walk away, to ignore the arrogant whelp, but Ma's leavings of steamed bass and *laap* and U-Tex rice noodles lie tantalizingly close. He thinks he smells pork and can't help salivating. His gums ache for the idea that he could chew meat again and he wonders if his teeth would accept the awful luxury…

Abruptly, Tranh realizes that he has been staring. That he has stood for some time, ogling the scraps of Ma's meal. And Ma is watching him. Tranh flushes and starts to turn away.

Ma says, "I didn't buy your watch to spite you, you know."

Tranh stops short. "Why then?"

Ma's fingers stray to the gold and diamond bauble, then seem to catch themselves. He reaches for his whiskey glass instead. "I wanted a reminder." He takes a swallow of liquor and sets the glass back amongst his piled plates with the deliberate care of a drunk. He grins sheepishly. His fingers are again stroking the watch, a guilty furtive movement. "I wanted a reminder. Against ego."

Tranh spits. "*Fang pi.*"

Ma shakes his head vigorously. "No! It's true." He pauses. "Anyone can fall. If the Three Prosperities can fall, then I can. I wanted to remember that." He takes another pull on his whiskey. "You were right to fire me."

Tranh snorts. "You didn't think so then."

"I was angry. I didn't know that you'd saved my life, then." He shrugs. "I would never have left Malaya if you hadn't fired me. I would never have seen the Incident coming. I would have had too much invested in staying." Abruptly, he pulls himself upright and motions for Tranh to join him. "Come. Have a drink. Have some food. I owe you that much. You saved my life. I've repaid you poorly. Sit."

Tranh turns away. "I don't despise myself so much."

"Do you love face so much that you can't take a man's food? Don't be stuck in your bones. I don't care if you hate me. Just take my food. Curse me later, when your belly is full."

Tranh tries to control his hunger, to force himself to walk away, but he can't. He knows men who might have enough face to starve before accepting Ma's scraps, but he isn't one of them. A lifetime ago, he might have been. But the humiliations of his new life have taught him much about who he really is. He has no sweet illusions, now. He sits. Ma beams and pushes his half-eaten dishes across the table.

Tranh thinks he must have done something grave in a former life to merit this humiliation, but still he has to fight the urge to bury his hands in the oily food and eat with bare fingers. Finally, the owner of the sidewalk stall brings a pair of chopsticks for the noodles, and fork and spoon for the rest. Noodles and ground pork slide down his throat. He tries to chew but as soon as the food touches his tongue he gulps it down. More food follows. He lifts a plate to his lips, shoveling down the last of Ma's leavings. Fish and lank coriander and hot thick oil slip down like blessings.

"Good. Good." Ma waves at the night stall man and a whiskey glass is quickly rinsed and handed to him.

The sharp scent of liquor floats around Ma like an aura as he pours. Tranh's chest tightens at the scent. Oil coats his chin where he has made a mess in his haste. He wipes his mouth against his arm, watching the amber liquid splash into the glass.

Tranh once drank cognac: XO. Imported by his own clippers. Fabulously expensive stuff with its shipping costs. A flavor of the foreign devils from before the Contraction. A ghost from utopian history, reinvigorated by the new Expansion and his own realization that the world was once again growing smaller. With new hull designs and polymer advances, his clipper ships navigated the globe and returned with the stuff of legends. And his Malay buyers were happy to purchase it, whatever their religion. What a profit that had been. He forces down the thought as Ma shoves the glass across to Tranh and then raises his own in toast. It is in the past. It is all in the past.

They drink. The whiskey burns warm in Tranh's belly, joining the chilies and fish and pork and the hot oil of the fried noodles.

"It really is too bad you didn't get that job."

Tranh grimaces. "Don't gloat. Fate has a way of balancing itself. I've learned that."

Ma waves a hand. "I don't gloat. There are too many of us, that's the truth. You were ten-thousand-times qualified for that job. For any job." He takes a sip of his whiskey, peers over its rim at Tranh. "Do you remember when you called me a lazy cockroach?"

Tranh shrugs, he can't take his eyes off the whiskey bottle. "I called you worse than that." He waits to see if Ma will refill his cup again.

Wondering how rich he is, and how far this largesse will go. Hating that he plays beggar to a boy he once refused to keep as a clerk, and who now lords over him… and who now, in a show of face, pours Tranh's whiskey to the top, letting it spill over in an amber cascade under the flickering light of the candles.

Ma finishes pouring, stares at the puddle he has created. "Truly the world is turned upside down. The young lord over the old. The Malays pinch out the Chinese. And the foreign devils return to our shores like bloated fish after a *ku-shui* epidemic." Ma smiles. "You need to keep your ears up, and be aware of opportunities. Not like all those old men out on the sidewalk, waiting for hard labor. Find a new niche. That's what I did. That's why I've got my job."

Tranh grimaces. "You came at a more fortuitous time." He rallies, emboldened by a full belly and the liquor warming his face and limbs. "Anyway, you shouldn't be too proud. You still stink of mother's milk as far as I'm concerned, living in the Dung Lord's tower. You're only the Lord of Yellow Cards. And what is that, really? You haven't climbed as high as my ankles, yet, Mr. Big Name."

Ma's eyes widen. He laughs. "No. Of course not. Someday, maybe. But I am trying to learn from you." He smiles slightly and nods at Tranh's decrepit state. "Everything except this postscript."

"Is it true there are crank fans on the top floors? That it's cool up there?"

Ma glances up at the looming highrise. "Yes. Of course. And men with the calories to wind them as well. And they haul water up for us, and men act as ballast on the elevator—up and down all day—doing favors for the Dung Lord." He laughs and pours more whiskey, motions Tranh to drink. "You're right though. It's nothing, really. A poor palace, truly.

"But it doesn't matter now. My family moves tomorrow. We have our residence permits. Tomorrow when I get paid again, we're moving out. No more yellow card for us. No more payoffs to the Dung Lord's lackeys. No more problems with the white shirts. It's all set with the Environment Ministry. We turn in our yellow cards and become Thai. We're going to be immigrants. Not just some invasive species, anymore." He raises his glass. "It's why I'm celebrating."

Tranh scowls. "You must be pleased." He finishes his drink, sets the tumbler down with a thud. "Just don't forget that the nail that stands up also gets pounded down."

Ma shakes his head and grins, his eyes whiskey bright. "Bangkok isn't Malacca."

"And Malacca wasn't Bali. And then they came with their machetes and their spring guns and they stacked our heads in the gutters and sent our bodies and blood down the river to Singapore."

Ma shrugs. "It's in the past." He waves to the man at the wok, calling for more food. "We have to make a home here, now."

"You think you can? You think some white shirt won't nail your hide to his door? You can't make them like us. Our luck's against us, here."

"Luck? When did Mr. Three Prosperities get so superstitious?"

Ma's dish arrives, tiny crabs crisp-fried, salted and hot with oil for Ma and Tranh to pick at with chopsticks and crunch between their teeth, each one no bigger than the tip of Tranh's pinkie. Ma plucks one out and crunches it down. "When did Mr. Three Prosperities get so weak? When you fired me, you said I made my own luck. And now you tell me you don't have any?" He spits on sidewalk. "I've seen windups with more will to survive than you."

"*Fang pi.*"

"No! It's true! There's a Japanese windup girl in the bars where my boss goes." Ma leans forward. "She looks like a real woman. And she does disgusting things." He grins. "Makes your cock hard. But you don't hear her complaining about luck. Every white shirt in the city would pay to dump her in the methane composters and she's still up in her highrise, dancing every night, in front of everyone. Her whole soulless body on display."

"It's not possible."

Ma shrugs. "Say so if you like. But I've seen her. And she isn't starving. She takes whatever spit and money come her way, and she survives. It doesn't matter about the white shirts or the Kingdom edicts or the Japan-haters or the religious fanatics; she's been dancing for months."

"How can she survive?"

"Bribes? Maybe some ugly *farang* who wallows in her filth? Who knows? No real girl would do what she does. It makes your heart stop. You forget she's a windup, when she does those things." He laughs, then glances at Tranh. "Don't talk to me about luck. There's not enough luck in the entire Kingdom to keep her alive this long. And we know it's not karma that keeps her alive. She has none."

Tranh shrugs noncommittally and shovels more crabs into his mouth.

Ma grins. "You know I'm right." He drains his whiskey glass and slams it down on the table. "We make our own luck! Our own fate. There's a windup in a public bar and I have a job with a rich *farang* who can't find his ass without my help! Of course I'm right!" He pours more whiskey. "Get over your self-pity, and climb out of your hole. The foreign devils don't worry about luck or fate, and look how they return to us, like a newly engineered virus! Even the Contraction didn't stop them. They're like another invasion of devil cats. But they make their own luck. I'm not even sure if karma exists for them. And if fools like these *farang* can succeed, than we Chinese can't be kept down for long. Men make their own luck, that's what you told me when you fired me. You said I'd made my own bad luck and only had myself to blame."

Tranh looks up at Ma. "Maybe I could work at your company." He grins, trying not to look desperate. "I could make money for your lazy boss."

Ma's eyes become hooded. "Ah. That's difficult. Difficult to say."

Tranh knows that he should take the polite rejection, that he should shut up. But even as a part of him cringes, his mouth opens again, pressing, pleading. "Maybe you need an assistant? To keep the books? I speak their devil language. I taught it to myself when I traded with them. I could be useful."

"There is little enough work for me."

"But if he is as stupid as you say—,"

"Stupid, yes. But not such a stupid melon that he wouldn't notice another body in his office. Our desks are just so far apart." He makes a motion with his hands. "You think he would not notice some stick coolie man squatting beside his computer treadle?"

"In his factory, then?"

But Ma is already shaking his head. "I would help you if I could. But the megodont unions control the power, and the line inspector unions are closed to *farang*, no offense, and no one will accept that you are a materials scientist." He shakes his head. "No. There is no way."

"Any job. As a dung shoveler, even."

But Ma is shaking his head more vigorously now, and Tranh finally manages to control his tongue, to plug this diarrhea of begging. "Never mind. Never mind." He forces a grin. "I'm sure some work will turn up. I'm not worried." He takes the bottle of Mekong whiskey and refills Ma's glass, upending the bottle and finishing the whiskey despite Ma's protests.

Tranh raises his half-empty glass and toasts the young man who has bested him in all ways, before throwing back the last of the alcohol in one swift swallow. Under the table, nearly invisible devil cats brush against his bony legs, waiting for him to leave, hoping that he will be foolish enough to leave scraps.

Morning dawns. Tranh wanders the streets, hunting for a breakfast he cannot afford. He threads through market alleys redolent with fish and lank green coriander and bright flares of lemongrass. Durians lie in reeking piles, their spiky skins covered with red blister rust boils. He wonders if he can steal one. Their yellow surfaces are blotched and stained, but their guts are nutritious. He wonders how much blister rust a man can consume before falling into a coma.

"You want? Special deal. Five for five baht. Good, yes?"

The woman who screeches at him has no teeth, she smiles with her gums and repeats herself. "Five for five baht." She speaks Mandarin to him, recognizing him for their common heritage though she had the luck to be born in the Kingdom and he had the misfortune to be set down in Malaya. Chiu Chow Chinese, blessedly protected by her clan and King. Tranh suppresses envy.

"More like four for four." He makes a pun of the homonyms. *Sz* for *sz*. Four for death. "They've got blister rust."

She waves a hand sourly. "Five for five. They're still good. Better than good. Picked just before." She wields a gleaming machete and chops the durian in half, revealing the clean yellow slime of its interior with its fat gleaming pits. The sickly sweet scent of fresh durian boils up and envelopes them. "See! Inside good. Picked just in time. Still safe."

"I might buy one." He can't afford any. But he can't help replying. It feels too good to be seen as a buyer. It is his suit, he realizes. The Hwang Brothers have raised him in this woman's eyes. She wouldn't have spoken if not for the suit. Wouldn't have even started the conversation.

"Buy more! The more you buy, the more you save."

He forces a grin, wondering how to get away from the bargaining he should never have started. "I'm only one old man. I don't need so much."

"One skinny old man. Eat more. Get fat!"

She says this and they both laugh. He searches for a response, something to keep their comradely interaction alive, but his tongue fails him. She sees the helplessness in his eyes. She shakes her head. "Ah, grandfather. It is hard times for everyone. Too many of you all at once. No one thought it would get so bad down there."

Tranh ducks his head, embarrassed. "I've troubled you. I should go."

"Wait. Here." She offers him the durian half. "Take it."

"I can't afford it."

She makes an impatient gesture. "Take it. It's lucky for me to help someone from the old country." She grins. "And the blister rust looks too bad to sell to anyone else."

"You're kind. Buddha smile on you." But as he takes her gift he again notices the great durian pile behind her. All neatly stacked with their blotches and their bloody weals of blister rust. Just like stacked Chinese heads in Malacca: his wife and daughter mouths staring out at him, accusatory. He drops the durian and kicks it away, frantically scraping his hands on his jacket, trying to get the blood off his palms.

"Ai! You'll waste it!"

Tranh barely hears the woman's cry. He staggers back from the fallen durian, staring at its ragged surface. Its gut-spilled interior. He looks around wildly. He has to get out of the crowds. Has to get away from the jostling bodies and the durian reek that's all around, thick in his throat, gagging him. He puts a hand to his mouth and runs, clawing at the other shoppers, fighting through their press.

"Where you go? Come back! *Huilai!*" But the woman's words are quickly drowned. Tranh shoves through the throng, pushing aside women with shopping baskets full of white lotus root and purple eggplants, dodging farmers and their clattering bamboo hand carts, twisting past tubs of squid and serpent head fish. He pelts down the market alley like a thief identified, scrambling and dodging, running without thought or knowledge of where he is going, but running anyway, desperate to escape the stacked heads of his family and countrymen.

He runs and runs.

And bursts into the open thoroughfare of Charoen Krung Road. Powdered dung dust and hot sunlight wash over him. Cycle rickshaws clatter past. Palms and squat banana trees shimmer green in the bright open air.

As quickly as it seized him, Tranh's panic fades. He stops short, hands on his knees, catching his breath and cursing himself. *Fool. Fool. If you don't eat, you die.* He straightens and tries to turn back but the stacked durians flash in his mind and he stumbles away from the alley, gagging again. He can't go back. Can't face those bloody piles. He doubles over and his stomach heaves but his empty guts bring up nothing but strings of drool.

Finally he wipes his mouth on a Hwang Brothers sleeve and forces himself to straighten and confront the foreign faces all around. The sea of foreigners that he must learn to swim amongst, and who all call him *farang.* It repels him to think of it. And to think that in Malacca, with twenty generations of family and clan well-rooted in that city, he was just as much an interloper. That his clan's esteemed history is nothing but a footnote for a Chinese expansion that has proven as transient as nighttime cool. That his people were nothing but an accidental spillage of rice on a map, now wiped up much more carefully than they were scattered down.

Tranh unloads U-Tex Brand RedSilks deep into the night, offerings to Potato God. A lucky job. A lucky moment, even if his knees have become loose and wobbly and feel as if they must soon give way. A lucky job, even if his arms are shaking from catching the heavy sacks as they come down off the megodonts. Tonight, he reaps not just pay but also the opportunity to steal from the harvest. Even if the RedSilk potatoes are small and harvested early to avoid a new sweep of scabis mold—the fourth genetic variation this year—they are still good. And their small size means their enhanced nutrition falls easily into his pockets.

Hu crouches above him, lowering down the potatoes. As the massive elephantine megodonts shuffle and grunt, waiting for their great wagons to be unloaded, Tranh catches Hu's offerings with his hand hooks and lowers the sacks the last step to the ground. Hook, catch, swing, and lower. Again and again and again.

He is not alone in his work. Women from the tower slums crowd around his ladder. They reach up and caress each sack as he lowers it to the ground. Their fingers quest along hemp and burlap, testing for holes, for slight tears, for lucky gifts. A thousand times they stroke his burdens, reverently following the seams, only drawing away when coolie men shove between them to heft the sacks and haul them to Potato God.

After the first hour of his work, Tranh's arms are shaking. After three, he can barely stand. He teeters on his creaking ladder as he lowers each new sack, and gasps and shakes his head to clear sweat from his eyes as he waits for the next one to come down.

Hu peers down from above. "Are you all right?"

Tranh glances warily over his shoulder. Potato God is watching, counting the sacks as they are carried into the warehouse. His eyes occasionally flick up to the wagons and trace across Tranh. Beyond him, fifty unlucky men watch silently from the shadows, any one of them far more observant than Potato God can ever be. Tranh straightens and reaches up to accept the next sack, trying not to think about the watching eyes. How politely they wait. How silent. How hungry. "I'm fine. Just fine."

Hu shrugs and pushes the next burlap load over the wagon's lip. Hu has the better place, but Tranh cannot resent it. One or the other must suffer. And Hu found the job. Hu has the right to the best place. To rest a moment before the next sack moves. After all, Hu collected Tranh for the job when he should have starved tonight. It is fair.

Tranh takes the sack and lowers it into the forest of waiting women's hands, releases his hooks with a twist, and drops the bag to the ground. His joints feel loose and rubbery, as if femur and tibia will skid apart at any moment. He is dizzy with heat, but he dares not ask to slow the pace.

Another potato sack comes down. Women's hands rise up like tangling strands of seaweed, touching, prodding, hungering. He cannot force them back. Even if he shouts at them they return. They are like devil cats; they cannot help themselves. He drops the sack the last few feet to the ground and reaches up for another as it comes over the wagon's lip.

As he hooks the sack, his ladder creaks and suddenly slides. It chatters down the side of the wagon, then catches abruptly. Tranh sways, juggling the potato sack, trying to regain his center of gravity. Hands are all around him, tugging at the bag, pulling, prodding. "Watch out—"

The ladder skids again. He drops like a stone. Women scatter as he plunges. He hits the ground and pain explodes in his knee. The potato sack bursts. For a moment he worries what Potato God will say but then he hears screams all around him. He rolls onto his back. Above him, the wagon is swaying, shuddering. People are shouting and fleeing. The megodont lunges forward and the wagon heaves. Bamboo ladders fall like rain, slapping the pavement with bright firecracker retorts. The beast reverses itself and the wagon skids past Tranh, grinding the ladders to splinters. It is impossibly fast, even with wagon's weight still hampering it. The megodont's great maw opens and suddenly it is screaming, a sound as high and panicked as a human's.

All around them, other megodonts respond in a chorus. Their cacophony swamps the street. The megodont surges onto its hind legs, an explosion of muscle and velocity that breaks the wagon's traces and flips it like a toy. Men cartwheel from it, blossoms shaken from a cherry tree. Maddened, the beast rears again and kicks the wagon. Sends it skidding sidewise. It slams past Tranh, missing him by inches.

Tranh tries to rise but his leg won't work. The wagon smashes into a wall. Bamboo and teak crackle and explode, the wagon disintegrating as the megodont drags and kicks it, trying to win free completely. Tranh drags himself away from the flying wagon, hand over hand, hauling his useless leg behind him. All around, men are shouting instructions, trying to control the beast, but he doesn't look back. He focuses on the cobbles ahead, on getting out of reach. His leg won't work. It refuses him. It seems to hate him.

Finally he makes it into the shelter of a protective wall. He hauls himself upright. "I'm fine," he tells himself. "Fine." Gingerly he tests his leg, setting weight on it. It's wobbly, but he feels no real pain, not now. *"Mei wenti. Mei wenti,"* he whispers. "Not a problem. Just cracked it. Not a problem."

The men are still shouting and the megodont is still screaming, but all he can see is his brittle old knee. He lets go of the wall. Takes a step, testing his weight, and collapses like a shadow puppet with strings gone slack.

Gritting his teeth, he again hauls himself up off the cobbles. He props himself against the wall, massaging his knee and watching the bedlam. Men are throwing ropes over the back of the struggling megodont, pulling it down, immobilizing it, finally. More than a score of men are working to hobble it.

The wagon's frame has shattered completely and potatoes are spilled everywhere. A thick mash coats the ground. Women scramble on their knees, clawing through the mess, fighting with one another to hoard pulped tubers. They scrape it up from the street. Some of their scavenge is stained red, but no one seems to care. Their squabbling continues. The red bloom spreads. At the blossom's center, a man's trousers protrude from the muck

Tranh frowns. He drags himself upright again and hops on his one good leg toward the broken wagon. He catches up against its shattered frame, staring. Hu's body is a savage ruin, awash in megodont dung and potato mash. And now that Tranh is close, he can see that the struggling megodont's great gray feet are gory with his friend. Someone is calling for a doctor but it is half-hearted, a habit from a time when they were not yellow cards.

Tranh tests his weight again but his knee provides the same queer jointless failure. He catches up against the wagon's splintered planking and hauls himself back upright. He works the leg, trying to understand why it collapses. The knee bends, it doesn't even hurt particularly, but it will not support his weight. He tests it again, with the same result.

With the megodont restrained, order in the unloading area is restored. Hu's body is dragged aside. Devil cats gather near his blood pool, feline shimmers under methane glow. Their tracks pock the potato grime in growing numbers. More paw impressions appear in the muck, closing from all directions on Hu's discarded body.

Tranh sighs. So we all go, he thinks. We all die. Even those of us who took our aging treatments and our tiger penis and kept ourselves strong are subject to the Hell journey. He promises to burn money for Hu, to ease his way in the afterlife, then catches himself and remembers that he is not the man he was. That even paper Hell Money is out of reach.

Potato God, disheveled and angry, comes and studies him. He frowns suspiciously. "Can you still work?"

"I can." Tranh tries to walk but stumbles once again and catches up against the wagon's shattered frame.

Potato God shakes his head. "I will pay you for the hours you worked." He waves to a young man, fresh and grinning from binding the megodont. "You! You're a quick one. Haul the rest of these sacks into the warehouse."

Already, other workers are lining up and grabbing loads from within the broken wagon. As the new man comes out with his first sack, his eyes dart to Tranh and then flick away, hiding his relief at Tranh's incapacity.

Potato God watches with satisfaction and heads back to the warehouse.

"Double pay," Tranh calls after Potato God's retreating back. "Give me double pay. I lost my leg for you."

The manager looks back at Tranh with pity, then glances at Hu's body and shrugs. It is an easy acquiescence. Hu will demand no reparation.

It is better to die insensate than to feel every starving inch of collapse; Tranh pours his leg-wreck money into a bottle of Mekong whiskey. He is old. He is broken. He is the last of his line. His sons are dead. His daughter mouths are long gone. His ancestors will live uncared for in the underworld with no one to burn incense or offer sweet rice to them.

How they must curse him.

He limps and stumbles and crawls through the sweltering night streets, one hand clutching the open bottle, the other scrabbling at doorways and walls and methane lamp posts to keep himself upright. Sometimes his knee works; sometimes it fails him completely. He has kissed the streets a dozen times.

He tells himself that he is scavenging, hunting for the chance of sustenance. But Bangkok is a city of scavengers, and the crows and devil cats and children have all come before him. If he is truly lucky, he will encounter the white shirts and they will knock him into bloody oblivion, perhaps send him to meet the previous owner of this fine Hwang Brothers suit that now flaps ragged around his shins. The thought appeals to him.

An ocean of whiskey rolls in his empty belly and he is warm and happy and carefree for the first time since the Incident. He laughs and drinks and shouts for the white shirts, calling them paper tigers, calling them dog fuckers. He calls them to him. Casts baiting words so that any within earshot will find him irresistable. But the Environment Ministry's patrols must have other yellow cards to abuse, for Tranh wanders the green-tinged streets of Bangkok alone.

Never mind. It doesn't matter. If he cannot find white shirts to do the job, he will drown himself. He will go to the river and dump himself in its offal. Floating on river currents to the sea appeals to him. He will end in the ocean like his scuttled clipper ships and the last of his heirs. He takes a swig of whiskey, loses his balance, and winds up on the ground once again, sobbing and cursing white shirts and green headbands, and wet machetes.

Finally he drags himself into a doorway to rest, holding his miraculously unbroken whiskey bottle with one feeble hand. He cradles it to himself like a last bit of precious jade, smiling and laughing that it is not broken. He wouldn't want to waste his life savings on the cobblestones.

He takes another swig. Stares at the methane lamps flickering overhead. Despair is the color of approved-burn methane flickering green and gaseous, vinous in the dark. Green used to mean things like coriander and silk and jade and now all it means to him is bloodthirsty men with patriotic headbands and hungry scavenging nights. The lamps flicker. An entire green city. An entire city of despair.

Across the street, a shape scuttles, keeping to the shadows. Tranh leans forward, eyes narrowed. At first he takes it for a white shirt. But no. It is too furtive. It's a woman. A girl. A pretty creature, all made up. An enticement that moves with the stuttery jerky motion of...

A windup girl.

Tranh grins, a surprised skeleton rictus of delight at the sight of this unnatural creature stealing through the night. A windup girl. Ma Ping's windup girl. The impossible made flesh.

She slips from shadow to shadow, a creature even more terrified of white shirts than a yellow card geriatric. A waifish ghost-child ripped from her natural habitat and set down in a city which despises everything she represents: her genetic inheritance, her manufacturers, her unnatural competition—her ghostly lack of a soul. She has been here every night as he has pillaged through discarded melon spines. She has been here, tottering through the sweat heat darkness as he dodged white shirt patrols. And despite everything, she has been surviving.

Tranh forces himself upright. He sways, drunken and unsteady, then follows, one hand clutching his whiskey bottle, the other touching walls, catching himself when his bad knee falters. It's a foolish thing, a whimsy, but the windup girl has seized his inebriated imagination. He wants to stalk this unlikely Japanese creature, this interloper on foreign soil even more despised than himself. He wants to follow her. Perhaps steal kisses from her. Perhaps protect her from the hazards of the night. To pretend at least that he is not this drunken ribcage caricature of a man, but is in fact a tiger still.

The windup girl travels through the blackest of back alleys, safe in darkness, hidden from the white shirts who would seize her and mulch her before she could protest. Devil cats yowl as she passes, scenting something as cynically engineered as themselves. The Kingdom is infested with plagues and beasts, besieged by so many bio-engineered monsters that it cannot keep up. As small as gray *fa' gan* fringe and as large as megodonts, they come. And as the Kingdom struggles to adapt, Tranh slinks after a windup girl, both of them as invasive as blister rust on a durian and just as welcome.

For all her irregular motion, the windup girl travels well enough. Tranh has difficulty keeping up with her. His knees creak and grind and he clenches his teeth against the pain. Sometimes he falls with a muffled grunt, but still he follows. Ahead of him, the windup girl ducks into new shadows, a wisp of tottering motion. Her herky-jerky gait announces her as a creature not human, no matter how beautiful she may be. No matter how intelligent, no matter how strong, no matter how supple her skin, she is a windup and meant to serve—and marked as such by a genetic specification that betrays her with every unnatural step.

Finally, when Tranh thinks that his legs will give out for a final time and that he can continue no longer, the windup girl pauses. She stands in the black mouth of a crumbling highrise, a tower as tall and wretched as his own, another carcass of the old Expansion. From high above, music and laughter filter down. Shapes float in the tower's upper-story windows, limned in red light, the silhouettes of women dancing. Calls of men and the throb of drums. The windup girl disappears inside.

What would it be like to enter such a place? To spend baht like water while women danced and sang songs of lust? Tranh suddenly regrets spending his last baht on whiskey. This is where he should have died. Surrounded by fleshly pleasures that he has not known since he lost his country and his life. He purses his lips, considering. Perhaps he can bluff his way in. He still wears the raiment of the Hwang Brothers. He still appears a gentleman, perhaps. Yes. He will attempt it, and if he gathers the shame of ejection on his head, if he loses face one more time, what of it? He will be dead in a river soon anyway, floating to the sea to join his sons.

He starts to cross the street but his knee gives out and he falls flat instead. He saves his whiskey bottle more by luck than by dexterity. The last of its amber liquid glints in the methane light. He grimaces and pulls himself into a sitting position, then drags himself back into a doorway. He will rest, first. And finish the bottle. The windup girl will be there for a long time, likely. He has time to recover himself. And if he falls again, at least he won't have wasted his liquor. He tilts the bottle to his lips then lets his tired head rest against the building. He'll just catch his breath.

Laughter issues from the highrise. Tranh jerks awake. A man stumbles from its shadow portal: drunk, laughing. More men spill out after him. They laugh and shove one another. Drag tittering women out with them. Motion to cycle rickshaws that wait in the alleys for easy drunken patrons. Slowly, they disperse. Tranh tilts his whiskey bottle. Finds it empty.

Another pair of men emerges from the highrise's maw. One of them is Ma Ping. The other a *farang* who can only be Ma's boss. The *farang* waves for a cycle rickshaw. He climbs in and waves his farewells. Ma raises his own hand in return and his gold and diamond wristwatch glints in the methane light. Tranh's wristwatch. Tranh's history. Tranh's heirloom flashing bright in the darkness. Tranh scowls. Wishes he could rip it off young Ma's wrist.

The *farang*'s rickshaw starts forward with a screech of unoiled bicycle chains and drunken laughter, leaving Ma Ping standing alone in the middle of the street. Ma laughs to himself, seems to consider returning to the bars, then laughs again and turns away, heading across the street, toward Tranh.

Tranh shies into the shadows, unwilling to let Ma catch him in such a state. Unwilling to endure more humiliation. He crouches deeper in his doorway as Ma stumbles about the street in search of rickshaws.

But all the rickshaws have been taken for the moment. No more lurk below the bars.

Ma's gold wristwatch glints again in the methane light.

Pale forms glazed green materialize on the street, three men walking, their mahogany skin almost black in the darkness, contrasting sharply against the creased whites of their uniforms. Their black batons twirl casually at their wrists. Ma doesn't seem to notice them at first. The white shirts converge, casual. Their voices carry easily in the quiet night.

"You're out late."

Ma shrugs, grins queasily. "Not really. Not so late."

The three white shirts gather close. "Late for a yellow card. You should be home by now. Bad luck to be out after yellow card curfew. Especially with all that yellow gold on your wrist."

Ma holds up his hands, defensive. "I'm not a yellow card."

"Your accent says differently."

Ma reaches for his pockets, fumbles in them. "Really. You'll see. Look."

A white shirt steps close. "Did I say you could move?"

"My papers. Look—"

"Get your hands out!"

"Look at my stamps!"

"Out!" A black baton flashes. Ma yelps, clutches his elbow. More blows rain down. Ma crouches, trying to shield himself. He curses, *"Nimade bi!"*

The white shirts laugh. "That's yellow card talk." One of them swings his baton, low and fast, and Ma collapses, crying out, curling around a damaged leg. The white shirts gather close. One of them jabs Ma in the face, making him uncurl, then runs the baton down Ma's chest, dragging blood.

"He's got nicer clothes than you, Thongchai."

"Probably snuck across the border with an assful of jade."

One of them squats, studies Ma's face. "Is it true? Do you shit jade?"

Ma shakes his head frantically. He rolls over and starts to crawl away. A black runnel of blood spills from his mouth. One leg drags behind him, useless. A white shirt follows, pushes him over with his shoe and puts his foot on Ma's face. The other two suck in their breath and step back, shocked. To beat a man is one thing… "Suttipong, no."

The man called Suttipong glances back at his peers. "It's nothing. These yellow cards are as bad as blister rust. This is nothing. They all come begging, taking food when we've got little enough for our own, and look." He kicks Ma's wrist. "Gold."

Ma gasps, tries to strip the watch from his wrist. "Take it. Here. Please. Take it."

"It's not yours to give, yellow card."

"Not… yellow card," Ma gasps. "Please. Not your Ministry." His hands fumble for his pockets, frantic under the white shirt's gaze. He pulls out his papers and waves them in the hot night air.

Suttipong takes the papers, glances at them. Leans close. "You think our countrymen don't fear us, too?"

He throws the papers on the ground, then quick as a cobra he strikes. One, two, three, the blows rain down. He is very fast. Very methodical. Ma curls into a ball, trying to ward off the blows. Suttipong steps back, breathing heavily. He waves at the other two. "Teach him respect." The other two glance at each other doubtfully, but under Suttipong's urging, they are soon beating Ma, shouting encouragement to one another.

A few men come down from the pleasure bars and stumble into the streets, but when they see white uniforms they flee back inside. The white shirts are alone. And if there are other watching eyes, they do not show themselves. Finally, Suttipong seems satisfied. He kneels and strips the antique Rolex from Ma's wrist, spits on Ma's face, and motions his peers to join him. They turn away, striding close past Tranh's hiding place.

The one called Thongchai looks back. "He might complain."

Suttipong shakes his head, his attention on the Rolex in his hand. "He's learned his lesson."

Their footsteps fade into the darkness. Music filters down from the highrise clubs. The street itself is silent. Tranh watches for a long time, looking for other hunters. Nothing moves. It is as if the entire city has turned its back on the broken Malay-Chinese lying in the street. Finally, Tranh limps out of the shadows and approaches Ma Ping.

Ma catches sight of him and holds up a weak hand. "Help." He tries the words in Thai, again in *farang* English, finally in Malay, as though he has returned to his childhood. Then he seems to recognize Tranh. His eyes widen. He smiles weakly, through split bloody lips. Speaks Mandarin, their trade language of brotherhood. "*Lao pengyou.* What are you doing here?"

Tranh squats beside him, studying his cracked face. "I saw your windup girl."

Ma closes his eyes, tries to smile. "You believe me, then?" His eyes are nearly swollen shut, blood runs down from a cut in his brow, trickling freely.

"Yes."

"I think they broke my leg." He tries to pull himself upright, gasps and collapses. He probes his ribs, runs his hand down to his shin. "I can't walk." He sucks air as he prods another broken bone. "You were right about the white shirts."

"A nail that stands up gets pounded down."

Something in Tranh's tone makes Ma look up. He studies Tranh's face. "Please. I gave you food. Find me a rickshaw." One hand strays to his wrist, fumbling for the timepiece that is no longer his, trying to offer it. Trying to bargain.

Is this fate? Tranh wonders. Or luck? Tranh purses his lips, considering. Was it fate that his own shiny wristwatch drew the white shirts and their wicked black batons? Was it luck that he arrived to see Ma fall? Do he and Ma Ping still have some larger karmic business?

Tranh watches Ma beg and remembers firing a young clerk so many lifetimes ago, sending him packing with a thrashing and a warning never to return. But that was when he was a great man. And now he is such a small one. As small as the clerk he thrashed so long ago. Perhaps smaller. He slides his hands under Ma's back, lifts.

"Thank you," Ma gasps. "Thank you."

Tranh runs his fingers into Ma's pockets, working through them methodically, checking for baht the white shirts have left. Ma groans, forces out a curse as Tranh jostles him. Tranh counts his scavenge, the dregs of Ma's pockets that still look like wealth to him. He stuffs the coins into his own pocket.

Ma's breathing comes in short panting gasps. "Please. A rickshaw. That's all." He barely manages to exhale the words.

Tranh cocks his head, considering, his instincts warring with themselves. He sighs and shakes his head. "A man makes his own luck, isn't that what you told me?" He smiles tightly. "My own arrogant words, coming from a brash young mouth." He shakes his head again, astounded at his previously fat ego, and smashes his whiskey bottle on the cobbles. Glass sprays. Shards glint green in the methane light.

"If I were still a great man…" Tranh grimaces. "But then, I suppose we're both past such illusions. I'm very sorry about this." With one last glance around the darkened street, he drives the broken bottle into Ma's throat. Ma jerks and blood spills out around Tranh's hand. Tranh scuttles back, keeping this new welling of blood off his Hwang Brothers fabrics. Ma's lungs bubble and his hands reach up for the bottle lodged in his neck, then fall away. His wet breathing stops.

Tranh is trembling. His hands shake with an electric palsy. He has seen so much death, and dealt so little. And now Ma lies before him, another Malay-Chinese dead, with only himself to blame. Again. He stifles an urge to be sick.

He turns and crawls into the protective shadows of the alley and pulls himself upright. He tests his weak leg. It seems to hold him. Beyond the shadows, the street is silent. Ma's body lies like a heap of garbage in its center. Nothing moves.

Tranh turns and limps down the street, keeping to the walls, bracing himself when his knee threatens to give way. After a few blocks, the methane lamps start to go out. One by one, as though a great hand is moving down the street snuffing them, they gutter into silence as the Public Works Ministry cuts off the gas. The street settles into complete darkness.

When Tranh finally arrives at Surawong Road, its wide black thoroughfare is nearly empty of traffic. A pair of ancient water buffalo placidly haul a rubber-wheeled wagon under starlight. A shadow farmer rides behind them, muttering softly. The yowls of mating devil cats scrape the hot night air, but that is all.

And then, from behind, the creak of bicycle chains. The rattle of wheels on cobbles. Tranh turns, half-expecting avenging white shirts, but it is only a cycle rickshaw, chattering down the darkened street. Tranh raises a hand, flashing newfound baht. The rickshaw slows. A man's ropey limbs gleam with moonlit sweat. Twin earrings decorate his lobes, gobs of silver in the night. "Where you going?"

Tranh scans the rickshaw man's broad face for hints of betrayal, for hints that he is a hunter, but the man is only looking at the baht in Tranh's hand. Tranh forces down his paranoia and climbs into the rickshaw's seat. "The *farang* factories. By the river."

The rickshaw man glances over his shoulder, surprised. "All the factories will be closed. Too much energy to run at night. It's all black night down there."

"It doesn't matter. There's a job opening. There will be interviews."

The man stands on his pedals. "At night?"

"Tomorrow." Tranh settles deeper into his seat. "I don't want to be late."

SOFTER

Jonathan Lilly slumped in hot water up to his neck and studied his dead wife. She half-floated at the far end of the bath, soap bubbles wreathing her Nordic face. Blond hair clung to bloodless skin. Her half-lidded eyes stared at the ceiling. Jonathan rearranged his position, shoving Pia's tangling legs aside to make more room for himself and wondered if this peaceful moment between crime and confession would make any difference in his sentencing.

He knew he should turn himself in. Let someone know that the day had gone wrong in Denver's Congress Park Neighborhood. Maybe it wouldn't be that bad. He might not even be in prison for so very long. He'd read somewhere that pot growers got more prison time than murderers, and he vaguely remembered that murder laws might provide leeway for unintended deaths like this one. Was it manslaughter? Murder in the second degree? He stirred soap suds, considering.

He'd have to Google it.

When he first jammed the pillow over Pia's face she hadn't fought at all. She might have even laughed. Might have mumbled something from under the pillow's cotton swaddle: "Cut it out," maybe, or "Get off." Or perhaps she told him he wasn't getting out of dish duty. That was what they'd been arguing about: the dishes in the sink from the night before.

She rolled over and said, "You forgot to do the dishes last night," and gave him a little nudge with her elbow. A little push to get him moving. The words. The elbow. And then he jammed the pillow over her face and her hands had come up and gently pushed against him, coaxing him to let her go, and it was all a joke.

Even he thought so.

He'd meant to lift the pillow and laugh and go start scrubbing dishes. And for one fragile crystal moment that had seemed possible. Purple lilac scent had slipped in through the half-opened windows and bees buzzed outside and lazy Sunday morning sunshine streamed in between shade slats. They lived lifetimes inside that moment. They laughed off the incident and went out for eggs Benedict at Le Central; they got a divorce after another fifteen years of marriage; they had four children and argued over whether Milo was a better baby name than Alistair; Pia turned out to be gay, but they worked it out; he had an affair, but they worked it out; she planted sunflowers and tomatoes and zucchini in their back-yard garden and he went to work on Monday and got a promotion.

He meant to take the pillow off her face.

But then Pia started struggling and screaming and beating on him with her fists and children and tomato plants and Le Central and a hundred other futures blew away like dandelion seeds and Jonathan suddenly couldn't bear to let her up. He couldn't stand to see the hurt and horror in her gray eyes when he lifted the pillow, the rancid version of himself that he knew he'd find reflected there, so he threw all his weight onto her struggling body and jammed the pillow hard over her face and rode her down to Hell.

She twisted and flailed. Her nails slashed his cheek. Her body bucked. She almost squeezed out from under him, twisting like an eel, but he pinned her again and buried her screams in the pillow as her hands scrabbled at his eyes. He turned his face away and let her rip at his neck. She thrashed like a fish but she couldn't force him off and suddenly he wanted to laugh. He was winning. For once in his life he was really winning.

Her hands whipped from his face to the pillow and back, an animal's panicked thoughtless movements. Gasping coughs filtered through the down. Her chest pumped convulsively, striving to suck air through the pillow. Her nails nicked his ear. She was losing coordination. She'd stopped bucking. Her body still writhed, but now it was easy to keep her trapped. It was only the muscle memories of struggle. He pressed harder with the pillow, putting his entire weight into killing her.

Her hands stopped scratching. They returned to the smothering pillow and touched it gently. A querying caress. As if they were a pair of creatures utterly separate from her, pale butterflies trying to discover the cause of their owner's distress. Two dumb insects trying to understand the nature of an airway obstruction.

Outside, a lawn mower buzzed to life, cutting back spring greenery. A meadowlark sang. Pia's body went slack and her hands fell away. Bright sunlight traced lazily across her blond hair where it tangled in the pillow and spread across the sheets. Slowly he became aware of wetness, the warmth of her releasing bladder.

Another lawnmower buzzed alive.

White soapsuds swirled, revealing one of Pia's pink nipples. Jonathan scooped up a blob of crackling bubbles and laid it gently over the breast, covering her again. He'd used half a bottle of moisturizing bath liquid, but still the bubbles kept fading, revealing her body and its increasing paleness as the blood settled deeper into her limbs. Her eyes stared away into the ceiling distance, at whatever things dead people saw.

Gray eyes. He'd thought they were creepy when he first met her. By the time he married her, he liked them. And now they were creepy again, half-lidded, staring at nothing. He wanted to lean over and close them, but hated the thought that rigor mortis might make them spring wide again. That he might find her staring at him, after he had pressed them closed. He shivered. He knew it was morbid to soak in the bathtub with his dead wife, but he didn't want to leave her. He still wanted to be close. He'd been washing her death-soiled body, and suddenly it had seemed so right, so appropriate, that he should climb in with her. That he should mutter an apology and climb into the overfilled tub and join her in a final soak. And so here he was in a cooling bath with a cooling corpse and all the consequences of his repressed angers settling heavy upon him.

He blamed spring sunshine.

If it had been a cloudy day, Pia would now be drawing up grocery lists instead of squeezed into the bath with her killer husband, her stiffening legs shoved to one side.

She'd never liked taking baths together. Didn't like having her space imposed on. It was her quiet time. A time to forget the irritations of a purchasing department that could never get its sourcing priorities in order. A time to close her eyes and relax completely. He'd respected that. Just like he respected her predilection for Amish quilts on their bed and her affection for wildlife photos on the walls and her pathological hatred of avocado. But now here they both were, sharing a tub that she'd never liked sharing, with her blood pooling into her ass and her face slipping under water every so often so that he had to shove her upright again, shove her up out of the suds like a whale surfacing, and every time her face came out of the water he expected her to gasp for air and ask what the fuck he'd been thinking keeping her down so long.

Sunshine. After months of winter gray and drizzling spring it had suddenly turned warm. That was the cause. The elms had budded green and the lilacs had bloomed purple and after years of gritted-teeth dutiful attendance to work and marriage and home ownership and oil changes, he woke to a day permeated with electric possibility. He woke up smiling.

The last time he remembered feeling so alive he'd been in fifth grade with a beat-up blue BMX that he'd raced through subdivision streets—jumping curbs and stealing chromie caps all the way—to pour his entire allowance into Three Musketeers, Nerds, and Bubblicious at a 7-Eleven.

And then Pia had rolled over and poked him with her elbow and reminded him that he'd forgotten to do the dishes.

Jonathan stirred the bath water. Their naked bodies rippled under the thinning suds: his pink, hers increasingly pale. He leaned out of the tub, jostling Pia's body and almost immersing her before he got hold of the bubble bath. He held the bottle high and let soap spill into the water, a viscous emerald tangle that trailed over her legs. He upended the bottle completely. *Green Tea Essence: Skin Revitalizing. Aloe, Cucumber and Green Tea extracts. Soaks away Tension, Softens and Moisturizes Skin, Revitalizes Spirit.* He tossed the empty bottle on the floor and turned on the water again. Scalding heat poured over his shoulders, filling the tub and gurgling down its overflow spout. He leaned back and closed his eyes.

He supposed this fit some pattern of domestic violence, some statistical map of human behavior. The FBI kept statistics: a murder every twenty minutes, a rape every fifteen, a shoplifting every thirty seconds. Someone had to kill their wife every so often to make the statistics work. It just turned out to be him. Statistical duty. In his job, he expected a certain amount of instability from the servers, from the hardware and software that hosted the applications he wrote. He planned for it. Just like the FBI did. Shit happens. While his friends were catching the last of Colorado spring skiing, or running to Home Depot for renovation projects, he was fulfilling statistical requirements.

From where he lay, he could just make out blue sky through the high bathroom window. The optimistic blue, infused with gaudy unrestrained sunshine. All he'd wanted was to do something nice with that sunshine. To go for a jog. Or a bike ride. Or go for brunch and read the paper.

And then Pia said there were dishes to do and all he could think about was that: the scabby lasagna pan, the stained sauce pots, the filmy wine glasses, the bread board crumbs, and the dishwasher that he'd also forgotten to run so he'd have to do more dishes by hand. And dishes led to taxes, April 15 bearing down on him like a tank. He should have talked to his investment advisor about his 401(k) but now it was Sunday and there wasn't anything he could do, and he'd probably forget again on Monday. And that led to the electric and phone bills that he'd forgotten to mail and that he should have set up for direct deposit but he kept blowing it off and now there was probably going to be a service fee and then there was his laptop lying on the living room floor where he'd dumped it, a beartrap of billable hours just waiting to get its jaws latched onto his leg. The Astai Networks project kept refusing to compile and his demo was set for eleven on Monday and he had no idea why the program was suddenly so completely screwed.

Lately, he'd been looking at Starbucks baristas and wishing he had their jobs. Tall, grande, latte, cappuccino, skinny, whatever. Not much complexity there. And when you left work at the end of the day you didn't have to think about a fucking thing. Who cared if they made shit for money? At least they wouldn't have to pay much in tax.

Taxes. Did murderers even do taxes? What was the IRS going to do? Arrest him now?

Jonathan frowned at the thought of arrest. He should call the police. Or Pia's mother, at least. Maybe 911? But that was for emergencies. And while the murder had been an emergency, this slow, soaking aftermath wasn't. He stared at Pia's dead body. He should cry. He should feel bad for her. Or at least for himself. He put wet fists in his eyes and waited for tears, but they didn't come.

Why can't I cry?

She's dead. Dead as doornail. You killed Pia. Everything about her is gone. She won't wear that blue and red peasant skirt you bought for her in San Francisco. She won't ask for a German shepherd puppy again. She won't call her mother and talk for three hours about whether to plant acorn squash or zucchini in the back yard.

He kept listing things that Pia wouldn't do again: no more lectures about flossing, no more holding hands after movies, no more Jelly Bellies and reading in bed… but it felt like a farce, just like the tears. A bit of play-acting, in case God was watching.

He pulled his knuckles from his eyes and stared up at the ceiling. *It was an accident.* He closed his eyes and concentrated on God, whatever

God was supposed to be like: a man with a white beard, some fat woman Gaia thing like in some of Pia's books, some round Buddha guy from when she'd been on her meditation kick.

I didn't mean to kill her. Really. You know that already, don't You? I didn't want to kill her. Forgive me, Father, for I have sinned…

He gave it up. He felt like he had when he'd been busted for stealing candy from the 7-Eleven after his allowance ran out. Faking the crying. Acting like he cared even though he couldn't summon sincerity. Mostly just wishing that they hadn't noticed the bandolier of Pez dangling from his pocket. He knew he should care. He did care, dammit. He didn't think Pia deserved to die with a pillow over her face and shit in her panties. He wanted to blame her nagging, but he was clearly the one in the wrong. But mostly he just felt… what?

Angry?

Frustrated?

Trapped?

Lost and without redemption?

He laughed to himself. That last one sounded trite.

Mostly he felt surprised. Stunned by his world's complete realignment: a life without a wife or taxes or a Monday morning deadline. *I'm a murderer.*

He tried the thought out again, saying it out loud. "I'm a murderer." Trying to make it mean something to him other than that he wasn't going to bother with the dinner dishes now.

A knock sounded at the front door.

Jonathan blinked, returning to the world around him: the dead wife rubbing against his hip, the cooling water. His hands were wrinkled with the bath. How long had he been soaking? The knocking came again. Louder. A thumping, insistent and authoritative. The police knocked like that.

Jonathan leaped out of the bath and ran dripping across the floor-boards to peek out between the shades. He expected cruisers and red and blue strobing lights and the neighbors all standing out on their porches, watching the drama unfold right on their quiet tree-lined street. A murder in the Denver suburbs. Instead, all he saw was his neighbor, Gabrielle Roberts. Gabby. A hyper-kinetic get-things-accomplished kind of girl he kept hoping would eventually be worn down by the disappointments of everyday life.

She spited him with summer mountain-biking expeditions, winter snow-boarding jaunts, a continuous stream of home improvement projects, and apparent pleasure in a job that had to do with telecom customer relations, the kind of thing that seemed perfect for deadening the soul, and which she nonetheless seemed to love.

She stood on the porch, black ponytail twitching, brows wrinkling as she leaned forward and beat on the door again. Bouncing from one foot to the other, moving to some internal techno beat that only she could hear. She had on shorts and a sweaty T-shirt that said "Marathoners Go Longer," along with soiled leather gloves.

Jonathan grimaced. Another home improvement project, then. He'd helped her move flagstones into her back yard one hot summer day a few years past, and she'd nearly broken him doing it. Pia had given him a back massage afterward and reminded him that he didn't have to do everything that people asked, but when Gabby had shown up at the door, he hadn't known how to refuse her. And now here she was again.

Couldn't she just stop and do nothing for a day? And why now, with Pia's body floating in the bath less than twenty feet away? How was he going to keep Gabby quiet? Would he have to kill her too? How would he do it? Not with a pillow, that was for sure. Gabby was fit. Hell, she was probably stronger than he was. A kitchen knife, maybe? If he could get her into the kitchen before she saw Pia in the bathtub, he could put a knife to her throat. She wouldn't be expecting that…

He shook off the thought. He didn't want to kill Gabby. He didn't want a mountain of bodies and blood piling up around him. He wanted this all to be over. He'd just tell Gabby what happened, she'd run screaming and call the cops, and he could wait on the front porch for them to arrive. Problem solved. They'd find him sitting in his bathrobe and his wife macerating in the tub and he'd go to jail for murder one, two, three, or four, or whatever it was and the neighbors would get their show.

They seemed like such a perfect couple.

But they were both so nice.

We had them take care of our cats when we went to Belize last year.

Fine. Bath time was over. Real life was starting up again. Time to face the music. He went to find a bathrobe and came back just as Gabby hammered on the door again.

"Hey! Jon!" Gabby grinned as he opened the door. "Didn't mean to wake you. Lazy Sunday?"

"I just killed my wife."

"Could I borrow your shovel? Mine broke."

Jonathan goggled. Gabby bounced expectantly.

Had he confessed or not? He thought he had. But Gabby wasn't running and screaming for the cops. She was breaking the script completely. She was bouncing back and forth from the ball of one foot to the other and looking at him like a golden retriever. He replayed the exchange in his mind. Had she not heard? Or had he not said it?

Gabby said, "You look really hungover. Late night last night?"

Jonathan tried to confess again, but the words lodged in his throat. Maybe he hadn't said it the first time. Maybe he'd only thought it. He rubbed his eyes. "What did you say you wanted?"

"I broke my shovel. Can I borrow yours?"

"You broke it?"

"Not on purpose. I tried to pry a rock out of the back yard and the handle snapped."

I killed my wife. She's soaking in the tub right now. Could you call the cops for me? I can't decide whether I should call 911 or the police department's main line. Or if maybe I should just wait until Monday and call a lawyer first. What do you think? Finally he said, "Pia had a shovel in the back shed. You want me to get it?"

"That would be great. Where's Pia?"

"In the tub."

Gabby seemed to notice Jonathan's bathrobe for the first time. Her eyes widened. "Oh. Sorry. I didn't mean to—"

"It's not what you think."

Gabby waved her hand, embarrassed, and stepped back from the open door. "I shouldn't have barged over here. I should have called. I didn't mean to interrupt things. I can get the shovel myself if you tell me where it is."

"Umm. Okay. You can go around through the side gate. It's in the shed, hanging off pegs by the door." Why didn't he come clean? He just kept playing the charade, pretending that he was still the man he'd been a few hours before.

"Thanks a ton. Sorry for barging in." Gabby turned and bounded down the steps, leaving Jonathan standing in the open doorway. He closed the door. Gabby's ponytail flashed briefly outside the living room window as she jogged past and slipped into the back yard. Jonathan wandered back into the bathroom and sat on the toilet's edge. Pia was floating.

"Nobody really cares, do they honey?"

He studied her stiffened body and then turned the faucet to add more hot water. Steam rose. He shook his head, watching as it poured into the tub. "No one pays any attention at all."

People died all the time. And yet people still did their chores and went to the store for their groceries and dug rocks out of their back yards. Life went on. The sun was still bright outside and the lilac-scented air was still there and it was still a beautiful day, and he wasn't going to have to do his taxes ever again. He shut off the water. Electric energy tingled in his limbs, an antsy youthful hunger for sun and movement. It really was a wonderful day for a jog.

The nice thing about completely ruining your life, Jonathan decided, was that it was finally possible to enjoy it. As he ran past his neighbors and waved and called out to them, he thought about how little they truly understood about how glorious this warm spring day had become. It was a thousand times better than he'd even guessed when he woke up in the morning. The last day of freedom felt so much better than a million days of daily grind. Sunny days were wasted on the guilt-free. Warm spring air enfolded him as he ran. He stopped at every stop sign, jogging in place and luxuriating in a world that was exactly the same as it had always been, except for his place in it.

It almost felt as if he was jogging for the first time. He felt every sweet breeze, smelled every bright flower, and saw every warm person and they were all beautiful and he missed them all terribly. He observed them from an incredible distance, and yet with extraordinary clarity, as if he was viewing them with a powerful telescope from the surface of Mars.

He ran and ran and sweated and gasped and rested and ran again and he loved it all. He wondered if this was what it was to be Buddhist. If this was what Pia had sought in her meditations. This centered sense, this knowledge that all was transient, that everything was effervescent and lost so easily. Perhaps it would never have existed, except for this sudden nostalgic love spurred on because he was about to lose it all. God, it felt good to run. To simply work every muscle and feel the pavement hit his shoes, to see the trees with their newly greened neon leaves, and to feel for once that he was paying attention to it all.

He kept waiting for someone to notice his difference, to recognize the fact that he was now a murderer, but no one did. He stopped at a 7-Eleven and bought a bottle of Gatorade, grinning at the clerk as he got his change and thinking, *I'm a murderer. I smothered my wife this morning.* But the old man behind the counter didn't notice Jonathan's scarlet letter M.

In fact, as Jonathan chugged his green electrolytes, he suddenly felt that he was not at all different from this lovely man behind the counter with his orange vest and corporate convenience logo on his back. He had the feeling that he could invite the wrinkled guy home and they could pull a couple bottles of Fat Tire Ale out of the fridge, or if the old man preferred something lighter, PBRs perhaps, whatever the guy wanted, they'd open their cans of watery beer and they'd go into the back yard and lie on the grass and soak up sunshine, and at some point Jonathan would mention casually that his dead wife was soaking in the bathtub and the man would nod and say, "Oh yes, I did something similar with mine. Do you mind if I take a look?"

And they would both go back inside and stand in the bathroom's doorway, studying Jonathan's floating lily and the clerk would nod his snowy head thoughtfully and suggest that she'd probably prefer to be buried in the back yard, in her garden.

After all, that was what his own wife had wanted, and she'd been a gardener, too.

On Monday, Jonathan emptied his bank accounts and IRAs and changed everything into cash: fifty and hundred dollar bills, fat wads of them that he stuffed into a messenger bag so that he walked out of the bank carrying $112,398. His life savings. The wages of sin. The profits of dutiful financial planning. The clerk had asked if he was getting a divorce, and he blushed and nodded and said it was something like that, but she didn't stop him from clearing out the account, and mostly seemed to think it was funny that he was beating his wife to the punch. He almost asked her on a date, before he remembered the reason she was counting all that cash onto the counter for him.

He came home and dropped his bag on the couch and carried the phone into the bathroom to sit with Pia while he bought himself some time. He called his job and told them his wife had family troubles and that he needed to take vacation and sick time early. Sorry about the Astai demo. Naeem could probably sort it out. He told a few of his and Pia's friends that Pia had a family emergency, and that she'd flown back to Illinois, to help. He notified Pia's work, saying that she'd be in touch when she knew more about what kind of emergency leave she might need. He chatted with Pia's parents and told them he was taking her on a surprise vacation for their anniversary and that phone service in Turkey would be unreliable. Every conversation closed doors of friendly inquiry. Every conversation lengthened the time between suspicion and discovery.

The steadiness of his voice surprised him. Somehow it was hard to be nervous when the worst was already done. He bought a pair of plane tickets in his and Pia's names to Cambodia with a departure a month away. From Vancouver, just to confuse things a little more. And when he was done, he made himself a gin and tonic and sat and soaked with Pia one last time in her macerate. There was a smell about her now, the rot of her guts, the gasses of her belly. The ruin wreaked by hot water on dead flesh. But he soaked with her anyway and apologized as best he could for remaking his life via her dead body. Then he went over and reclaimed his shovel from Gabby.

By the light of a few alley street lamps, he buried Pia in the back yard under a part of the garden. He left a note for the police, describing generally what had happened—including an apology—for when he was finally caught and needed some faceless court to forgive him and let him out in less time than they would have demanded of a pot grower. He scattered sunflower and poppy and morning glory seeds on the mound and thought that the 7-Eleven clerk would approve.

That night, he drove across the mountains. He wondered if he had finally crossed the line between Manslaughter and Murder, or Murder Two and Murder One, but didn't really care. A bit of travel just seemed in order. A long vacation before a longer prison sentence. Really, it wasn't much different from changing jobs. A bit of a break before the new job started.

He sold his car in Las Vegas for another five thousand in cash, pretending to be a gambling junkie sure his luck would turn around. Then he struck off down the road, headed for the interstate and the wider world beyond.

On a desert on-ramp he stuck out his thumb. He wondered if his luck would keep holding and then he wondered how much he really cared. He marveled that he had ever worried about something as trivial as a 401(k) allocation. He was on the road to Mexico with its sun and sand and pleasant rhythms and... who knew? Perhaps he would be caught. Or perhaps he would simply disappear into his strange new life.

Jonathan had once read that Japanese samurai lived as if they had already died. But he doubted even they had any idea what that really felt like. Standing beside the hot Nevada interstate with gritty winds and big rigs blowing past him, he thought he might have an inkling.

By the time he'd pulled Pia from the bath and buried her, he'd feared she would fall apart from all her soaking. His mother used to say that if you stayed in a bath too long you'd shrivel up and disappear. But Pia had held together all right, even after a couple days. She was gone, but still recognizable. He, on the other hand, was still around—and yet utterly changed.

A sporty RAV4 hit the on-ramp. It whipped past him in a flash of white, then slowed suddenly and pulled onto the margin. Jonathan jogged after it, his messenger bag of cash jouncing against his hip. He yanked open the little SUV's door. A kid with a crushed cowboy hat studied him through mirrored Ray-Bans.

"Where you headed?"

"San Diego?"

"You pay gas?"

Jonathan couldn't help grinning. "Yeah. I think I can help with that."

The kid motioned him in, gunned the little engine and accelerated onto the highway.

"What are you doing in San Diego?"

"I'm actually going to Mexico. Somewhere with beaches."

"I'm going to Cabo for spring break. Gonna get drunk, suck titties, and go native."

"Sounds nice."

"Yeah man. It's gonna be great."

The kid cranked up the stereo and whipped the RAV4 into the passing lane, zipping past eighteen-wheelers and late weekend traffic returning from Vegas to L.A.

Jonathan rolled down the window, reclined his seat, and closed his eyes as the stereo throbbed and the kid yammered on about how he wanted to be in a skateboard video someday and how much he was going to get laid in Mexico and how you could buy phat weed down there for nothing.

The miles sped by. Jonathan let himself relax and think again about Pia. When he pulled her from the bath, he'd been amazed at how soft her skin had become.

The next time he got married, he hoped he'd be softer, too.

PUMP SIX

The first thing I saw Thursday morning when I walked into the kitchen was Maggie's ass sticking up in the air. Not a bad way to wake up, really. She's got a good figure, keeps herself in shape, so a morning eyeful of her pretty bottom pressed against a black mesh nightie is generally a positive way to start the day.

Except that she had her head in the oven. And the whole kitchen smelled like gas. And she had a lighter with a blue flame six inches high that she was waving around inside the oven like it was a Tickle Monkey revival concert.

"Jesus Christ, Maggie! What the hell are you doing?"

I dove across the kitchen, grabbed a handful of nightie and yanked hard. Her head banged as she came out of the oven. Frying pans rattled on the stovetop and she dropped her lighter. It skittered across the tuffscuff, ending up in a corner. "Owwwwww!" She grabbed her head. "Oooowwww!"

She spun around and slapped me. "What the fuck did you do that for?" She raked her nails across my cheek then went for my eyes. I shoved her away. She slammed into the wall and spun, ready to come back again. "What's the matter with you?" she yelled. "You pissed off you couldn't get it up last night? Now you want to knock me around instead?" She grabbed the cast-iron skillet off the stovetop, dumping NiftyFreeze bacon all over the burners. "You want to try again, trogwad? Huh? You want to?" She waved the pan, threatening, and started for me. "Come on then!"

I jumped back, rubbing my cheek where she'd gouged me. "You're crazy! I keep you from getting yourself blown up and you want to beat my head in?"

"I was making your damn breakfast!" She ran her fingers through her black tangled hair and showed me blood. "You broke my damn head!"

"I saved your dumb ass is what I did." I turned and started shoving the kitchen windows open, letting the gas escape. A couple of the windows were just cardboard curtains that were easy to pull free, but one of the remaining whole windows was really stuck.

"You sonofabitch!"

I turned just in time to dodge the skillet. I yanked it out of her hands and shoved her away, hard, then went back to opening windows. She came back, trying to get around in front of me as I pushed the windows open. Her nails were all over my face, scratching and scraping. I pushed her away again and waved the skillet when she tried to come back. "You want me to use this?"

She backed off, eyes on the pan. She circled. "That's all you got to say to me? 'I saved your dumb ass'?" Her face was red with anger. "How about 'Thanks for trying to fix the stove, Maggie,' or 'Thanks for giving a damn about whether I get a decent breakfast before work, Maggie.'" She hawked snot and spat, missing me and hitting the wall, then gave me the finger. "Make your own damn breakfast. See if I try to help you again."

I stared at her. "You're dumber than a sack of trogs, you know that?" I waved the skillet toward the stove. "Checking a gas leak with a lighter? Do you even have a brain in there? Hello? Hello?"

"Don't talk to me like that! You're the trogwad—" She choked off mid-sentence and sat, suddenly, like she'd been hit in the head with a chunk of concrete rain. Just plopped on the yellow tuffscuff. Completely stunned.

"Oh." She looked up at me, wide-eyed. "I'm sorry, Trav. I didn't even think of that." She stared at her lighter where it lay in the corner. "Oh, shit. Wow." She put her head in her hands. "Oh… Wow."

She started to hiccup, then to cry. When she looked up at me again, her big brown eyes were full of tears. "I'm so sorry. I'm really really sorry." The tears started rolling, pouring off her cheeks. "I had no idea. I just didn't think. I…"

I was still ready to fight, but seeing her sitting on the floor, all forlorn and lost and apologetic took it out of me.

"Forget it." I dropped the pan on the stove and went back to jamming open the windows. A breeze started moving through, and the gas stink faded. When we had some decent air circulation, I pulled the stove out from the wall. Bacon was scattered all over the burners, limp and thawed now that it was out of its NiftyFreeze cellophane, strips of pork lying everywhere, marbled and glistening with fat. Maggie's idea of a home-made breakfast. My granddad would have loved her. He was a big believer in breakfasts. Except for the NiftyFreeze. He hated those wrappers.

Maggie saw me staring at the bacon. "Can you fix the stove?"

"Not right now. I've got to get to work."

She wiped her eyes with the palm of her hand. "Waste of bacon," she said. "Sorry."

"No big deal."

"I had to go to six different stores to find it. That was the last package, and they didn't know when they were going to get more."

I didn't have anything to say to that. I found the gas shut-off and closed it. Sniffed. Then sniffed all around the stove and the rest of kitchen.

The gas smell was almost gone.

For the first time, I noticed my hands were shaking. I tried to get a coffee packet out of the cabinet and dropped it. It hit the counter with a water balloon plop. I set my twitching hands flat on the counter and leaned on them, hard, trying to make them go still. My elbows started shaking instead. It's not every morning you almost get yourself blown up.

It was kind of funny, though, when I thought about it. Half the time, the gas didn't even work. And on the one day it did, Maggie decided to play repairman. I had to suppress a giggle.

Maggie was still in the middle of the floor, snuffling. "I'm really sorry," she said again.

"It's okay. Forget it." I took my hands off the counter. They weren't flapping around anymore. That was something. I ripped open the coffee packet and chugged its liquid cold. After the rest of the morning, the caffeine was calming.

"No, I'm really sorry. I could have got us both killed."

I wanted to say something nasty but there wasn't any point. It just would have been cruel. "Well, you didn't. So it's okay." I pulled out a chair and sat down and looked out the open windows. The city's sky was turning from yellow dawn smog to a gray-blue morning smog. Down below, people were just starting their day. Their noises filtered up: Kids shouting on their way to school. Hand carts clattering on their way to deliveries. The grind of some truck's engine, clanking and squealing and sending up black clouds of exhaust that wafted in through the window along with summer heat. I fumbled for my inhaler and took a hit, then made myself smile at Maggie. "It's like that time you tried to clean the electric outlet with a fork. You just got to remember not to look for gas leaks with a fire. It's not a good idea."

Wrong thing to say, I guess. Or wrong tone of voice.

Maggie's waterworks started again: not just the snuffling and the tears, but the whole bawling squalling release thing, water pouring down her face, her nose getting all runny and her saying, "I'm sorry, I'm sorry, I'm sorry," over and over again, like a Ya Lu aud sample, but without the subsonic thump that would have made it fun to listen to.

I stared at the wall for a while, trying to wait it out, and thought about getting my earbug and listening to some real Ya Lu, but I didn't want to wear out the battery because it took a while to find good ones, and anyway, it didn't seem right to duck out while she was bawling. So I sat there while she kept crying, and then I finally sucked it up and got down on the floor next to her and held her while she wore herself out.

Finally she stopped crying and started wiping her eyes. "I'm sorry. I'll remember."

She must have seen my expression because she got more insistent. "Really. I will." She used the shoulder of her nightie on her runny nose. "I must look awful."

She looked puffy and red-eyed and snotty. I said, "You look fine. Great. You look great."

"Liar." She smiled, then shook her head. "I didn't mean to melt down like that. And the frying pan…" She shook her head again. "I must be PMS-ing."

"You take a Gynoloft?"

"I don't want to mess with my hormones. You know, just in case…" She shook her head again. "I keep thinking maybe this time, but…" She shrugged. "Never mind. I'm a mess." She leaned against me again and went quiet for a little bit. I could feel her breathing. "I just keep hoping," she said finally.

I stroked her hair. "If it's meant to happen, it will. We've just got to stay optimistic."

"Sure. That's up to God. I know that. I just keep hoping."

"It took Miku and Gabe three years. We've been trying, what, six months?"

"A year, month after next." She was quiet, then said, "Lizzi and Pearl only had miscarriages."

"We've got a ways to go before we start worrying about miscarriages." I disentangled and went hunting for another coffee packet in the cabinets.

This one I actually took the time to shake. It heated itself and I tore it open and sipped. Not as good as the little brewer I found for Maggie at the flea market so she could make coffee on the stove, but it was a damn sight better than being blown to bits.

Maggie was getting herself arranged, getting up off the floor and starting to bustle around. Even all puffy faced, she still looked good in that mesh nightie: lots of skin, lots of interesting shadows.

She caught me watching her. "What are you smiling at?"

I shrugged. "You look nice in that nightie."

"I got it from that lady's estate sale, downstairs. It's hardly even used."

I leered. "I like it."

She laughed. "Now? You couldn't last night or the night before, but now you want to do it?"

I shrugged.

"You're going to be late as it is." She turned and started rustling in the cabinets herself. "You want a brekkie bar? I found a whole bunch of them when I was shopping for the bacon. I guess their factory is working again." She tossed one before I could answer. I caught it and tore off the smiling foil wrapper and read the ingredients while I ate. Fig and Nut, and then a whole bunch of nutrients like dextro-forma-albuterolhyde. Not as neat as the chemicals that thaw NiftyFreeze packets, but what the hell, it's all nutritional, right?

Maggie turned and studied the stove where I'd marooned it. With hot morning air blowing in from the windows, the bacon was getting limper and greasier by the second. I thought about taking it downstairs and frying it on the sidewalk. If nothing else, I could feed it to the trogs. Maggie was pinching her lip. I expected her to say something about the stove or the wasting bacon, but instead she said, "We're going out for drinks with Nora tonight. She wants to go to Wicky."

"Pus girl?"

"That's not funny."

I jammed the rest of the brekkie bar into my mouth. "It is to me. I warned both of you. That water's not safe for anything."

She made a face. "Well nothing happened to me, smarty pants. We all looked at it and it wasn't yellow or sludgy or anything—"

"So you jumped right in and went swimming. And now she's got all those funny zits on her. How mysterious." I finished the second coffee packet and tossed it and the brekkie bar wrapper down the disposal and ran some water to wash them down. In another half hour, they'd be whirling and dissolving in the belly of Pump Two. "You can't go thinking something's clean, just because it looks clear. You got lucky." I wiped my hands and went over to her. I ran my fingers up her hips. "Yep. Lucky. Still no reaction."

She slapped my hands away. "What, you're a doctor, now?"

"Specializing in skin creams…"

"Don't be gross. I told Nora to meet us at eight. Can we go to Wicky?"

I shrugged. "I doubt it. It's pretty exclusive."

"But Max owes you—" she broke off as she caught me leering at her again. "Oh. Right."

"What do you say?"

She shook her head and grinned. "I should be glad, after the last couple nights."

"Exactly." I leaned down and kissed her.

When she finally pulled back, she looked up at me with those big brown eyes of hers and the whole bad morning just melted away. "You're going to be late," she said.

But her body was up against mine, and she wasn't slapping my hands away anymore.

Summer in New York is one of my least favorite times. The heat sits down between the buildings, choking everything, and the air just… stops. You smell everything. Plastics melting into hot concrete, garbage burning, old urine that effervesces into the air when someone throws water into the gutter; just the plain smell of so many people living all packed together. Like all the skyscrapers are sweating alcoholics after a binge, standing there exhausted and oozing with the evidence of every-thing they've been up to. It drives my asthma nuts. Some days, I take three hits off the inhaler just to get to work.

About the only good thing about summer is that it isn't spring so at least you don't have freeze-thaw dropping concrete rain down on your head.

I cut across the park just to give my lungs a break from the ooze and stink, but it wasn't much of an improvement. Even with the morning heat still building up, the trees looked dusty and tired, all their leaves drooping, and there were big brown patches on the grass where the green had just given up for the summer, like bald spots on an old dog.

The trogs were out in force, lying in the grass, lolling around in the dust and sun, enjoying another summer day with nothing to do. The weather was bringing them out. I stopped to watch them frolicking—all hairy and horny without any concerns at all.

A while back someone started a petition to get rid of them, or at least to get them spayed, but the mayor came out and said that they had some rights, too. After all, they were somebody's kids, even if no one was admitting it. He even got the police to stop beating them up so much, which made the tabloids go crazy. They all said he had a trog love child hidden in Connecticut. But after a few years, people got used to having them around. And the tabloids went out of business, so the mayor didn't care what they said about his love children anymore.

These days, the trogs are just part of the background, a whole parkful of mash-faced monkey people shambling around with bright yellow eyes and big pink tongues and not nearly enough fur to survive in the wild. When winter hits, they either freeze in piles or migrate down to warmer places. But every summer there's more of them.

When Maggie and I first started trying to have a baby, I had a nightmare that Maggie had a trog. She was holding it and smiling, right after the delivery, all sweaty and puffy and saying, "Isn't it beautiful? Isn't it beautiful?" and then she handed the sucker to me. And the scary thing wasn't that it was a trog; the scary thing was trying to figure out how I was going to explain to everyone at work that we were keeping it. Because I loved that little squash-faced critter. I guess that's what being a parent is all about.

That dream scared me limp for a month. Maggie put me on perkies because of it.

A trog sidled up. It—or he or she, or whatever you call a hermaphrodite critter with boobs and a big sausage—made kissy faces at me. I just smiled and shook my head and decided that it was a him because of his hairy back, and because he actually had that sausage, instead of just a little pencil like some of them have. The trog took the rejection pretty well. He just smiled and shrugged. That's one nice thing about them: they may be dumber than hamsters, but they're pleasant-natured. Nicer than most of the people I work with, really. Way nicer than some people you meet in the subway.

The trog wandered off, touching himself and grunting, and I kept going across the park. On the other side, I walked down a couple blocks to Freedom Street and then down the stairs into the command substation.

Chee was waiting for me when I unlocked the gates to let myself in. "Alvarez! You're late, man."

Chee's a nervous skinny little guy with suspenders and red hair slicked straight back over a bald spot. He always has this acrid smell around him because of this steroid formula he uses on the bald spot, which makes his hair grow all right for a while, but then he starts picking at it compulsively and it all falls out and he has to start all over with the steroids, and in the meantime, he smells like the Hudson. And whatever the gel is, it makes his skull shine like a polished bowling ball. We used to tell him to stop using the stuff, but he'd go all rabid and try to bite you if you kept it up for long.

"You're late," he said again. He was scratching his head like an epileptic monkey trying to groom himself.

"Yeah? So?" I got my work jacket out of my locker and pulled it on. The fluorescents were all dim and flickery, but climate control was running, so the interior was actually pretty bearable, for once.

"Pump Six is broken."

"Broken how?"

Chee shrugged. "I don't know. It's stopped."

"Is it making a noise? Is it stopped all the way? Is it going slowly? Is it flooding? Come on, help me out."

Chee looked at me blankly. Even his head-picking stopped, for a second.

"You try looking at the troubleshooting indexes?" I asked.

Chee shrugged. "Didn't think of it."

"How many times have I told you, that's the first thing you do? How long has it been out?"

"Since midnight?" He screwed up his face, thinking. "No, since ten."

"You switch the flows over?"

He hit his forehead with the palm of his hand. "Forgot."

I started to run. "The entire Upper West Side doesn't have sewage processing since LAST NIGHT? Why didn't you call me?"

Chee jogged after me, dogging my heels as we ran through the plant's labyrinth to the control rooms. "You were off duty."

"So you just let it sit there?"

It's hard to shrug while you're running full-out, but Chee managed it. "Stuff's broken all the time. I didn't figure it was that bad. You know, there was that bulb out in tunnel three, and then there was that leak from the toilets. And then the drinking fountain went out again. You always let things slide. I figured I'd let you sleep."

I didn't bother trying to explain the difference. "If it happens again, just remember, if the pumps, any of them, die, you call me. It doesn't matter where I am, I won't be mad. You just call me. If we let these pumps go down, there's no telling how many people could get sick. There's bad stuff in that water, and we've got to stay on top of it, otherwise it bubbles up into the sewers and then it gets out in the air, and people get sick. You got it?"

I shoved open the doors to the control room, and stopped.

The floor was covered with toilet paper, rolls of it, all unstrung and dangled around the control room. Like some kind of mummy striptease had gone wrong. There must have been a hundred rolls unraveled all over the floor. "What the hell is this?"

"This?" He looked around, scratching his head.

"The paper, Chee."

"Oh. Right. We had a toilet paper fight last night. For some reason they triple delivered. We didn't have enough space in the storage closet. I mean, we haven't had ass wipes for two months, and then we had piles and piles of it— ,"

"So you had a toilet paper fight while Pump Six was down?"

Something in my voice must have finally gotten through. He cringed. "Hey, don't look at me that way. I'll get it picked up. No worries. Jeez. You're worse than Mercati. And anyway, it wasn't my fault. I was just getting ready to reload the dispensers and then Suze and Zoo came down and we got into this fight." He shrugged. "It was just something to do, that's all. And Suze started it, anyway."

I gave him another dirty look and kicked my way through the tangle of t.p. to the control consoles.

Chee called after me, "Hey, how am I going to wind it back up if you kick it around?"

I started throwing switches on the console, running diagnostics. I tried booting up the troubleshooting database, but got a connection error. Big surprise. I looked on the shelves for the hard copies of the operation and maintenance manuals, but they were missing. I looked at Chee. "Do you know where the manuals are?"

"The what?"

I pointed at the empty shelves.

"Oh. They're in the bathroom."

I looked at him. He looked back at me. I couldn't make myself ask. I just turned back to the consoles. "Go get them, I need to figure out what these flashers mean." There was a whole panel of them winking away at me, all for Pump Six.

Chee scuttled out of the room, dragging t.p. behind him. Overhead, I heard the Observation Room door open: Suze, coming down the stairs. More trouble. She rustled through the t.p. streamers and came up close behind me, crowding. I could feel her breathing on my neck.

"The pump's been down for almost twelve hours," she said. "I could write you up." She thumped me in the back, hard. "I could write you up, buddy." She did it again, harder. *Bam.*

I thought about hitting her back, but I wasn't going to give her another excuse to dock pay. Besides, she's bigger than me. And she's got more muscles than an orangutan. About as hairy, too. Instead, I said, "It would have helped if somebody had called."

"You talking back to me?" She gave me another shove and leaned around to get in my face, looking at me all squinty-eyed. "Twelve hours down-time," she said again. "That's grounds for a write-up. It's in the manual. I can do it."

"No kidding? You read that? All by yourself?"

"You're not the only one who can read, Alvarez." She turned and stomped back up the stairs to her office.

Chee came back lugging the maintenance manuals. "I don't know how you do this," he puffed as he handed them over. "These manuals make no sense at all."

"It's a talent."

I took the plastirene volumes and glanced up at Suze's office. She was just standing there, looking down at me through the observation glass, looking like she was going to come down and beat my head in. A dimwit promo who got lucky when the old boss went into retirement.

She has no idea what a boss does, so mostly she spends her time scowling at us, filling out paperwork that she can't remember how to route, and molesting her secretary. Employment guarantees are great for people like me, but I can see why you might want to fire someone; the only way Suze was ever going to leave was if she fell down the Observation Room stairs and broke her neck.

She scowled harder at me, trying to make me look away. I let her win. She'd either write me up, or she wouldn't. And even if she did, she might still get distracted and forget to file it. At any rate, she couldn't fire me. We were stuck together like a couple of cats tied in a sack.

I started thumbing through the manuals' plastic pages, going back and forth through the indexes. as I cross-referenced all the flashers. I looked up again at the console. There were a lot of them. Maybe more than I'd ever seen.

Chee squatted down beside me, watching. He started picking his head again. I think it's a comfort thing for him. But it makes your skin crawl until you get used to it. Makes you think of lice.

"You do that fast," he said. "How come you didn't go to college?"

"You kidding?"

"No way, man. You're the smartest guy I ever met. You totally could have gone to college."

I glanced over at him, trying to tell if he was screwing with me. He looked back at me, completely sincere, like a dog waiting for a treat. I went back to the manual. "No ambition, I guess."

The truth was that I never made it through high school. I dropped out of P.S. 105 and never looked back. Or forward, I guess. I remember sitting in freshman algebra and watching the teacher's lips flap and not understanding a word he was saying. I turned in worksheets and got Ds every time, even after I redid them. None of the other kids were complaining, though. They just laughed at me when I kept asking him to explain the difference between squaring and doubling variables. You don't have to be Einstein to figure out where you don't belong.

I started piecing my way through the troubleshooting diagrams. No clogs indicated. Go to Mechanics Diagnostics, Volume Three. I picked up the next binder of pages and started flipping. "Anyway, you've got a bad frame of reference. We aren't exactly a bunch of Nobel Prize winners here." I glanced up at Suze's office. "Smart people don't work in dumps like this." Suze was scowling down at me again. I gave her the universal salute. "You see?"

Chee shrugged. "I dunno. I tried reading that manual about twenty times on the john, and it still doesn't make any sense to me. If you weren't around, half the city would be swimming in shit right now."

Another flasher winked on the console: amber, amber, red… It stayed red.

"In a couple minutes they're going to be swimming in a lot worse than that. Believe me, buddy, there's lots worse things than shit. Mercati showed me a list once, before he retired. All the things that run through here that the pumps are supposed to clean: polychlorinated biphenyls, bisphenyl-A, estrogen, phlalates, PCBs, heptachlor…"

"I got a Super Clean sticker for all that stuff." He lifted his shirt and showed me the one he had stuck to his skin, right below his rib cage. A yellow smiley face sticker a little like the kind I used to get from my grandpa when he was feeling generous. It said SUPER CLEAN on the smiley's forehead.

"You buy those?"

"Sure. Seven bucks for seven. I get 'em every week. I can drink the water straight, now. I'd even drink out of the Hudson." He started scratching his skull again.

I watched him scratch for a second, remembering how zit girl Nora had tried to sell some to Maria before they went swimming. "Well, I'm glad it's working for you." I turned and started keying restart sequences for the pumps. "Now let's see if we can get this sucker started up, and keep all the neighbors who don't buy stickers from having a pack of trogs. Get ready to pull a reboot on my say-so."

Chee went over to clear the data lines and put his hands on the restart levers. "I don't know what difference it makes. I went through the park the other day and you know what I saw? A mama trog and five little baby trogs. What good does it do to keep trogs from getting born to good folks, when you got those ones down in the park making whole litters?"

I looked over at Chee to say something back, but he kind of had a point. The reboot sequences completed and Pump Six's indicators showed primed. "Three... Two... One... Primed full," I said. "Go. Go. Go."

Chee threw his levers and the consoles cleared green and somewhere deep down below us, sewage started pumping again.

We climbed the skin of the Kusovic Center, climbing for heaven, climbing for Wicky. Maggie and Nora and Wu and me, worming our way up through stairwell turns, scrambling over rubble, kicking past condom wrappers and scattering Effy packets like autumn leaves.

Wicky's synthesized xylophones and Japanese kettle drums thrummed, urging us higher. Trogs and sadsack partiers who didn't have my connections watched jealously as we climbed. Watched and whispered as we passed them by, all of them knowing that Max owed me favors and favors and favors and that I went to the front of the line because I kept the toilets running on time.

The club was perched at the very top of the Kusovic, a bunch of old stock broker offices. Max had torn down the glass cubicles and the old digital wallscreens that used to track the NYSE and had really opened the space up. Unfortunately, the club wasn't much good in the winter anymore because we'd all gotten rowdy one night and shoved out the windows. But even if it was too damn breezy half the year, watching those windows falling had been a major high point at the club. A couple years later people were still talking about it, and I could still remember the slow way they came out of their frames and tumbled and sailed through the air. And when they hit bottom, they splashed across the streets like giant buckets of water.

At any rate, the open-air thing worked really good in the summer, with all the rolling brownouts that were always knocking out the A/C.

I got a shot of Effy as we went in the door, and the club rode in on a wave of primal flesh, a tribal gathering of sweaty jumping monkeys in half-torn business suits, all of us going crazy and eyeball wide until our faces were as pale and big as fish wallowing in the bottom of the ocean.

Maggie was smiling at me as we danced and our whole oven fight was completely behind us. I was glad about that, because after our fork-in-the-outlet fight, she acted like it was my fault for a week, even after she said she forgave me. But now, in the dance throb of Wicky, I was her white knight again, and I was glad to be with her, even if it meant dragging Nora along.

All the way up the stairs, I'd tried to not stare at Nora's zit-pocked skin or make fun of her swollen-up face but she knew what I was thinking because she kept giving me dirty looks whenever I warned her to step around places where the stairway was crumbling. Talk about stupid, though. She's about as sharp as a marble. I won't drink or swim in any of the water around here. It comes from working with sewage all the time. You know way too much about everything that goes in and out of the system. People like Nora put a Kali-Mary pendant between their tits or stick a Super Clean smiley to their ass cheek and hope for the best. I drink bottled water and only shower with a filter head. And sometimes I still get creeped out. No pus rashes, though.

The kettle drums throbbed inside my eyeballs. Across the club, Nora was dancing with Wu and now that my Effy was kicking into overdrive, I could see her positive qualities: she danced fast and furious... her hair was long and black... her zits were the size of breasts.

They looked succulent.

I sidled up to her and tried to apologize for not appreciating her before, but between the noise and my slobbering on her skin, I guess I failed to communicate effectively. She ran away before I could make it up to her and I ended up bouncing alone in Wicky's kettle drum womb while the crowds rode in and out around me and the Effy built up in ocean throbs that ran from my eyeballs to my crotch and back again, bouncing me higher and higher and higher...

A girl in torn knee socks and a nun's habit was mewling in the bathroom when Maggie found us and pulled us apart and took me on the floor with people walking around us and trying to use the stainless steel piss troughs, but then Max grabbed me and I couldn't tell if we'd been doing it on the bar and if that was the problem or if I was just taking a leak in the wrong place but Max kept complaining about bubbles in his gin and a riot a riot a RIOT that he was going to have on his hands if these Effy freaks didn't get their liquor and he shoved me down under the bar where tubes come out of vats of gin and tonic and it was like floating inside the guts of an octopus with the waves of the kettle drums booming away above me.

I wanted to sleep down there, maybe hunt for the nun's red panties except that Max kept coming back to me with more Effy and saying we had to find the problem, the bubbly problem the bubbly problem, take some of this it will clear your damn head, find where the bubbles come from, where they fill the gin. No no no! The tonic the tonic the tonic! No bubbles in the tonic. Find the tonic. Stop the RIOT, make it all okay before the gag-gas trucks come and shut us down and dammit what are you sniffing down under there?

Swimming under the bar... Swimming long and low... eyeballs wide... prehistoric fishy amongst giant mossy root-laced eggs, buried under the mist of the swamp, down with the bar rags and the lost spoons and the sticky slime of bar sugar, and these huge dead silver eggs lying under the roots, growing moss and mildew but nothing else, no yolky tonic coming out of these suckers, been sucked dry, sucked full dry by too many thirsty dinosaurs and of course that's the problem. No tonic. None. None at all.

More eggs! More eggs! We need more eggs! More big silver tonic dispensing eggs need to rumble in on handtrucks and roll in on white-jacketed bow-tie bartender backs. More eggs need to take the prod from the long root green sucking tubes and then we can suck the tonic of their yolk out, and Max can keep on making g-and-t's and I'm a hero hey hey hey a hero a goddamn superstar because I know a lot about silver eggs and how to stick in the right tubes and isn't that why Maggie's always pissed at me because my tube is never ready to stick into her eggs, or maybe she's got no eggs to stick and we sure as hell aren't going to the doctor to find out she's got no eggs and no replacements either, not a single one coming in on a handtruck and isn't that why she's out in the crowd bouncing in a black corset with a guy licking her feet and giving me the finger?

And isn't that why we're going to have a RIOT now when I beat that trogwad's head in with this chunk of bar that I'm going to get Max to loan me… except I'm too far underwater to beat up boot licker. And little smoking piles of Effy keep blooming on the floor, and we're all lapping them up because I'm a goddamn hero a hero a hero, the fixit man of all fixit men, and everyone bows and scrapes and passes me Effy because there isn't going to be a RIOT and we won't get shut down with gag-gas, and we won't do the vomit crawl down the stairwells to the streets.

And then Max shoves me back onto the dance floor with more shots of Effy for Maggie, a big old tray of forgiveness, and forgiveness comes easy when we're all walking on the ceiling of the biggest oldest skyscraper in the sky.

Blue kettle drums and eyeball nuns. Zits and dinner dates. Down the stairs and into the streets.

By the time we stumbled out of Wicky I was finally coming out of the Effy folds but Maggie was still flying, running her hands all over me, touching me, telling me what she was going to do to me when we got home. Nora and Wu were supposed to be with us, but somehow we'd gotten separated. Maggie wasn't interested in waiting around so we headed uptown, stumbling between the big old city towers, winding around sidewalk stink ads for Diabolo and Possession, and dodging fishdog stands with after-bar octopi on a stick.

The night was finally cool, in the sweet spot between end of midnight swelter and beginning of morning smother. There was a blanket of humidity, wet on us, and seductive after the club. Without rain or freezes, I barely had to watch for concrete rain at all.

Maggie ran her hands up and down my arm as we walked, occasionally leaning in close to kiss my cheek and nibble on my ear. "Max says you're amazing. You saved the day."

I shrugged. "It wasn't a big deal."

The whole bar thing was pretty hazy, bubbled-out by all the Effy I'd done. My skin was still singing from it. Mostly what I had was a warm glow right in my crotch and a stuttery view of the dark streets and the long rows of candles in the windows of the towers, but Maggie's hand felt good, and she looked good, and I had some plans of my own for when we got back to the apartment, so I knew I was coming down nice and slow, like falling into a warm feather bed full of helium and tongues.

"Anyone could have figured out his tonic was empty, if we hadn't all been so damn high." I stopped in front of a bank of autovendors. Three of them were sold out, and one was broken open, but there were still a couple drinks in the last one. I dropped my money in and chose a bottle of Blue Vitality for her, and a Sweatshine for me. It was a pleasant surprise when the machine kicked out the bottles.

"Wow!" Maggie beamed at me.

I grinned and fished out her bottle. "Lucky night, I guess: first the bar, now this."

"I don't think the bar thing was luck. I wouldn't have thought of it." She downed her Blue Vitality in two long swallows, and giggled. "And you did it when your eyes were as big as a fish. You were doing hand-stands on the bar."

I didn't remember that. Bar sugar and red lace bras, I remembered. But not handstands. "I don't see how Max keeps that place going when he can't even remember to restock."

Maggie rubbed up against me. "Wicky's a lot better than most clubs. And anyway, that's why he's got you. A real live hero." She giggled again. "I'm glad we didn't have to fight our way out of another riot. I hate that."

In an alley, some trogs were making it. Clustered bodies, hermaphro-ditic, climbing on each other and humping, their mouths open, smiling and panting. I glanced at them and kept going, but Maggie grabbed my arm and tugged me back.

The trogs were really going at it, all in a flounder, three of them piled, their skins gleaming with sweat slick and saliva. They looked back at us with yellow eyes and not a bit of shame. They just smiled and got into a heavy groaning rhythm.

"I can't believe how much they DO it," Maggie whispered. She gripped my arm, pressing against me. "They're like dogs."

"That's about how smart they are."

They changed positions, one crouching as though Maggie's words had inspired them. The others piled on top of him... or her. Maggie's hand slid to the front of my pants, fumbled with the zipper and reached inside. "They're so.... Oh, God." She pulled me close and started working on my belt, almost tearing at it.

"What the hell?" I tried to push her off, but she was all over me, her hands reaching inside my pants, touching me, making me hard. The Effy was still working, that was for sure.

"Let's do it, too. Here. I want you."

"Are you crazy?"

"They don't care. Come on. Maybe this time it'll take. Knock me up." She touched me, her eyes widening at my sudden size. "You're never like this." She touched me again. "Oh God. Please." She pressed herself against me, looking over at the trogs. "Like that. Just like that." She pulled off her shimmersilk blouse, exposing her black corset and the pale skin of her breasts.

I stared at her skin and curves. That beautiful body she'd teased me with all night long. Suddenly I didn't care about the trogs or the few people walking by on the street. We both yanked at my belt. My pants fell down around my ankles. We slammed up against the alley wall, pressing against old concrete and staring into each other's eyes and then she pulled me into her and her lips were on my ear, biting and panting and whispering as we moved against each other.

The trogs just grinned and grinned and watched us with their big yellow eyes as we all shared the alley, and all watched each other.

At five in the morning, Chee called again, his voice coming straight into my head through my earbug. In all the excitement and Effy, I'd forgotten to take it out. Pump Six was down again. "You said I was supposed to call you," he whined.

I groaned and dragged myself out of bed. "Yeah. Yeah. I did. Don't worry about it. You did good. I'll be there."

Maggie rolled over. "Where you going?"

I pulled on my pants and gave her a quick kiss. "Got to go save the world."

"They work you too hard. I don't think you should go."

"And let Chee sort it out? You've got to be kidding. We'd be up to our necks in sludge by dinner time."

"My hero." She smiled sleepily. "See if you can find me some donuts when you come back. I feel pregnant."

She looked so happy and warm and fuzzy I almost climbed back into bed with her, but I fought off the urge and just gave her another kiss. "Will do."

Outside, light was just starting to break in the sky, a slow yellowing of the smog. The streets were almost silent at the early hour. It was hard not to be bitter about being up at this ungodly hungover time, but it was better than having to deal with the sewage backup if Chee hadn't called. I headed downtown and bought a bagel from a girly faced guy who didn't know how to make change.

The bagel was wrapped in some kind of plastic film that dissolved when I put it in my mouth. It wasn't bad, but it ticked me off that bagel boy got confused with the change and needed me to go into his cash pouch and count out my own money.

It seems like I always end up bailing everyone out. Even dumb bagel guys. Maggie says I'm as compulsive as Chee. She would have just stood there and waited until bagel boy sorted it out, even if it took all day. But I have a damn hard time watching some trogwad drop dollars all over the sidewalk. Sometimes it's just easier to climb out of the oatmeal and do things yourself.

Chee was waiting for me when I got in, practically bouncing up and down. Five pumps down, now.

"It started with just one when I called you, but now there's five. They keep shutting off."

I went into the control room. The troubleshooting database was still down so I grabbed the hardcopy manuals again. Weird how the pumps were all going off-line like that. The control room, normally alive with the hum of the machines was quieter with half of them down. Around the city, sewage lines were backing up as we failed to cycle waste into the treatment facilities and pump the treated water out into the river.

I thought about Nora with her rash, thanks to swimming in that gunk. It could really make you nervous. Looks clean, makes you rash. And we're at the bottom of the river. It's not just our crap in it. Everyone upstream, too. Our treatment plants pump water up from underground or pipe it in and treat it from lakes upstate. At least that's the theory. I don't really buy it; I've seen the amount of water we move through here and there's no way its all coming from the lakes. In reality, we've got 20-million-odd people all sucking water that we don't know where it's coming from or what's in it. Like I said, I drink bottled water even if I have to hike all over the city to find it. Or soda water. Or… tonic, even.

I closed my eyes, trying to piece the evening back together. All those empty canisters of tonic under the bar. Travis Alvarez saves the world while flying to the moon on Effy, and two rounds of sex yesterday.

Hell, yeah.

Chee and I brought the PressureDynes up one by one. All of them came back online except Pump Six. It was stubborn. We reprimed it. Fired. Reprimed. Nothing.

Suze came down to backseat drive, dragging Zoo, her secretary, be-hind her. Suze was completely strung out. Her blouse was half-tucked in, and she had big old fishy Effy eyes that were almost as red as the flashers on the console. But her fishy-eyes narrowed when she saw all the flashers. "How come all these pumps went down? It's your job to keep them working."

I just looked at her. Zoned out of her mind at six A.M., romping around with her secretary girlfriend while she tried to crack the whip on the rest of us. Now that's leadership. Suddenly I thought that maybe I needed to get a different job. Or needed to start licking big piles of Effy before I came to work. Anything to take the edge off Suze.

"If you want me to fix it, I'll need you to clear out so I can concentrate."

Suze looked at me like she was chewing on a lemon. "You better get it fixed." She poked my chest with a thick finger. "If you don't, I'm making Chee your boss." She glanced at Zoo. "It's your turn on the couch. Come on." They trooped off.

Chee watched them go. He started picking at his head. "They never do any work," he said.

Another flasher went amber on the console. I flipped through the manual, hunting for a reason. "Who does? A job like this, where nobody gets fired?"

"Yeah, but there ought to be a way to get rid of her, at least. She moved all her home furniture into the office, the other day. She never goes home now. Says she likes the A/C here."

"You shouldn't complain. You're the guy who was throwing t.p. around yesterday."

He looked at me, puzzled. "So?"

"Never mind. Don't worry about Suze. We're the bottom of the pile, Chee. Get used to it. Let's try the reboot again."

It didn't work.

I went back to the manual. Sludge was probably coming up a hundred thousand toilets in the city by now. Weird how all the pumps shut down like that: one, two, three, four. I closed my eyes, thinking. Something about my Effy spree kept tickling the back of my head. Effy flashbacks, for sure. But they kept coming: big old eggs, big old silver eggs, all of them sucked dry by egg slurping dinosaurs. Wow. That was some kind of weird spree. Nuns and stainless steel eggs. The urinals and Maggie... I blinked. Everything clicked. Pieces of the puzzle coming together. Cosmic Effy convergence: Emptied silver eggs. Max forgetting to restock his bar.

I looked up at Chee, then down at the manuals, then back up at Chee. "How long have we been running these pumps?"

"What do you mean?"

"When did they get installed?"

Chee stared at the ceiling, picked his head thoughtfully. "Hell if I know. Before I came on, that's for sure."

"Me too. I've been here nine years. Have we got a computer that would tell us that? A receipt? Something?" I flipped to the front of the manual in my hands. "PressureDyne: Hi-Capacity, Self-Purging, Multi-Platform Pumping Engine. Model 13-44474-888." I frowned. "This manual was printed in 2020."

Chee whistled and leaned over to finger the plasticized pages. "That's pretty damn old."

"Built to last, right? People built things to last, back then."

"More than a hundred years?" He shrugged. "I had a car like that, once. Real solid. Engine hardly had any rust on it at all. And it had both headlights. But too damn old." He picked something out of his scalp and examined it for a second before flicking it onto the floor. "No one works on cars anymore. I can't remember the last time I saw a taxi running."

I looked at him, trying to decide if I wanted to say anything about flicking scalp on the floor, then just gave it up. I flipped through the manual some more until I found the part I wanted: "Individual Reporting Modules: Remote Access, Connectivity Features, and Data Collection."

Following the manual's instructions, I opened a new set of diagnostic windows that bypassed the PressureDynes' generalized reports for pump station managers and instead connected directly with the pumps' raw log data. What I got was: "Host source data not found."

Big surprise.

The rest of the error text advised me to check the remote reporting module extension connectors, whatever those were. I closed the manual and tucked it under my arm. "Come on. I think I know what's wrong." I led Chee out of the control room and down into the bowels of the tunnels and plant system. The elevator was busted so we had to take the access stairs.

As we went deeper and deeper, darkness closed in. Grit and dust were everywhere. Rats skittered away from us. Isolated LEDs kept the stairwell visible, but barely. Dust and shadows and moving rats were all you could see in the dim amber. Eventually even the LEDs gave out. Chee found an emergency lantern in a wall socket, blanketed with gray fluffy dust, but it still had a charge. My asthma started to tickle and close in, sitting on my chest from all the crud in the air. I took a hit off my inhaler, and we kept going down. Finally, we hit bottom.

Light from Chee's lantern wavered and disappeared in the cavern's darkness. The metal of the PressureDynes glinted dimly. Chee sneezed.

The motion sent his lantern rocking. Shadows shifted crazily until he used a hand to stop it. "You can't see shit down here," he muttered.

"Shut up. I'm thinking."

"I've never been down here."

"I came down, once. When I first came on. When Mercati was still alive."

"No wonder you act like him. He trained you?"

"Sure." I hunted around for the emergency lighting.

Mercati had shown the switches to me when he brought me down, nearly a decade before, and told me about the pumps. He'd been old then, but still working, and I liked the guy. He had a way of paying attention to things. Focused. Not like most people who can barely say hello to you before they start looking at their watch, or planning their party schedule, or complaining about their skin rashes.

He used to say my teachers didn't know shit about algebra and that I should have stayed in school. Even knowing that he was just comparing me to Suze, I thought it was a pretty nice thing for him to say.

No one knew the pump systems as well as he did, so even after he got sick and I took over his job, I'd still sneak out to the hospital to ask him questions. He was my secret weapon until the cancer finally took out his guts.

I found the emergency lighting and pulled the switches. Fluorescent lights flickered, and came alive, buzzing. Some bulbs didn't come on, but there were enough.

Chee gasped. "They're huge."

A cathedral of engineering. Overhead, pipes arched through cavern dimness, shimmering under the muted light of the fluorescents, an interconnecting web of iron and shadows that centered in complex rosettes around the ranked loom of the pumps.

They towered over us, gleaming dully, three stories tall, steel dinosaurs. Dust mantled them. Rust blossoms patterned their hides in complex overlays that made them look like they'd been draped in oriental rugs. Pentagonal bolts as big as my hands studded their armored plating and stitched together the vast sectioned pipes that spanned the darkness and shot down black tunnels in every compass direction, reaching for every neighborhood in the city. Moisture jewels gleamed and dripped from ancient joints. The pumps thrummed on. Perfectly designed. Forgotten by everyone in the city above. Beasts working without complaint, loyal despite abandonment.

Except that one of them had now gone silent.

I stifled an urge to get down on my knees and apologize for neglecting them, for betraying these loyal machines that had run for more than a century.

I went over to Pump Six's control panel, and stroked the dinosaur's vast belly where it loomed over me. The control panel was all covered with dust, but it glowed when I ran my hand over it. Amber signals and lime text glowing authoritatively, telling me just what was wrong, telling me and telling me, and never complaining that I hadn't been listening.

Raw data had stopped piping up to the control room at some point, and had instead sat in the dark, waiting for someone to come down and notice it. And the raw data was the answer to all my questions. At the top of the list: Model 13-44474-888, Requires Scheduled Maintenance. 946,080,000 cycles completed.

I ran through the pump diagnostics:

Valve Ring Part# 12-33939, Scheduled for Replacement.

Piston Parts# 232-2, 222-5, 222-6, 222-4-1, Scheduled for Replacement.

Displacement Catch Reservoir, Part# 37-37-375-77, Damaged, Replace.

Emergency Release Trigger Bearing, Part# 810-9, Damaged, Replace.

Valve Kit, Part# 437834-13, Damaged, Replace.

Master Drive Regulator, Part# 39-23-9834959-5, Damaged, Replace.

Priority Maintenance:

Compression Sensors, Part# 49-4, Part# 7777-302, Part# 403-74698

Primary Train, Part# 010303-0

Gurney Belt Valve, Part# 9-0-2…

The list went on. I keyed into the maintenance history. The list opened up, running well into Mercati's tenure and even before, dozens of maintenance triggers and scheduled work requests, all of them blinking down here in the darkness, and ignored. Twenty-five years of neglect.

"Hey!" Chee called. "Check this out! They left magazines down here!"

I glanced over. He'd found a pile of trash someone had stuffed under one of the pumps. He was down on his hands and knees, reaching underneath, rooting things out: magazines, what looked like old food wrappers. I started to tell him to quit messing with stuff, but then I let it go. At least he wasn't breaking anything. I rubbed my eyes and went back to the pump diagnostics.

For the six years I'd been in charge, there were over a dozen errors

displayed, but the PressureDynes had just kept going, chugging away
as bits and pieces of them rattled away, and now, suddenly this one had
given way completely, coming apart at the seams, loyally chugging until
it just couldn't go on anymore and the maintenance backlog finally
took the sucker down. I went over and started looking at the logs for
the nine other pumps.

Every one of them was riddled with neglect: warning dumps, data
logs full of error corrections, alarm triggers.

I went back to Pump Six and looked at its logs again. The men who'd
built the machines had built them to last, but enough tiny little knives
can still kill a big old dinosaur, and this one was beyond dead.

"We'll need to call PressureDyne," I said. "This thing is going to need
more help than we can give it."

Chee looked up from a found magazine with a bright yellow car on
the cover. "Do they even exist anymore?"

"They better." I grabbed the manual and looked up their customer
support number.

It wasn't even in the same format as our numbers. Not a single letter
of the alphabet in the whole damn thing.

Not only did PressureDyne not exist, they'd gone bankrupt more than
forty years ago, victims of their overly well-designed pump products.
They'd killed their own market. The only bright spot was that their
technology had slouched into the public domain, and the net was up for
once, so I could download schematics of the PressureDynes. There was a
ton of information, except I didn't know anyone who could understand
any of it. I sure couldn't.

I leaned back in my desk chair, staring at all that information I couldn't
use. Like looking at Egyptian hieroglyphs. Something was there, but
it sure beat me what I was supposed to do with it. I'd shifted the flows
for Pump Six over to the rest of the pumps, and they were handling
the new load, but it made me nervous thinking about all those maintenance warnings glowing down there in the dark: Mercury Extender
Seal, Part# 5974-30, Damaged, Replace... whatever the hell that meant.
I downloaded everything about the PressureDynes onto my phone bug,
not sure who I'd take it to, but damn sure no one here was going to be
able to help.

"What are you doing with that?"

I jumped and looked around. Suze had snuck up on me.

I shrugged. "Dunno. See if I can find someone to help, I guess."

"That's proprietary. You can't take those schematics out of here. Wipe it."

"You're crazy. It's public domain." I got up and popped my phone bug back into my ear. She made a swipe at it, but I dodged and headed for the doors.

She chased after me, a mean mountain of muscle. "I could fire you, you know!"

"Not if I quit first." I yanked open the control room door and ducked out.

"Hey! Get back here! I'm your boss." Her voice followed me down the corridor, getting fainter. "I'm in charge here, dammit. I can fire you! It's in the manual! I found it! You're not the only one who can read! I found it! I can fire you! I will!" Like a little kid, having a fit. She was still yelling when the control room doors finally shut her off.

Outside, in the sunshine, I ended up wandering in the park, watching the trogs, and wondering what I did to piss off God that he stuck me with a nutjob like Suze. I thought about calling Maggie to meet me, but I didn't feel like telling her about work—half the time when I tried to explain stuff to her, she just came up with bad ideas to fix it, or didn't think the things I was talking about were such a big deal—and if I called up halfway through the day she'd definitely wonder why I'd left so early, and what was going on, and then when I didn't take her advice about Suze she'd just get annoyed.

I kept passing trogs humping away and smiling. They waved at me to come over and play. I just waved back. One of them must have been a real girl, because she was distendedly obviously pregnant, bouncing away with a couple of her friends, and I was glad again that Maggie wasn't with me. She had enough pregnancy hang-ups without seeing the trogs breeding.

I wouldn't have minded throwing Suze to the trogs, though. She was about as dumb as one. Christ, I was surrounded by dummies. I needed a new job. Someplace that attracted better talent than sewage work did. I wondered how serious Suze had been about trying to fire me. If there really was something in the manuals that we'd all missed about hiring and firing. And then I wondered how serious I was about quitting. I sure hated Suze. But how did you get a better job when you hadn't finished high school, let alone college?

I stopped short. Sudden enlightenment: College. Columbia. They could help. They'd have some sharpie who could understand all the

PressureDyne information. An engineering department, or something. They were even dependent on Pump Six. Talk about leverage.

I headed uptown on the subway with a whole pack of snarly pissed-off commuters, everyone scowling at each other and acting like you were stealing their territory if you sat down next to them. I ended up hanging from a strap and watching two old guys hiss at each other across the car until we broke down at 86th and we all ended up walking.

I kept passing clumps of trogs, lounging around on the sidewalks. A few of the really smart ones were panhandling, but most of them were just humping away. I would have been annoyed at having to shove through the orgy, if I wasn't actually feeling jealous. I kept wondering why the hell was I out here in the sweaty summer smog taking hits off my inhaler while Suze and Chee and Zoo were all hanging around in air-con comfort and basically doing nothing.

What was wrong with me? Why was I the one who always tried to fix things? Mercati had been like that, always taking stuff on and then just getting worked harder and harder until the cancer ate him from the inside out. He was working so hard at the end I think he might have been glad to go, just for the rest.

Maggie always said they worked me too hard, and as I dragged my ass up Broadway, I started thinking she was right. Then again, if I left things to Chee and Suze, I'd be swimming up the Broadway River in a stew of crap and chemicals instead of walking up a street. Maggie would have said that was someone else's problem, but she just thought so because when she flushed the toilet, it still worked. At the end of the day, it seemed like some people just got stuck dealing with the shit, and some people figured out how to have a good time.

A half-hour later, covered with sweat and street grime and holding a half-empty squirt bottle of rehydrating Sweatshine that I'd stolen from an unwary trog, I rolled through Columbia's gates and into the main quad, where I immediately ran into problems.

I kept following signs for the engineering building, but they kept sending me around in circles. I would have asked for directions—I'm not one of those guys who can't—but it's pretty damn embarrassing when you can't even follow a simple sign, so I held off.

And really, who was I going to ask? There were lots of kids out in the quad, all sprawled out and wearing basically nothing and looking like they were starting a trog colony of their own, but I didn't feel like talking to them. I'm not a prude, but you've got to draw the line somewhere.

I ended up wandering around lost, going from one building to the next, stumbling through a jumble of big old Roman- and Ben Franklin-style buildings: lots of columns and brick and patchy green quads—everything looking like it was about to start raining concrete any second—trying to figure out why I couldn't understand any of the signs.

Finally, I sucked it up and asked a couple half-naked kids for directions.

The thing that ticks me off about academic types is that they always act like they're smarter than you. Rich-kid, free-ride, prep-school ones are the worst. I kept asking the best and brightest for directions, trying to get them to take me to the engineering department, or the engineering building, or whatever the hell it was, and they all just looked me up and down and gibbered at me like monkeys, or else laughed through their Effy highs and kept on going. A couple of them gave me a shrug and a "dunno," but that was the best I got.

I gave up on directions, and just kept roaming. I don't know how long I wandered. Eventually I found a big old building off one of the quads, a big square thing with pillars like the Parthenon. A few kids were sprawled out on the steps, soaking up the sun, but it was one of the quietest parts of the campus I'd seen.

The first set of doors I tried was chained, and so was the second, but then I found a set where the chain had been left undone, two heavy lengths of it, dangling with an old open padlock on the end. The kids on the steps were ignoring me, so I yanked open the doors.

Inside, everything was silence and dust. Big old chandeliers hung down from the ceiling, sparkling with orangey light that filtered in through the dirt on the windows. The light made if feel like it was the end of day with the sun starting to set, even though it was only a little past noon. A heavy blanket of dust covered everything; floors and reading tables and chairs and computers all had a thick gray film over them.

"Hello?"

No one answered. My voice echoed and died, like the building had just swallowed up the sound. I started wandering, picking doorways at random: reading rooms, study carrels, more dead computers, but most of all, books. Aisles and aisles with racks full of them. Room after room stuffed with books, all of them covered with thick layers of dust.

A library. A whole damn library in the middle of a university, and not a single person in it. There were tracks on the floor, and a litter of Effy packets, condom wrappers, and liquor bottles where people had come and gone at some point, but even the trash had its own fine layer of dust.

In some rooms, all the books had been yanked off the shelves like a tornado had ripped through. In one, someone had made a bonfire out of them. They lay in a huge heap, completely torched, a pile of ash and pages and backings, a jumble of black ash fossils that crumbled to nothing when I crouched down and touched them. I stood quickly, wiping my hands on my pants. It was like fingering someone's bones.

I kept wandering, running my fingers along shelves and watching the dust cascade like miniature falls of concrete rain. I pulled down a book at random. More dust poured off and puffed up in my face. I coughed. My chest seized and I took a hit off my inhaler. In the dimness, I could barely make out the title: "Post-Liberation America. A Modern Perspective." When I opened it, its spine cracked.

"What are you doing here?"

I jumped back and dropped the book. Dust puffed around me. An old lady, hunched and witchy, was standing at the end of the aisle. She limped forward. Her voice was sharp as she repeated herself. "What are you doing here?"

"I got lost. I'm trying to find the engineering department."

She was an ugly old dame: Liver spots and lines all over her face. Her skin hung off her bones in loose flaps. She looked a thousand years old, and not in a smart wise way, just in a wrecked moth-eaten way. She had something flat and silvery in her hand. A pistol.

I took another step back.

She raised the gun. "Not that way. Out the way you came." She motioned with the pistol. "Off you go."

I hesitated.

She smiled slightly, showing stumps of missing teeth. "I won't shoot if you don't give me a reason." She waved the gun again. "Go on. You aren't supposed to be here." She herded me back through the library to the main doors with a brisk authority. She pulled them open and waved her pistol at me. "Go on. Get."

"Wait. Please. Can't you at least tell me where the engineering department is?"

"Closed down years ago. Now get out."

"There's got to be one!"

"Not anymore. Go on. Get." She brandished the pistol again. "Get."

I held onto the door. "But you must know someone who can help me." I was talking fast, trying to get all my words out before she used the gun. "I work on the city's sewage pumps. They're breaking, and I don't know how to fix them. I need someone who has engineering experience."

She was shaking her head and starting to wave the gun. I tried again. "Please! You've got to help. No one will talk to me, and you're going to be swimming in crap if I don't find help. Pump Six serves the university and *I don't know how to fix it!*"

She paused. She cocked her head first one way, then the other. "Go on."

I briefly outlined the problems with the PressureDynes. When I finished, she shook her head and turned away. "You've wasted your time. We haven't had an engineering department in over twenty years." She went over to a reading table and took a couple swipes at its dust. Pulled out a chair and did the same with it. She sat, placing her pistol on the table, and motioned me to join her.

Warily, I brushed off my own seat. She laughed at the way my eyes kept going to her pistol. She picked it up and tucked it into a pocket of her moth-eaten sweater. "Don't worry. I won't shoot you now. I just keep it around in case the kids get belligerent. They don't very often, anymore, but you never know…" Her voice trailed off, as she looked out at the quad.

"How can you not have an engineering department?"

Her eyes swung back to me. "Same reason I closed the library." She laughed. "We can't have the students running around in here, can we?" She considered me for a moment, thoughtful. "I'm surprised you got in. I'm must be getting old, forgetting to lock up like that."

"You always lock it? Aren't you librarians—"

"I'm not a librarian," she interrupted. "We haven't had a librarian since Herman Hsu died." She laughed. "I'm just an old faculty wife. My husband taught organic chemistry before he died."

"But you're the one who put the chains on the doors?"

"There wasn't anyone else to do it. I just saw the students partying in here and realized something had to be done before they burned the damn place down." She drummed her fingers on the table, raising little dust puffs with her boney digits as she considered me. Finally she said, "If I gave you the library keys, could you learn the things you need to know? About these pumps? Learn how they work? Fix them, maybe?"

"I doubt it. That's why I came here." I pulled out my earbug. "I've got the schematics right here. I just need someone to go over them for me."

"There's no one here who can help you." She smiled tightly. "My degree was in social psychology, not engineering. And really, there's no one else. Unless you count them." She waved at the students beyond the windows, humping in the quad. "Do you think that any of them could read your schematics?"

Through the smudged glass doors I could see the kids on the library steps, stripped down completely. They were humping away, grinning and having a good time. One of the girls saw me through the glass and waved at me to join her. When I shook my head, she shrugged and went back to her humping.

The old lady studied me like a vulture. "See what I mean?"

The girl got into her rhythm. She grinned at me watching, and motioned again for me to come out and play. All she needed were some big yellow eyes, and she would have made a perfect trog.

I closed my eyes and opened them again. Nothing changed. The girl was still there with all of her little play friends. All of them romping around and having a good time.

"The best and the brightest," the old lady murmured.

In the middle of the quad, more of the students were stripping down, none of them caring that they were doing it in the middle of broad daylight, none of them worried about who was watching, or what anyone might think. A couple hundred kids, and not a single one of them had a book, or a notebook, or pens, or paper, or a computer with them.

The old lady laughed. "Don't look so surprised. You can't say someone of your caliber never noticed." She paused, waiting, then peered at me, incredulous. "The trogs? The concrete rain? The reproductive disorders? You never wondered about any of it?" She shook her head. "You're stupider than I guessed."

"But…" I cleared my throat. "How could it… I mean…" I trailed off.

"Chemistry was my husband's field." She squinted at the kids humping on the steps and tangled out in the grass, then shook her head and shrugged. "There are plenty of books on the topic. For a while there were even magazine stories about it. 'Why breast might not be best.' Stuff like that. " She waved a hand impatiently. "Rohit and I never really thought about any of it until his students started seeming stupider every year." She cackled briefly. "And then he tested them, and he was right."

"We can't all be turning into trogs." I held up my bottle of Sweatshine. "How could I buy this bottle, or my earbug, or bacon, or anything? Someone has to be making these things."

"You found bacon? Where?" She leaned forward, interested.

"My wife did. Last packet."

She settled back with a sigh. "It doesn't matter. I couldn't chew it anyway." She studied my Sweatshine bottle. "Who knows? Maybe you're right. Maybe it's not so bad. But this is the longest conversation that I've had since Rohit died; most people just don't seem to be able to pay attention to things like they used to." She eyed me. "Maybe your Sweatshine bottle just means there's a factory somewhere that's as good as your sewage pumps used to be. And as long as nothing too complex goes wrong, we all get to keep drinking it."

"It's not that bad."

"Maybe not." She shrugged. "It doesn't matter to me, anymore. I'll kick off pretty soon. After that, it's your problem."

It was night by the time I came out of the university. I had a bag full of books, and no one to know that I'd taken them. The old lady hadn't cared if I checked them out or not, just waved at me to take as many as I liked, and then gave me the keys and told me to lock up when I left.

All of the books were thick with equations and diagrams. I'd picked through them one after another, reading each for a while, before giving up and starting on another. They were all pretty much gibberish. It was like trying to read before you knew your ABCs. Mercati had been right. I should have stayed in school. I probably wouldn't have done any worse than the Columbia kids.

Out on the street, half the buildings were dark. Some kind of brownout that ran all the way down Broadway. One side of the street had electricity, cheerful and bright. The other side had candles glimmering in all the apartment windows, ghost lights flickering in a pretty ambiance.

A crash of concrete rain echoed from a couple blocks away. I couldn't help shivering. Everything had turned creepy. It felt like the old lady was leaning over my shoulder and pointing out broken things everywhere. Empty autovendors. Cars that hadn't moved in years. Cracks in the sidewalk. Piss in the gutters.

What was normal supposed to look like?

I forced myself to look at good things. People were still out and about, walking to their dance clubs, going out to eat, wandering uptown or downtown to see their parents. Kids were on skateboards rolling past and trogs were humping in the alleys. A couple of vendor boxes were full of cellophane bagels, along with a big row of Sweatshine bottles all glowing green under their lights, still all stocked up and ready for sale. Lots of things were still working. Wicky was still a great club, even if Max needed a little help remembering to restock. And Miku and Gabe had their new baby, even if it took them three years to get it. I couldn't let myself wonder if that baby was going to turn out like the college kids in the quad. Not everything was broken.

As if to prove it, the subway ran all the way to my stop for a change. Somewhere on the line, they must have had a couple guys like me, people who could still read a schematic and remember how to show up for work and not throw toilet paper around the control rooms. I wondered who they were. And then I wondered if they ever noticed how hard it was to get anything done.

When I got home, Maggie was already in bed. I gave her a kiss and she woke up a little. She pushed her hair away from her face. "I left out a hotpack burrito for you. The stove's still broke."

"Sorry. I forgot. I'll fix it now."

"No worry." She turned away from me and pulled the sheets up around her neck. For a minute, I thought she'd dozed off, but then she said, "Trav?"

"Yeah?"

"I got my period."

I sat down beside her and started massaging her back. "How you doing with that?"

"S'okay. Maybe next time." She was already dropping back to sleep. "You just got to stay optimistic, right?"

"That's right, baby." I kept rubbing her back. "That's right."

When she was asleep, I went back to the kitchen. I found the hotpack burrito and shook it and tore it open, holding it with the tips of my fingers so I wouldn't burn myself. I took a bite, and decided the burritos were still working just fine. I dumped all the books onto the kitchen table and stared at them, trying to decide where to start.

Through the open kitchen windows, from the direction of the park, I heard another crash of concrete rain. I looked out toward the candle-flicker darkness. Not far away, deep underground, nine pumps were chugging away; their little flashers winking in and out with errors, their maintenance logs scrolling repair requests, and all of them running a little harder now that Pump Six was down. But they were still running. The people who'd built them had done a good job. With luck, they'd keep running for a long time yet.

I chose a book at random and started reading.

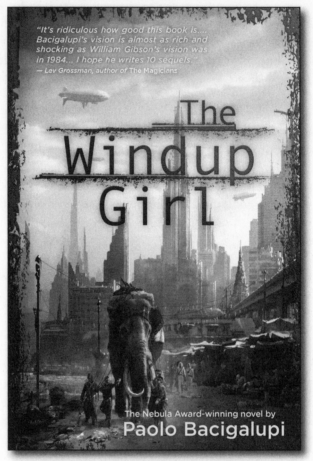

Night Shade Books Is an Independent Publisher of Quality SF, Fantasy and Horror

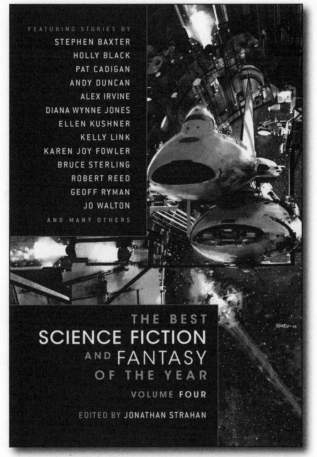

FEATURING STORIES BY
STEPHEN BAXTER
HOLLY BLACK
PAT CADIGAN
ANDY DUNCAN
ALEX IRVINE
DIANA WYNNE JONES
ELLEN KUSHNER
KELLY LINK
KAREN JOY FOWLER
BRUCE STERLING
ROBERT REED
GEOFF RYMAN
JO WALTON
AND MANY OTHERS

THE BEST
SCIENCE FICTION
AND FANTASY
OF THE YEAR
VOLUME FOUR
EDITED BY JONATHAN STRAHAN

ISBN: 978-1-59780-171-3, Trade Paperback; $19.95

A ruthless venture capitalist finds love—or something chemically similar—in an Atlanta strip club; a girl in grey conjures a man from a handful of moonshine; a boy becomes a man by mastering the sword; a rebellious young woman suffers a strange incarceration; an astronaut shares a lifeboat—and herself—with an unfathomable alien; an infected girl counts the days until she becomes a vampire; an aviatrix and an inventor square off against saboteurs and monstrous brains; a big man travels to a tiny moon to examine an ancient starship covered with flowers...

The depth and breadth of science fiction and fantasy fiction continues to change with every passing year. The twenty-nine stories chosen for this book by award-winning anthologist Jonathan Strahan carefully map this evolution, giving readers a captivating and always-entertaining look at the very best the genre has to offer.

Night Shade Books Is an Independent Publisher of Quality SF, Fantasy and Horror

ISBN: 978-1-59780-174-4, Trade Hardcover; $24.95

Nasim Golestani, a young Iranian scientist living in exile in the United States, hopes to work on the Human Connectome Project—which aims to construct a detailed map of the wiring of the human brain. When government funding for the project is canceled and a chance comes for Nasim to return to her homeland, she chooses to head back to Iran. Fifteen years later, Nasim is in charge of the virtual world known as Zendegi, used by millions of people for entertainment and business. When Zendegi comes under threat from powerful competitors, Nasim draws on her old skills, and data from the now-completed Human Connectome Project, to embark on a program to create more lifelike virtual characters and give the company an unbeatable edge…but Zendegi is about to become a battlefield.

Night Shade Books Is an Independent Publisher of Quality SF, Fantasy and Horror

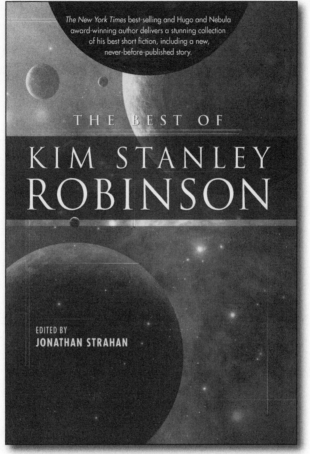

The New York Times best-selling and Hugo and Nebula award-winning author delivers a stunning collection of his best short fiction, including a new, never-before-published story.

THE BEST OF

KIM STANLEY
ROBINSON

EDITED BY
JONATHAN STRAHAN

ISBN: 978-1-59780-184-3, Trade Hardcover; $27.95

Adventurers, scientists, artists, workers, and visionaries—these are the men and women you will encounter in the short fiction of Kim Stanley Robinson. In settings ranging from the sunken ruins of Venice to the upper reaches of the Himalayas to the terraformed surface of Mars itself, and through themes of environmental sustainability, social justice, personal responsibility, sports, adventure and fun, Robinson's protagonists explore a world which stands in sharp contrast to many of the traditional locales and mores of science fiction, presenting instead a world in which Utopia rests within our grasp.

From Kim Stanley Robinson, award-winning author of the Mars Trilogy (*Red Mars, Green Mars, Blue Mars*), the Three Californias Trilogy (*The Wild Shore, The Gold Coast, Pacific Edge*), the Science in the Capital series (*Forty Signs of Rain, Fifty Degrees Below, Sixty Days and Counting*), *The Martians*, and *The Years of Rice and Salt*, comes *The Best of Kim Stanley Robinson*.

Paolo Bacigalupi's debut novel *The Windup Girl* has won the Nebula Award, the Locus Award, the Compton Crook Award, and the John W. Campbell Award, and has been nominated for the Hugo Award. His short stories have appeared in *The Magazine of Fantasy & Science Fiction*, *Asimov's Science Fiction*, and the environmental journal *High Country News*, and numerous best of the year anthologies. His short fiction has been nominated for the Nebula and Hugo awards, and has won the Theodore Sturgeon Memorial Award for best SF short story of the year. His YA novel *Ship Breaker* was recently published. His non-fiction essays have appeared in *Salon.com* and *High Country News*, and have been syndicated in numerous newspapers including the *Idaho Statesman*, the *Albuquerque Journal*, and the *Salt Lake Tribune*. He lives in Western Colorado with his wife and son, where he is working on his next novel.

Find out more about the author online at http://windupstories.com.